SIMON MAYO

CORGI BOOKS

ITCH ROCKS
A CORGI BOOK 978 0552 56551 6

First published in Great Britain by Doubleday
an imprint of Random House Children's Publishers UK
A Random House Group Company

Doubleday edition published 2013
Corgi edition published 2013

3 5 7 9 10 8 6 4

The Random House Group Limited supports the Forest Stewardship Council®
(FSC®), the leading international forest-certification organisation. Our books
carrying the FSC label are printed on FSC®-certified paper. FSC is the only
forest-certification scheme supported by the leading environmental organisations,
including Greenpeace. Our paper procurement policy can be found at
www.randomhouse.co.uk/environment

Set in Bembo MT by Falcon Oast Graphic Art Ltd.

Corgi Books are published by Random House Children's Publishers UK,
61–63 Uxbridge Road, London W5 5SA

www.**randomhousechildrens**.co.uk
www.**totallyrandombooks**.co.uk
www.**randomhouse**.co.uk

Addresses for companies within The Random House Group Limited
can be found at: www.randomhouse.co.uk/offices.htm

THE RANDOM HOUSE GROUP Limited Reg. No. 954009

A CIP catalogue record for this book is available from the British Library.

Printed and bound by CPI Group (uk) Ltd, Croydon, CR0 4YY

Praise for ITCH

'A great debut . . . you'll be itching to read more'

'Teenage intrigue and heart-in-mouth escapades'
The Guardian

'An exciting and nail-biting thriller'
Booktrust

Praise for ITCH ROCKS

'With its explosive mix of action and adventure, chemistry
lessons will never be the same again'
Daily Express

'There is kinetic energy all over these pages, with film-show
presenter Mayo definitely envisaging this as a wide-screen
blockbuster'
The Bookbag

www.totallyrandombooks.co.uk

Also available from Simon Mayo:

For Ben, the adventurer, Natasha, the keeper of the
Cake flame, and Joe, the original element hunter

Ikoyi Prison, Lagos, Nigeria
July

She lay motionless on her iron bed. Any movement would trigger a series of metallic creaks and scrapes and she needed to listen. It was never quiet in prison, not even at three a.m., but she filtered out the usual sounds of crying and snoring. She was listening for footsteps. Her eyes were open, but her head was turned to the wall in case one of the others noticed she was awake. There were nine of them in the cell but she was the one they would be watching.

She had earned the right to the bottom bed. She'd broken a few noses to get there but no one questioned her position as wing 'president' now. Most of the other prisoners did as she said, and if they resisted her friends would quietly explain the rules. Remind them she could get cross very quickly.

So she stared unseeing at the damp and peeling wall and cursed the occupants of the bed above her. They had started to stir and the old springs were creaking loudly. The beds were stacked on top of each other and there were no mattresses to muffle the sound. The whole cell seemed to fill with noise and she kicked the metalwork above her, hard. The restless movement stopped.

'Sorry, Shivvi,' said a tiny voice no more than a metre overhead, quickly followed by another.

'Yeah, sorry, Shivvi.'

'Get to sleep, Johanna, you're driving me mad. You too, Olufemi. Last warning.'

From the slight, moving indentations, Shivvi Tan Fook reckoned that the two twelve-year-olds lying above her had just curled into a ball and probably wouldn't move till sunrise. She was annoyed with herself for letting the whole cell know that she was awake; how long before they were all asleep again? Thirty minutes she reckoned, maybe more. The heat was unbearable again tonight. Even after three years inside, the combination of thirty-five-degree heat, the stench from their toilet − a hole in the ground − and the constant whine of mosquitoes meant that sleep was always a difficult task. Her long dirty nails picked at the wall as she ran through her plan again. She was ready, she knew she was ready; she just needed to hear those footsteps.

She sat up after five minutes, her usual patience deserting her. The two bunks above her were silent and the stack of three opposite were still too, save for an occasional grunt and mutter from deep in someone's dream. The three new arrivals slept on tattered mats on the floor, their arms and legs tangled with a number of plastic bowls. The mouldy remains of beans and cassava were scattered everywhere.

She was about to make for the door when she heard a key in the lock. She held her breath as it turned slowly and the ancient pin-tumbler mechanism strained and then clicked. It seemed deafening to Shivvi and she tensed, glancing around the cell, but no one stirred. She counted to twenty, then moved to the door, pushing against its steel panels. It opened slowly and light from the prison landing fell on one of the floor sleepers. A squinting face looked up at Shivvi who, turning round, drew her finger sharply across her neck. The girl understood the threat well enough and lowered her head to the mat. Shivvi slipped out of the cell.

She had memorized her route to the outside world so many times. She knew the corridors she had to slip down, the rooms she could hide in and the doors and gates that would be open. She had paid enough. The bribes were at last coming good and soon she would be free. Crouching low to avoid being seen from any of the cells, she ran towards the two metal doors at the end of the corridor; she could already see that they were slightly ajar. Her bare feet were noiseless as she sprinted and then slowed down, slipping through them both in a second.

Her wing was on the fourth floor of a block that ran parallel with the front gates of the prison. But as she flew down the flights of stairs – the steel doors stood open at each floor – she knew she was heading in the other direction. There were three staff entrances: one for the caterers and cleaners at the side of the prison and two for the wardens and guards. She had paid for the nearest one to be unmanned and unlocked. She would be there in one minute; the deal was that it would be locked again in three.

The stairs came out at a courtyard which was at the centre of the prison. The air was warm and humid, but in comparison with the fetid stench of the prison, Shivvi thought it was the freshest thing she had ever smelled. She inhaled deeply. She had exercised here many times, but as she looked across to the far side where her open door would be found, she realized she had never seen it empty before. As she checked her route around the cobbled periphery, she briefly caught a familiar stale perfume and whirled round. The vast bulk of Zuma, one of the senior guards, was hurtling towards her. Shivvi jumped sideways – but not quickly enough to escape Zuma's grabbing hands, which closed around her ponytail. Attempting to throw her to the ground, the guard pulled down sharply, but Shivvi had been here before. In countless street fights and prison battles she had found herself attacked by bullies and thugs who assumed that because of her 1.6-metre, 45-kilo frame, she would be a pushover. They were wrong. As Zuma tugged her down, Shivvi smashed her palm into the guard's face, splintering her nose instantly. It was her speciality. Zuma let go and put her hands in front of her face, gasping as blood poured between her fingers. Shivvi ran behind her and kicked at her knees. Zuma's legs buckled and she fell to the ground, groaning.

'Lie down. Lie down, Zuma or I'll smack your nose again,' she half whispered, half shouted in the guard's ear. Zuma did what she was told. 'You stay here for ten minutes. You don't make a sound.' Shivvi bent down and looked her in the eye. 'You made my life a misery for three years. I hope you go as mad in here as I have.' And using Zuma's head as a starting block, she sprinted for the gate.

The altercation in the courtyard had cost Shivvi some crucial minutes, and as she approached staff entrance A, skipping round open doors and ducking under lit windows, she recognized the silhouette of the guard who had been unlocking the doors for her. With keys in hand, she was about to close up.

'No!' called Shivvi, closing fast, and the guard,

looking up, stood aside. They exchanged the briefest of glances, and the former Greencorps oil analyst, convicted polluter and killer, squeezed her way out of the prison and onto the dark back streets of Lagos.

Hiding behind a garden wall, Shivvi Tan Fook retied the band in her black hair and produced a pair of sandals from under her shirt. She slipped them on and looked around, smiling. If anyone had been watching they would have marvelled at the effect that one smile could have on a face. Despite her twenty-five years – the last three spent in one of the most notorious prisons in Africa – she could still look like a teenager.

'Now,' she said out loud, 'Dr Nathaniel Flowerdew.' She spat the words. 'I believe we have an appointment.' And she started to run through the still-dark streets, away from the prison and towards the harbour.

1

Cornwall, England
November

The most protected boy in the world was in his bed-room making chlorine gas. Having failed in his attempts to buy any, he was mixing his own. Nowadays, the only time he had to himself was before everyone got up, so he had been setting his alarm for six a.m. A tattered old book lay open on the floor, and Itch, kneeling down in his pyjamas, read the instructions aloud.

'*Add five grams of manganese dioxide . . .*' He scooped up a small quantity of black powder from a dish and tipped it into his test tube. '*Now add the hydrochloric acid and heat gently.*'

From an old biscuit tin he produced a small bottle of clear liquid and measured the suggested 3ml, dripping in the exact amount. Warming the mixture with an old lighter, he picked up another test tube, ready to catch the gas. It wasn't the most efficient way of collecting a sample of element number 17 for his collection, but it would have to do.

As the mixture began to bubble, Itch leaned eagerly towards the tube. Unfortunately he miscalculated by a few centimetres. The error was small but the effect was huge. Chlorine gas seared into his lungs like fire and he dropped the test tube. His gasp sounded like he was being throttled. In the quiet house, it was like an alarm going off.

Seemingly from nowhere, three figures crashed through his bedroom door.

'Call Fairnie!' shouted the leader, scooping Itch up in her arms. 'And check the room.' She carried him, coughing and retching, back down the stairs.

'Are you OK, Itch?' asked the woman, setting him down on a kitchen chair. 'Can you breathe?'

Itch nodded, his eyes pressed tightly together but watering anyway. The back door was open, and through it appeared a small, athletic man with a neat black moustache.

'Chlorine gas, sir,' barked the woman, her voice loud in the kitchen. 'Small tube. Self-inflicted.'

'Take him outside,' sighed Dr Jim Fairnie. 'He needs the air.'

She led Itch out into the floodlit back garden and sat him on the kitchen step. After he had taken a few deep breaths, Fairnie knelt down beside him.

He tapped Itch on the shoulder and waited for him to open his eyes. 'Idiot,' he said.

'Sorry,' croaked Itch. 'Thought I could bottle some before school—' He broke off, coughing.

Fairnie looked up as Nicholas and Jude Lofte appeared behind them in the kitchen. They were both tall – Nicholas easily six four – but it was Jude that Itch most closely resembled; their hair both mousy, wavy and uncontrolled. 'He's fine! He's fine!' he called before they could say anything. 'Just a little chlorinated mouthwash to start the day. He'll be OK just as soon as his lungs have stopped burning. Give him five minutes.'

Itch's parents stared at their son, then at the man in charge of his security.

'But what happened?' asked his father. 'It's six in the morning, for heaven's sake!'

As if in answer to Nicholas's question, the two men who had been checking Itch's bedroom appeared in the doorway holding a bag of smashed chemistry equipment.

Jude Lofte rolled her eyes. 'You have got to be kidding . . .'

Itchingham Lofte had been allowed home at the beginning of October, after three months in a military hospital.

And 'home' was now very different.

9

MI5 had taken over his house and forced the neighbours to move. Dr Fairnie – who was also a colonel in the British army – ran a cell of seven agents from what had been the Cole family's house next door. There were three on duty, three off, twenty-four hours a day. (The final member of the team had moved in with Itch's cousin Jack and her family.) On every window, the Lofte house now had steel shutters that could be lowered if there was a perceived threat. There was a very visible CCTV at the front and back of the property, and a complex alarm system triggered by laser beams that criss-crossed the garden. Inside, there were cameras downstairs but, by common agreement, none upstairs.

The fence between the two semi-detached houses had been removed and replaced with powerful lighting, a satellite dish and a generator. In the Coles' house, the living rooms were now stuffed with a battery of monitors running images from inside and outside the next-door house. Other cameras showed the roads around the town and the Cornwall Academy, the school attended by Itch and his eleven-year-old sister, Chloe.

The agents tried to interfere with family life as little as possible, keeping to the kitchen as much as they could. The on-duty team would have one member watching the screens next door while the other two patrolled the garden.

And all this because a man called Cake had given Itch a rock. It had looked unremarkable enough – largely brown and pebble-sized – but that rock had turned out to consist of the previously undiscovered element 126. Highly radioactive and extremely powerful, its value was incalculable – but so was the danger it presented. Depending on who controlled it, element 126 had the potential to solve the world's energy crisis or make its owner a nuclear power overnight.

Itch's science teacher, Dr Nathaniel Flowerdew, had been quick to spot its value. He'd stolen it from Itch, who promptly stole it back, with the help of Chloe and their cousin Jack. When Cake died from radiation poisoning, they found that he had left behind seven more of the radioactive rocks, and the Loftes had been forced to go on the run to keep them out of Flowerdew's hands.

In the end, Itch had managed to evade Flowerdew and leave the rocks in the bottom of a very deep well. By the time he had completed his mission he was almost dead from radiation poison-ing. Itch didn't know who it was who had carried him out of the well and left him at a nearby hospital, but his mysterious rescuer was the only other person who could locate the final resting place of element 126. The identity of this person was a continual worry to Itch: whoever it was knew his secret. Would they go and retrieve the rocks he had gone to such lengths to hide? What were their motives? If it was Flowerdew or Greencorps, surely they would have acted by now?

The reward for Itch's heroics had been an emergency bone-marrow transplant, followed by three months of recovery and interrogation by MI5, who were desperate to know where the rocks were hidden. When it became clear that Itch wasn't going to tell them, the British government finally allowed him to go home. But, of course, they couldn't run the risk of anyone else forcing him to give up his secret. And so the government had come with him . . .

The Loftes now lived with MI5. Nicholas had given up his job on the oil rigs and was living at home permanently for the first time that Itch could remember. Chloe, who had recovered from her own, less serious, radiation poisoning, had made the adjustment to their new lifestyle with ease. Itch suspected she secretly rather enjoyed the drama that Fairnie and his team brought with them. She had certainly made herself popular with her home-made biscuits.

Itch and Chloe had an older brother, Gabriel, who was away at Warwick University. Apart from a brief visit when Itch was discharged from hospital, he hadn't come home – a fact that Jude Lofte was not very happy about. In fact, apart from having Itch back home and – all things considered

– healthy, his mother, a solicitor, didn't seem happy about very much at all. She didn't like the way MI5 'messed up the garden', or the disruption they caused to her normal routines; she certainly didn't like having them in the house. Itch suspected that she secretly wished that he would just tell Fairnie where he had hidden the rocks, just so they could all go back to living their normal lives.

That November morning found Itch and Chloe having breakfast with two of the daytime security team, Sam Singh and Tina Greaves. The third member was a former marine called Moz Taylor, doubtless watching them from the monitors next door. Tina was the team leader and ex-army, while Sam was as much of a science nut as Itch, and was giving him a hard time about the chlorine:

'I would have thought you'd put your body through enough without inhaling poison gas for fun.'

Itch was irritated – both by the criticism and by his mistake. 'I know, I know,' he snapped. 'I told Colonel Fairnie I was sorry, didn't I? It was only a tiny amount. I didn't need rescuing like that. Now Mum's mad again.'

'Mum is *always* mad,' said Chloe, pouring herself a cup of tea. 'You know that. But if I'd heard you choking, I might have raised the alarm too.'

'You need a history lesson, Itch,' said Sam. 'Try looking up how chlorine gas was used in the First

World War and then see if you still want to inhale some.'

'I wasn't trying to . . . Oh, never mind. I'll do without chlorine. Go for something more fun, like mercury, instead.' Itch checked the clock. 'Time to go?'

'Give me five,' said Chloe.

Tina spoke into the tiny pin-sized microphone built into her sleeve. 'School run in five minutes.'

The 'school run' was actually shorthand for the complex operation needed to get Itch and Chloe to and from school; it required the whole cell. The walk to the Cornwall Academy was the same as it had ever been: down the hill towards the sea, across the golf course, then through the town. Itch and Chloe used to go on their own. Now they had two agents walking twenty metres in front and another two twenty metres behind. Two more followed in a white van with blacked-out windows. All six were in constant radio contact, while Colonel Fairnie monitored events from the Coles' house.

When Itch and Chloe first returned to school, Jude and Nicholas had assumed that they would be driven there in the van, but Jim Fairnie had said no.

'If they want to carry on walking, we can cover that. So much has changed for them, it would be good to keep some things the same. We can always change the routine if anyone is unhappy.'

The parents had agreed, and so the twice daily 'run' began.

Initially, both Itch and Chloe had been very conscious of all the attention, and laughed and cringed with embarrassment all the way. After all, this level of security was normally reserved for prime ministers, presidents and royalty. But after two weeks the routine had come to feel almost normal.

Tina's radio crackled, and Colonel Fairnie's voice came through: 'School run, your route is clear.'

'Roger that,' replied Tina. 'OK, let's go.'

The two agents stationed at the front door, Sam Singh and ex-policewoman Kirsten Jones, opened it and stepped out. Casually dressed in jeans and leather jackets, they looked like a couple going to work or shopping in town, not agents from MI5 on a security detail. Itch knew better though. He knew that their clothing had to conceal a Glock 17 pistol. All the agents carried firearms 24/7 – another thing that upset Jude Lofte, who hated the idea of guns in the house. Itch thought it was pretty cool. He'd asked to examine one and been refused.

After ten seconds Tina called, 'OK, Itch, Chloe – your turn,' and they walked out of the house.

The security team's van, with Danny Stein, the youngest of Fairnie's team, and Chris Lakeman, both ex-policemen, was idling in the middle of the road. As the Loftes headed down the hill, it followed a few metres behind them. Completing the procession, Tina left the house with Moz. They walked side by side on the other side of the road behind Itch and Chloe. Every few seconds one of them would turn and walk backwards for a few steps, checking the surrounding area for anything out of the ordinary. Itch had originally assumed they'd all walk together, but Fairnie had vetoed that.

'Close protection is only used when the threat is, frankly, assassination. Here it is kidnap that we are preventing, so twenty metres is best.'

'You see, Chloe,' Itch had said grimly, 'we're not going to be assassinated. I told you everything would be fine.'

When they reached the golf course, the van peeled off. The route had been approved by Fairnie, even though it had to drive round and meet the rest of the group on the other side. Crossing the golf course was much quicker and meant they usually encountered fewer people. On the edge of one of the fairways they passed an impressive two-metre pile of wood, ready for Bonfire Night.

'I hope you're not planning anything involving fireworks,' said Chloe, smiling. 'You shouldn't be allowed anywhere near them!'

'Yeah, that's pretty much what Fairnie said,' replied Itch. 'Which is a shame — I could probably put on quite a show.'

'I think that's what they're afraid of.'

They walked on, passing the eleventh green and its perfectly semicircular bunker. 'I hate that first bit,' said Itch. 'I just feel watched all the time.'

'We *are* watched all the time,' Chloe pointed out. 'You should know that by now.'

'Not by our lot, by . . .' Itch waved his arms around. 'By everyone. Out of their windows, behind curtains. At school I can't go anywhere without nods and winks and comments. No one really spoke to me before, but at least they weren't *scared* of me. Now, as soon as they see Moz or Tina, they either flatten themselves against the wall to let me pass or turn round and go the other way.'

'You might not have noticed,' said Chloe, 'but some of the girls in my class actually follow you at lunch just to see if anything happens. Ever since you disappeared, they reckon you're a spy or something. Apparently loads of people thought you were dead. They saw us at the school jazz concert that evening, then we disappeared with Mr Watkins. When none of us turned up for school, the rumours started. The head couldn't say anything as she didn't know much either.'

'Yeah,' said Itch. 'Jack told me that Potts started a *What's Happened to Lofte?* Facebook group – most of the school were on it before Fairnie found out and got it taken down.'

The colonel and his team had managed to keep

a pretty tight information blackout on Itch and element 126. Facebook and Twitter were under constant surveillance back in London, and any online discussion disappeared as soon as it had been uploaded. On the first day of the school run, one early-morning golfer had made the mistake of trying to film the unlikely procession on his phone. Five seconds later he was flat on his face in a bunker with his phone smashed by a five-iron, courtesy of Moz Taylor.

Despite the information blackout though, everyone in town seemed to know that something had gone on; just not precisely what. They also understood that whatever had happened to Itch was serious; serious enough to involve people with firearms. The unfortunate golfer's fellow players all noticed — and reported to their friends — that the agent had a gun inside his jacket.

A small group of golfers was watching them now, Itch realized, gawping at them like they were some sort of local tourist attraction.

'What are they watching?' he shouted. 'Do they expect me to be shot or something? Is that what they want?' He smiled at them sarcastically and they looked away, embarrassed.

Itch picked up his pace. In front and behind, the security agents lengthened their own stride.

'Why are we hurrying?' asked Chloe. 'You usually make this bit last as long as possible.'

Itch and his sister often walked slowly on the way to school – with their home full of cameras and MI5 agents, it was the only time they felt they could speak openly to each other, without being overheard.

'I hate golf. I hate golfers. Stupid trousers, stupid game,' said Itch.

Chloe said nothing but hurried after him.

As they approached the edge of the course, they spotted their cousin, Jacqueline Lofte, always known as Jack, walking up the hill. They called out to her and she crossed the road to join them, waving at the blacked-out van that was idling on the corner. A few metres behind, her own bodyguard jogged to catch up.

'Hi, you guys!' called Jack. She was fifteen, the same age as Itch, and almost as tall; the whole Lofte clan were several centimetres taller than their peers. Her black hair had grown back since the radiation-induced close crop of the summer, but it was still short and pixie-like, making her look more like Chloe. Her bodyguard fell in with Tina and Moz, who were waiting by the thirteenth green as the three cousins greeted each other.

'How are you getting on with your security?' asked Itch, nodding towards the young blonde woman in tracksuit and baseball cap who had been accompanying his cousin.

'Rachel's nice,' replied Jack. 'Quiet, but that's OK.

And we're used to having people to stay. Just not used to them following me everywhere.' Rachel Taylor was Jack's 'minder', and had moved into her house. 'But it is so weird not being able to walk through town without it becoming a major hassle for everyone. I went to get some shopping for Mum at the weekend, and Rachel had to go ahead first. She radioed back just to say that Tesco was OK!'

'We should keep going,' said Itch. 'Our friends are looking nervous.'

Ahead, the two lead bodyguards, Sam and Kirsten, had stopped by a newsagent's, waiting for the Loftes to set off again. They were glancing from cars to pedestrians, checking for anything unusual.

'Come on, then,' said Chloe, and the trio set off down the high street. Five minutes later, the disjointed column of agents and pupils walked in through the gates of the Cornwall Academy.

2

With temperatures set at freezing, the winds running at forty knots, and sleet and snow swirling around the heli-pad, a group of oil workers hurried into the galley. They were exhausted and hungry after a gruelling six-hour shift, and needed hot food and drink – fast.

They crashed through the doors, and the warmth and smells of the kitchen overwhelmed them. As they cheerfully shed their many layers of waterproofing, they noticed an unusual sight at the far table. The galley chef, an enormous red-faced American by the name of George Sanders, had one of his colleagues face down in a pizza. Sanders's chef's apron and overalls strained to enclose his bulk as he twisted the tomato- and cheese-smeared face left and right on the table.

'You all right, George?' called one of the men.

'Hell, yes! Just meting out some chef's justice!' Sanders smiled at the new arrivals. 'Some folk just seem to forget who's in charge here. They think they can tell me what to do. Imagine that! I'm just reminding my assistant here that it's, er, unwise.' Three other galley hands were watching from the serving counter, laughing and clapping. The chef held the man's curly white hair with one hand, while the other wiped what was left of the pizza over his face like a flannel.

'Who's in charge here, blossom? Huh, bud? Geddit?' Sanders laughed as the remains of the twelve-inch margarita flopped onto the floor.

'Yes, I get it . . .' The man spat out tomato sauce and globs of cheese.

The chef pulled him up and spun him round to face him. 'Say, *Sorry, chef.*'

A moment's pause, then: 'Sorry, chef.'

'What have you learned, bud?'

'I have learned,' said the chef's assistant in a clipped, educated voice, 'that you are in charge and I am not.'

'Too right, Flowerman, too right. Now, go and wash some dishes. And no, you can't go and clean up first. You look just fine as you are.'

The oilmen laughed as Dr Nathaniel Flowerdew,

22

fourth galley assistant, made his way behind the counter and disappeared into the kitchen.

Flowerdew had arrived on the rig a month ago. The multinational oil company Greencorps owned the Ocean Bar, and a stint on the rig had been doled out as punishment. They had not taken kindly to their agent losing the most valuable rocks of all time – the newly discovered element 126.

The Greencorps bosses had toyed with the idea of sending Flowerdew to their project in Baffin Bay, Greenland, but in the end had opted for the utter remoteness of the Falkland Islands, at the very southern tip of South America. The rig was thirty miles out from the capital, Port Stanley, which had the only airport for hundreds of miles.

This was punishment Greencorps-style. Flowerdew's prison was a twenty-year-old semi-submersible oil rig that had been towed from its previous site in the North Sea. It was surrounded by the stormy Atlantic waves and populated by a hundred of the toughest oilmen and -women in the business. All they were told about their new arrival was that he was a thief, a crook and not to be trusted. And life as a galley assistant was proving every bit as uncomfortable for Flowerdew as Greencorps had intended it to be.

Flowerdew's shift finished at midnight. The oil exploration and drilling was a twenty-four-hour-a-day operation, so the catering had to be too. A new galley shift had arrived, and Flowerdew was the first out of the doors. The roar of the freezing wind took his breath away, and he paused to zip his coat up to his chin. Pulling a black cap low over his eyes, he hurried past the enormous S-61 helicopter and hauled himself up the steps to the living quarters. He wanted to get to the bar first, and avoid the queue – and the jokes.

'Large whisky, please. No ice, no water.' He knew the face of the man behind the bar but couldn't remember his name, so he just smiled and hoped he'd be served. The steward was in his twenties, with cropped hair and a ready smile.

'It's Alejandro. Remember? I showed you around when you arrived.'

'Oh yes, of course,' said Flowerdew without conviction. 'Now – that whisky . . .'

Alejandro pointed to the corner of the room. 'Your friend has already bought you one.' He nodded to a sofa, where a small hunched figure was sitting with his back to him.

'Friend? Unlikely.' Flowerdew could see two whiskies on the low table and walked over. He tried to make out the reflection of the face in the glass surrounding the small bar, but whoever it was had their face buried deep in a magazine. He took a seat opposite his visitor and reached for the whisky. He didn't make it.

'Hello, Nathaniel.'

Shivvi Tan Fook lowered the magazine and stared at her old boss.

Flowerdew froze. His hand was centimetres from the glass, but his eyes were now wide with shock and fear. He was already pale, but now the blood seemed to have left his face completely. He sat back quickly.

'But you're in prison . . .' He swallowed hard.

'I got out.'

'Twenty-five years, I thought . . .'

'Three was enough.'

He stared blankly at the glass wall.

Shivvi sat forward. 'Is that it? No apologies, no explanation?' She spoke bitterly, her face flushed. 'That should have been *you* in prison. The Nigerian deep drill was *your* idea; the spill *your* fault. The deaths of those workers were *your* fault. My three years in Ikoyi – *your* fault. The beatings I took – *your* fault. This here' – she showed him the livid scar on the back of her neck – 'a broken bottle from point-blank range. *Your* fault, you scumbag.'

Flowerdew had shrunk back in his chair. 'Now, Shivvi, we worked on that project together. You and your little group of divers were closely involved, as I recall.' His tone was gentler now, and he even tried a smile. 'I argued with the board – honestly I did. I told them that they should help you too, but they said—'

25

Before he could finish his sentence, he felt the point of a knife in his ribs and gasped. He looked desperately around the bar, but there was nobody there.

'You are a liar and a crook, Flowerdew. You'd do anything, say anything, to save your pathetic neck. Well, this time it's not working.' Shivvi pushed the knife in a little further. 'I've thought about this moment every day for three years, you know. And it is every bit as good as I thought it would be.'

Flowerdew's forehead was beaded with sweat. 'Please, Shivvi, let's talk this through. I have money—'

'You have nothing. Really, you have nothing.' She was speaking millimetres from his ear. 'And when you fall overboard, no one will notice and no one will care.'

Just then, Alejandro the barman came and set down a tray of drinks at a nearby table; three customers followed him, and Shivvi backed off. 'Don't even think of calling for help,' she hissed as she perched on the arm of Flowerdew's chair. The knife disappeared back up her sleeve.

'Can I tell you a story?' he said.

'No. Shut up.'

'Just until they go away.' He gestured at the drinkers. 'Then you can push me overboard.'

'What sort of story?'

'The most incredible story you've ever heard,

actually. About a boy and some . . . precious stones.'

'How long will it take?'

'Oh, not long,' said Flowerdew.

'Who's the boy?'

'Ah. His name is Itchingham Lofte.'

'Stupid name,' said Shivvi.

'Yes, it is, isn't it?'

Flowerdew looked longingly at the whisky. Shivvi nodded, so he picked up the glass and took a large mouthful.

The tale of the pieces of element 126 did not take long. In Flowerdew's version, he was the victim and Itch the thief; Shivvi listened impassively. He finished the story – then the whisky, wiping his mouth with the back of his hand.

'We could work on this, Shivvi. We could—' He felt the knife back in his ribs and gasped.

'Walk,' she said, sliding off the arm of the chair. 'And slowly. Like we're two old friends who have just agreed a deal.'

Flowerdew stood up and winced as the knife pierced the skin of his side. Shivvi put her arm around him as though she was helping him.

'But we can agree a deal . . .' Flowerdew was breathing hard now. 'We ran Lagos for years, and we can run this show too.' He felt blood running down his side as Shivvi held the knife firm, her other arm steering him outside.

The cold and wind hit them as they emerged, but

Flowerdew continued to plead as he was pushed down the steps. 'I have the contacts, Shivvi! I lined up Agu Osiegbe to buy the 126 – you remember him? He has the money ready – he wants them, I know it— Argh!' He shouted into the gale as Shivvi edged the knife sideways along a rib; the tip had now found bone.

'You're too late, Flowerdew,' she shouted. 'Way, way too late. And I'm in a hurry. Shame you didn't think of me when I was in solitary confinement.' They had passed the heli-pad and Shivvi picked up the pace, marching him along now. 'Or when I was getting beaten by the wardens.'

Flowerdew tried to break free, but she forced him into a run. He was resisting as much as he could, his feet dragging across the tarmac, but the whisky and the months without access to a gym had softened him.

Shivvi was shouting again. 'Or maybe when I had Lassa fever and was vomiting everywhere. It would have been so good to see a familiar face.' She leaned in till her mouth was next to Flowerdew's ear. 'BUT I WAS ON MY OWN. AS YOU ARE NOW!' she yelled. 'BUT THANKS FOR THE BOY WITH THE STUPID NAME. I'M SURE I'LL BE ABLE FIND HIM – AND WITHOUT YOU.'

Ahead of them, a white line marked the end of the deck; there was no fence or railing between them and the hundred-metre drop to the sea. Suddenly Shivvi kicked sharply at the back of Flowerdew's knees and he tumbled forward. Using his momentum, she grabbed his coat, sending him toppling towards the edge. He scrambled round, trying to speak, but Shivvi was in his face in an instant.

'This is how we get rid of trash. Remember? You taught me well . . . Goodbye, Nathaniel.' She stood and kicked hard.

Flowerdew felt her boot in his chest, and fell into the darkness.

3

It had been two weeks since MI5 had become part of life at the Cornwall Academy, and people weren't quite used to it yet. Staff liked the calmer, quieter atmosphere, but they realized it came at a price.

'Amazing what you can achieve when everyone knows the man outside the classroom has a gun,' is how Jim Littlewood, the history teacher, put it.

'Next we could have armed teachers,' physics man Chris Hopkins had suggested. 'Even my Year Eight class would have to shut up.'

At first pupils had reacted with a mixture of excitement, fear and curiosity. They had been warned about putting anything to do with Itch on Facebook or Twitter, and the threat of 'dire consequences' had been enough to scare most of them into silence. They had also been told not to speak to the 'special policemen', as Dr Felicity Dart, the head teacher, had called them. But the agents had begun to give the odd word of greeting or thanks to the students, and the tense atmosphere of the first few days had relaxed somewhat.

The morning arrival of the Loftes and their security detail was, however, still a novelty. Moz and Tina led the way into the building. Staff and pupils scattered in all directions. With brisk efficiency, they made their way through the corridors to Itch and Jack's form room. Moz entered first, and the buzz and chatter of form 10W died away instantly.

A quick visual sweep of the room was followed by a check of the store cupboard. As Itch and Jack's form teacher, John Watkins, was the academy's head of geography, his cupboard contained nothing more threatening than a selection of weather instruments, maps and tea bags. Satisfied that the room was secure, Moz beckoned the Loftes inside.

They went into the recently hushed classroom while Moz took up position by the door. He would stay there during registration, and then follow Itch and Jack as they moved around the school. Assembly, games, maths – whatever it was, they were watched. If the cousins were apart, Jack's bodyguard Rachel would appear and continue her surveillance. The remaining team members roamed the school grounds.

The academy had been built on cliffs above the Atlantic, with the science labs backing onto the footpath that marked the school boundary.

The coastal walk was spectacular – popular with hikers and a distraction for pupils. Dr Dart had had a two-metre fence erected to run the length of the academy's grounds; this was now patrolled hourly.

'Good morning, boys!' bellowed John Watkins as he arrived in his classroom; he didn't really mean to ignore the girls – it was just what he always said, and everyone had given up correcting him. 'My, how lovely and quiet you all are!' He took the register at top speed, as he always did, aiming to get through it in under thirty-five seconds, which was his record. 'Right, a busy day ahead. Mr Logan is ill, I'm afraid, so no maths from him in period three. I will nurse you through, however.' He beamed.

'But, sir, you hate maths!' shouted Ian Steele.

'And you told us you're rubbish at it too!' said Sam Jennings.

'Indeed! So I did. We can all pool our ignorance then. Dismissed, Ten W! Itch – a word, if I may.'

As the class got up to leave, Itch shuffled to the front. 'Yes, sir? If it's about the flour mill explosion project, it's nearly finished. I'm just drawing the spark from the conveyer belt that lights the dust . . .'

Watkins laughed. 'No, no, it's not that. I was just wondering if everything was all right, Itch. How are you taking to your, er, new friends?'

'Fine, I guess,' he replied.

'Really?'

'Well. Given that I'm told terrorists and criminals from around the world want to kidnap me, I'd rather Colonel Fairnie and co. were here, yes. Life at home isn't much fun, and making friends isn't easy, but if the pieces of 126 are to stay' – he thought carefully about his next words – 'out of sight . . . then I don't really have any choice.'

Itch had disposed of the eight rocks down the Woodingdean Well near Brighton, and now his old rucksack, with its extremely radioactive contents, lay 1,285 feet below ground *and* under 885 feet of water.

'No, I suppose you don't,' said Watkins. 'And so neither do we.'

Watkins gathered his papers together. 'How are you getting on with Mr Hampton?'

Over the summer, an American called Henry Hampton had been appointed head of science, replacing the disgraced Nathaniel Flowerdew.

'Fine,' said Itch. 'Only had a couple of lessons with him, but at least he doesn't appear to hate us. So that's an improvement.'

Watkins laughed uneasily. Dr Nathaniel Flowerdew had made no secret of his dislike of his pupils. 'Fair point, Itch, fair point. Anyway, this science club is his idea, and I think he's hoping you'll go along. Only a few keen souls made it last week. He asked me to remind you.'

'How does he know I like science? I deliberately

didn't answer any questions in class and I haven't handed any homework in yet.'

'Oh well, teachers talk, you know. And you are, by some distance, the most talked-about pupil right now.'

Itch shrugged. 'Well, it sounds OK, I suppose. I'll give it a go – he's guaranteed to have one of my armed friends along too, isn't he? Two for the price of one! Tell Mr Hampton I'll be there.'

'Right-o – good lad. Run along then, or you'll miss Mr Littlewood's excellent Weimar Germany lesson.'

Itch hoisted his new rucksack onto his shoulder. Its 118 pockets had been a Fairnie joke. The colonel had taken a standard model and got one of his team to stick and sew on an extra 109 compartments, one for each element on the Periodic Table, and label them accordingly. *H 1* was for hydrogen, *He 2* for helium, and *Li 3* for lithium – they were the first pockets on the outside of the rucksack – running to *As 33*, which was arsenic. Inside, around the circumference of the bag and across its partition ran pockets *Se 34* to *Uuo 118*. As everything above element ninety-two was unstable, the last twenty-six pockets were just for show, but it made for a rucksack with many hiding places. There were zips, poppers, Velcro and webbing all over the toughened nylon fabric.

As he left his form room, he found Jack waiting

for him outside; Moz was at the end of the corridor, ready to escort them both to double history. As they approached, he turned and began climbing the stairs.

'Everything OK? What did Watkins want?' asked Jack.

'Just making sure I go to the science club thing at lunch. Fancy it?'

Jack laughed. 'Not likely! I've had enough science to last me a lifetime, thank you very much. You and radiation were made for each other. I'm even avoiding the microwave if I can help it.'

Itch was laughing when he heard steps behind him. Before he could turn round, he recognized the familiar leering voice of James Potts.

'Well, well, it's the weirdo cousins again,' he said. The horse-like laugh of Darcy Campbell indicated that Potts had brought his favourite stooge with him. Potts leaned close to Itch's ear. 'You think you're so special, don't you? Everyone says you're some kind of special agent, but I know you're *nothing*, Lofte. Apart from a *freak*, that is. The radiation's made you grow another metre.'

Itch slowly turned to face him. 'Leave me alone, Potts.'

The bully's grin widened. 'Or what?' he replied, prodding Itch in the chest with his history folder.

It was a mistake. In a flash, Moz had jumped down eight steps. While the abuse stayed verbal, he had been prepared to let it go. But with the use of force he went into action, and landed perfectly balanced, right next to Potts and Campbell. The transformation was startling – even for Itch, who knew Moz's background in the Royal Marines. He had appeared relaxed – sloppy even – in his jeans, sweatshirt and boots. Now, as he grabbed hold of Potts with one hand and Campbell with the other, he was every inch the trained soldier. He pulled their faces towards his; so close there was no way they could miss the winged tattoo showing above his collar.

'Was there something you wanted to say to Mr Lofte?' he said quietly.

The snared pupils looked absolutely terrified. Campbell just whimpered and shook her head; Potts managed a 'N-no – it's nothing,' and went limp.

Moz slowly released them. 'I really, really wouldn't try that again. And you can tell your nasty little friends – in case they really are so thick they hadn't realized – that we are here to protect Mr Lofte. We are authorized to use force against anyone who threatens him. *Anyone*. I hope that's clear. Now, off you go, children . . .'

Potts and Campbell took off up the stairs without looking back.

'Wow,' said Jack, 'that was cool! But how does Potts know about the radiation? That's all supposed to be secret, isn't it?'

'My bone-marrow transplant seems to be known about somehow,' said Itch, 'and the rest must be guesswork. With you and Chloe getting treated too, that's a lot of people to keep quiet.'

'Presumably those two are some of the kids you told us about?' Moz nodded in the direction of the departing Potts and Campbell.

Itch sighed. 'Yeah. Thought it might ease off this term, but maybe I was wrong.'

Moz grinned. 'Well, the message will get around. They'll leave you alone now. I can't abide bullying. Saw enough of it in the army to last a lifetime. Come on – let's get you to history.'

That lunch time Itch made his way to the chemistry lab. A gang of Year Sevens flattened themselves against the wall as he walked past; some girls from Year Eight took one look at him and made a U-turn, disappearing into the nearest form room. Head down, Itch tried to ignore them all.

As he entered the lab, he was still half expecting to see Dr Flowerdew behind the long wooden bench at the front. But instead of the curly white hair, athletic build and permanent scowl of his former teacher, Itch was greeted by the genial smile of the short-haired Henry Hampton – the new head of science.

'Hi there!' Hampton's American accent echoed loud and clear through the lab. 'Itch, you're very welcome. Do come in. Does your friend want to join us too?' He took off his wire-rimmed glasses and gestured at the huge figure of Moz, who had taken up position by the door.

'No, he'll be fine outside,' said Itch.

Hampton looked disappointed but smiled a welcome anyway. 'Well, come in, come in! So glad you're joining us.'

Itch looked around. He counted twelve others, most of whom he didn't know. The only other boy from his class was Craig Murray, who had famously vomited on Flowerdew after Itch had accidentally poisoned his class with arsenic. There was Lucy Cavendish from Year Eleven, who had always been friendly to him and who was the last student to talk to him before his kidnap by Flowerdew. There were a couple of boys he thought he recognized from Chloe's class, and a lot of people he was sure he'd never seen before, some A-level students, he guessed.

'I was just suggesting a few things for us to look at this half term,' continued Hampton. 'What do you think?' He stood by the whiteboard, felt tip in hand. 'Did you know that the smallest motor in the world is just six atoms long? How about that! So I thought we could do some nano-technology.' He wrote *nano-technology* on the board. 'There's a lot of interest in rare earth mining at the moment. I can tell you all about my time at the Mountain Pass

38

mine in California . . .' *Rare earths* appeared on the board. 'And what else, guys? Any suggestions?' He waved his arms expansively, as though addressing five hundred students, not twelve.

There was a brief, embarrassing silence before one of the Year Sevens, a round boy with equally round glasses, said, 'Sir, Henderson was wondering if we could we look at the effects of methane in a small room . . .' He dissolved into giggles.

Itch rolled his eyes. *This is going to be a waste of time*, he thought.

'Hilarious, Cox!' said Hampton. 'We can, of course, study methane. It is a fascinating gas but, you should know, odourless. I imagine you are talking about breaking wind, yes?' More giggles and nodding from the Year Sevens. 'A whole lunch time to play with and you want to talk flatulence. My, my. Well, if you really want to know, the gas you are talking about is mainly nitrogen and hydrogen, with smaller amounts of carbon dioxide and, yes, methane. It is called flatus. If you wish to learn more, may I suggest you continue in your own time and at home . . .?' The other pupils laughed. 'Now, who else has something for us?'

He looked around, and one of the older girls – a slight Asian girl who must have been in the top year – put her hand up. Her hair was cropped short and Itch noticed three empty piercings in each ear. *Cool*, he thought.

'Yes, Mary,' said Hampton. 'What do you have for us?'

The girl leaned forward and smiled. 'My dad works in the petrochemicals industry and he's always bringing home interesting stuff. He just came back with a large glass tube which has some shiny silvery metal in it. It's solid most of the time, but when it's hot it turns liquid. I'm sure he wouldn't mind—'

'Sir, that's caesium!' shouted Itch, suddenly paying attention. 'That's amazing! Where did he get it?'

'No idea,' said Mary, 'but it's got CCCP stamped on it.'

Henry Hampton looked impressed. 'That's interesting, Mary. That'll be caesium from the old Soviet Union, by the sound of it. CCCP is Russian for USSR, the Union of Soviet Socialist Republics. It fell apart at the end of the 1980s, but some samples of their extraordinary array of chemicals do turn up from time to time. I do hope your father has kept it safe. Caesium is fantastically reactive. It'll explode if it gets wet. In fact, it'll burst into flames if any air gets to it at all.'

'Well, the glass is pretty thick,' said Mary. 'So as long as no one drops it, I'm sure I could bring it in. I've got a photo somewhere . . .' She scrolled through some pictures on her phone. 'Here we are . . .' She held up a photo of what looked like a

40

glass torpedo, about a metre long, with a white label and a red wax seal stamped on it.

Itch whistled his appreciation, and Hampton wrote *Caesium, Cs, atomic number 55* on the board.

'I'll need to speak to Dr Dart about it,' he said. 'I'm not too sure she'd want a highly explosive metal in her school.' He shot a glance at Itch. 'I think she's had her fill of, er, unnecessary chemistry. For quite a while.'

'But, sir, if Mary's father says it's OK—' Itch began.

'Oh, calm yourself,' said a scornful voice. Itch turned round, puzzled, and saw that it was Lucy Cavendish from the year above him. 'It's not *that* exciting.'

'Really? Caesium is cool! Don't they use it in clocks, sir?'

Mr Hampton nodded. 'Yes, Itch, they do. Caesium fountain clocks are the most accurate in the world.'

'There you go,' Itch told Lucy. 'I said it was interesting.'

But Lucy had her arms folded and was staring at the floor. Itch thought he heard her say 'loser'.

'Anyone got any other suggestions?' asked Hampton. He looked hopefully at Itch, who sighed. *I thought this might happen.* He was about to shake his head, keen to talk to Mary, when he remembered his work for Mr Watkins.

'Could you do something on dust fires maybe? There's a mill in Kentucky that blew up . . .'

'Oh sure,' said Hampton. 'Those explosions are terrifying. We can do that. No one thinks of flour as an explosive, but dispersed as a fine powder, that's exactly what it is. That's how the Great Fire of London started. Good call, Itch.'

They spent the rest of the lunch break talking about the Higgs boson and the Large Hadron Collider, with Mr Hampton showing them some photos he had taken while visiting CERN in the summer. When he had finished, Itch made a beeline for Mary. Although she was clearly older than Itch, she was several centimetres shorter. But then, most people were.

'That caesium sounds amazing,' he said. 'Does your dad bring home other stuff like that?'

'Yeah, quite often.' She smiled. 'How come you're so interested?'

'Oh, I'm an element hunter. I collect—'

'Don't tell me! The Periodic Table, right?' Itch looked astonished and Mary laughed. 'That's what my dad calls himself. That's why he brings all this stuff home. Our house is full of it.'

Itch didn't know where to start. 'Really? He's an element hunter? You're kidding, right? He's got more of . . .? Where did you say he . . .? I've never . . . Sorry, I'm not making any sense.'

Mary laughed. 'That's OK. Hopefully I'll be able

to bring some of it in. I'll find something less scary that won't give Mr Hampton a fit.'

'I think it's the head who's the problem, really,' said Itch. 'We had a few . . . well, problems, last term.'

'Yes, I heard.'

'Are you new?' Itch realized he had no idea who he was speaking to.

'Yes. We just moved. My dad's job means he has to travel, and we follow him around. He likes it that way.'

'Where were you before?'

'Stockholm. We loved it there, but Cornwall is so much warmer! We'll be fine here as long as I get the A-levels I need.'

'Are you in Year Thirteen?' asked Itch.

'Yeah, the end of school is nigh!' She picked up her bag and was about to leave when she turned and said, 'Did Mr Hampton just call you Itch? Is that a nickname?'

She didn't say it unpleasantly, but Itch still flushed with embarrassment and shrugged. 'No. It's just a name. What's yours, anyway?'

'Mary Lee.'

'OK. Bye, Mary Lee. Tell your dad there's an element hunter at school.'

Mary laughed. 'OK, I will. And I'll try and bring something interesting for next time. Bye!'

Itch watched her go, his head buzzing.

'Found someone who'll talk to you?' Itch turned

to see Lucy Cavendish with her bag over her shoulder. It looked as though she had been waiting around to speak to him.

'Well, I—'

'Once she's found out what you're really like, she'll join the rest of us.'

'What do you mean?' Itch was starting to go red again.

Lucy's eyes narrowed. 'In finding you totally embarrassing. The biggest, stupidest jerk in the school. She'll join us in hating you, Lofte.'

4

The 'home run' was at 4.15. With the exception of those with games or after-school clubs, the students had left by the time the Loftes gathered in the academy's reception hall. Itch, Chloe and Jack all had to leave at the same time.

Jack waved at the security van pairing of Danny and Chris. They smiled in acknowledgement as Tina led the way out into the gathering gloom; a soft sea mist hung in the air. Sam, and Jack's body-guard, Rachel, were with her 'on point', Moz and Kirsten following.

'Tell Chloe about your girl trouble,' said Jack.

'You what?' exclaimed Chloe, her eyes wide. 'Itch? You have girl trouble?' She started jumping up and down with excitement.

'It's not like that!' said Itch. 'They were at the science—'

'*They?* There's more than one?' Chloe clapped

45

her hands together and squealed. 'This *will* be a fun walk home.'

Jack laughed. 'He's told me most of it. That new science club might be more interesting than I thought!'

Itch explained what had happened at lunch time, with Lucy Cavendish being spiteful and new girl Mary Lee telling him about her element-collector father.

'I thought Lucy was the girl who always smiled when you turned up. Wasn't she the one who came to see how you were in the first-aid room after you were attacked by Flowerdew? I *thought* she fancied you,' said Chloe.

'Well, she obviously doesn't fancy me now,' said Itch. 'She said she hated me.'

'Doesn't mean she doesn't fancy you . . .' Jack was smiling.

'No, seriously,' protested Itch. 'You should have been there. She was wide-eyed and . . . staring.'

Jack and Chloe laughed.

'You'll win her round with your charm and your elements,' said Chloe.

Itch was feeling exasperated. 'Oh, ha ha. I'm not trying to *win her round*! Anyway, at least Mary was pleasant and knows about caesium—'

'The perfect girl!' cried Jack. 'Good-looking and knows about caesium!'

Chloe stifled another laugh.

'I know you're making fun of me, but actually caesium is really smart stuff. Her sample sounded as though it could be worth thousands,' Itch told them.

Jack and Chloe grinned at each other as Itch crossed the road to the golf course with the others just behind.

'Here's Rachel. Be seeing you guys!' Jack said. The tracksuited Rachel Taylor had peeled away from Sam and Tina and was waiting by the deserted thirteenth green.

'Might call you about that English essay!' called Itch as she crossed the road.

'Thought you might!' she shouted back.

As Itch and Chloe walked across the golf course, evening protection protocol had their minders at least five metres closer than in daylight. The course was deserted – sunset was in ten minutes. Sam and Tina, were keeping to the right of the course, by the road. It was brighter there – Itch watched the sodium vapour lamps pool their orange light on the damp tarmac.

'You OK?' asked Chloe.

'S'pose,' said Itch. He kicked a stone out of his way. 'I was really hoping to get to talk to more people this year – make more of an effort. You know, try to make a few friends. But that seems unlikely, the way things are going. Campbell and Potts got a scare from Moz, which will shut them up for a bit, but everyone just avoids me all the more.'

'Anyone you'd like to invite over? Maybe watch a film or something? Other than Mary or Lucy, obviously!' Chloe laughed, but tugged at Itch's sleeve reassuringly.

'Thanks . . . No, not really. Tom Westgate and Ian Steele aren't actually mean to me, but that's hardly best mates, is it?' Itch brushed his hair out of his eyes; the moisture in the air had plastered it to his forehead. 'When I was in Year Seven, just after we moved here, there was a day when I was feeling rubbish and asked to be excused. From maths, I think. I went to sit in the toilets, and Tom came in. He said Mr Logan had asked for a friend of mine to go and see if I was OK, but no one had put their hand up. So he volunteered Tom to go anyway. I don't know why he felt he had to tell me that, really. But he did.'

Chloe didn't say anything but tugged again at her brother's sleeve as they walked on.

Ahead, Tina and Sam had stopped. The pile of logs on the patch of scrubland at the corner of the golf course was alight. The agents each held up a hand, and Itch and Chloe stood still, while behind them Moz and Kirsten closed in slightly, looking around. A steady stream of vehicles were headed both up and down the hill, most with headlights and windscreen wipers on. Looking seaward, the golf course appeared empty – even the flags that marked the holes had been taken in for the night. A few silhouetted figures were hurrying along the path above the beach. The agents took all this in in seconds; they saw nothing to alarm them unduly. They could hear the flames crackling now and see the outlines of a few people gathered around the fire. Sam and Tina approached slowly and the procession moved on behind them.

'Bit early to light the fire, isn't it?' said Itch. 'I thought it was for the weekend.'

It is,' said Chloe, frowning. 'Maybe it was a mistake. The weather's getting worse, so perhaps they thought they might as well light it before the rain set in . . .'

Itch turned round, seeking reassurance, and Kirsten, unsmiling, nodded for them to continue. Ahead, Tina reached the fire first, with Sam just behind. The damp burning wood was spitting and hissing, but Itch clearly heard Tina ask, 'Who's in charge?'

And the bonfire exploded.

The flash was a brilliant yellow and orange, the explosion deafening, and it started to rain burning wood. Itch and Chloe were thrown to the ground, ash and flames landing all around them; they started swatting at their clothes and hair to extinguish the little fires that had landed on them. Itch was just picking himself up when the bunker behind them erupted. With a roar, sand and earth were blasted in all directions. Lumps of smoking soil crashed to the ground. Shaking sand out of his eyes, Itch realized he couldn't see Kirsten or Moz. Looking back down the hill, he couldn't see Sam or Tina either.

His stomach lurched. 'Whoa. We're in trouble!' His ears were ringing as he grabbed Chloe's hand. He looked round for the van, but all he could see was a row of stationary cars with their hazard lights flashing.

'Itch?' There was panic in Chloe's voice, and it spurred him into action.

Turning up the hill, he pulled her along through the smoke. They had only gone a few metres when they saw a large motorbike climbing the bank from the road. It shot up into the air, landed, and headed straight for them.

'He's not one of ours!' shouted Itch. They spun round and started back down the course, when three black-clad figures came running towards them through the smoking ruins of the bonfire.

'This way!' Itch gripped his sister's hand tighter and they ran into the darkness, towards the beach. His legs felt heavy – a reminder that he wasn't as fast as he had been before his bone-marrow transplant – but fear drove him on.

They could hear the roar of the motorbike's engine getting closer – it had changed course to intercept them from the left, while the three men were sprinting from the right.

'Where are we going?' cried Chloe.

'I don't know,' Itch panted. 'Maybe if we can get to the beach, we can lose them in the rocks. Head for the cliff path!'

He and Chloe weren't slow, but they could tell from the roar of the bike that it would reach them long before they got to the edge of the course. Its powerful headlights hadn't picked them up yet, but there was still enough light from the western sky to pick out two figures running at speed.

'What are we going to do?' Chloe sobbed.

Itch didn't answer – he was looking over his shoulder towards dual beams of light that were now throwing long double shadows across the wet grass. Halfway up the course, the security van was hurtling towards them. It was still fifty metres behind the motorbike, but closing the gap with every second.

'There! Look!' Itch shouted, pointing.

Chloe glanced up as the motorbike rider suddenly realized he had company. He started to change course but he was too slow. The van's front bumper ploughed into the motorbike's back wheel, sending the rider flying in an arc before he crumpled in a heap onto the twelfth green. He didn't move.

Itch and Chloe had paused only briefly to watch

the van, but within seconds the men from the bonfire were on them. One pushed Chloe roughly to the ground while the other two rugby-tackled her brother. Lying stunned on the grass, Itch twisted round desperately. Straining to get free, he caught sight of his attacker taking a syringe from his pocket. Itch cried out, but then heard a double thud, and the man on his chest was blown away from him, like leaf tossed by a gust of wind. He crumpled and lay face down on the turf; a gun and his glistening needle lay on the ground between them.

The remaining two men flung themselves down in front of him, their guns drawn. Their only visible target was the still stationary van, and they both started firing. Itch had flattened himself on the ground; a few metres away, a wide-eyed Chloe had done the same. He crawled towards her until he could touch her fingers.

'Stay low!' he mouthed, and she nodded. More shots, and Chloe screwed her eyes shut. Itch didn't know where the shot that had hit the man with the syringe had come from – he still couldn't see any of their protection force. How many of them had survived the twin explosions? Were the agents in the van OK? Itch decided he didn't want to wait and find out. He grabbed Chloe's hand, and she opened her eyes.

The two gunmen looked huge to Itch; their enormous black boots were barely a metre from his face. He could now see that they both wore balaclavas; their heads flicked nervously between the van and the remains of the bonfire. With no agents to aim at, they kept peppering the van with bullets. The noise gave Itch the confidence to speak to Chloe.

'Come on!' he said, and started to shuffle backwards to put some distance between him and the enemy. Chloe saw what he was doing and followed suit. It was a snake-like slither, but when Itch judged they were far enough away, they rose to a crouching run. They had covered nearly twenty metres before they heard loud shouts of alarm. Itch didn't recognize the language, but it sounded East European – Russian, maybe.

'They've spotted us! Hurry!' he cried, and they sprinted across the rough grass that marked the outer edge of the golf course. It was a gentle climb, and then a sharp descent to the cliff path, fifty metres away. Itch glanced over his shoulder; both men were up and giving chase. A burst of fire from the direction of the van: one of them crashed to the ground, screaming with pain.

The pair crested the ridge and flew downhill, but their remaining pursuer was too fast. A gloved fist made contact with Chloe's cheek and she stumbled to the ground. With the next step the man had grabbed Itch and forced him down too.

A black-jacketed arm came round Itch's throat

and the balaclava'd face was close to his ear. 'You struggle, I kill your sister.' The man pointed his gun at Chloe's head. 'Is not a problem for me.' His accent was thick but the words were clear enough.

'OK, OK!' cried Itch. 'Please! Whatever . . . I won't struggle! Leave her, leave her, please! She doesn't know anything!'

The man nodded. 'Get up. Down there . . .' He pointed towards the beach. 'Go. You try any-thing . . .' He gestured towards Chloe.

'No! I'll come with you! Please don't!'

The man grabbed Itch and, leaving Chloe behind, they half ran, half stumbled down towards the coastal path. It appeared to be deserted now, as did the parade of huts that sloped down along the beach front. At the far end stood a streetlamp; the mist had become a steady drizzle and the raindrops briefly shone yellow as they fell around it. There was still a thin line of light on the horizon too – just enough to see the dark mass of black granite rocks that ran out into the Atlantic and formed the south-ern end of the beach.

The man shoved Itch against the first beach hut and held him there while he spoke rapidly into a radio. The response squawked back and he scanned the beach. He produced a small pair of binoculars and looked again along the rocky promontory. Itch looked too, but saw nothing. The man spoke into his handset again, and this time they both heard a powerful outboard motor approaching from the south. Holding Itch by the collar, the man stepped out from the cover of the beach hut – and Itch wondered why it had taken him so long to realize what was happening.

He was being kidnapped.

5

Nicholas Lofte was in the garden, raking up the last fall of autumn leaves, when he heard the explosions. He dropped the rake and ran towards the next-door house. Fairnie was already emerging, his Glock 17 held in front of him.

'What's happened?' Nicholas's voice was urgent, demanding.

'There's an attack underway. Danny and Chris are in the van but the traffic's solid and they can't reach them. You have to stay here.'

'Like hell I will,' said Nicholas, sprinting away.

He was a hundred metres down the road before Fairnie caught up with him. 'Listen. He's your son, but he's *my* responsibility and this is an MI5 operation. Got it? If you're with me, you take orders, OK?'

Nicholas looked at him, but didn't reply. They turned the corner at the bottom of the hill and saw the full chaos and destruction that the twin explosions had caused. Splinters of wood and clods of earth covered the parked cars. There was a large hole in the ground; some of the logs had fallen back in and were burning fiercely. They ran across the road and saw Sam Singh and Tina Greaves lying face down, covered in sand.

Nicholas knelt down beside them while Fairnie ran over to the bunker. He found Moz Taylor still standing, but swaying as he bent to help Kirsten.

'Where's Itch?' the colonel yelled over the roar of the flames.

Moz shook his head. 'I don't know, sir.'

'There!' Nicholas was at Fairnie's shoulder, pointing at the edge of the course. The unmistakable figures of Itch and Chloe were silhouetted against the darkening sky. An assailant followed swiftly behind them.

'This way!' Fairnie ran right, along the road that led straight to the car park and the beach. Nicholas heard him talking to Kirsten and Moz, who were already back in action. 'Moz, you and Kirsten get Danny and Chris, and follow them. I'm going round to the right!'

They stormed through the car park and skidded round the corner of the first beach hut.

And froze.

Fairnie and Nicholas stared at the man who held Itch in one hand and a gun in the other.

'Itch!' Nicholas yelled as Fairnie pushed him into the gap between the first two huts.

'Dad!'

The man now had his right arm around Itch's neck. With his gun in his left hand, he dragged Itch in front of him and held him firm.

Fairnie emerged slowly, his gun aimed at the man's head. For a few seconds no one dared move. Then, from the slope behind, the clatter of guns being loaded made the man turn round. Moz and Kirsten were scrabbling down to the path, lining up their weapons as they ran. But they pulled up fast.

'Chloe's back there. She's hurt!' called Itch before his kidnapper tightened his grip, choking off any further words.

'OK – we'll find her!' Fairnie shouted. 'I'll get Chris to pick her up. Don't worry about her now – we'll make sure she's safe! Keep calm and do what he says!'

The man was walking backwards towards the steps that led down to the beach, the gun still pointing at Itch's left temple, his right arm still firmly across his windpipe.

Fairnie's voice filled the beach front again: 'You know you're not going anywhere. I'm counting three guns pointing straight at you. Give the boy up now!'

'And I have one gun pointing at his head,' called the man in the balaclava, his voice cracked and hoarse. 'I think I'm getting wherever I want to go. And you will let me.' He reached the steps, barely thirty metres from Fairnie and Nicholas, and, his eyes darting between the agents, descended onto the beach. He turned his head and shouted something in the direction of the rocks. In reply, the outboard motor roared back into life.

Still holding Itch tightly, the kidnapper walked backwards across the sand. None of the agents could risk a shot: attacker and hostage were approximately the same height, and in the near darkness the two figures had effectively merged. All they could see was one rapidly retreating shadow. At one end of the huts, Fairnie and Nicholas crawled across to the railings that ran a metre above the beach, while Kirsten mirrored their movements at the other end. She had the advantage of her Yukon Tracker night-vision goggles: she could see the infrared image of Itch, wide-eyed but not struggling, being dragged towards the rocks.

She spoke into her lapel mic. 'They're nearly at the rocks. The boat looks like a seven-metre rigid-inflatable, two engines. At least one man on board. It's a fast one – let's not let it go.'

Fairnie, cursing his lack of night vision, spoke fast. 'Moz, Danny – do you see them?'

'Got them,' came Danny's voice. 'I'm south of the rocks, twenty metres away, Moz is in the water.'

A few seconds passed before Moz's whisper came

through. 'I'm closing on the RIB. There's two on board, repeat two. Both armed, but we could take them! I'll have a clear shot in thirty seconds.'

'Not yet.' Fairnie's voice was firm. 'While Itch is a human shield, we can't risk it.'

Nicholas was beside himself with frustration. 'What's happening, Fairnie? Surely one of you can take a shot?'

Flashes of orange, and then two shots came from the rocks and the colonel had seen enough. 'Kirsten, you're my eyes. I'm going in. Give me cover.'

Kirsten's Glock 17 started firing; a deeper, thudding sound. She was aiming high, but close enough to draw the attackers' attention away from her boss.

Fairnie swivelled under the railings and hit the sand running. He hadn't spoken to Nicholas because he knew there was no point. He could hear him at his shoulder, matching him stride for stride.

'Sir! He has his back to you now! He's pushing Itch up onto the rocks!' Kirsten's voice was more urgent now, and Fairnie lined up his Glock.

As he sprinted across the sand, he saw Itch being herded towards the boat. It was rising and falling as its twin engines churned in the swell. Two men, also in balaclavas, crouched inside – one in the bow, the other at the stern, both facing the shore. Kirsten's sweeping fire was keeping them down. They were returning shots, but without taking proper aim.

Itch and his captor were crawling across the rocks towards them. Itch kept slipping over barnacles and into rock pools, and felt the barrel of the gun in his back, urging him to hurry towards the RIB. Then, just beyond the boat's stern, he saw Moz surface, let off three rounds at the boat, then sink again. The two men aimed their guns down into the water.

Now Danny started firing from behind the largest boulder he could find. The kidnapper loosened his grip just a little to correct his aim, and Itch realized he had to act swiftly. He twisted out from under the arm, and threw himself down on the granite.

'Itch on the ground! Clear shot! *Now now now!*'

Ten rounds came from Kirsten's Glock, followed by five from Fairnie. The kidnapper's head and chest exploded with blood, and he was thrown off the rocks and splashed into the sea.

'Itch, run!' yelled Fairnie. 'Straight to me!'

Itch picked himself up, but his right foot caught in a gap between two boulders and his ankle twisted painfully. Crying out, he crashed back down onto the rocks. As the fire-fight continued, Nicholas launched himself forward. Fairnie provided the covering fire as Nicholas ran to his son, and in one easy movement scooped him up and carried him off the rocks.

'Keep low!' called the colonel. 'Get him to a

beach hut and stay there! Go! We'll clear this up as quickly as we can!'

Nicholas, with Itch in his arms, ran for the steps. The agents intensified their fire to keep the kidnappers pinned down, and as he jumped up onto the promenade, he put his boot to the door of the nearest beach hut.

He gently laid Itch down on the wooden bench, then turned and pushed the door shut. The lock had buckled, so he propped it shut with a couple of deck chairs. They would provide no security, but he and Itch simply needed to disappear; if the attackers came back this way, there would be no indication of where they had hidden. He knelt on the sandy concrete floor and peered through the curtained window. He couldn't see what was happening on the rocks – the darkness and his limited field of vision saw to that. The shooting continued, how-ever, so it was clear the agents still had work to do.

'Thought of just taking you home, but Fairnie said to stay here,' he whispered to his son. 'I suppose we don't know who else is out there. Who are those guys, anyway?'

Itch sat up slowly and swung his legs down, wincing as his right foot touched the floor.

'Rest it,' said his father. 'You might need it very soon. Hopefully it's just a sprain.'

Itch felt gingerly around his ankle. 'It'll be fine. What's happening out there?'

Nicholas peered through the window. 'Can't see much. Can't see anything actually. But they're still shooting.' He slid to the floor with the buckets and crabbing lines, and rested one boot against the door. 'What happened to Chloe?' he said. 'Is she all right, do you think?'

'The kidnapper punched her in the face,' said Itch, 'but she was conscious – Fairnie said Chris was picking her up, didn't he?'

Nicholas nodded and they sat in silence.

'Thanks,' said Itch in the darkness.

'It's what dads do,' Nicholas replied.

'No, it isn't.' Itch managed a laugh. 'It really isn't.'

'Well, it seems to be what I do.'

There was silence in the hut, and Itch's mind started to whirl. He shifted his weight on the bench. If there had been any light, Nicholas would have seen his son's eyes widening. 'What do you mean?'

Nicholas didn't reply.

'Have . . . Have you . . . done that before, then?' asked Itch, his voice strained and his throat tightening.

There was a long pause. In the distance, two more shots.

Nicholas coughed nervously. 'Well, there was that time when we were camping in France and you—'

'Not then,' said Itch. Another pause. 'I don't mean then.'

63

'Yes,' said his father in a whisper. 'I *have* done this before.'

'Carried me to safety?'

'Yes, carried you to safety.'

'Where from?' said Itch. 'Where have you carried me from?' He barely registered that he was shaking from top to toe.

'I carried you out of the well, Itch,' said his father. 'It was me who rescued you from the well.'

6

In the dampness and darkness of the beach hut, Itch slid off the wooden bench, ignored the shooting pain in his ankle, and embraced his father. With both arms tightly round his neck, he sobbed quietly into Nicholas's jacket. A thousand questions were crowding into his brain, but for now the sheer relief of finding out who had saved him from certain death down the Woodingdean Well was all that mattered.

It hadn't been Flowerdew, and it hadn't been anyone from Greencorps. It had been his dad!

For some time, neither of them moved, briefly oblivious to the fighting a few hundred metres away. Eventually Itch pulled away and, sitting down on the damp floor, grinned broadly at his father. Nicholas smiled back, but his look was haunted, Itch thought. Both father and son wiped their eyes.

'I can't believe it was you!' cried Itch. 'How did you know where I was? How come—?'

'I guess there are a thousand things you need an answer to,' interrupted his father, 'but this is not the best time or place really . . . I never intended to tell you like this.' He sighed. Itch thought it was the longest, weariest sigh he had ever heard.

Nicholas suddenly realized that the shooting had stopped, but he still couldn't see any movement. The pale streetlight at the car park end of the promenade didn't help.

'Look, Itch, we are in a lot of danger still, and until Fairnie comes to get us we need to be alert. Those criminals, or whoever they are, could come back any time. Who's to say there aren't more of them out there?'

'Sure, Dad – but you need to tell me something! I've been worrying about who got me out of the well ever since I woke up in hospital! Don't you realize what a difference this makes – the fact that it was you? Wait till Fairnie hears this!'

'No way, Itch! Sorry, but absolutely no,' said Nicholas firmly. 'This is just for you. Really. No one else.'

'Presumably Mum knows . . . ?'

'Er, no, she doesn't, actually.'

Itch gasped. 'What? Well, what does she—?'

'OK, listen.' His father peered out of the window

again. 'In brief . . .' He sighed again. 'Remember, just for you, OK?'

Itch nodded.

'I haven't worked on the rigs for quite a while now, Itch. The reason we moved here is because I was offered a job by Jacob Alexander at the—'

'You work at the mining school?' said Itch, incredulous.

'No, no – not usually, no. I'm mostly in London. Listen, son, this will take ages if you don't let me talk, and who knows how long we have? I've been desperate to tell you this stuff, so . . . here goes. I started to hate the rig, and pretty much the whole oil industry. Corners were being cut, safety compromised – there were injuries that could have been avoided. Greencorps were the worst, so I left them years ago. I thought the smaller companies would be better, and some are, but mostly they seemed just as grubby, just as bent. So when Jacob offered me a job, I jumped at the chance.'

Itch was bursting to cut in – he remembered Dr Alexander well: his enthusiasm for the Gaia theory – viewing the Earth as a living planet that looked after itself; his dream of clean, green nuclear energy – but his father didn't stop.

'I realized I couldn't tell your mother. Things . . . well . . . you might have noticed that things are a bit tense at home. Between your mum and me. It sort of suited both of us that I wasn't there very much.'

Itch bit his lip.

'Also,' his father continued, 'she thinks Jacob is a bit of a crackpot. She would have hated me leaving the rigs for him. So I decided just to . . . not tell anyone.'

'And move us all to Cornwall?'

'That was always the plan anyway, and with my new job being in London, I thought it would be easier to keep the secret. It's fascinating work Jacob does, Itch. You'd really—'

'Dad, Dad, there'll be time for that, but tell me how you found me, please. Fill me in on all this other stuff, sure, but I need to know how you got to the well.'

Three distant shots – then footsteps running on concrete. Itch and Nicholas froze. Two shadows moved outside – too quickly to be identified.

'Lie down! There!' Nicholas pointed under the wooden bench and Itch eased himself into his hiding place. His father flattened himself against the door. They could hear each hut door being rattled and kicked. Whoever it was, they were working their way down the row. They would be outside in a matter of seconds.

'Dad! We can't just wait here! Let's make a run for it!'

'You can't run on that ankle, Itch, remember.' The voices were closer now.

'I don't want to be kidnapped, Dad. Not again! Please!'

'It's too late to run. Wait . . .'

Suddenly they heard a woman's voice: 'Itch! It's Kirsten. Moz too. Are you there?'

Nicholas sprang up and peered through the window into the darkness. Itch heard him sigh again, but this time with relief. He opened the door. 'Here!' he called, and suddenly the hut was full of drenched and bloody agents cradling their guns and talking at the same time. The hut filled with the smells of sulphur, smoke and saltwater.

Itch and Nicholas sat down while Kirsten and Moz radioed Fairnie.

'Found them, sir! Hut twenty-six, both good.' Kirsten and Moz listened to Fairnie's reply through their earpieces. 'Yes, sir,' they said together.

'Fairnie says we're to head straight back,' Kirsten reported.

Nicholas stood up. 'What about Chloe? . . . Where's my daughter?'

'Chris took her home – she's with your wife. That's all I know.'

Nicholas thought for a moment. 'Are we OK now?'

'Think so, yes,' said Moz. 'They put up quite a fight – they wanted you bad, Itch, that's for certain.' A thin stream of blood ran down his face from a cut in his scalp, and he was still dripping wet. 'You ready to go?'

'How're Tina and Sam?' asked Itch.

'Not great,' replied Moz. 'Sam seems OK, but Tina took the full force of that bonfire explosion.'

'Will she . . . will she be OK?'

Moz shrugged. 'I don't know. But they're on their way to hospital now. She's in good hands. Come on, let's go.'

That night, the three Lofte cousins were gathered together in the unfamiliar surroundings of the next-door house. Fairnie had insisted that, with fewer agents fit to guard them, Jack should join the others in the Coles' house until the situation had been assessed. It was a squeeze, but with the agents sharing rooms, everyone was accommodated.

Itch hadn't realized how much he'd been looking forward to being just with Jack and Chloe again. The three of them would now be sleeping – more like camping, really – in the guest room that Sam had been using. The steel blinds had been lowered – no light from the streetlamps seeped in.

Jack and Itch's sleeping bags lay on the floor, but they had joined Chloe on the bed, sitting with their backs against the wall; Jack had her arm around Chloe. The lights had been switched off earlier, but when it became clear that no one could sleep, they had put the bedside light back on. The clock radio now showed 00.09.

Jack and her parents had been brought over in the van and hadn't stopped asking questions. Itch and Chloe had answered as many as they could, but Fairnie still hadn't returned, and he was the one with the answers. He was still checking on Sam and Tina in the hospital. Tina was in intensive care but stable.

'They said you'd be a target, Itch, but I never really believed them, you know,' said Jack. 'I mean, not here! Not on the way back from school!'

'Same here,' Chloe agreed. 'But I changed my mind.' She was holding an ice pack to her face, but it had arrived too late to prevent her left eye closing. A purple bruise had spread out over most of her nose and cheek.

'Has your head stopped throbbing?' Itch asked her. 'That was some punch you took.'

'Painkillers helped a bit. But not really, no.' There was silence, then she added, 'Does today change anything?'

'Do you mean, am I about to tell Fairnie where the 126 is? Answer: no. Will they stop us going to school? Don't know. There's a chance, I suppose.'

'Will the school want us?' said Jack, handing round some cheese biscuits she had brought. 'Now that men with guns have been shooting up the beach, will *anyone* want us?'

'Maybe not. Guess all those party invitations will be drying up, then,' said Itch, smiling. The others laughed.

'You seem pretty made up for someone who's just been kidnapped and shot at,' commented Jack.

'Do I? Oh. Well, it must be relief, I suppose.' And he grinned again.

'You're so weird,' said Chloe through a mouthful of biscuit, and closed her eyes.

Itch was feeling better than either Jack or Chloe knew. The knowledge that it was his father who had rescued him from the well was still sinking in. He could feel himself relaxing more with each passing minute. He had tried in vain to get Nicholas on his own once they were all back in the Coles' house, but his father had been constantly in meetings with the agents, on the phone or talking to Itch's mother. Jude had arrived home, horrified, shortly after Itch and Nicholas. Itch wanted more details of his rescue from the well in the Fitzherbert School, but it could wait. He felt a strange lightness now. He knew he was still in danger, and that this evening had proved how deadly matters had become, but in spite of that, he found himself smiling.

When Chloe had finally drifted off to sleep, the ice pack still against her face, Itch and Jack got back into their sleeping bags.

'How long . . . ? Wait,' said Jack. 'Are we OK to talk here? Will it be bugged?'

'No, it's Sam's room,' Itch told her. 'Why would they? It wouldn't make sense. Keep it quiet, though.'

'OK . . . How long were you hiding in the hut with your dad?' whispered Jack. 'You must have been terrified.'

Itch thought about it. All he remembered was his dad telling him about the well, so he had to guess. 'Dunno, really. Ten minutes? Something like that. And it wasn't so bad.'

'Excuse me?' Jack propped herself up and stared at her cousin. 'Did you really just say, *It wasn't so bad?* Really? Weren't you wondering if the guys with guns would come back and find you?'

'Well, yes, I suppose we were,' said Itch, 'but it wasn't really like that.'

Jack waited for Itch to continue, but when he stayed silent, she tried again. 'Well, what was it like then?'

'Er . . . I . . .'

Itch remembered that his father had sworn him to secrecy, but he would *have* to tell Jack. They had gone through so much and become so ill getting rid of the radioactive 126, she deserved the truth. Or as much of it as he knew, anyway.

He glanced at his sister – she was sound asleep. His whispered voice was tense with excitement. 'Jack! Dad said it was *him*! It was *him* who rescued me!'

'You what?'

73

Itch sat up and leaned towards his cousin. 'You know, after I'd got rid of the 126 I was in a bad way . . . and then I turned up in Crawley hospital with a radioactive sticker on me? It was Dad who pulled me out! It was him all along! I don't know how he knew where I was, but somehow he did. I haven't been able to get the details yet, but I'll talk to him in the morning.'

Now it was Jack's turn to be silent.

'Well, what do you think?' asked Itch. 'Jack? Don't you think that's amazing?'

Jack stared at her cousin, and Itch suddenly thought he saw the gleam of tears.

'Jack, what's the matter?'

'Look, Itch, this is difficult, OK?' Jack paused, searching for the right words. 'It sounds like you'll find this out tomorrow anyway, and I'd rather you heard it from me.'

'Heard *what* from you? Jack, what's going on?'

She wiped her eyes with her sleeve. 'OK. Well, remember when we were in the toilets at Victoria Station? And I wanted to give up?'

Itch nodded. 'You were very sick, Jack.'

'Then you told me to leave you. And that you needed to do the next bit on your own.'

'Yes, of course I remember. You ended up being followed by that Greencorps guy with the burned hair.'

'But before that . . .' Jack swallowed. 'Itch, don't

be mad, please . . . Before that, I hid round the corner from the toilets and waited for you. I saw you leave, buy the train ticket, then throw up under those stairs. I watched you get on the train to Brighton.'

Itch was flabbergasted. 'Jack! The whole point was that no one would know where I was going. Even *you*!'

'I know what the point was, Itch, but I couldn't just leave you on your own! So once I knew you were on the Brighton train, I called Mr Watkins.'

Itch gaped. 'You rang Watkins?'

'You were watching the platform for ages. I checked the board: Platform Ten was the Brighton train, and I knew there was a reason you'd picked it. It took me a while to get it, but then I remembered that Watkins had taught there once. And that story about the Woodingdean Well is a favourite of his, isn't it? I realized that was where you must be heading. Anyway, he said he'd do his best. Which I guess must have meant ringing your dad.' Her eyes were pleading. 'Say something, Itch! I know you wanted it to be a secret, but I thought . . . think I was helping. I was right, wasn't I?'

'So . . . you rang Watkins, he rang my dad and my dad rescued me. He must have been in London to be able to reach me so soon.' Itch shook his head. 'This is too much! I've been living with this secret since the summer – every minute of every day wondering who came for me – and all along *my dad* knew, *Watkins* knew and *you* knew! *Everyone* knew! Anyone else I haven't worked out yet?'

'Itch, don't be mad! I thought . . . you were going to die, Itch. I really thought I'd never see you again.'

Itch's head was spinning. 'Wow. Wow,' he said softly, and looked at Jack. 'You saved my life. You actually saved my life. I'd still be down that well if you hadn't made that call.'

Jack grinned. 'Yes, I think so.'

They sat there for a moment, aware of the hum of adult conversation downstairs.

'Does Chloe know any of this?' asked Itch.

Jack shook her head.

Slowly and painfully, Itch told Jack the full story of how he had travelled to Brighton and dispatched the 126 rocks to the bottom of the Woodingdean Well.

Jack listened in silence with wide eyes and a hand over her mouth. 'I think that's the most amazing story I've ever heard,' she said quietly when he had finished. 'I guessed it had been rough, but I never knew . . . I never realized . . .' She tailed off, and neither of them said anything for several minutes.

Eventually Jack said quietly, 'You know Cake would be proud, don't you?'

Even in the darkness, she could see Itch's eyes glisten as he thought of the mineral seller who had first found the rocks.

Then he smiled. 'I hope so. He told me to get rid of them, and I did my best.'

'How deep was it?'

'1,285 feet.'

'What's that in metres?'

'391.668,' said Itch, and Jack laughed.

'That's a very Itchingham Lofte answer!'

'Well, it's just the answer to the question,' replied Itch, 'and I had a long time to work it out.'

'Is that it then?' asked Jack. 'End of the story?'

'Doesn't feel like it, does it?' said Itch. 'And now, you realize you're in danger too, don't you? And my dad. And Watkins,' he added.

Jack dropped her voice even further. 'Only if anyone realizes that we know where the 126 is. But I'm glad of my protection all the same.'

'Watkins has nothing, though. Nobody's watching him,' said Itch. 'Maybe we should talk to him.'

The sound of a large car arriving interrupted their conversation.

'Fairnie's back,' said Itch.

A few seconds later they heard him enter the kitchen, exchange a few words and then bound up the stairs. A single knock on the door, and there he was, still grimy from the beach fight, his face smeared with grease, sand on his trousers and boots.

'Thought you'd still be up. I've spoken to your folks and your head teacher. You need to sleep, but you're going to school tomorrow. Same as usual. OK? Nothing changes.'

'Really?' said Jack. 'I thought they'd want us out of there . . .'

'No,' said Fairnie. 'The school just think it was a November the Fifth prank that went wrong. And I have given your parents certain assurances.' He wiped his moustache with his thumb and forefinger. 'We are tightening our security. And they are fine with that.'

And before they could ask about Sam and Tina, he was gone.

7

'Want some company?' Alejandro, the sometime oil-rig barman approached his patient.

Eyes closed, his face blue and green with bruises, Nathaniel Flowerdew barely moved his lips. 'Do I look like I want company?' His voice was weak and he coughed, wincing at the effort.

'No.' The Argentinian smiled. 'Doesn't mean you're not getting it though.' He pulled up a chair, placing fresh water on the bedside table. 'I suppose the thanks-for-saving-my-life stuff can wait.'

'Fair enough,' said Flowerdew. 'Thanks for saving my life. Where am I? I'm afraid to open my eyes in case I'm still on the rig with that lunatic woman.'

'You're on the north coast of the Malvinas – or

the Falkland Islands, if you prefer. Little place called Green Cove. You're safe.'

'Safe from who?'

Alejandro laughed. 'It's remote here. So, safe from the British. Safe from Greencorps. Safe from everything bar the rockhopper penguins.'

Flowerdew managed to open one eye a few millimetres. 'But you're just a barman.'

That laugh again. 'Of course! The barman who saw you being thrown off the rig; the barman who got the helicopter crew to pull you out and transfer you to Stanley; the barman who made you disappear under the noses of your bosses. And the barman who reckons you're the scientist who had some rocks to sell.'

Flowerdew was silent for a few moments. 'It's . . . Alejandro, isn't it?'

'I'm flattered you remembered my name; that must have taken some effort.'

Flowerdew closed his eyes again. 'I didn't know the Spanish did sarcasm.'

'It's *Argentinian*. I'm Argentinian and my name is Alejandro Loya. We hear enough *sarcasmo* from you Brits to get quite good at it ourselves.'

Flowerdew opened both eyes now and looked around. He was in a small, neat room with a log fire at one end and a curtained bay window filtering sunshine at the other. The room was sparsely furnished but it was clean and there was a smell of bacon wafting in from somewhere.

'OK, let me guess,' he said. 'You have to be Secretaria de Intelligencia. Am I right?'

The Argentinian smiled.

'Well I never . . .' Flowerdew attempted to whistle but failed – his swollen lips just made a wet blowing sound. 'The notorious SI. The Argentinian secret service on an oil rig off the Falklands? What were you doing there?'

'What do you think?' said Loya, peering through the curtains. 'We watch what is ours and what we want to be ours.'

'Don't think you're getting the oil. There was a war, remember?' Flowerdew shut his eyes again and tried to sip some water.

'I don't need a history lesson,' said the Argentinian, 'and I don't mean the oil. I mean *you*.'

Flowerdew opened both eyes once more. 'Well well. Two surprises in one morning. So you saved me for a reason, not just because you felt sorry for me. I'm grateful, of course . . .'

The bedroom door opened, and a stocky, bearded man came in, balancing a tray laden with bacon sandwiches and a teapot and mug. 'Good morning, Dr Flowerdew. I am Peter Voss. I've got some food here, if you fancy something to eat?'

Loya produced another chair and they both sat down facing Flowerdew.

The Englishman was frowning. 'And that's a

South African accent . . . Afrikaans. This is one strange international operation.'

'We work with many agencies and individuals around the world to get what we want,' said Loya.

'And what does Peter bring to the party?' said Flowerdew. 'Apart from breakfast.'

'My history is in mining, Dr Flowerdew, but I have learned many new skills that may assist us all.'

'So you're not a South African agent?'

'I was once.'

'Thrown out?'

'We had our disagreements.'

'I'm sure you did. So, Alejandro, what is it you want? I'm listening.' Flowerdew leaned back on the pillows and removed the bacon from the sandwich, nibbling it carefully.

The Argentinian and the South African nodded at each other.

'We have admired your skills over many years, Dr Flowerdew.' It was Loya who led the conversation. 'You combine a flare for finding oil and other valuable deposits with a certain – shall we say – *enthusiasm* for results.'

'You mean *ruthless*. The word you're looking for is *ruthless*.'

Both agents nodded. 'Thank you for helping me with my English,' said Loya, straight-faced. '*Ruthless* is good – *despiadado*! We were planning an approach anyway, but when your former colleague kicked you off the rig, we had to move quickly. The chopper got you out fast but I thought you would be dead.'

'I remember nothing after hitting the water,' said Flowerdew. 'Did I sink?'

'You kicked around for long enough for the heli-crew to reach you. We had you medi-vaced to Port Stanley, and then I made the detour to this cottage owned by Peter here. It's a safe house we've used before. It's fine but limited. Greencorps will realize you're not in hospital and come looking for you. The weekly flight to Santiago leaves in three hours: you need to be on it.'

'And in return?'

'I think you know what we want,' said Loya.

Flowerdew rubbed his white curls. 'Ah – you've heard about the 126, I assume.'

The South African Voss smiled. 'We have a client who is very interested in acquiring it.'

'So I get to Chile . . . then what?'

'You wait,' said Voss. 'Then we put you on a flight to London. A passport will be with you shortly.'

'And then? Once I've done all this waiting?' Flowerdew sounded impatient already.

Alejandro Loya leaned in close. 'You get the rocks for us.'

Flowerdew sipped some more water. 'But I don't know where they are.'

'We'll help you find them.'

'My delightful ex-colleague Shivvi Tan Fook – the woman who pushed me into the sea – is already on the case. I told her about the 126.'

Loya and Voss exchanged glances.

'Then we need to be fast,' said the South African.

Flowerdew, his voice steady, said, 'OK. What's the deal?'

'You'll get a generous percentage of what we make,' said Loya.

'Define generous.'

'Twenty per cent. And you're hardly in a position to negotiate.'

Flowerdew looked in pain again and closed his eyes. Then he nodded.

The Argentinian stood up. 'Good. Let's get you out of here.'

8

Whatever Fairnie had said, the school run was different now. At Jude Lofte's insistence, all the children went to school in the security van with Danny and Chris, and Colonel Fairnie went with them. There was silence as they left the house – none of the usual joking about.

They drove past the golf course, the sites of the twin explosions marked by deep holes in the ground and police tape cordoning off the area. Sand and charred logs were scattered across the lower part of the course. In the light of day, the wreckage was all the more stark and shocking. Small groups of onlookers stood around; they looked up as the van passed by.

'Loads of people heard the explosions,' Jack said, peering out of the tinted rear window. 'Natalie, Sam, Jay and Matt have all changed their Facebook status to things like *The golf course exploded!* and *Whoa! Who's attacking us now?* Then there's loads of comments; some people said they went down last night to see what had happened.'

Fairnie swivelled round. 'What else was posted? Anyone hear the shooting on the beach?'

'Yeah, a few,' Jack replied. '*Did anyone hear the gun-fire? What was happening on the beach?* That kind of thing.'

Fairnie swore quietly.

'What are the chances that this will be picked up by the local news? Or in the paper?' asked Itch.

'Now that it's on Facebook, I would say every chance. They've been cooperative so far, but nothing has been this public until now.'

'What do you mean, *they've been cooperative*? Do they know about me?'

Colonel Fairnie ignored Itch's question. 'The police are saying it was just a bonfire that got out of control, and that should keep it quiet for a while. But if evidence of the gunfight gets out, that might be . . . a problem. Fireworks will take the blame for most of it, so let's hope that's good enough.'

He looked at Itch in the mirror. 'Where did you say you'd hidden the rocks?' He smiled, and Itch managed a laugh. This had been their joke back in the military hospital in the summer, when every-body had been trying to tease the 126's location out of Itch.

Itch and Jack avoided each other's gaze.

The van swung into the academy car park, where Kirsten, Moz and Rachel were waiting for them.

'Feels like we're arriving at a movie premiere,' said Chloe.

In the mêlée of the reception area, a familiar face caught Itch's attention.

'Hi, Itch.' It was Mary Lee, the new girl in Year Thirteen. 'Did you hear the explosions last night? Isn't the golf course near you? Are you OK?'

'Oh, thanks,' said Itch, blushing already. Chloe and Jack moved away a little, grinning to each other. 'Yeah, I'm fine. We were at home; think it was some fireworks that went wrong or something.'

'So it wasn't that Year Eleven girl trying to blow you up?' Mary smiled.

'Oh – Lucy, you mean?' said Itch. 'No, she's just mad at me for some reason. What's that you've got . . . ?' His raging embarrassment was overcome by curiosity. Mary held a small cardboard box in her hand.

'Oh, well, I guess the caesium really *is* too dangerous for school, so I brought this in instead.' She held out the box, but before Itch could take it, Moz was beside him.

'Can I see that, please?' He grabbed it, and Mary looked irritated.

'It's perfectly safe, you know.'

'So you say,' replied Moz. 'What is it?'

'Show him – he'll know.' Mary pointed at Itch.

Moz removed the lid and looked at the large crystal sitting inside on some cotton wool. He showed it to Itch, who grinned.

'Wow, it's beautiful,' he said, reaching forward to pick it up. He held it to the light. It was about two centimetres square and seemed to be made up of thin layers of metallic pinks, blues and yellows. Its neat square edges made it look like a missing piece of a futuristic building kit.

'Safe?' asked Moz.

'Pretty much,' said Itch. 'It used to be the last of the stable elements.'

'What is it now, then?'

Itch smiled. 'It's fine, Moz. Really.'

Mary clapped her hands. 'Told you! You got it!' She smiled at Moz. 'You haven't a clue though, have you? Tell him, Itch.'

Itch glanced at Mary, uncomfortable with her treatment of Moz. 'It's bismuth,' he said. 'Number eighty-three on the Periodic Table. If she'd brought in the next one along, Moz, then you'd have had a problem.' Moz raised a quizzical eyebrow. 'Polonium. Ten one-billionths of a gram could kill you. But this is fine. It's beautiful, isn't it?'

'It's quite pretty if you like that kind of thing, I suppose,' he agreed. 'Now, can we move along? You have lessons, I think . . .'

Itch put the crystal back in the box and handed it back to Mary.

'No, you keep it for a bit.' She pushed it back at Itch. 'My dad won't miss it. He's off travelling again anyway. See you around, Itch!' And she turned and jogged away down the corridor.

Itch watched her go.

'Stop gawping,' said Moz quietly in his ear. 'Let's go.'

All morning, Itch kept looking at the crystal. He had seen pictures of bismuth, of course, but had never been tempted to buy any. He hadn't realized how beautiful it was and wondered how much the crystal was worth.

'Does it have *I Love You* inscribed on it?' asked Jack at the start of ICT.

Itch punched her lightly on the arm. 'Oh, ha ha, Jack. You are *so* funny. It's just a crystal . . .'

'From her dad's collection!' laughed Jack. 'And you only met her yesterday.'

'Jack, she's Year Thirteen. Use your head.' He put the crystal back in its box. 'It's just that there aren't exactly many element hunters around, so when you find one – even the daughter of one – you have stuff to talk about. That's all.' He felt himself start to blush again and pushed the box deep into his rucksack.

Jack leaned over again. 'Anyway, if you can tear

yourself away from your new rock friend, don't forget my hockey match at lunch time,' she whispered. 'Bit of support would be nice . . . It might be quite a tough one.'

'Sure,' said Itch. 'I'll be there. And I'll flash my bismuth crystal to blind the opposition if they dare to score.'

The explosions on the golf course were the only topic of conversation at school that morning. Itch heard a number of theories, including a car running into the bonfire, a hidden cache of fireworks going off and – from an excited Year Eight boy – a terrorist rocket attack. Although no one seemed to have been an eyewitness, most assumed that it was something to do with Itch. After the lectures from the MI5 agents about the dangers of on-line discussion about him, this wasn't surprising.

Potts and Campbell were keeping well away after the previous day's run-in with Moz, but on the way out to the playing fields at lunch time, huddled against a fine drizzle blowing in off the Atlantic, Itch had more than Moz for company.

'Was that you on the golf course yesterday?' asked Tim Abbott. 'Did you blow up the bonfire? Bet it was you! That's so cool!'

'I reckon it was your bodyguards,' said Craig Murray, pointing at Kirsten, who was, as ever, ten metres in front of Moz. 'They probably saw someone hiding in the wood and just took him out.'

'Maybe the whole golf course is covered in land mines. Under every bunker and green.' This was Matt Colston's theory. 'Whaddya think, Itch? They know you walk across the golf course, and eventually you'll step on one and . . . *boom!*' Everyone laughed, including Itch.

'Yeah, thanks, Matt. But no, I was at home. As were my *bodyguards*.'

'Then why was the ambulance called?' asked Tim. 'I heard some of your guys got taken out. Is that right?'

'I . . . I don't know actually,' replied Itch.

As they approached the hockey pitch, Itch saw Chloe coming over; she too appeared to have a gang of inquisitors firing questions at her. She waved at her brother and shrugged.

A decent crowd of around thirty students had come out for the match – a practice match: Year Ten versus Year Eleven. Both teams had important games coming up, and this was the warm-up – a try-out too for some new hopefuls. There was scattered applause as the two teams ran out. Rachel Taylor was, as usual, just behind Jack, looking like she was about to referee the match. The players warmed up, flicking hockey balls at each other and hitting shots goalwards; the well-padded goal-keepers threw themselves about theatrically.

Jack's team of Year Tens had only played one match this term, a 3–0 defeat to Launceston

College, so they were all keen to improve. Itch studied the Year Elevens, who looked so much bigger, and hoped it wasn't going to be embarrassing. Lucy Cavendish was the only player he recognized on their team, and he remembered how unpleasant she'd been yesterday. He was still puzzling it over when Craig Harris, the games teacher, blew his whistle. A few shouts of encouragement came from the students spread thinly around the pitch. Itch noticed that Mary Lee had come out to watch, standing on her own behind the Year Tens' goal.

Both sides were in the academy colours of black and white quarters, with the Year Tens wearing diagonal yellow sashes to mark them out. In the November gloom and mud, the match soon became a messy and foul-strewn affair; Mr Harris had to warn both teams about their tactics and language. Fiona Bones, the Year Eleven captain, had a nasty tangle with Darcy Campbell in the Year Tens' goal, and had to be held back by her teammates. Itch found himself hoping Bones would thump Campbell and get them both sent off; he guessed Jack was thinking the same.

The most combative player on the pitch was Lucy Cavendish. Playing in Year Elevens' midfield, she was at the heart of everything her team did. She was ferocious: on two occasions Year Ten players lost their grip on their sticks after a crunching

Cavendish tackle. She yelled at her teammates and rubbished her opponents. Itch tended to watch Jack more than the ball, so he spotted Lucy saying quite a lot to his cousin, particularly when Mr Harris wasn't watching.

Jack seemed to be ignoring her – the usual Lofte response to verbal abuse from classmates, though they'd never had trouble with older students. As he watched, Lucy ran past Jack and let a trailing stick catch her shin. Jack cried out and Lucy put her hands up in apology, but Itch was sure she'd done it on purpose.

The Year Tens thought so too. Debbie Rice, playing in their defence, pointed at Lucy. 'Mr Harris! Sir!' she called. 'Cavendish fouled Jack! Watch her!'

Jack was rubbing her leg where the stick had broken her skin, but was playing on.

The Year Elevens had a short corner, and as the ball was played to Lucy, the Year Tens rushed out to defend their goal. Lucy swung her stick at the ball, missed, but found the head of Izzy Batstone – a new Year Ten girl – instead. As the girl dropped to her knees, Natalie Hussain pushed Lucy and grabbed hold of her ponytail, but Fiona Bones, the Elevens' captain, charged over and smacked Natalie in the face.

This was the cue for a scrap that involved almost every player apart from the Elevens' goalkeeper, who couldn't get there in time. Jack had scratches on her face and was pushing a Year Eleven away by the time Craig Harris finally got control. This was due in no small measure to agents Kirsten and Rachel jogging over 'to see if they could help'.

With tempers calmed, Mr Harris gave them all a final warning and allowed play to continue.

Itch hadn't watched a hockey match for years — maybe ever — but he was surprised how violent it was. 'You OK?' he called as Jack ran past.

She nodded quickly as she faced up to another Year Eleven attack. Being fast and tricky made her a useful player; being as tall as a Year Eleven made her invaluable. Itch still sometimes felt weak after his bone-marrow transplant in the summer, but Jack appeared to be at full strength again.

After fifteen minutes Darcy Campbell, in the Tens' goal, kicked the ball clear, and Izzy Batstone flicked it through to Jack. Pushing the ball past a stocky Year Eleven girl twenty metres out, Jack had a clear sight of goal, with only the goalkeeper, Jackson Baker, to beat. As Baker came rushing out, Lucy Cavendish and another Year Eleven closed in on Jack from behind, one on each side. Running without the ball, they were soon within tackling distance.

Itch heard Lucy shout, 'She's mine!' and as Jack ran wide to find an angle to shoot from, she barged into her. Losing her balance, Jack shortened her stride but found Lucy's stick between her feet. Realizing she was falling, Jack dropped her stick to break her fall. As her hands hit the turf, one of Lucy Cavendish's studded boots stamped hard on her fingers. The crunch echoed around the pitch.

The players raced towards Jack, who was lying on her side, cradling a damaged right hand. Led by the huge padded figure of goalkeeper Darcy Campbell, the Year Tens surrounded Lucy, and the slapping, hair-pulling and scratching started up again. Mr Harris waved his hands and blew his whistle, but it was Kirsten who restored order. She pulled a bloodied Lucy Cavendish out from under two Year Tens – her shirt ripped at the neck and her ear starting to swell.

'Go away. Now. And take your team with you,' Kirsten yelled at Lucy. No one argued, and the teacher gratefully accepted her help.

The Year Tens turned their attention to their stricken teammate. Jack was lying in the mud, sobbing quietly, when Itch got there, but Rachel, kneeling beside her, asked everyone to keep back. She was quickly joined by Kirsten.

'You need to show me the damage, Jack. Let's see your hand.'

Jack shook her head, her eyes and mouth screwed shut.

'OK. Hold still. Got some painkillers on the way.' Rachel took off her padded coat and draped it over Jack, who had started to shake from shock.

Itch noticed that Mr Harris was jogging after the departing Year Elevens and he ran to catch up. The games teacher shouted, 'Lucy, a word please.'

Flushed and bloody, Lucy Cavendish turned and trotted over to him, her hockey stick over her shoulder. She ignored Itch. 'Sir?'

'Well, what do you think, Lucy? What happened there?'

'Just an accident, sir. She fell and I trod on her hand, sir. I tried to avoid her, but we were running so fast I couldn't get out of the way in time. Sorry, sir.'

'You may well be. That was the worst-tempered match I have ever seen, and you were a part of the problem. I couldn't see what was going on through the tangle of legs, but I'll talk to Jack when she's in less pain. You'd better go and clean up. Don't go home till I've spoken to you.'

Lucy nodded, and had turned to go when Itch stepped in front of her.

'Excuse me,' she said. 'If you don't mind, I need to go and shower.' She smiled sweetly.

'But I saw you! I *saw* you.' Itch knew he was shouting, but he didn't care; he was furious. 'I *saw* you and I *heard* you. You said *She's mine*, then pushed Jack over. And you *could* have avoided her hand; in fact, I think you stamped on her hand on purpose!'

Mr Harris pushed him away. 'Itch, leave it for

now. We'll sort this out in school once everyone has calmed down. Lucy, go and shower. Itch, walk away. We have to get Jack to hospital, then we can deal with . . . all of this.'

Kirsten was coming towards them. 'Jack is clearly suffering from shock as well as broken bones; Rachel has called the ambulance – she'll go with her. My guess is three broken fingers but we'll find out soon enough. She's asking for you, Itch, by the way.'

They both ran back to where Rachel crouched beside Jack. Most of the Year Ten team were still standing around, incensed about what had happened to their teammate. Itch knelt down in the mud next to Jack, who managed a weak smile for her cousin.

'Hospital again, then?' Itch smiled.

'Looks like it,' she said hoarsely. 'Did you hear the crack?'

Itch winced again. 'Everyone did. You've got noisy bones. Can I see?'

Jack slowly raised her right hand, which she'd been cradling in her left. It looked as though Lucy's studs had crushed every finger – they looked like badly cooked sausages. She whispered something, but Itch didn't catch it; he leaned in closer.

'She spoke to me, you know. After she'd trod on my hand. Lucy. It must have looked as though she was just seeing if I was all right, but you'll never guess what she said.' Itch leaned in closer, and she clutched at his sleeve with her good hand. 'She said, *You had that coming, bitch.*'

He recoiled and gasped at the same time.

'You all right?' asked Rachel.

'Er, yeah . . . sure.' Itch was reeling with shock. 'You. Are. Kidding. Me,' he said to Jack. It didn't make sense. What had happened to turn Lucy against them? 'Why would she do that?' he whispered.

'No idea,' said Jack, closing her eyes.

She seemed to be shutting off the conversation and Itch thought he'd let the painkillers do all their work before trying again. The sound of an ambulance siren suggested that the questions would have to be resumed in Stratton General Hospital.

9

Sam Singh and Tina Greaves were recovering well. Sam had burns to his face and neck, along with concussion and bruised ribs. Tina had been hit by flying debris, splinters and nails embedding themselves in her legs and torso. Both agents, desperate not to be replaced, insisted that they were well enough to rejoin Fairnie's team. The colonel had said he would talk to their doctors today, but as it turned out, he had another patient to attend to.

Jack travelled in the ambulance with Rachel, while Moz, Chris and Danny Stein raced ahead in Moz's Alfa Romeo. Itch followed in the van with Fairnie and Kirsten.

'Nothing like organizing a simple trip to A&E,' said Itch. He was getting used to the complicated arrangements that followed him everywhere, and after the attack on the golf course was glad they were in place. But he would have preferred to go in the ambulance with Jack. Her injuries were all Lucy's fault, but Itch still felt responsible.

It was the rocks. It all came back to the rocks. The priceless element 126, lying at the bottom of the Woodingdean Well. He thought again of his old rucksack, now under 1,285 feet of water, and smiled at the thought that it was his father who had found him. There were still so many questions he needed to ask, as soon as everything calmed down.

The rolling grey clouds streamed inland from the Atlantic as Stratton General received its string of unusual visitors. Avoiding the main doors, Jack went into A&E via the emergency entrance, and from there went straight to X-ray. Afterwards, she was shown to a private room. Kirsten was standing guard, and Itch was waiting for her.

They grinned at each other. 'How's the hand?' asked Itch.

'Dunno yet,' said Jack, holding her right arm, now sporting four finger splints and a fresh white sling. 'But I heard the guy taking the X-ray say *Ouch* when he was looking at my hand.'

They both sat on the bed. 'I've been thinking, Jack. We should probably tell Fairnie what Lucy called you.'

'I was wondering about that,' said Jack, 'but she's hardly a terrorist or a criminal, is she? Just a horrible little git.'

'Agreed. But she's a horrible git who set out to

hurt you and chose the only place she could get near you. On the sports field. If she'd tried that in school, one of the agents would have been onto her in a flash.'

'But when did this all start, Itch?' asked Jack. 'She was OK last year. Always smiled, said hello, that kind of thing.'

'Same here,' said Itch. 'In fact, looking back, I think she was trying to be friends with us. I don't pick up on that sometimes, I know, but in comparison with how she is now . . .'

The door opened and the small room quickly filled up with Fairnie, Jack's father, Jon, and two doctors, one of whom removed X-rays from a brown envelope.

Jon Lofte – tall and stooped – embraced his daughter gently. 'Let's have a look at you, my girl! The colonel here says it's broken fingers . . .'

'Well, the doctor here agrees.' The medic with the X-rays shook Jack's good hand. 'I'm Mr Haddington and this is Dr Hepworth.' He held the film up to the window. 'Three fingers broken, four breaks in total. You see, your index finger has two small fractures, just above and below the knuckle. We'll give you a proper splint before you go, of course – Dr Hepworth here will sort you out. Don't think you'll be writing much before Christmas, though. Any questions?'

'Yes. I have one,' said Jon Lofte. 'How much

pressure would be needed to do that amount of damage?'

'A lot,' said Dr Hepworth. 'I'm surprised it's just a hockey boot that did this – must have landed with some force.' Everyone looked at Jack.

'She's got big legs, if that helps,' she said, and everyone laughed.

After the splint had been fixed, Jack was free to go. Her father had to return to work, so she opted to travel back with Itch in the van, as they had decided they wanted to tell Fairnie about Lucy. He and Kirsten listened intently as Jack described what had happened on the hockey pitch and what Lucy had whispered in her ear afterwards.

Fairnie whistled.

'What a cow,' said Kirsten.

'Yeah, that's pretty much what we think,' said Itch.

Kirsten was driving slowly along the twisty roads. 'Why would you have *had that coming*? What did she mean?' She glanced at the cousins in her rearview mirror; they both shrugged.

'Haven't a clue,' said Jack. 'We've barely spoken to each other. And when we have, it's been dead friendly.'

Fairnie looked at Kirsten. 'Maybe we should pay Miss Cavendish a visit. Find out what she has to say for herself . . .'

Kirsten nodded. 'Good idea.'

'Really?' said Jack. 'Is that necessary? We were just telling you 'cos you said you need to know this stuff. Didn't realize you'd go to her house.'

The colonel turned round to face them. 'Our job is to keep you guys safe until such time as the threat to you has receded. If that threat is from men with guns and boats like yesterday, we'll deal with it. If it is from schoolgirls with hockey sticks who can't keep their cool on the sports field, we'll deal with that too. Don't worry. We'll just . . . calm her down a little.'

Kirsten smiled.

The temporary move next door meant that Jude Lofte was no longer in charge of her own house. In fact, she wasn't in charge of anything any more, and she didn't like it one bit. With the imminent return of Sam and Tina, the agents would return to full strength and the Loftes could return to their respective houses. But this evening saw another crowded meal around the kitchen table, and yet more pizzas eaten out of cardboard boxes. Jude's irritation was temporarily forgotten as she fussed over her wounded niece.

Jack explained what had happened again, leaving out Lucy's final comment, and Jon described what the X-rays had shown.

'This family!' exclaimed Jude. 'What has

happened to us! It's one thing after another.' She looked at Chloe's bruised face and Jack's splinted hand.

Please don't say this is all my fault, thought Itch. *It's what I'm thinking anyway, I don't need you to say it.*

Jude looked at him, but just smiled her tired smile.

I know what that means, but at least you kept it to yourself. Itch caught his uncle and aunt glancing surreptitiously at him.

Chloe must have done too. 'Well, I think this family is actually cool,' she said. 'People might think we're weird, but I think *they're* just boring.'

Jack high-fived her cousin with her good hand, and Nicholas and Jon Lofte led a small round of applause.

Itch nodded and smiled. 'Thanks, Chloe.'

'Apparently we can start moving stuff back,' said Jude. 'If we all grab a few things we'll be ready for when Sam and Tina return tomorrow.'

'Itch and I will do it,' said Nicholas, clearing away the pizza boxes.

Itch took his cue. 'Sure. You stay here, Mum, watch some TV. Do some work or something. Dad and I can sort it – there isn't much, anyway.'

'OK,' said Jude suspiciously, 'if you say so.'

She watched as Itch and Nicholas collected cases and bags of food. Watched over by Moz, they walked across the now-adjoining gardens to their own back door. The lights had been left on and shone out into the gloom. They quickly dropped the bags in their appropriate rooms and Itch, back in his own room, started to unpack some clothes and get some clean uniform from his drawers.

His father came in and sat on his bed. He sighed. 'So where were we . . . ?'

'I've spoken to Jack, Dad. She told me what happened. She said she followed me at the station and called Mr Watkins when she realized I was going to Brighton.'

'Yes. Then Watkins called me. I knew you'd stumbled onto something because Jacob called me from the mining school. Told me – ha! – told me he'd sort you and the girls out, but to get to the labs in London because you'd brought in something very special. When Watkins called me, I went straight to Victoria Station and caught the next train. He told me how to find the Fitzherbert School, and I followed your tracks. You made quite a mess in there! There was blood and sick everywhere – it led me to the labs and that extraordinary well.'

Itch shuddered as the memory of the aching, exhausting, desperate sickness returned.

'You OK?'

'Yeah, go on.'

'I could hear you down there, but it was impossible to see anything much. With my torches I could just make you out—'

'Wait!' said Itch. '*Five lights!* I remember now! There were *five* lights at the top of the well and I'd only left three! I couldn't really think straight though, and then . . . it all went black. Don't remember anything more.'

'It was the most terrifying sound I've ever heard,' said Nicholas quietly, 'and I've heard some bad ones on the rigs. It was a muffled shuddering to start with. Then the walls of the well started to move – actually move; I thought it was about to collapse in on you. I was panicking really, but there was nothing I could do. I heard the water rush before I saw it – a gushing, sucking noise. As soon as I saw the water level started to rise, I knew it would reach you and . . . I have to say, Itch, I thought that . . . would be *that*, really.' He swallowed hard. 'When the water had gone down, I saw that you'd been thrown back onto the ledge. I knew I had to go down there and get you out somehow.'

'Wasn't I pretty radioactive by then?' asked Itch.

'No, you weren't. You'd been exposed to acute external radiation, which made you so sick – Jacob had told me how toxic that 126 was – but I had brought a radiation suit from the London labs anyway.'

'You pulled me out of the well wearing a radiation suit?' Itch was astonished.

'Had to leave the helmet behind – but yes; I didn't know where all the rocks had ended up. And you weren't taking questions. Anyway, you're a skinny thing. Fireman's lift sorted you, no problem.'

'I'm amazed those rungs held.'

'Some of them didn't,' said Nicholas, 'but enough did.' He smiled. 'You did an astonishing thing, you know, Itch. Truly astonishing. Stupid too, but most riggers I know would not have had the guts . . .'

'Do you understand why, Dad?'

'Why you did it? I think so. The rocks aren't safe – too dangerous to be trusted to anyone. Something like that?'

'They killed Cake. He didn't realize the power in those rocks until it was too late.'

'That mineral seller? Really? My God, I didn't know,' said Nicholas. 'No wonder you ran. I didn't know . . .'

'He was dead, Dad. And he left me a note saying I had to get rid of them. So I did. Don't know what happened to him. I went back to the spoil heap out at St Haven, and his caravan had gone. There was no sign he'd ever been there.'

There was a silence in the house. Father and son sat staring at Itch's poster of the Periodic Table. Nicholas stood up and, taking a pen from Itch's bedside table, added *126* under the middle column.

'Nice one,' said Itch.

Back next door, he started to pack his rucksack for school the next day. He was filling Jack in on the conversation with his father when his hands closed around the box holding the bismuth crystal.

'You should give that back,' said Jack, 'or Mary might think you're keeping it. To remind you of her.' She laughed, and Itch blushed.

'Shut up, Jack. I *will* give it back, of course. You know she's got some old Russian caesium which is seriously rare and—'

'Boring.'

'Actually, it's anything but boring.'

'Boring. Stop now,' said Jack, smiling. 'Really. If you want to see her dad's collection, get Fairnie to sort it. Then you can bore each other for as long as you like.'

Fairnie took Kirsten with him to see Lucy Cavendish and her mother. Sam and Tina would rejoin the team the next day – the doctors had reluctantly given permission – but until then, Kirsten was a must-have. He had decided to let her take the lead in the questioning; she was less threatening and more approachable than him. He had spoken to Dr Dart, the head teacher of the Cornwall Academy, about Lucy. She had been shocked about the fight on the hockey pitch and had gasped when told of the language Lucy had used.

'She has been difficult this term, it is true,' she admitted, 'but nothing like this has happened before, as far as I know.' She had been unhappy to have the disciplinary measures taken out of her hands, but had been given no choice in the matter.

Fairnie and Kirsten took the steep and dark narrow road out of town that headed east and inland. On the outskirts of town, they found the small cul-de-sac of modern semi-detached houses they were looking for. A thick-set woman in her mid-forties answered their knock.

Through the small crack allowed by the security chain, she peered at her visitors through black-rimmed glasses. 'Not more missionaries! I told the last lot we were—'

Kirsten held up her ID. 'I'm Kirsten Jones; this is Jim Fairnie. Mrs Cavendish, we are government agents working at the academy. Can we speak to your daughter, please? It's important or we wouldn't trouble you tonight.'

'Are you police?' asked Mrs Cavendish.

'No, we are MI5 actually, but we are working with the local police. Can we—'

'MI5? What like in *Spooks*, you mean?' Lucy's mother looked incredulous. 'Here? Is this a joke? Are you students?' She glanced at Jim Fairnie, who smiled, and then nodded to herself. 'No – too old.'

'Could we come in, Mrs Cavendish? I'm sure we won't take up much of your time. Please. We just need Lucy to clear up a few things.'

Mrs Cavendish nodded and slid the chain off the

door. The agents followed her into a cosy lounge: the TV was on mute, and a steaming bowl of pasta sat on the table.

'Sorry to interrupt your meal, Mrs Cavendish. Is Lucy in?' A thumping bass line from upstairs suggested the answer was yes.

'Just call me Nicola, please. And I'm not Mrs. That's her noise upstairs. She in trouble?'

'Well, there was a fight at school today, during hockey actually. She might have told you about it . . .?'

Nicola Cavendish sat down at the table. 'No. She said everything was "fine". Everything is always "fine", even when things are clearly *not* fine.' She ate a mouthful of spaghetti. 'Actually, I'm not surprised to hear she's been in a fight. She's pretty angry most of the time these days. I get her meals and keep clear.' She looked up at Kirsten and Fairnie as though expecting a rebuke. When she didn't get one, she continued eating.

Now Fairnie spoke. 'Has she always been like this, Nicola? I mean, I know teenagers can be difficult, of course . . .'

'Been bad since the summer, really. A phase, I hope, but . . . she used to be so sweet and thoughtful. And affectionate! Now she barely says a civil word to me.' The thumping from the bedroom upstairs cranked up a few decibels.

Kirsten looked at the smiling school photos and

mother-and-child shots from sunny beaches and campsites. 'Excuse me for asking, but is there a father around at all . . . ?'

'Ha! He didn't hang around long. Cleared off soon after Lucy was born. I don't think we were quite what he was hoping for.' Nicola cleared her plate away. 'Shall I get her down? It might take some time, that's all.'

She took the stairs two at a time, and Fairnie and Kirsten heard a loud knocking. The music stopped, and muffled voices went to and fro before Lucy emerged slowly, peering down the steps as she came. Fairnie stood up as she reached the bottom of the stairs.

Lucy spoke first. 'It was an accident. Really it was.' She spoke fast and sounded scared. 'I was running for the ball, but I just . . . got my feet wrong, that's all. When she fell, I . . . I couldn't help it. I knew she was badly hurt, but then they all went mad and everyone was fighting.'

Kirsten nodded. 'I know hockey can be vicious and these things happen. But according to Jack you said something to her afterwards. While she was lying on the ground. Do you remember what that was, Lucy?'

Fairnie and Kirsten both noticed Lucy redden.

'No. I think I just asked her how she was. Or something like that.'

'So you didn't use a particularly cruel and

111

vicious word and tell her, *You had that coming*?'

Nicola gasped. 'Lucy?'

Lucy's face grew even redder, but she just shook her head.

Kirsten told Nicola what Jack had reported hearing and Lucy's mother put her hand in front of her mouth. 'You'd never say anything like that, would you, Lucy?' she said in a voice that suggested that she may well have.

'I told you what I said! What's the point of asking if you don't believe me!' Lucy turned and stormed off upstairs. Her bedroom door slammed, and the music started up again.

The adults stood looking at each other, and then Fairnie went towards the stairs.

'Nicola, with your permission I'd like to have a final word with Lucy. Would you lead the way?'

Nicola Cavendish laughed. 'A final word? Best of luck! I haven't managed that for three years.' Without knocking, she went upstairs and pushed her daughter's door open. 'Be my guest . . .' And all three of them walked in.

Lucy was sprawled on her unmade bed, with an open laptop in front of her. The carpet was barely visible through piles of discarded clothes and shoes. The wardrobe doors were ajar and a knocked-over chair lay under a desk that was covered in magazines, folders and seven or eight tumblers of water, squash and juice. Jars and powders littered the shelves and an overflowing wastepaper basket sat at the end of the bed. Nicola marched over to the iPod speakers and pulled out the plug. Lucy opened her mouth to protest, but Fairnie got in first. He spoke quietly but firmly; he was clearly not expecting any interruption.

'Lucy, my team have a job to do. We are here to look after Itch and Jack. Certain threats have been made, which we take very seriously. So do the police. And the government. And the Prime Minister. So, when we hear of another threat, we have to investigate it. Do you understand? Even if it was on a sports field. I imagine that if anything like this were to happen again, someone somewhere might think the threats were connected. And want to make arrests.'

There were sharp intakes of breath from Lucy and her mother. Fairnie let the words hang for a few moments. 'I hope that's clear.' He glanced at Nicola, then back at Lucy. 'Sorry for interrupting your evening. We'll show ourselves out.'

Fairnie drove. 'Well? What do you think?' he asked Kirsten.

'Guilty as charged, your honour. But we still don't know *why* she said it,' she replied.

'Agreed, but she won't be so foolish again.'

'That was a strange smell in her room, didn't you think?' said Kirsten.

'I was trying not to pay it too much attention,' said Fairnie, laughing.

'Didn't it remind you of anything?' Kirsten was still serious.

'Teenage bedrooms the world over, maybe? What are you saying?'

'Oh, probably nothing. It was just . . . the smell – it reminded me of something, that's all. Just can't remember what. But it'll come to me . . .'

10

Lucy Cavendish allowed herself three minutes for breakfast. Her alarm had given her longer, but she chose to spend more time under the duvet. At the last moment, she rolled out of bed and into the shower. Retrieving some school uniform from under one of the piles on the floor, she was washed, dressed and at the kitchen table before her mother was up. She used to take the bus to the academy, but had missed it so often she now preferred to cycle.

From upstairs, her mother shouted, 'Have a good day, darling,' which Lucy pretended not to hear – and then she was gone.

Retrieving her bike from the side of the house, she forced a helmet over her wild and wiry hair and her school bag over her shoulders. In moments, she was freewheeling down the hill and picking up speed – this was her favourite part of the journey. The hill was steep, and the high-hedged, twisty roads made the speed all the more exhilarating. Lucy rode standing on the pedals, her hands poised on both brakes, and she felt the cold, and damp morning air on her face and legs. This was the way to wake up.

Blood pumping, she sped towards the T-junction at the bottom of the lane. Her routine was that if she could hear any other vehicle approaching, she would slow enough to gauge what it was and how fast it was moving. If there was silence, she would take the left turn as fast as she could, often sending up a spray of loose stones into the road with her rear wheel. From there, the main roads into town required a more cautious riding style.

As she stood higher on the pedals to listen for traffic, she caught the sound of another set of tyres on the tarmac behind her. Craning her neck round, she was astonished to see another cyclist, crouched low and closing on her fast. Helmeted and wearing tinted goggles, whoever it was looked more like a downhill skier. Lucy found herself braking instinctively – she was unnerved and didn't want a race. If this cyclist wanted to beat her to the junction, that was fine by her.

As Lucy slowed, so did the other cyclist. Lucy had just taken in her slim, black-Lycra-clad frame when she suddenly disappeared into Lucy's slipstream. Lucy wanted to turn round to find out what exactly this cyclist was doing, but the main road was approaching and she needed eyes front. She squeezed her brakes harder, and for a second they worked. Then she felt a jolt from behind, and her bike picked up speed again. Spinning round in her saddle, she saw that the Lycra cyclist's front wheel was hard up against her own back wheel and her pursuer was pedalling hard; the result was that Lucy was now heading for the crossroads at an uncomfortably fast speed. Lucy turned her handlebars, and drew away momentarily before she felt a hand grab her jacket, holding and pushing her. She was squeezing both brakes as hard as she could, but knew she couldn't stop in time.

Screaming wildly, she was propelled across the junction. Two cars slowed and blew their horns. Lucy, realizing the hill was steeper here – both bikes were accelerating dangerously – took one hand off the handlebars to push her attacker away. But the Lycra cyclist had been expecting her move and instantly leaned back, leaving Lucy's hand flapping uselessly in mid-air. Frantically steering around the twisty, pot-holed road, Lucy realized she was going to have to jump. She tried to stand up in the saddle but felt herself held firmly. As she glanced over her shoulder, the rider smiled broadly and mouthed some words. Lucy barely had time to register what was happening before a Lycra-clad arm swung towards her. Lucy felt

117

head-exploding pain as the palm of her attacker's hand smashed the bones in her nose and she crashed to the ground, her bike sliding ahead of her down the hill. Lucy rolled across the tarmac and into a ditch, branches cutting through her clothes and into her face and legs. She lay motionless, blood pouring from her face onto the rotting leaves.

Itch and Jack were the last into the form room that morning. After registration, Jack nudged Itch.

'We really should talk to Mr Watkins. About getting security.' Itch looked up at their form teacher, dressed today in a green shirt, yellow tie and khaki chinos.

'You're right. And dressed like that, if he's a target, they'll spot him from miles away. Let's do it now.'

They both picked up their bags and hesitated by Watkins's desk.

'Ah, Jack! Itch! How are things?' He beamed at them. He would never be so unprofessional as to have favourite students, but after he had signed the Official Secrets Act forbidding him to talk about the radioactive 126, he always enjoyed catching a few private words with the Loftes. 'What did you make of your mega-cities lesson yesterday? Not sure everyone was quite, er, fully participating. Young Darcy was asleep until I asked her to point out Singapore on a map. She pointed at Sydney, poor thing. Bit sleepy.'

'Bit stupid,' said Jack.

'Yes, well . . .' Mr Watkins started collecting his books together.

'I thought it was, er, fine, sir. Really,' said Itch. 'But we wanted to talk to you about *you*.'

'Me? Nothing to discuss, really. What's up?'

Itch and Jack both glanced at the door, where Moz was waiting.

'You need someone like that,' said Itch, pointing at him.

'What? Really . . .? I mean . . .' Watkins was colouring slightly, but Jack clarified matters.

'You need some security, sir,' she said softly. 'Itch knows I called you from Victoria station.' Itch nodded.

'Ah, I see. Well, I'm quite happy as I am, thank you. No one knows what I know, and I like my freedom to come and go, you see.'

'But, sir, you're the only one who's on his own. If Colonel Fairnie realized what you know—'

'Yes, but he doesn't, and you're not going to tell him. I appreciate your concern – really I do – but I've seen how the team work and I don't think I could bear it.'

Jack protested, 'But, sir, it wouldn't be like that—'

'My mind is made up, Jack. And it's a no.'

Watkins smiled. 'But thank you again – and you're late for Mr Logan's marvellous maths lesson. Off you go.'

'Well, we tried,' said Itch as they rejoined the security operation that swept them along to maths.

Mr Hampton's science club meeting that lunch time had fewer members than before. Itch counted nine in total before the head of science bustled in, calling out a cheery 'Hi there, folks!' and sitting on the desk at the front. He smiled, removing his wire-rimmed glasses and cleaning them with a cloth.

'You'll have noticed we have lost a few of our younger friends. I thought maybe they could have their own . . . club some other time.'

'No great loss,' muttered Craig Murray, who had been sitting next to Lofte-baiter James Potts when Itch arrived. Now that Itch had taken the seat on Craig's other side, Potts got up and sat on his own. After his embarrassment at the hands of Moz Taylor, he wasn't going to try anything bolder. He managed to pull a face at Itch, but then quickly shot a glance at the back-on-duty Tina Greaves. She was standing in the doorway, watching the lunch-time corridor activities and didn't notice.

'Ah, Mary, welcome!' called Mr Hampton as Mary Lee jogged in, taking the seat right behind Itch. Itch faced the front and tried to listen to the science teacher, but found it hard to concentrate.

'Is Lucy coming today? Anyone know?' asked Mr Hampton.

'Not here today, sir,' called another Year Eleven girl.

Mary leaned in between Itch and Craig. 'Got some stuff to show you!' she whispered. 'Got five minutes afterwards?'

He nodded, blushed and gave her a thumbs-up, all at the same time. Mr Hampton was telling them about his time working at the Large Hadron Collider at CERN in Switzerland, but the only thoughts in Itch's head were: *Why did I do that ridiculous thumbs-up gesture? That was so lame. She'll think I'm an idiot. I'll just talk to Craig afterwards. Does the back of my neck go red?*

'We were all working to understand the science behind nuclear power,' continued Henry Hampton.

She'll probably never talk to me again, Itch told himself.

Hampton showed a presentation of images he'd taken inside the maze of underground tunnels at CERN, but Itch wasn't watching; he was too busy kicking himself.

When Mr Hampton had wrapped up, Itch quickly started talking to Craig Murray. The conversation wasn't a long one, as Craig immediately looked up and nodded over Itch's shoulder.

'I think she's waiting for you,' he said.

'Oh, hi,' said Itch, turning round and feigning surprise.

Mary Lee was unpacking a small duffel bag, from which she produced a wooden box. 'It's part of my dad's collection. Thought I'd show you.'

'It's not the caesium, is it?' said Itch, glancing over at Mr Hampton. 'He'll go mad!'

Mary shook her head. 'No, no, don't worry yourself so.' Itch thought he detected a slight mocking tone in her voice. 'These are all safe, trust me. Even Dr Dart would like them.' She opened the box to reveal three drawstring bags, each with a stencilled number on. 'It's a test, of course!' she told him. 'All my dad's collection is in bags like this. What do we have here, Mr Element Hunter?'

Again, Itch felt he was being made fun of, but he couldn't resist the challenge. He picked up the bag marked *12*; it was heavy, and contained a small square block. 'Well, that'll be magnesium.'

Mary nodded. 'Good. Open it up!'

Itch tipped a square of silvery metal encased in plastic onto the bench. It was marked *Mg 12*.

'Yup, magnesium – atomic number twelve. That was the easy one,' said Mary. 'Next!'

The second bag weighed virtually nothing, but Itch could feel the outline of something like a small coin. He had to think for a moment, his mind running along and down the Periodic Table. 'What colour is it?' he asked.

'Blue. Shiny,' said Mary.

Five rows down and five along.

'Wow – this should be niobium. Can I look?'

Mary nodded, and Itch found a tiny but dazzling blue coin on his palm. It sparkled as he held it up to the light, and he was keen to know more, but Mr Hampton had wandered over.

'Whaddya have here, Itch?'

'Oh, it's some of Mary's father's element collection, sir. Look at this – it's beautiful, isn't it?' He held out the coin. 'It's niobium, sir.'

'Ah, of course,' the teacher said appreciatively. 'Two things, Mary. Firstly, this is a very fine piece of anodized niobium; and secondly, I'm just glad it's not a rocket.'

Mary looked puzzled.

'Niobium is used in rockets as it doesn't corrode even at high temperatures,' he explained. 'And what's this last one?'

Mary was picking up the bag marked 73 when Jack appeared at the door.

'Itch! It's Lucy! She's . . . she's . . . in hospital, unconscious. Itch – she might have been attacked!'

By the start of afternoon lessons the only topic of conversation was Lucy Cavendish. The school had been told that she was in Stratton General after being found in a ditch by a passing motorist. She had a badly broken nose and deep cuts to her arms and legs. The driver who found her didn't know how long she'd been lying there; at first he thought she might be dead. Dr Dart had gone straight to the hospital; meanwhile, at the academy, speculation was running wild.

Lucy's friends were quick to point the finger at Jack. Even though her hand was still heavily strapped and she had round-the-clock security, it didn't stop the theories.

'She got her police friends to do it,' was one that Itch and Jack heard as they headed for the final class of the day.

'She's still got one good hand,' Peter Williams, a Year Seven boy, was saying as the cousins passed.

'Maybe she got her dad to do it,' another boy suggested.

Itch had heard enough. He stepped in front of them. 'Really?' he shouted. 'You really think Jack could have attacked Lucy? Look!' He pointed to Moz, who was closest to them. 'We have these guys with us all the time! Do you think they'd let that happen? Well, do you?' The Year Sevens had shrunk back against the wall, but Itch hadn't finished. 'And you think she's the kind of person who'd just attack someone like that?' Moz was about to step in when Jim Littlewood, the history teacher and Lucy's form teacher, arrived.

'Everyone just move on, please. Williams, you can see me after school. The rest of you, clear off.'

Peter Williams, embarrassed, dropped his head and slunk off; Moz Taylor ushered Itch and Jack away.

'You need to tell everyone that we all arrived together this morning,' Itch told him. 'That Jack couldn't have attacked Lucy.'

'Agreed,' said Moz. 'I'll get the colonel on it.'

'Even if she might have wanted to,' added Jack quietly.

'Even if she might have wanted to,' repeated Itch, smiling.

At Stratton hospital A&E, Felicity Dart and Nicola Cavendish were sitting outside Lucy's room, both drinking something that tasted like a mixture of tea, coffee and hot chocolate out of polystyrene cups.

A nurse put her head round the door. 'She's asking for you, Mrs Cavendish.'

'Would you come with me?' Nicola asked Dr Dart. Her eyes were red-rimmed, her hair straggly and unkempt. 'Please? I might say the wrong thing . . .'

Reluctantly, Dr Dart went into Lucy's room with her, and couldn't stop herself from holding her hand to her mouth. Lucy had bandages covering her nose, cheeks and ears, but the bruising was still visible: red and purple skin showing around the edges. Her left eye was swollen and blue, her bottom lip split in two places. Her arms were covered in cuts, many closed with stitches.

'Oh my . . .' said Dr Dart quietly, and they both sat down by the bed.

Hearing the creak of the ancient chairs, Lucy turned her head towards them and opened her one good eye. She managed a slight smile before her lips started to crack and bleed. 'Hi, Mum,' she whispered.

Nicola Cavendish got up to pass her daughter a tissue and to cover her own tears. 'Hi, dear. You don't need to talk – just rest up.'

Lucy nodded and closed her eyes. 'I'll be OK.' She noticed her head teacher sitting next to her mother. 'Oh hi, Dr Dart. Glad you're here.'

Felicity Dart looked surprised. 'You just get better as soon as possible. All the school send their best wishes. What a terrible, terrible accident. Do you remember what happened?'

Lucy took a deep breath and exhaled slowly. The monitor beeped and the oxygen mixer hummed as she tried to prop herself up on her pillows. Her mother jumped up again to help her.

'It wasn't an accident, Mum. There was another cyclist – she pushed me off.'

Horrified, Nicola looked at Felicity Dart, then back to her daughter. 'What!' she gasped. 'Who would do—?'

Lucy cut her off. 'Couldn't see.' She swallowed

twice, and Nicola handed her some water, which she sipped before resuming. 'But she . . . I'm sure it was a she . . . She mouthed two words at me before' – she closed her eyes and waved down at her body – 'before any of this happened.'

'What did she say – if it was a "she"?' asked Nicola.

'She said, *Naughty girl*, Mum. She said, *Naughty girl.*'

11

Lucy Cavendish stayed in hospital for two days. As she had what they called 'nasal trauma' to the bridge of her nose, they needed to check for 'cerebrospinal fluid leak', which sounded bad, but finally she'd been given the all clear. Her mother had had to go work, and was unable to pick her up, so an ambulance had been summoned. She was waiting in the back for the paramedic to arrive.

She had not been told that she would have company.

Suddenly the back door opened, and Itch and Jack Lofte climbed in, Jack cradling a new cast to her hand. Lucy looked up in surprise, then froze. The three of them stared at each other, and Lucy quickly tried to leave, but her path was blocked. She sat back down and stared at the resuscitation equipment.

While Jack was having her hand examined and

new splints fitted, she had found out that Lucy was waiting to leave hospital. Itch had persuaded her that they should take the opportunity to talk to Lucy. Jack hadn't been keen: 'Not sure I can do this,' she had said. 'You know what she called me. That hurts almost as much as this . . .' She waved her splinted fingers.

'We don't *have* to do it,' said Itch. 'We can go back in the car. Would be a shame though, don't you think? It's a good opportunity to talk to her – or let her talk to us.'

Jack sighed. 'OK, let's do it. But I'm not sitting next to her, all right?'

Itch explained to Tina and Sam that they wanted to return in the ambulance and why. Fairnie OK'd the plan; Tina would sit next to the ambulance driver, with Sam following in the car.

The ambulance door closed behind them and they sat down facing Lucy. As it moved off, all three of them stared at the blank monitors, the swaying cables – anything but each other.

Itch turned to look at Jack. 'You OK?' He had spoken quietly, but it seemed loud in the close confines of the ambulance. Jack nodded but stayed silent, her damaged hand cradled on her lap for all to see.

As the ambulance swung onto the main road, the chatter of its radio clearly audible above the engine noise and the metallic rattling of the shifting medical equipment, the paramedic radioed in his status and destination. While he chatted to the call handler and Tina sitting next to him, Itch tried again.

'Does it hurt?' he said to Jack. She shook her head. He thought for a moment. 'As you can't do the essay for the Brigadier, fancy helping me with mine?'

'OK.' Jack pressed her lips together, not trusting herself to say much more. Itch could see that she was struggling to stay in control, but he wasn't sure whether to keep a conversation going or just sit in silence. He wasn't used to being the one who had to think of things to say.

'Can you use a laptop for English? I'm sure—'

Jack put her good hand on Itch's arm and shook her head. 'Later, OK? We'll talk later.'

He nodded. *Got that one wrong then*, he thought.

Itch glanced at Lucy. She looked terrible and spectacular at the same time. The bruising from the assault had spread around her eyes and cheeks and turned yellow. Her nose was protected by what looked like a mass of protective padding and tape, and her face and neck were still covered in deep scratches from the hedge. Despite all that unwanted colour, she was still very pale, and her long wiry hair was barely controlled by a black band. As far as Itch could tell, she hadn't moved since they had sat down, but he saw her wince as the ambulance negotiated a pothole and realized she must still be in pain. With a quick glance at Jack, he asked, 'You OK?'

Lucy and Jack both looked at him at the same time. Jack's astonished expression was clear; it meant: *Excuse me – you're bothered about how she's feeling?*

'I think she's in pain, Jack,' Itch said quietly. 'I'm only asking.' By the time he looked back, Lucy had resumed her staring at the canister of oxygen in front of her. He caught himself about to say that the atmosphere was twenty-one per cent oxygen. *Not quite the time*, he thought.

Just when it seemed that he would be spending the journey between two furious, silent girls, Lucy said, 'Like *you* care.'

Itch's jaw dropped.

Jack, eyes full of tears, shook her head. 'Don't bother, Itch. This was a mistake. We know what she's like. It's not worth it. Please. We'll be back soon.'

Itch thought about that. Normally he would have taken Jack's advice: she always judged these situations better than he did. But when would he have a better chance to talk to Lucy? Certainly not at school. She clearly hated him, hated Jack, and probably hated Chloe too; but he didn't know why. This wasn't the usual antagonism he faced at school, this was vicious: Jack's broken hand was proof of that. He felt responsible for what had happened because ultimately, he was sure, this was his fault.

'I'm sorry for what happened to you,' he told Lucy. 'It looks painful.'

'You're *sorry*?' she shot back. 'Don't make me sick.' And she turned to face forward and watch the road.

'I *am* sorry! Why wouldn't I be?' said Itch.

Silence.

'Look, I know that, for whatever reason, you attacked Jack, but that doesn't mean I wanted you to . . . get hurt like this. I don't know why you hate us so much, Lucy, but Jack's fingers are badly broken. And we all saw you do it. But that doesn't mean we aren't sorry for what happened to you.'

The driver was dividing his attention between the road and the conversation in the back of his ambulance. Tina had twisted round in her front seat.

'So it's just a coincidence, is it?' Lucy had spun round now, her eyes fiery and angry. 'I stand on her hand and the next morning a cyclist knocks me off my bike and smashes my nose with her hand. It just *happened*? Really? That's just stupid. And whoever it was said I was a *naughty girl*! I don't know who it was, but your security buddies here have got to be the most likely thugs, wouldn't you say?'

'They said you were *what*?' said Itch. Jack too had turned to look at Lucy.

'A *naughty girl*. And I guess it's unlikely she was talking about my messy room. So who else would be out to get me, apart from friends of yours?'

'I haven't got any friends,' said Itch. 'Not really.'

'True. So that leaves your private army.' Lucy leaned forward. 'I mean, come on, who would *you* blame?' She sat back then, and pressed some of the bandage tape back flat on her face, wincing again as she did so.

Itch and Jack sat there for a while, considering what Lucy had said.

Then Jack spoke. 'You're right. If I was you, I'd be blaming me too. But here's the thing: you don't know who bust your nose, but I know precisely who stood on my hand.' There was silence as the ambulance slowed down to turn into Lucy's drive. 'And what she said afterwards . . .'

'Why did you do it, Lucy?' pleaded Itch. 'We don't understand. You seemed friendly last year. At that jazz evening last term you seemed happy to chat . . . If there's something we've done . . .'

They had arrived at Lucy's house and she stood up slowly. The paramedic opened the door, and as the wintry afternoon light flooded in, they saw Lucy's tired, beaten face was streaked with tears.

'Yes, you could say there is *something*,' she said. 'Just a small *something*. You should be able to work it out. You know it, anyway.'

The paramedic helped her out and was just about to close the door again when Itch stood up.

'Hope you feel better soon!' he called after her. Then added, 'And honestly, we had nothing to do with it!' They watched as she headed for the front door and disappeared inside.

'Finished?' asked the paramedic. Itch nodded, and they climbed out as Sam pulled up behind. In the car, the cousins were silent as they headed down the hill. They drove past the section of road where Lucy had been attacked; police tape still marked the place where she had been found.

'So,' said Jack. 'She stamped on my hand and broke my fingers. She's been foul to both of us all term. And now I'm feeling sorry for her.' She glanced at Itch. 'What's that about?'

Chloe looked up as her brother came into the kitchen. They had now, with relief all round, returned to their house.

'How's Jack's hand?' she asked as Itch rummaged around in the biscuit tin.

'Not bad, considering,' said Itch through a mouthful of biscuit. 'And you'll never guess who we shared a lift with coming back . . .' He told her what had happened at the hospital and on the journey home with Lucy.

'Wow,' said Chloe. 'She really *is* messed up. I asked about her after that hockey match. A couple

134

of the sports crowd knew she was tough, but they said they'd never seen her play that dirty before.'

'So it was just for Jack.'

'Seems like it.'

The kitchen door opened and Nicholas appeared. 'Hey, you two. Anyone fancy giving me a hand with this garden rubbish? I need another pair of hands. I'd ask Sam or Moz, but they usually say they have other things to do.'

'Like protect us from terrorists and criminals – that kind of thing?' said Itch.

'Yeah, they're not paid to do the gardening really, Dad.' Chloe laughed.

Their dad smiled and nodded. 'Good point. Which leaves you, Itch – come on.'

'What about Chloe?' protested Itch. 'I was just about to do some homework!'

Nicholas and Chloe both laughed.

'Yeah, right,' said Chloe.

'Nice try, son. Your homework can wait – I'd like to get this garden cleared and tidied up for winter. It'll be dark soon. Won't take long.'

Itch sighed and put his jacket on again. Taking another biscuit, he followed his father into the garden. As Nicholas raked up the leaves, Itch piled them onto the compost heap.

'Did you know that there are twenty-five thousand aerobic bacteria in a gram of soil, Dad?'

This was exactly the kind of statement that drove everyone apart from his father mad.

'Is this a lesson in the chemistry of composting?' asked Nicholas. 'The carbon and nitrogen balance required for the perfect hot pile – that kind of thing?'

'Not really. I just remember that you could get twenty-five thousand of them, end to end. If that was your idea of fun. They're all here, millions of them, busy decomposing this stuff and giving off heat in the process. Smart guys, really.'

Nicholas smiled at that. 'Yup. Smart indeed.'

They worked on in silence with each of them knowing there was much to discuss, but not knowing how long they'd have before they'd be interrupted. After all the leaves and twigs had been cleared, Itch checked that they weren't being overlooked or overheard, glancing back at the kitchens of both his house and next door's.

'How's work?' he asked.

Nicholas picked up the secateurs. 'Bring the waste bag, Itch,' he said, and set off for the far end of the garden. Itch followed with a green plastic holdall-sized container. In what remained of the day's sun, his father began pruning the shrubs and dropping the stems into the bag Itch held open. 'Work is interesting, thank you for asking.' He stopped and laughed, shaking his head. 'There is so much you don't know, but let me tell you a little anyway. You know . . . Jacob Alexander doesn't just run the mining school. His main work is trying to find new energy sources. All governments have realized that someone has to think the unthinkable because they certainly can't. Coal is gone, oil and natural gas are going – we maybe have enough for forty years. Then what? Some kind of nuclear, that's what. So we go around the world planning, experimenting, researching. Trying to find out how we're going to survive in a world with no power. That's why, when Jacob analysed your rocks of 126, he went – he tells me – a little crazy.'

'You could say that!' Itch said, remembering the moment when Alexander had analysed the X-rays coming from the rocks. '*It's what we've been hoping for!* – that's what he said when he tested them! *It's what we've been hoping for.* No wonder he was going mental. And . . . and . . . and what else?' Itch walked in a circle, trying to recall his words. 'That's it! He said, *Your dad did well.* He was praising me for look-ing after the rocks, and he said, *Your dad did well.* I thought it was kind of weird at the time, but then . . . other stuff happened.'

Nicholas moved on to another bush and resumed the trimming. 'Other stuff did indeed happen.'

'Does Dr Alexander know about my rescue? After all, he called you about the rocks in the first place.'

'Nothing about the rescue,' Itch's dad replied. 'At

137

least, I don't think so. He alerted me to the 126, but the call about you came from Mr Watkins via Jack. Jacob's had to sign the Official Secrets Act, of course, as has Mr Watkins. But it's driving him mad – knowing he had the world's most extraordinary energy source in his hands, only to lose it again.' He looked at Itch. 'This is what he had been hoping to find all his life. Well, as long as he can remember, anyway. The fact that I know where they are is . . . difficult.'

'Does he suspect you rescued me?' said Itch. 'After all, you effectively disappeared and then reappeared after I'd turned up. He must have thought about it.'

'Don't think so, Itch, no. He was in hospital recovering from the attack by the Greencorps agents; he was in no position to know what I was doing. They'd hit him pretty hard, you know.'

Itch nodded, remembering how the two Greencorps men had set upon Alexander in the mining-school car park.

Nicholas continued. 'I went back to the Fitzherbert School, you know . . .'

'You what?' exclaimed Itch. 'You went *back*? Why?'

'Well, you'd left it in quite a mess and I wanted to see what had been done about it. I pretended to be a prospective parent and was shown around.'

Itch looked flabbergasted, but his father went on, 'Everything had been tidied up, of course – no sign of the break-in, and the well had been covered and, I imagine, sealed. There was a security van of some alarm company parked outside; don't think it'll be as easy to break in again!'

'And why would I ever want to do that?' said Itch, quieter now.

His father turned. 'No reason. Of course. Sorry.'

They worked on in the near dark. They had run out of bushes to prune but wanted to continue talking.

'This is like mime-gardening,' said Nicholas, 'but we'll need to go in soon.'

Itch nodded. 'This organization of Alexander's you work for – where do you fit in?' he asked, finding some more leaves to tidy.

'Well, one of my jobs on the rigs was to analyse aerial photos for possible oil fields,' said Nicholas. 'Now I analyse photos for all sorts of energy possibilities; that's one of my jobs.'

'Why don't you tell Mum? I don't really understand that bit.'

'Well, what we do is pretty secret. But someone – some people – need to take responsibility for getting the Earth through the coming hot stage. And that's us. That is what we are doing. No one is supposed to know about us. I certainly shouldn't be telling you. Jacob started on this years ago, but the whole deal is that no one knows what he's working on. He was asked to think the unthinkable on energy, and the trouble with the unthinkable is that it's pretty unpopular, especially if the answer is nuclear. Or vast numbers of wind farms around the coast. No one would vote for it, so no politician wants to talk about it. If there's a climate-based, earth-shattering disaster, people will sit up and demand answers. Until that happens, we just get on with it.'

Itch was relieved. 'So it's not because of Mum, then . . .'

His dad laughed. 'Not *mainly* because of your mum, no. Jacob wanted things kept as quiet as possible and, well, it just seemed easier not to say anything.' He took off his gardening gloves. 'Do you understand, Itch?'

Itch thought about it. 'Kind of. But seeing as you pulled me out of the well, whether I understand it or not, I'm glad you're doing it. Whatever it is.'

They both laughed.

'Let's call it a day,' said Nicholas. 'How do you fancy meeting up with Jacob again? He'd love to talk 126 with you. I'm sure that's not against the Official Secrets Act.'

'Does that involve listening to his crazy theory about the Earth looking after itself again?' asked Itch.

His dad laughed. 'Ah, the Gaia Theory! Yes, probably.'

They'd reached the back door and could see

Chloe and Jude in the kitchen. Nicholas turned to his son, but Itch cut him off, anticipating what he was going to say.

'I know. Secret. Don't tell Mum. Right?'

His father nodded, and they went in.

12

Mary Lee was living in an old farmhouse rented from a local estate agent. On the outskirts of the town, it was the first time it had been asked for outside of the holiday season, and the retired dairy farmer had been more than happy to have the extra income. Rented in the name of John Lee, he had been told it was a father and daughter from Sweden. They'd paid up front, and caused no trouble.

It was an unremarkable but well-kept two-storey building with a few outhouses that once upon a time had held livestock. Originally there had been land – thirty acres or more – but that had long disappeared to the developers. What was left was an unkempt border of trees and shrubs which provided the house with some privacy from both the road and the new arrivals on the nearby housing estate.

They also gave Lucy Cavendish plenty of places to hide.

Since she had climbed over the fence from one of the new houses, leaving her bike behind someone's shed, Lucy had been sitting with her back to a large beech tree. It had taken a full five minutes for her heart to stop thumping and her nose to stop hurting. Finally she got up and peered at the rear of the house. She had been watching it for ages: she decided that Mary must have gone to school and that her father was away. She needed to move now. She wasn't sure how long the house would remain empty – and she was freezing.

Lucy had spent Sunday wondering about the conversation with Itch and Jack in the ambulance. She had come to the conclusion that Itch had been telling the truth when he said they had had nothing to do with the attack. Furthermore, she was sure her attacker was female and very slight – and that description didn't match any of his bodyguards.

But then who was the mystery cyclist? Lucy had run through everyone at school who might have seen what she'd done to Jack, and one image kept recurring: the lone figure of Mary Lee standing behind the goal. The goal that Jack had been attacking when Lucy stamped on her hand.

Of course. It *had* to be Mary.

She was new to the academy, and no one knew

that much about her, but she had been so friendly to Itch at Mr Hampton's science club – chatting and laughing about this element thing they seemed to have in common.

She looked athletic. She was small.

And she had witnessed what Lucy had done to Jack.

Lucy had no desire to confront Mary. If she was right, the throbbing in her nose and cheekbones was all the reminder she needed of the other girl's strength and brutality. But the more she thought about it, the more certain she was that there was a mystery surrounding this new sixth-former. She had been accepted, of course; no one had been curious about a new Year Thirteen student, even one who said she had just arrived from Sweden. Lucy had messaged some friends from the sixth form; none had been to Mary's house or seen her father. She didn't appear to be on Facebook, and Google found no record of a John Lee working in pharmaceuticals. Hardly proof of anything, Lucy realized; but when her mother left for work, thinking her daughter would spend the day in bed, continuing to recover, she knew she wanted to investigate further.

Now that she was outside Mary's house, however, she realized she had no idea what she was going to do next.

★ ★ ★

Jack's suggestion that Fairnie should fix up a meeting for Itch and Mary to talk element hunting had been much discussed back at the Lofte house. Nicholas and Jude were happy, the agents were happy, and Chloe had plenty of material to tease her brother with.

'So today will be your first-ever date, won't it?' she had said that morning before school. 'I mean, I don't think you've ever—' She had popped her head round Itch's door, and a biro cap hit her on the ear.

'Oh, ha-ha, Chloe, you are so funny. I've told you – her dad's got an element collection. It's here, in town. There's no Cake to find me new stuff now.'

'OK.' Chloe smiled. 'I believe you.'

'And she's Year Thirteen, dummy.' Itch was finding some uniform and hiding his red cheeks. 'She's bound to have boyfriends back in Sweden, anyway,' he said.

'Or a husband – as she's so old!'

'If it makes it funnier for you, yes, maybe a husband. Happy now?'

Chloe called, 'Nice new deodorant, by the way!' as she left his room. The rest of the biro followed swiftly afterwards.

Fairnie had agreed that Mary could bring her elements to school on Monday. She had the use of her father's car, and it seemed the safest way to transport a delicate collection.

At break, Itch and Jack had passed Mary in the corridor. 'See you in Mr Hampton's labs later!' she told them.

'Where's all the stuff?' said Itch.

'Going home to get it at lunch time,' she called over her shoulder.

Jack had giggled as they walked on to ICT. 'You're as bad as Chloe,' Itch muttered.

Lucy stood in the damp, cold autumn air outside Mary's back door. With her heart thundering like a train against her ribs, she tried the handle. Locked. She looked around; the windows were all shut, apart from one she hadn't noticed earlier – on the first floor above a small conservatory. It wasn't open by much, but it gave Lucy an idea. The conservatory had once been painted white but had weathered back to the wood. Some of the glass looked loose and there was some uninviting jagged brass decoration on the top, but it was the only way up.

As Lucy found a foot-hold on the first window ledge, she was glad she had opted for her combat boots and jeans. Reaching for the guttering, she tested its strength, pulling hard. It was heavy and made of iron, but rust had sapped all its strength. A length of it snapped off and came away; Lucy fell with it to the ground. Pain shot through her whole face and she cried out. Once her eyes had stopped watering, her first instinct was to run, but she fought against it and, leaving the half-pipe where it lay, tried again on the other side of the conservatory. This time the gutter held and she was able to haul herself onto the roof.

Lying flat and straddling the ornamental brass frill, she found the open window right above her head. She pushed up the metal catch and, reaching for the sill, pulled herself up and through, sliding on her stomach over the ledge.

Itch, Jack and Chloe sat having lunch together.

'Thought you'd be in the labs,' said Jack. 'Wasn't that the plan?'

Itch nodded. 'Fairnie thought the best thing would be for Mary to go home and pick up the elements in her car. She left a few minutes ago – she won't be long, so I have to hurry.' He shovelled great forkfuls of pasta in his mouth.

'Itch, you're revolting,' said Chloe as she watched his food disappear. 'She won't like you if you're burping and farting all afternoon.'

Jack laughed but Itch wasn't impressed. 'For the last time, Chloe, I don't care if she doesn't like me! It's the elements her dad has that I want to see.' He sprayed some pasta over his sister and cousin as he spoke, and apologized. 'Look. It'll be ten minutes—'

Jack held up her hand. 'Itch, calm down. We're only messing. Forget it. Hope she brings in some cool stuff, not just boring old tin.'

'Tin isn't boring. As you well know!' Itch was going to explain further, but Jack's hand was up again.

'I know. I'm messing!'

Itch smiled weakly and nodded. 'OK – see you after lunch,' he said, clearing his plate.

'Don't forget, it's the Oscars first period this afternoon!' called Chloe as her brother left his tray in the hatch. He waved his acknowledgement and headed for the labs.

The Oscars were a new idea of CA principal Dr Dart. The embarrassment of losing their head of science after he'd attacked Itch and his fellow teachers had been followed by some terrible publicity. Local TV and radio – as well as some of the national papers – had covered the story in what Dr Dart thought was 'an unnecessarily lurid way'. There had been public meetings questioning her competence – along with that of the teachers and the board of governors. The Parents and Teachers Association had had some heated meetings.

So the 'Oscars' were intended to bring some pride back to the school. The Academy's Awards, as they were officially called, were handed out monthly for any special work that had been brought to the head's attention. Given that the winners received a certificate and – more importantly – vouchers, they had become quite a talking point.

'You got any work in for an award, Jack?' asked Chloe.

'Not sure. Littlewood liked my last history essay, but who knows? You? Are you allowed to win two in a row?'

Chloe shrugged; she had won an Oscar for a maths homework on angles. 'Dunno. Think they're making this up as they go along.'

Jack nodded. 'I don't suppose Itch will win anything. But then, he won't be concentrating much on anything this afternoon!'

Lucy had landed in a bedroom. Crouched under the windowsill, she allowed her aching body to be warmed by the room's heat. It smelled of showers, shampoo and wet towels. She was next to a large made-up bed; with a pile of books, newspapers and magazines under a bedside table. They were in a precarious pile and Lucy glanced at them, afraid to touch or rearrange anything. Instead of the celebrity magazines she expected, she found old copies of *The Times*, a magazine called *Newswatch* and a few *National Geographics*. The smell of the room said it was Mary's, but no girl Lucy knew only had this sort of reading material. The books on her shelves looked just as boring.

Maybe her father was here, after all.

She stood up slowly and walked around the room. No clothes on the floor, all drawers closed. Did anyone of her generation really live like this? Realizing her boots were leaving marks in the carpet, Lucy leaned on the wardrobe to remove them. She placed them under the window and walked around the bed into the en-suite bathroom. She smiled – there was no doubt this was a girl's domain. Make-up, deodorant and perfumes lined the windowsill. A razor and more bottles stood in the shower's soap dish.

Out on the landing there were two other doors leading onto smaller bedrooms. They looked unused: each had a single bed with fresh bedding folded up neatly at one end. There was no trace of Mary's father. Lucy wondered for the first time if there really *was* a Mr Lee.

Moving more quickly now, Lucy padded down the stairs. Both front rooms were shuttered and dark, the light in the hall coming from the frosted window in the front door at one end and the kitchen at the other. Drawn to the warmth coming from the old Aga cooker, she walked round the kitchen, looking for . . . what exactly? All Lucy had was an idea: that there was something not quite right about Mary, and that her house must hold a clue somewhere. But the kitchen felt an unlikely place for secrets. The fridge and larder held a few items, essentials really. The drawers and dresser contained the tired cutlery and crockery used by everyone who had ever rented the house. A pair of straw-coloured sandals were propped up against the heat of the Aga.

Lucy was just heading for the first of the shuttered front rooms when she heard a car pull up outside.

Mary had returned.

She ran back into the kitchen, her heart pumping and her eyes wide. By the back door she found a small utility room and an open door to an office she hadn't seen before. There was the sound of a car door slamming, swiftly followed by a key in the lock. Lucy dived into the darkness of the utility room and slid behind a clothes horse with jeans, T-shirts and underwear draped over it. She sat on the cold tiled floor with her back against a bucket and mop and started to shake. As her eyes grew accustomed to the dark, the clothing she was hiding behind came more into focus and a flash of fluorescent green caught her eye. Her stomach lurched and another shot of adrenaline flooded her body. She recognized the bright logo of a famous cycling sportswear manufacturer. She touched the black fabric. Lycra.

The woman on the bike. It *had* been Mary. Instinctively, Lucy covered her damaged face with both hands.

She hadn't had time to shut the utility door properly – she must be visible from the kitchen. She listened to Mary's movements, praying that what she wanted was in one of the front rooms. It sounded as if she was carrying something out of the house – presumably to the car; Lucy waited to hear the door slam before she moved. Then she jumped as a shrill, warbling ringtone came from the office. Lucy recognized the sound: it was an incoming Skype call.

Mary came running back into the house. She flew past the utility room and into the office; immediately she started shouting at the screen. Through the door Lucy could hear a disembodied female voice arguing with her. She was sure it was an argument even though it wasn't in English; in fact she didn't recognize a single word. Mary kept repeating, 'Leila' – the other person's name maybe – and the other voice, 'Shivvi'. Was that Mary's nickname?

The conversation finished with 'Leila' saying, '*Selamat jalan*,' and Mary repeating, '*Selamat jalan*.'

Lucy caught a glimpse of Mary as she passed the door, and seconds later heard the front door close and the car pull away. Still not wanting to move, she stayed on the floor by the washing and reached for her phone. She typed in different spellings of the words she had just heard, and after two attempts she was close enough for Google to suggest, *Do you mean* selamat jalan? She clicked on the first suggestion:

'Selamat jalan – *Malay interjection meaning* bon voyage/*goodbye.*'

Lucy switched off her phone and went into the office. On the computer screen the Skype log said the call was from LEILA S, and the image was of a smiling black-haired woman in her twenties. For a mad moment Lucy was tempted to call back. She hovered by the computer, then sat down.

Wow, Mary's Malaysian, she thought and, her hands trembling again, clicked on the *MAIL* icon. Long lists of emails appeared, and she scanned the first few. They were mostly in a foreign language – Malay presumably – but they were all addressed to 'Shivvi'.

She searched for correspondence from 'Leila S', and there were three emails. As she scanned the incomprehensible text, three words jumped out at her. In the second paragraph there was a reference to *Greencorps*, who she knew were the sponsors of the Cornwall Academy. This was followed by *Nathaniel Flowerdew*, and Lucy shivered. What did Mary – or Shivvi – have to do with her disgraced head of science? Risking a few more seconds at the computer, she Googled *Shivvi + Greencorps + Flowerdew*.

Two minutes later, her head spinning, she clicked

CLEAR HISTORY, and stared at the screen. The computer's screensaver appeared, and Lucy leaned closer: six wet-suited divers squinted and smiled out at her. They appeared to be standing on the deck of an oil rig, and behind them, her arms spread wide and beaming proudly, was Mary Lee.

13

'No one here yet,' called Moz from the chemistry lab. 'How can we entertain ourselves while we are waiting for the lovely Mary?'

'Don't *you* start,' groaned Itch, following him and Kirsten into the room. 'It's bad enough with Chloe and Jack.'

Moz laughed as he walked around the lab, inspecting jars and bottles.

'Anyway,' said Itch, 'you don't really want me to start showing you experiments, do you? Not sure the colonel would be happy.'

'You're right. I stand corrected. Just sit down. I'm sure she won't keep us waiting too long.'

Kirsten walked down the corridor to look out at the car park. 'Black Volvo just arrived. Nice wheels for a school kid.' She watched as Mary Lee jumped out and reached into the back seat for what looked like two large blue plastic toolboxes.

She met her at the school door. 'Hi, Mary. We were just wondering if you were coming—'

'I'm sure you were.' Mary made to sweep past her.

Kirsten stepped in front of her, blocking her way. 'Sorry, but I need to open the boxes before you go any further.'

Mary Lee stared at her. 'Is there any point? Would you know what you are looking at?'

Kirsten tucked a stray lock of hair behind her ears and forced a smile. 'I won't know till I see what's inside, will I? So, both boxes open. Now.'

For a moment they stared at each other, and then Mary smiled.

'Of course you can see. I'm sorry. I've just had an argument with my dad and I'm still mad.' She set the boxes down and opened them.

'I thought he was abroad . . . ?'

'He is. Still argued, though. We argue more when he's away, for some reason. Anyway, here you are. Some of his element collection; I'm not sure what they all are myself, to be honest, but have a look.'

Kirsten knelt down to inspect the collection, and realized that Mary was right: she hadn't a clue what she was looking at. She picked up a Perspex box with two shiny silver beads rolling around in it and 77 etched on the outside. 'What's this?' she asked.

Mary checked on one of the box lids. 'Iridium.'

'Never heard of it.'

'Me neither.'

'Itch will love it,' said Kirsten.

Mary smiled. 'I hope so.'

Moz made a formal announcement of Mary Lee's arrival. 'Miss Lee to see you, Itch,' he said.

Itch spun round as Mary walked in.

'Sorry I'm late!' She smiled at him. 'I was busy shouting at my dad.'

'I thought . . .'

'I know. He's still away – we just shout a lot on Skype.' She walked over to where Itch was sitting and swung the boxes up onto the bench. 'We've got several of these at home,' she said. 'See what you think of these two.'

Itch unclipped the first box, to reveal six separate compartments. Each contained a muslin bag with a number and letters stencilled in black ink.

'Forty to forty-seven,' Itch murmured reverently. 'Zirconium to silver.'

It wasn't that they were particularly rare – Itch had samples of both himself – it was the way they were presented; as though they were as valuable as the Crown Jewels. In the lid of the box was a typed, plastic-coated sheet detailing where Mary's father had acquired each element. Itch stared.

'Have a look,' said Mary impatiently. 'Didn't bring them here for you just to gawp at them.'

He smiled awkwardly and nodded. His hand

hovered over the bags as he decided which one to open first. He plumped for the bag with *45* and *Rh* on it, and felt the weight of the rhodium metal inside. Pulling open the drawstring, he tipped a two-pound-coin-sized strip of silvery metal onto his hand. It had jagged edges, like a piece of torn thick kitchen foil, with a crystalline rim. He held it up to the light.

'It's beautiful . . . Where did your dad find this? Never seen rhodium like this before . . .'

'No idea, I'm afraid. It'll all be in the notes, if you're that bothered.' Mary pointed at the sheet in the lid. 'But let's see what we have here . . .' She picked up the next bag – marked *46* and *Pd*.

'Palladium,' said Itch, turning to look at the chunk of silvery-grey metal now sitting in Mary's hand. She placed bag and palladium on the bench and continued to pick up the bags and tip out the element inside. When the first box was empty she started on the second.

Itch was transfixed. 'Forty-eight to fifty-four. Hey, slow down there, Mary! I can't keep up!'

But Mary took no notice. 'How did you start all this, Itch?' she asked. 'My dad says it was *his* dad who gave him some rare samples of thorium or something that got him going.'

'Me too,' said Itch, watching Mary unpack the bags. 'My dad gave me an old chemistry book of my grandpa's, and that started the collecting thing. A few months back I had quite a collection, but . . . well . . .'

'What happened?' asked Mary, opening a bag marked *51* and *Sb*.

Eyes fixed on a container of antimony, Itch replied, 'Oh, I had to . . . They sort of got lost, I suppose.'

'Lost?' said Mary.

'Well, the old science teacher here went a bit nuts and attacked me. It's a long story, but he trashed my house looking for a rock I had.'

'Wow,' said Mary, her eyes wide. 'Were you OK? What happened?'

'He banged my head against the wall a few times but I was OK . . .'

Mary had stopped unpacking and was staring at Itch. 'Is this the Flowerdew guy I've heard of? Sounds like a nutcase.'

Itch nodded. 'You're right there.'

'What was so special about the rock? Was it gold or something?'

Itch paused only briefly. 'It was amazingly radioactive. Really dangerous.' He was aware that he might be showing off, but it was the truth, wasn't it?

'What happened next?' asked Mary, unwrapping the bag marked *54* and *Xe*.

Itch spotted the small canister and laughed. '*That*

happened,' he said, pointing at the metal tube. 'Xenon is what happened. It's an anaesthetic and I used some to put Flowerdew and an idiot friend of his to sleep.'

'That's so cool!' said Mary. 'You did that? I'm impressed! So you must have taken the rocks and made a run for it. Where did you go?'

Itch was too busy studying the xenon to notice the glint in her eyes.

Lucy Cavendish knew it was time to leave. She had been sitting at the computer in a daze for a few minutes before daring to move. Half expecting 'Leila S' to Skype again, she scrambled out of the study and went back upstairs to the bedroom. She was certain there was much more to learn in the house, but she felt as though she had ridden her luck already. She had to get out while she could. Retracing her steps to the window, she leaned against the wardrobe to pull her boots on.

She paused mid lace-up, a thought forming in her mind, and took them off again. Running downstairs, she headed straight for the Aga and the sandals that were propped up against it. And there it was. The one sandal that was sole-up had black writing on it. In thick felt tip, someone had written *TF*. She picked up the other sandal – warm to the touch – and turned it over. In the same capital letters it said *SHIVVI*.

'Got you,' said Lucy.

She pushed the sandals into her jacket pocket and ran upstairs. With her boots back on, she reversed out of the window and crouched on top of the conservatory. There was no easy way to the ground. It was too high to jump and her face had started throbbing again. A slow, careful backwards shuffle took her to the edge. Then, easing herself over the guttering, she let herself down. With the edge gripped tightly and her arms fully extended, Lucy dangled by her fingertips for a few seconds before letting go.

The drop was little more than a metre, but she landed awkwardly and pain shot through her nose and eye sockets. She winced and dropped to her knees, waiting for the burning and throbbing to pass. Fresh blood dropped onto her jeans.

'Well, I can't say where I went,' said Itch. 'I just decided I had to get rid of them.'

'But why? Couldn't you have done lots of good with them!'

'Maybe — but it wasn't worth the risk.' Itch looked at Mary as she handed him another bag. 'There are some good things you can do with them, but a whole load more of bad things. Which is why some seriously evil guys were after me. And still are. That's why I need Moz and friends. The big-time criminals will try anything to find those rocks.' Itch had looked away by the time Mary blinked and swallowed.

'Would you ever go back to get them?' asked Mary. 'You know, if you really had to.'

Images of the dark, never-ending well, and the smell and taste of the filthy water, flooded back, and Itch closed his eyes briefly. 'No,' he said quietly. 'I couldn't go back down there again.'

A small flicker of triumph flashed across Mary's face. *Down there*. He had said, *down there*. It wasn't much, but it was new.

'And I was pretty messed up when I came out too.'

Before Mary could follow this up, Jack and Chloe appeared in the doorway, grinning. 'You know it's the Oscars now?' said Jack. And they both pulled funny faces and hurried away along the corridor.

And the spell was broken.

Itch suddenly realized he'd said too much and stood dumbstruck, furious with himself. He looked at Mary and the elements laid out on their bags in front of him. How could he have been so stupid? All at once he wanted to leave. Now. He checked the lab clock.

'Er, sorry, Mary – I said I'd sit with Jack for the Oscars.' He got up to go, catching Kirsten and Moz by surprise. 'But thanks – they're really beautiful and . . .' But he'd run out of words. He turned and hurried out of the lab, closely followed by his minders.

Behind him there was a cry of 'Itch! Come back!' followed by the sound of something breaking into many pieces.

14

'What the hell was that?' asked Moz, running to catch up, but Itch didn't want to explain just yet; he was still cursing his stupidity.

'Rather you didn't take off like that,' Kirsten told him. 'One of us needs to be ahead of you. At all times. They're the rules, Itch, you know that.'

'Sorry. Just needed to get out, that's all.'

Moz went ahead and Kirsten fell back. The throng of students heading into the hall opened up as they saw the familiar security routine in operation. Normally Itch protested that he wanted to queue along with everybody else. But this time he followed the path that appeared in front of him and, spotting Jack, marched straight over.

He slumped down, and Jack, who was clearly about to carry on the teasing, opened her mouth and closed it again. Itch just stared at the floor.

'You OK? What's happened, Itch?' she whispered.

After a pause he replied, 'I nearly told her, Jack! If you guys hadn't come past, I might have . . . said too much.'

Jack looked stunned. 'But why? What was she asking you?'

'She was handing me these amazing samples. She had the most beautiful rhodium, Jack – you should have seen it – and she was asking about what happened with Flowerdew, and it just . . . sort of . . . went on from there.'

'What did you tell her?'

'I only said, *I couldn't go back down there.* But I could easily have said more, Jack – I could so easily have said more.' He shook his head.

'Showing off?' asked Jack.

'Probably.'

They both watched as the school hall filled up.

'Reckon you're fine, actually,' said Jack. 'There's nothing there that could tell anyone very much. *Down there* could mean anything: a basement, a dungeon, a cave, anything! Don't worry.'

Itch didn't reply, but he was grateful for the reassurance.

'You going to win anything, Itch?' asked Ian Steele, who had just dropped into the seat next to him.

'Unlikely. What about you?'

'No chance at all,' he said cheerily. 'Reckon it'll be Natalie and Debbie if anyone wins from Ten W.'

'What about Darcy Campbell?' Itch looked along the row. 'She looks pretty confident to me . . .'

'No chance,' said Ian. 'It's just the way her face was made. She always looks like that.'

In spite of his mood, Itch laughed, but Jack elbowed him in the ribs. 'Too loud, Itch. You need to learn to laugh quietly.'

Six seats along, Darcy Campbell was giving all three of them her scary face. This had the unfortunate effect of making Itch laugh even louder. People turned round to see what was so funny but, on realizing it was Itch, gave a shrug or a raised eyebrow.

'OK, you can stop now,' said Jack. 'It wasn't that funny.'

It was only the arrival on the platform of Dr Dart that stopped Itch's attack of the giggles. Most of the teachers filed in behind her, shuffling along to take their seats. Everyone fell quiet, and Dr Dart started to announce the winners of last month's Oscars. She started with the youngest classes. Each name was greeted with whoops and claps, the volume depending on the popularity of the recipient. Itch found himself hoping he hadn't won anything in case no one clapped.

'From Seven R, Asa Ahmed for English and Max Lawson for science.' Enthusiastic applause greeted the latest winners, who stood up, grinning, and made their way to the front. More names from Years

Eight and Nine were called out. Small groups of smiling pupils began to form on the stage.

'From Ten W, Jacqueline Lofte for history, and Sam Jennings for geography.'

Itch sat up and clapped loudly. 'Hey, Jack, that's you! Well done!'

Jack looked as astonished as Darcy Campbell was annoyed. Seeing her furious pout started Itch laughing again, and this time Ian Steele joined in.

'Darcy spent ages flirting with Mr Littlewood, you know,' he said as they both applauded hard. 'Reckoned it might get her the prize! Ha!'

'When all she had to do was write something that proved she wasn't a complete idiot,' said Itch, 'and she clearly failed.'

'Might be worth avoiding her for a while,' said Ian.

'Like the next four years?'

They both carried on laughing, missing the moment when Jack shook hands with Dr Dart.

The Year Eleven and Twelve winners joined a crowded stage, and then the applause died down before the final awards. The oldest students were trying to look cool and uninterested, but there was still some nudging as Dr Dart picked up her final certificates and envelopes.

She smiled down at her school. 'So, finally, our Year Thirteen. For exceptional work in drama, Polly Morrison . . .' She paused, and a large smiling girl with red hair jumped up and bounded towards the stage to whoops of delight. 'And for really advanced work . . .'

Itch suddenly knew what she was going to say.

'. . . in chemistry . . .'

There was only one person who was going to get called now.

'Mary Lee.'

Of course. Polite applause broke out around the hall. Because she was a new girl, no one had a strong opinion about her. Mary had kept herself to herself, so no one was particularly bothered either way. Itch kept his head down and clapped quietly.

As Mary stood up and made her way to the front, Itch became aware of some turned heads and then gasps of astonishment. But they weren't directed at Mary. Itch had to twist round to see what was causing the disturbance. And the next gasp was his.

Standing at the back of the hall, just by the door, he saw Lucy Cavendish. And she was terrifying. Her face was a mess of tape and blood, her re-opened wound bleeding freely over her clothes. Dressed in boots, jeans, Barbour jacket and hoodie pulled up over her thick, long hair, she pushed away all offers of help. On her cycle ride to the academy, she had tried to wipe away the blood from her nose with her jacket sleeve. As a result, she had streaks of dried blood smeared across her cheek and small congealed knots of it sticking to the strands of her hair that had escaped from her hoodie. In her left hand, she held the sandals.

Dr Dart hadn't noticed the commotion; she was greeting the Year Thirteen winners. Lucy – spotting the gap left by Jack – went over to her vacated seat and sat down slowly. Itch and Ian Steele stared at her, open-mouthed, but she seemed unaware of them, her eyes fixed on the stage.

'Lucy! What happened?' asked Itch. She ignored him, or maybe she hadn't heard, and Itch followed the direction of her stare.

Dr Dart had given Polly her certificate and voucher, and had turned to Mary. 'Dr Hampton tells me that this piece of work on acids and bases was quite wonderful.' Then, addressing the school, 'She's only been with us a few weeks, but Mr Hampton is very impressed. He says Mary handed in an extraordinarily advanced piece of work. Well done, Mary – our final award for today.' She handed over the envelope and card. 'And before you go to your next lesson, a big Cornwall Academy round of applause for this month's winners.'

Itch clapped and cheered for Jack, but froze as he saw Lucy stand up, pull her hood back and climb onto her seat. The applause started to die away as everyone turned. The teachers who had started to file out stopped in their tracks.

'Stop!' shouted Lucy. 'Stop now!'

Itch felt the seats tremble. Dr Dart, who had been leading the applause and smiling at the winners, held up her hands. Mary took a step back, behind the principal. Everyone was now staring at Lucy – those who hadn't noticed her earlier gasping in shock at her appearance. The hall went silent.

Lucy was swaying slightly, and Itch wondered if he should help her, but thought better of it. Mr Watkins, who was the nearest member of staff, started to approach her, but stopped as Dr Dart spoke.

'Good heavens, Lucy, why are you here? You should be in hospital! Mr Watkins, will you—'

But then Lucy spoke again. Wiping the blood from her mouth, she pointed her smeared finger at Mary Lee. 'It . . . was . . . her!' she shouted, her voice cracking. 'It . . . was . . . *her*!' The last word was more of a scream. 'She's the one who attacked me and did this!' Mr Watkins was now at Lucy's side and made to reach for her arm, but she brushed him away.

On the stage all the award-winners were dividing their attention between the impassive Mary Lee and the demented Lucy Cavendish. Jack looked from Lucy to Itch, and then noticed Chloe in the front row with her hands over her mouth. A few students who had been taking photos of the award-winners had swung their phones round and were now videoing Lucy. Their close-ups showed her bloodied and bruised face, her matted hair and her wild, tear-filled eyes.

Dr Dart found her voice again. 'Lucy, stop that now – get down from the chair and we'll discuss this in my office. If you—'

But Lucy hadn't finished; Itch saw and heard her take a huge breath.

'And her name isn't Mary!' The words rang around the old hall. Now Lucy held up the sandals so Mary could see them.

The only movement was from Kirsten, Moz and Sam Singh, who had heard enough and were starting to edge their way closer to the front.

'Her name isn't Mary Lee!' Lucy, her voice now higher and louder, pointed at the stage again. 'Her name is Shivvi Tan Fook!'

15

The impact of the name on Itch, Jack and Chloe was instantaneous. They each looked stunned, and then terrified.

Shivvi . . .

The woman who had gone to prison after the catastrophic oil leak in Nigeria.

Flowerdew's colleague.

It was *her*.

Itch's mind was a confused whirl and he looked around frantically for Moz; when their eyes met, he shouted, 'Get Jack!'

The award-winners on the stage looked confused and awkward. Dr Dart spun round just in time to see Shivvi leap up the steps to the backstage area and disappear into the corridor.

Moz vaulted onto the stage and grabbed Jack. Itch helped Lucy down from the chair, and Mr Watkins led her slowly out of the hall. Itch climbed over the seats to Chloe, at which point Sam pulled them both down onto the floor and held them there.

'Tina, get the car here now!' he called into his lapel mic. 'Rachel, get Mary Lee – she's probably coming your way.' Rachel Taylor was out patrolling the grounds, but was far away on the playing fields.

Seeing the security team in action caused panic. Some pupils screamed and ran for the exits. Once the rush had begun, most of the others joined in. Dr Dart called for calm, but no one was listening, and within seconds she was the only one left on the stage. When the main doors became jammed with students, some of the staff opened the emergency exits, triggering the fire alarms. Hundreds of students ran out of the hall and onto the playing fields; a hardy few lurked in the doorways, recording what they could. And then running.

As the hall emptied, Itch, Jack and Chloe remained crouched on the floor, with Moz and Sam standing over them, hands hovering near their holsters.

'Take charge out there, Dr Dart, and we'll sort it in here!' Sam shouted above the clanging bells.

Itch, Jack and Chloe all started talking and shouting at the same time:

'That was *her*! Oh my God, I can't believe it,' said Jack.

'Shivvi? That *can't* have been her!' Chloe still looked stunned.

Moz and Sam both asked, 'Who's Shivvi?'

'Shivvi Tan Fook. She worked for Greencorps and was Flowerdew's mate,' said Itch. 'She went to prison instead of him after they caused that oil spill in Lagos. We found her name when we were look-ing up stuff on Flowerdew.'

Sam whistled. 'That was her? Sure? Doesn't look old enough to have been in prison.'

'Well, she ran away, didn't she?' Itch pointed out. 'If she really was Mary Lee, she wouldn't have legged it.'

'But how did Lucy know?' asked Jack. 'Where did she get Shivvi's name from?'

Kirsten Jones ran into the hall. 'Tina's ready – let's go!' She led the way past the deserted labs and classrooms to the reception hall, then bundled them into the waiting van.

As they roared away, Moz called Rachel. 'Where is she, Rach? Need to know! Now!'

Rachel Taylor's breathless voice crackled into his earpiece, 'Never saw her. The car's gone too. I was the other side of the grounds. Sorry.'

A week of squally showers and plunging temper-atures accompanied Itch, Jack and Chloe's 'house arrest', as they had taken to calling it. After the revelation of Shivvi's infiltration of the school, serious questions were being asked about the entire security operation. And while that was happening, the academy was out of bounds. In fact, anywhere outside the two houses was out of bounds. And Colonel Fairnie had once again asked for Jack to move into her cousins' house. The confinement was driving everybody crazy.

Itch and Chloe had their own rooms, and Jack had taken Gabriel's. The three of them enjoyed each other's company – it was just everything else that was getting tiresome. The security team were on edge, and Nicholas and Jude were doing lots of shouting – sometimes at the children, sometimes at the MI5 team, but most of the time at each other. One morning Itch and Chloe had sat on the stairs for twenty minutes waiting for a particularly nasty argument to finish.

Jude's 'I see no reason why I should ever trust you again!' had distressed Chloe the most. Appalled, she looked at Itch and mouthed 'Why is she saying that?' Itch had merely shrugged and studied the carpet. As a result, they spent lots of time in Gabriel's – now Jack's – room. Out of everybody's way.

They had texted everyone they knew to ask about Lucy. Dr Dart had apparently called an ambulance and accompanied her to Stratton hospital herself. Lucy now had twenty-four-hour police protection. The academy had opened as usual the following morning.

★ ★ ★

In the meantime the Loftes played every game they could find in the house and online. Jack and Chloe's patience was tried by Itch's constant changing of the rules. They were quite happy to stick with the conventional way of playing, but Itch always liked to tinker. Games with seven cards now had to be tried with ten; chess had to be played without pawns, and Monopoly's Chance cards all had to be re-written.

Not content with this, Itch said he was going to design a Periodic Table version of Monopoly, which got him quite excited for a while. He had designed the board on his laptop, with hydrogen and oxygen as the first two 'properties', and gold and platinum as the last two.

'Not sure about that,' he said as he studied the new board. 'Californium is worth more per gram than gold, but there's hardly any around. No one will want to collect that.'

They were lying on the floor in Jack's room. It was the largest of the three, had less clutter, along with the strongest wi-fi signal. As it was in the attic, it was also furthest away from the shouting.

'Itch, no one will want to collect *any* of it. I wouldn't worry,' said Chloe.

But her brother hadn't heard. 'What if I put oxygen, sulphur and selenium together? That'd be a cool set, wouldn't it? And fluorine, chlorine and bromine would go together . . . Do you think the sets should be vertical or horizontal? C'mon, guys, what would look best? Help me out here.'

'I've got one,' said Jack. 'How about if you land on arsenic you go directly to jail?'

Chloe snorted. 'Nice one, Jack!' It had been Itch's sample of arsenic that had once been responsible for making most of his class sick.

Itch looked up. 'Oh well, thanks a lot. If you're not going to take it seriously . . .'

'Itch,' said Jack. 'An element hunter's Monopoly set is a great idea. Really it is. *If* you're an element hunter. But I only know one, and he's quite enough for anybody.' She got up to take a look at the screen. 'Anyway, shouldn't the most valuable square be you-know-what?'

'Quite right,' said Chloe. 'Who wants boring, reliable gold and platinum when there's much more exciting lofteium to collect?'

Fairnie had told Itch that element 126 might well end up being called this, if they ever found any more. Again, the memories of the Woodingdean Well flooded Itch's mind and he shivered.

'I'll be very happy if I never see any more 126 in my life.'

'Same here,' agreed Jack. 'It can all stay exactly where it is. For ever.'

'I know you can't tell us, but I still wonder where it ended up. I reckon you threw it down a mine somewhere,' said Chloe. 'I know you're protecting

Jack and me, but sometimes I'd love to be able to talk to you about it. There's no one else . . .' She caught the look that passed between Itch and Jack. '*What?* What did *that* mean? *Jack?*'

There was a silence. Jack and Itch glanced at each other. Itch closed the laptop.

'Jack knows,' he said.

Chloe gasped.

'Look, it's complicated, Chloe.'

'Try me,' she said, arms folded.

What can I say? thought Itch. *She would be in so much more danger if she knew the location of the 126. And I can't tell her about Dad not working on the rigs. Telling Jack was one thing, but Dad would spot it if Chloe knew too.*

'She kinda guessed, really. She worked it out . . . and you really *are* better off not knowing. Trust me.'

'Really?' said Chloe. 'You worked it out, Jack? Anyone else know, or is it just me that's in the dark?'

Itch had alarm bells going off in his head now. *That's what I said when Jack told me she knew what had happened, but if I mention my dad or Mr Watkins she might start to piece the story together. And I've put her in enough danger already. I'm not going to make it worse. Even if it makes her cross.*

'Chloe, I'd tell you if I could. Really. It would be great to sit here and chat about it all, but I don't think—'

She went over to the door. 'It's fine. You just talk

to Jack about it. Maybe tell me when I'm older,' she muttered as she left the room.

'When did she get to be so sarcastic?' said Itch.

'She's got a point,' said Jack uncomfortably. 'But she has protection and doesn't know anything. Mr Watkins knows everything and hasn't got *anyone* looking after him.'

'I know. You're right; maybe we should talk to Fairnie. Maybe he can persuade him.'

There was a silence. Itch had been waiting for Jack's question.

'Do you think you'd have told Shivvi anything? You know, if she'd brought in that caesium you wanted to see, for example?'

'I've asked myself that, Jack. I was certainly amazed by that element collection . . .'

'Which she'd so obviously just bought.'

Itch nodded. 'Which it looks like she bought. There was certainly no father around, that's for sure.'

'And you fancied her.'

'Jack, she's twenty-five! She might look eighteen, but come on . . .'

'Well, you know she's twenty-five *now*. You didn't when she was flashing her titanium and arsenic around, did you!'

They both grinned. They had the same smile and the family resemblance became – briefly – striking.

'OK, OK,' said Itch. 'But listen, we have to work

out whether Shivvi was operating on her own or not. Who would she work with? Greencorps?'

'Possibly,' said Jack. 'In which case she might have had access to Flowerdew. Wherever he is.' She rubbed her hands together. 'Maybe she's locked him up instead. Or cast him adrift. As long as he's miserable.'

There was a knock at the door and Sam looked in. 'Kitchen in five please. The colonel wants a chat.' She smiled and disappeared.

'Hmm,' said Jack. 'That's never good news.'

'Unless he has news of how miserable Flowerdew is,' said Itch.

'Agreed. And if the answer is "very", that'll be a good day.'

Everyone was crammed into the Lofte kitchen. Itch, Jack and Chloe, Nicholas and Jude were sitting around the table, with the MI5 team standing. Colonel Fairnie had just come in, finishing a phone call as he did so.

'Oh hi – thanks, everyone. Here's the latest for you. We've emptied the house Shivvi was staying in. Obviously she wasn't expecting to leave as quickly as she did. Her laptop was useful, and her communications interesting. There weren't too many photos, no videos – just a record of contacts here and in Nigeria. We think she escaped from prison in Lagos a few months ago, but the authorities there aren't being helpful. Where she went after that isn't known, but she came to the UK from Chile in August.' He looked at Tina, who checked her papers.

'Yes. The house here was rented online. The farmer says Lee paid monthly, up front, for a long-term let. No cleaner.'

'There's a surprise,' said Jack.

Jude Lofte had been tapping a pen against a magazine on the table, waiting her moment.

'So,' she said, 'a criminal who had just busted herself out of prison flew to England and got herself enrolled at our local school. My son and daughter and niece, the most heavily protected children of all time, were sharing a classroom with a murderer. Is that – roughly – right?'

Itch was familiar with this warm-up routine. *Please let no one interrupt*, he thought.

'That does appear to be—' the colonel began, but Jude hadn't finished. She held up her hand to stop him.

'And this – forgive me – was just a few days after an armed gang of criminals from Russia tried to kidnap my son and would have succeeded if it hadn't been for Nicholas.' She paused, then added, 'And they punched Chloe.' Nicholas started to say something, but he too was cut off. 'You will forgive me, Colonel, if I don't feel that this is going particularly well.'

There was an awkward silence before Itch, with a flushed face, said quietly, 'They saved my life, Mum. Out there on the golf course and on the beach, they saved me. Dad was great, but if these guys hadn't been there . . .' He tailed off, but then added, 'You're being unfair.' He swallowed hard and Chloe smiled at him. He was expecting a volcano-sized eruption from his mother, but this was headed off by Nicholas.

'Maybe you can assure us that the school and MI5 will vet any future pupils better from now on? And of course, we are both grateful for the risks you're all taking every day.' He smiled reassuringly while Jude stared straight ahead.

'Procedures are in place,' said Fairnie, 'and you are right to be angry about Shivvi Tan Fook. So am I. We should have spotted her and we didn't. We are sorry about that.'

'Do we know where she is?' asked Jack.

'Unfortunately we have no sightings. She escaped in her car. She'll be holed up somewhere – Cornwall's an easy place to hide yourself away in. Police, ports and airports all have her details – she's listed on Interpol now as an escaped prisoner – but my guess is she's not going anywhere. Itch is who she wants, and she'll be back.'

'Did she leave all her element collection behind? It's obviously not her father's . . .' Itch ignored the groans from Chloe and Jack. 'It's just that she had some cool stuff, by the sound of it.'

'She certainly did,' said Fairnie, 'and we cata-logued what's been left behind. Some nice pieces. If no one claims them in three months, they're yours.' Everyone laughed – even Jude. 'Seriously, Itch, there's nothing dangerous there, so once we've finished with fingerprints . . . if it's all right with your parents . . .' The colonel was looking at Jude, but Itch was frowning and he put his hand up.

'Er, excuse me – well, there's the caesium, of course. That counts as dangerous surely? Did you check that's OK?'

Fairnie looked at Sam, who had the inventory from Shivvi's house; he started flicking through the pages.

'Element fifty-five,' said Itch, trying to be helpful.

'Thank you,' said Sam irritably. 'Surprisingly, we didn't catalogue them in order of atomic weight' – he flicked over a few pages – 'but no, there was no caesium in the house.'

'Are you sure she had some?' asked Fairnie.

'She showed me photos,' said Itch. 'It's in a glass tube – an old Russian one, according to Mr Hampton. He told her she couldn't bring it into school.'

'Well, they got that right,' said Nicholas.

'Remind me . . . ?' said Jude to Itch.

'It's a solid metal but turns liquid beyond 28.4 degrees Celsius,' said Itch. 'It's the most reactive of the alkali metals. Burns immediately on contact with air. Explodes on contact with water.'

'My God,' said Jude. 'Here we go again.' There was a silence in the room.

'OK, thanks for the heads up, Itch. We don't know she has any caesium for certain – who knows where the photo came from – but we do need to treat her as extremely dangerous. If she does re-surface, we'll be ready for her.' Fairnie looked around. 'OK, that's it, folks.'

Itch, Jack and Chloe returned to Gabriel's/Jack's room. 'I don't like the sound of Shivvi with that caesium, Itch,' said Chloe. 'Do you think she has it?'

'Well, she seemed keen to bring it in, but who knows – maybe she was bluffing.' He sounded unconvinced.

'Anyway,' said Chloe. 'Good speech. Mum had lost it down there.' She high-fived her brother, and Jack joined in.

'She was out of order about the Russians, but she has a point about no one spotting Shivvi. Mind you, we're the only ones who've seen a picture of her and we didn't realize it was her.'

'A grainy image on a website hardly counts, Jack,' said Itch, 'and she'd cut her hair since then.'

'Wonder where she went . . .' said Chloe.

Jack frowned. 'Let's hope we never have to find out . . .'

16

Nathaniel Flowerdew threw his phone against the wall, where it cracked a photo frame holding a picture of himself on an African oil rig. The battery flew out of the handset and both crashed to the floor. He cursed loudly and banged the table with his hand.

'Damn that woman! She's messing everything up all over again!'

Alejandro Loya and Peter Voss realized they were not expected to reply. Both men were in Flowerdew's London flat by the Thames, a private investment made through an offshore company while he was working for Greencorps in Nigeria. He had barely been there, but it was the perfect place from which to plot the recovery

185

of the rocks. From wherever they were.

'She might be a brilliant diver, but that's all she is. My Interpol friend says she's on the run after *an incident at the academy*. At the academy, for God's sake! Whatever her plan was, it's over now – the security around the children will be much tighter.'

Loya smiled. 'It's a treasure hunt, Dr Flowerdew. *La equis marca el lugar*. X marks the spot, yes? And instead of doblòns – doubloons, as you say – our treasure is more valuable.'

Before Flowerdew could throw anything else, Voss passed him some tea. 'So. We have to be smarter. From the beginning. Every fact, every detail matters. Staff, pupils, how you found the rock, where you took the boy and his cousin . . . everything. Conversations you had that Itchingham might have heard . . .'

'Don't call him Itchingham – it sounds ridiculous. Like you're his dad or something.'

'What do you want me to call him?'

'Don't call him anything. Or "that boy", if you need to.'

'OK,' Loya said. 'Things that boy might have said – either to you or to other members of staff – that might give us some clue to where he might have gone to hide the 126. It'll be in there somewhere. We have time. Begin . . .'

Flowerdew found a coin in his pocket and began

to work it around his fingers, weaving it in and out, the fifty-pence piece spinning as it moved from one side of his hand to the other. His long frame stretched low in the chair as he thought through the thousands of conversations, meetings and people. Apart from his fingers, nothing moved; the Argentinian sat waiting with his laptop open and a pen in his hand.

Then, with a sudden snap of his wrist, Flowerdew tossed the coin in the air and caught it. 'OK, here's what happened,' he said, and starting with the first time he'd passed the academy's Geiger counter over the piece of 126, he told Loya and Voss everything he could remember. He held nothing back – why should he? If they wanted the 126 as much as he thought they did, they wouldn't be too bothered about a few British laws that he had broken.

As Flowerdew gathered speed, Loya struggled to keep up. Scribbled page followed scribbled page, each full of names, opinions and rants. Occasionally the Argentinian would ask Flowerdew to pause as he looked up some information online; then the tirade would start again. Flowerdew had got to the capture of 'the detestable Lofte children' and their flight from the mining school. He described the theft of the Lexus, the drive to London; how he and his driver Kinch had been drugged, allowing the cousins to escape. 'Xenon, apparently! Gassed by xenon! I never even knew it was an anaesthetic. I'd told Kinch to check his rucksack, but the idiot missed it.'

'Cars like that are sometimes fitted with tracking devices,' said Voss. 'Weren't you worried you'd be caught?'

Flowerdew shook his head. 'Never really thought about it. We just—' He sat bolt upright, banging the table with his knees as he did so, his eyes wide.

'You have thought of something?' Loya looked intrigued.

'*Tracking devices*. You said *tracking devices*,' said Flowerdew quietly.

'On the car, on the Lexus . . .'

'No. Not on the car, stupid. On my laptop . . . on my *laptop*!'

'I'm not with you.'

'Of course you're not. When they escaped, the accursed Lofte children stole my case and my laptop. While in Nigeria I was persuaded by a business colleague to have a tracker fitted to my laptop – it seemed a laughable idea at the time, but he insisted. He said I had too much dangerous information to take the risk. Had it done there and then.'

'When was this?' said Voss.

'Ages back. Forgotten about it till ten seconds ago.'

'And your laptop never turned up?'

'Obviously not.' The sneer was unmistakable.

Loya stood up and started pacing around Flowerdew. 'A tracker on a laptop would have its own battery, or maybe run from the laptop's. Either way, it's unlikely to be still charged. It'll be dead by now.'

'Yes, yes, of course, but it worked with a website, I think. I'm sure he said that this tracker left co-ordinates every hour or something. You just log in and it'll tell you where it is.'

'What's the website?' asked Voss.

'No idea. Absolutely no idea.'

After ten minutes on the phone, Loya was back at his laptop. 'There aren't that many sites that do this tracker operation. Any of these look familiar?' he said.

Flowerdew joined him in front of the screen as he typed in a series of web addresses. When, one by one, the home pages flashed up, Flowerdew shook his head, exasperated. 'I never logged on, I never checked it. I never needed to. This is useless.'

'No, let's try something else,' said Voss. 'Men of your age usually keep the same login and password. You're told to change it regularly, but you don't. Am I right?'

'Possibly. Let's try. How many sites?'

'Eight, I think. Here – try to log in.' Loya moved aside so that Flowerdew could enter his details. As he typed, Loya and Voss could sense his excitement rising. The fifth site was called boxsecure.com: Flowerdew typed in his password, and the now-familiar •••••••••••••••••••••••• came up.

'That's a long password.'

'It's part of a DNA sequence of a protein,' said Flowerdew, and hit ENTER. 'You beauty,' he said as the screen showed a new array of security questions. Typing furiously now, he tore into answer boxes and hit ENTER again. The screen momentarily went blank; then, suddenly, an array of tiny black figures filled the screen, and Loya and Voss leaned forward to take in the information.

'Dates on the left, coordinates on the right!' shouted Loya.

'And the last date is in June – that'll be when the battery died.' Flowerdew was following the last entries on the screen with his finger. 'And all the coordinates are in the same place. It didn't move for six days! We need a map! Where is 50.8288 degrees north and 0.1411 degrees west? Write it down!'

Alejandro Loya smiled again. 'I think it's easier than that. Look.' He clicked on the coordinates and the screen moved into Google maps. The image zoomed in on blocks of colour which, when focused, revealed a mass of railway tracks by a park.

'Dyke Road Park? Where's that?' said Flowerdew, his voice loud and tense.

Loya pulled the focus out, and a mass of blue appeared at the bottom of the screen.

'Well, well,' said Flowerdew, smiling. 'Hello, Brighton. Now what, I wonder, was Lofte doing there?'

'The school run just got cancelled!' Itch had put his head round Jack's door just as she was putting on her school sweatshirt. From underneath it, she called, 'You what?' Pulling it over her head, she stared at Itch. 'What's happened?'

'Two sightings of Shivvi. One at a clothes shop in Launceston, the other in Tesco.'

'You're joking.' Jack ruffled her hair, making it stick up. 'Tesco? Like she's going to be shopping?'

'Kirsten is checking the CCTV footage, but until they know what's happening we're staying here. Too much of a threat.'

'*Wild Prisoner Attacks Van with Her Shopping! Crazy Woman Throws Beans at Students!* That kind of danger, do you mean?'

They were still laughing when they entered the kitchen. Chloe was sitting at the table with Nicholas and Fairnie.

'I know what you're thinking!' said the colonel. 'But we can't allow you to go to school if Tan Fook is still around. I guessed she'd be back, but not this soon.'

'And not shopping in Tesco,' said Jack.

Fairnie smiled. 'Agreed. But we can check that one. The sighting at Launceston is trickier. Reports

191

point to someone small and female buying gentlemen's clothes. Could be her.' Everyone looked doubtful. 'OK, OK, it sounds unlikely, but we've taken a lot of heat for not getting this right. From many quarters.' He glanced at Nicholas. 'And Jude was right to be cross. So, we take no chances.'

'But I'd quite like to go home,' said Jack. 'It's nice here with everyone, of course, but . . .'

Fairnie was shaking his head. 'Sorry, Jack. Not yet. You can go home when you can go to school. We're sending Chris to Tesco for a while to see if he can help from there. Meantime you're still stuck here, I'm afraid.'

From then on, things got increasingly tetchy and difficult for everyone.

Jack, realizing she was rooming at Itch and Chloe's for an unknown amount of time, spent longer on her own in Gabriel's room.

Itch realized he was annoyed with her for wanting to be at home, and Chloe was missing her friends.

'It's fun for a few days,' she said, 'but then it just gets boring.'

Itch had catalogued his element collection twice – once in alphabetical order and then in atomic number order. But then he too had got bored.

'Got a friend for you to meet,' Nicholas called up to Itch's room, and was surprised to find his son jumping down the stairs.

'Really? We don't really get visitors any more. Who is it?'

Nicholas led the way to the kitchen, where Jacob Alexander, the director of West Ridge School of Mining, sat drinking tea. He smiled broadly and got to his feet when he saw Itch. Itch hadn't seen him since running away from his labs with the pieces of 126. Just before being kidnapped by Flowerdew.

'Hi, Itch! Great to see you!' The scientist was dressed in a suit, his broad frame straining the fabric in a number of places. He offered his hand and Itch shook it tentatively.

'Oh. Hi.'

It was Dr Alexander who had analysed and identified the 126 and then been attacked by Greencorps agents when he had refused them entry. And, as Itch had learned in that startling beach-hut confession, he was now his dad's boss. He didn't know where to start . . .

'You OK now?' he asked at last. 'That was quite a kicking you took in the car park.'

Alexander smiled and his tanned face crinkled. 'I was going to ask how *you* are! That was some dose of radiation you must have taken.'

'Yes. Bone-marrow transplant, blood transfusions – that kind of thing. But I'm OK now, I think.'

'Found any more of those rocks?'

'Haven't been looking. I'm stuck in here or at school these days. Can't say I'd be that keen to find any more, anyway.'

'No, no, of course,' said Alexander, rubbing his closely cropped grey hair. 'I was going to suggest going for a walk, but your dad says that's not possible.'

'Not at the moment, no. No school, no town, no nothing. There's always the garden, if you want some air.' Itch looked through the kitchen window into the misty gloom. 'We've some neatly trimmed hedges to have a look at.'

His father smiled, but he seemed on edge and subdued. *He's obviously set this meeting up*, thought Itch. *This is all for me.* And when he thought about it, he realized that this chat was always going to happen at some point. But if his dad needed him to listen to Dr Alexander, then he wanted to hear what he had to say.

The three of them pulled on jackets and wandered into the darkening garden.

'What's really weird,' said Itch, 'is that, er, until recently I didn't even know you knew each other.'

'Well, this is just a social chat, of course. I've really come to see your dad . . .'

'While my mum's out.'

'Yes, while your mum's out. So this is awkward in a number of ways. But let me get to the point – your dad says we can speak safely here.'

'Unless they've bugged the flowerbeds, yes. As far as I know.'

They set off around the garden.

'I know that you know I don't just run the mining school. I also head up a group of scientists around the world who are trying to plan for when the world has run out of energy. Which will happen much, much sooner than anyone realizes. Until now we have been concentrating on hydraulic fracturing – *fracking*, as it's known – but when you came along with the 126, everything changed. It is a source of great frustration to me that I had in my hands . . . for just a few moments – an energy source that could revolutionize everything. But then we . . . lost them. And it would break my heart to think that they might be lost for ever.'

'Can I just say something?' said Itch as they started their second lap of the garden.

'Of course.'

'Well, it's just that I know all this . . . I don't mean to be rude or – or disrespectful, but I had scientists and politicians telling me this all summer. I know the good stuff it can do, but I know the bad stuff too. A friend told me, *Don't trust anyone*, and I don't. And I'm not going to. Sorry, but there it is.'

'Was that Cake?'

Itch paused, and his father almost bumped into him. 'You know him?' Itch was incredulous.

'Oh, not very well, but we all had dealings with him over the years. I knew him when he was called Mike.'

Itch stopped again, and this time his father did bump into him. 'Mike? He was called *Mike*? You're kidding . . . Anyway, he died.'

'Yes, I heard. I'm sorry.'

'Radiation.'

'Yes. A nasty way to go, but then, you know all about that. My point, Itch, is that Cake was wrong. You *can* trust some people.'

'People like you?'

'Yes, actually, people like me. And your dad. If the future is left to the oil companies and politicians, we're stuffed. But scientists can make a difference – *we* can make a difference. If we had the 126, we could ensure that it was only used for powering ships, cars and aeroplanes. In a power station it could make its own energy by fission – where a particle would split, produce free neutrons and gamma rays and a whole lot of energy—'

'I know what fission is, Dr Alexander.'

'Sorry. Of course you do. Anyway, we'd probably get element 127 out of that little lot.'

Nicholas put his hand on Itch's shoulder as they walked. 'I've explained to Jacob that you won't be telling anyone where the rocks are, but he just wanted to give it a go, that's all.'

'We've started searching for the 126 elsewhere,' Alexander said. 'We're looking in northern France now. Geologically, the rocks in Brittany are the closest match to Cornwall's – almost certainly they were joined at one time. Seems like the best place to start, but nothing yet. It's still just your rocks, I'm afraid.'

'I'm sorry, Dr Alexander, but as I keep telling everyone, they aren't *my* rocks. And I have no intention of *ever* seeing them again.'

17

With the arrival of December and no sightings of anything suspicious for many days, Fairnie gave permission for the cousins to return to school and for Jack to go home. Chloe and Jack celebrated by going Saturday shopping, while Itch realized he didn't really have anywhere to go. Or anyone to go anywhere with. He had hoped to make some friends this term, but it hadn't worked out like that. In fact, since returning from military hospital he'd had even less contact with even fewer people.

The morning post brought a parcel for Itch. All packages had to be inspected, and Kirsten had already opened it when she walked into the kitchen and passed it to Itch.

'Looks like your kind of thing, Itch – this your latest order?'

'Yup,' said Itch, and tipped out a small box containing some silvery crystals and a square of torn foil. Pointing at each in turn, he said, 'That's scandium and rhodium. And this . . .' He held up a clear packet containing a white powder. 'It's fifty-two on the Periodic Table. Come on then, Kirsten – you must have studied this at school. What's this?'

'I could pretend to try and remember, but to be honest I don't think I've ever known. Surprise me.'

'Tellurium,' said Itch, weighing the bag of powder in his hand. 'Atomic weight 127.6, melting point 449.51 degrees Celsius. It's not pure, un-fortunately – sodium tellurite is the best I could do.' He put it down on the table, and saw her expression. 'Well, you *did* ask.'

'How do you get all this stuff?' asked Kirsten.

'It's difficult. Without Cake, and with all you guys around, there aren't too many places. I'm having to restock my collection after . . . what happened . . . and I'm back up to forty elements now. Different collectors swap stuff, and some websites will sell to fifteen-year-olds. There's a new arts shop opening in town apparently – they may be able help.'

'An arts shop? What good is that?'

'Glazes, dyes – that kind of thing. Should be able to get me some vanadium, that kind of thing,' said Itch. 'It would help if I could do ebay. You don't fancy getting me some stuff, do you, Kirsten?'

'Yeah, that would go down well with the colonel!' she laughed.

On cue, Fairnie's head appeared round the door. 'What would go down well with me? You planning something, Itch?'

'I was thinking of this experiment. I'd love some iodine crystals and some concentrated ammonia really, but—'

'That'll be a no, then,' interrupted Fairnie. 'I remember enough of my chemistry, and that particular experiment ends in a bang. Correct?'

Itch fiddled with his packets and boxes. 'Might do . . .' He smiled. 'Some other time maybe.'

'Not while I'm in charge.'

Itch gathered his new elements together. 'Not even outside?'

'Especially outside. Large bangs coming from the Lofte house is just not a good idea.'

'Yes, sir,' muttered Itch as he left the kitchen.

Kirsten and Fairnie watched him go. When they heard his bedroom door slam, Kirsten turned to Fairnie.

'Oh, Colonel, you know I said the smell in Lucy Cavendish's room reminded me of something? Well, I've realized what it is.'

Fairnie raised an eyebrow.

'Itch's bedroom smells exactly the same. Just thought I'd mention it.'

John Watkins had lived by the canal ever since he'd started teaching at the Cornwall Academy five years previously. There was a row of six fishermen's cottages: four were second homes to London folk, and the fifth had its roof off, awaiting major repair work. His cottage was the last one before the dunes and the Atlantic, and he had fallen in love with it as soon as he saw it. If he wasn't at school, the only place he wanted to be was here, by the sea.

That Sunday, nearing the end of a particularly windy and cold walk along the beach, Watkins recognized the familiar grouping escorting the cousins along the expanse of sand that the low tide had exposed: two agents leading the way, the cousins twenty metres behind them, and two more agents at the rear. Watkins knew that the van wouldn't be far away; sure enough, looking back, he saw it in the car park near his cottage.

He waved, and as the Loftes realized who was approaching, they waved back. Watkins nodded his greeting as the couple on point passed him. Pulling his coat closer he shook hands with Itch, Jack and Chloe, which seemed rather weird to them.

'Where are you heading?' he called over the noise of the wind. 'You all look freezing!'

'We're just escaping the house, sir. It can get a bit tense sometimes, particularly during a meal. We're walking it off,' Itch told him.

'Of course, of course. Well, why don't you all warm up at my place? I can offer you a hot drink.'

He gestured to the four MI5 officers: Danny, Sam, Moz and Kirsten.

'OK – thanks,' said Itch. He wasn't actually sure about visiting teachers' houses, even his form teacher's. But they were indeed frozen. 'That'd be nice.'

'Excellent! Come on then!'

Moz and Kirsten secured the cottage; when they had given it the all-clear, the Loftes went in gratefully. Mr Watkins dispensed tea or hot blackcurrant, then handed round shortbread. The agents went back out with their drinks, eyes scanning the beach, minds still on the job. The Loftes were left alone with Mr Watkins.

'This is weird,' said Chloe. 'But nice weird,' she added quickly.

'Weird for me too,' said Watkins. 'Don't get many passers-by at this time of year. But it's nice to see you all.'

We weren't exactly passing by, thought Itch; *you came and got us*. But he was happy to see where his teacher lived. The kitchen was all old wood units and flooring, with a battered old Aga. A pile of newspapers and magazines lay on one end of the table, and Itch idly took one from the top.

'*Times Educational Supplement*,' he read out loud. 'Is this a magazine just for teachers?'

'Yes, it is indeed. I've read the TES for many years. You can borrow one if you want.'

Itch dropped it. 'No thanks!'

Jack picked it up and started flicking through the pages.

'It's where I saw the advert for the Cornwall Academy many years ago,' Mr Watkins added. 'Without it I might never have met you lot.'

'Have you thought any more about what we were talking about at school the other day?' asked Itch.

'The security thing, you mean? No – forgive me, I haven't. If one's mind is made up, there really is no point in thinking any more about it, is there?' Watkins stopped, noticing that Jack had gone rather pale. 'What is it, Jack?' he asked.

She had pushed the magazine towards Itch and pointed to a brief article and photograph. He read it and felt the blood drain from his face.

The Mondo group of international hotels today announced the purchase of the Fitzherbert School in Brighton. The school, which was established in 1845, has been struggling to attract new pupils, and when the surprise offer was made to the governors last month, they felt they had to accept. The school will close at Christmas, and alternative places are being found for all existing pupils. A spokesman for Mondo Holdings said they would be demolishing the building and opening a five-star resort hotel on the site in two years' time.

There was a small photo of the school from what looked like many decades ago. It looked cleaner and brighter, but still sent a chill through Itch; he passed the article to his form teacher. While he was reading it, Chloe was looking between Jack and Itch.

'What is it? What's happened?' she asked sharply. 'Jack? Itch? One of you! What's in the article?' Still no one spoke.

Watkins finished reading and put the magazine down. 'It isn't necessarily bad news,' he said eventually. 'We have no idea who Mondo group are, but they might just be who they say they are.'

Chloe reached over for it. 'Well, as no one will tell me . . .' she said, and started reading. 'The Fitzherbert School . . . Do we know it?'

'I used to teach there many moons ago,' said Watkins softly.

They were all waiting for Chloe to finish the article. Jack gave her a concerned look, but Itch shrugged. 'I guess she's going to have to know now,' he said.

Chloe had started to re-read the article when the penny dropped and she looked at her brother, open-mouthed. '*This* is where you went, isn't it? *This* is where you hid the rocks!'

By saying it out loud, it was as though a spell had been broken and Itch felt he had to tell Chloe everything that had happened after they left her at the mining school. He hadn't really realized quite how much he had wanted to tell his sister the whole story, but now it came out in a torrent. Chloe and John Watkins listened in astonishment as Itch finished with the final flourish – that it had been his father who had rescued him.

'*Dad?* Are you kidding me?' Chloe was reeling.

Itch knew he was going to have to break his father's confidence again. As he started to explain where Nicholas had been working these past few years, Watkins stood up and put his hands over his ears.

'No – I don't need to know any of this. I've heard enough, thank you very much! I'll put the kettle on again – don't mind me.' He gathered up the mugs and retreated to the kitchen. The cousins heard him go outside and start up a conversation with the MI5 officers.

Itch continued to tell Chloe about their father. 'But you can't let him know I told you – he swore me to secrecy. I just think you deserve to know everything that we do, that's all.'

'So he's lied to us all this time. All the North Sea stuff, the troubles on the rig . . . all of it.'

'I think it's for a good reason, Chloe. And if he hadn't been in London when Mr Watkins called, he'd never have been able to reach me down the well. So, all things considered . . .'

Chloe nodded as Mr Watkins returned with more drinks.

'If you have quite finished talking about things I don't need to know, I'll come back in. So . . .' He sat down and looked at them.

Itch felt he was expected to say something. 'OK, well, let's assume Mondo aren't good people at all. So far, that's been a safe bet where the rocks are concerned. Somehow they know about the 126 and intend to get them. If that's the case, then it's all over and I need to talk to Fairnie now.'

'I've just Googled Mondo: they *do* run hotels around the world,' said Jack, showing her phone to Itch. 'Barcelona, Los Angeles, Buenos Aires . . . They might be OK . . .'

'Might be.' Itch was thoughtful. 'But it seems suspicious, don't you think? School struggles for years – according to that article – then acquires some valuable rocks down the well, and all of a sudden they're snapped up by a big company.'

'I agree it needs investigating further,' said Watkins. 'Why don't I call the school on Monday – I think I still know some of the staff down there – see what I can find out?'

Chloe looked relieved. 'That sounds like a plan,' she said. 'But then what? What happens next?'

'Why don't you come to our form room after school on Monday, Chloe? Jack and Itch will be there last thing anyway, and I'll fill you in on what I've learned,' Watkins suggested.

Itch was agitated now and pacing the room, frowning. 'Can we wait that long? If it is Greencorps that have bought the school, we need to act now. If I tell Fairnie tonight, the school would be sealed off within hours.'

'And if it's nothing?' said Mr Watkins. 'If it's just a hotel company buying up an old building? What then?'

'I know, I know,' said Itch. 'Then I might just as well have handed them over months ago.' *This is my decision: they're waiting for me on this*, he thought. He sighed. 'OK, let's wait. But only till tomorrow. Then, if there's anything you don't like about what your friends at the Fitzherbert School are telling you, I'll go to Fairnie.'

'Agreed,' said Jack.

Watkins nodded. 'I'll call as soon as I can on Monday. I might have to call from here just to keep things private.'

'We should get back,' said Jack, and they all stood up.

Moz and the team immediately came back in, ready to leave. Reverting to their previous form-ation, they marched out into the December gloom, calling their thanks to Watkins.

'Well, quite a gang, aren't we?' he said.

When the walking expedition returned, it was dark, and Jude Lofte was preparing supper for whoever was in. The cousins sat around the kitchen table with steaming bowls of soup. Jack and Itch talked homework; Chloe was silent. The MI5 team were just filing out when Fairnie appeared at the door and they all trooped back in.

'We have a problem. I just spoke to Dr Dart. She has just received an email that appears to be from Shivvi: she's threatening to burn the school down.' There were sharp intakes of breath all round the kitchen. 'And you were right about the caesium, Itch. The email is signed off with $Cs + H_2O = a$ *whole lot of fun.*'

'Sounds like her,' he replied.

Fairnie looked at his team and nodded; they started to move, knowing what Fairnie was about to say. 'We must find Shivvi. I'll call the police for extra manpower. Let's get to the school.'

The officers disappeared next door and the colonel addressed the Lofte family. 'Jack, you're here tonight again. I need as many members of my team as possible on this one. I'll call your parents. I don't need to tell you what a chemical fire would mean. We have to assume that Shivvi has the caesium – and God knows what else. I'll leave Danny here and the full house armour on – shutters, the lot. No one leaves. Clear?'

Everyone nodded, and he strode out of the kitchen.

★ ★ ★

Chloe and Itch spent the rest of the evening in Jack's room at the top of the house.

'At least we're safe here,' said Chloe, sitting on the floor with her back to the bed.

'Yes, 'cos it certainly doesn't sound safe out there,' said Jack. 'Would Mary – sorry, Shivvi – really burn the academy down, Itch?'

'Just what I was wondering,' said Itch. 'We only knew Mary, not Shivvi, who caused the oil spillage and the deaths and went to jail. If she was planning to get the 126 through me, she failed – maybe she's pretty hacked off. Who knows what she's capable of?'

Jack had her laptop open. 'Do you think we can Facebook people about this? Shouldn't we warn them to stay inside or something?'

Itch shook his head. 'No – that would be too public. We could text, though . . .'

And so Jack and Chloe spent the next few minutes texting friends a general warning, while Itch contacted Mr Watkins.

After his visitors left, John Watkins had tidied up and settled down to prepare the next week's lessons. Some classes were easing off for Christmas, but those with exams in the New Year still needed plenty of attention and he took a pile of Year Twelve essays out of his bag. The house was warm, the tea freshly brewed, but the first essay on globalization was atrocious and his attention wandered. His eyes were heavy and the armchair comfortable . . .

The next thing he knew was his heart racing as, nearby, a police siren wailed past. It was unusual to hear one at all – sometimes the summer tourists triggered a few, but in winter and this close it was rare indeed. As he sat still trying to clear his head, another siren joined the first, and Watkins knew that something serious was happening. He stood up and peered through his curtains, but the darkness in the garden and on the towpath was total.

But there was something else, he thought . . . and he stood uneasily by the window. The siren had certainly woken him, but having lived on his own for so long, and knowing every creak and rattle of the old house, he knew it felt different. He stood motionless, his heart pounding again. He walked into the hall, and stood there too. He then peered into the room he used as his study; the light was off but the shadows in there looked different . . . wrong . . . Maybe he'd forgotten to draw the curtains. He stepped into the room and froze.

'Hello, sir.'

Watkins wheeled round, and in the near dark saw a small figure standing against the wall. 'What the—!' He thumped the desk light on.

Shivvi stood by the bookcase, grinning, her hoodie pulled low over her face.

'Mary? What are you doing here? How dare you! I'll—'

Shivvi produced a baseball bat from behind her back and Watkins fell silent.

'As you know, my name isn't Mary,' she said. 'It's Shivvi Tan Fook. Originally from Malaysia, but not long out of the Ikoyi Prison in Lagos. That's in Nigeria. But then, as a geography teacher, you'll know all about that.' She pulled her hood back, her shaven head making her look even younger and smaller. Her smile, however, was not the easy-going glance of the teenager that Watkins had seen at the academy. This was a mean, cold grimace and she looked to him like a killer.

18

'What do you want? I . . . I haven't got anything particularly valuable, I'm afraid. Do you need money? I could lend you some money . . .' John Watkins was trembling as he stared at Shivvi Tan Fook.

She leaned on the baseball bat and laughed; though the brown eyes that were fixed on him were hard.

'I don't need money. There's nothing here I could possibly want. It's all junk, anyway.' And before Watkins realized what was happening, Shivvi swung the baseball bat, smashing it into the bookshelves. The wood splintered, and scores of books crashed to the floor. Watkins gasped, then jumped with each new blow as she worked her way around the room. She paused as another police car sped by on its way to town, siren blaring, and nodded with satisfaction. Then the bat swung

again: a vase . . . the computer screen . . . a paint-
ing. Papers went flying – an old radio – a photo
frame with two smiling elderly faces in it.

Watkins gasped. 'My parents! Why are you doing
this?' He bent down to pick up the photograph, but
found the bat being pushed into his chest.

'I'm doing it to show you I'm not a schoolgirl,'
said Shivvi with narrowed eyes. 'And when I ask for
information, I will expect an answer.'

'What information would you like?' asked John
Watkins, swallowing hard. 'I'm just a geography
teacher. I'm not likely to have anything you could
want. Should we perhaps have some tea? I
could put the kettle on . . .' The knot in his
stomach told him he had a good idea where this
questioning was heading, but he wanted to delay
the moment if he could.

She shook her head and went into the lounge,
beckoning for him to follow. She sat on the sofa,
muddy boots tucked under her legs, the baseball bat
across her lap. 'Let's talk. Now.'

He perched on an armchair, aware that the bat
could come flying his way at any minute. Shivvi
looked up and he shivered.

'I would like your phone, please.'

'My what?' The question caught him off-guard.

'Your mobile phone.'

Watkins fetched it from the kitchen, noticing that
he had received a text.

'Give it to me.' Shivvi held her hand out. 'You have an unread message,' she said, looking at the screen. She pressed a key and smiled. She read aloud: '*Shivvi in town. Maybe to attack CA? Itch.* Well, well. That has made everything so much easier. I was going to get you to send him a message. But this is so much neater: you can just reply.'

Watkins swallowed. 'What do you want me to say?'

'Oh. I'll say it for you, I think. And I shall say just enough to make him come running.'

'No! Don't do that! I'm sure I can help somehow. Please, leave him alone!'

'How sweet,' said Shivvi. 'OK, let me try one question. Where did Itchingham Lofte leave the element 126? How about that?'

Despite being ready for some kind of question about the rocks, hearing it spoken out loud took his breath away.

Shivvi smiled. 'And I see from your reaction that you *do* know. Well?'

Watkins shifted on the edge of his chair. '126? What's that? You're asking the wrong person, I'm afraid. I'm not the elements man at school . . .'

Shivvi picked up the baseball bat. 'Oh, I think you can do better than that. So much better than that. You forget, I worked in the oil industry for five years. I can spot a liar if I need to.'

Shaking now, John Watkins was thinking fast.

'Of course, you worked alongside Nathaniel Flowerdew, didn't you? You went to prison instead of him.'

Shivvi nodded. 'You got that right. He taught me everything I know. Including the effectiveness of this.' And she swung the baseball bat through the air.

'If I tell you where the rocks are,' said Watkins, 'will you leave Itch alone? Surely you won't need to involve him.'

But Shivvi shook her head. 'No, I want him here. He can show me. He'd make a better guide, don't you think? I might need him.'

She typed something into Watkins's phone and pressed SEND. 'That should do it. Let's see how long it takes for our hero to arrive.'

Itch, Jack and Chloe were monitoring events in town via Facebook updates: *Anyone know what's happening in town? . . . Big deal in the high street — what's going on? . . . More police round CA than Glasto.* After Fairnie and his team had left the house in lockdown, with only Danny Stein watching it, the sound of sirens filled the night. The cousins didn't know Cornwall even had that number of emergency vehicles. Fairnie was obviously preparing for a major incident, and if they had been able to look through the bedroom window, Itch, Jack and Chloe would have seen the town's Christmas illuminations utterly overwhelmed by countless flashing blue lights.

'You guys want to watch a film? I'm just starting one . . .' Jude Lofte had put her head round the door.

Itch looked at Jack and Chloe. 'No, we're fine, thanks, Mum.'

'Done all your homework?'

'Yes,' Chloe said, 'but I doubt we'll be going to school tomorrow.' They all listened again to the wailing sirens.

'You may be right there,' agreed Jude. 'Got everything you need, Jack? I've spoken to your dad; he says things are pretty wild down there. He's happy, anyway.'

'Thanks,' said Jack. 'Yes, I'm fine.'

Her aunt nodded and, with a final glance at Itch and Chloe, went back downstairs.

Itch's phone bleeped and he picked it up. As he had only sent the one text, he guessed who it was from.

'It's from Mr Watkins . . . This is weird . . .'

'Show me,' said Jack and he chucked the phone to her.

'*Gweres*. What does *gweres* mean?' She passed it to Chloe.

'Is it a spell-check mistake?' she asked, and tried the letters out on her phone. 'No, nothing here.'

Itch was back at his laptop. 'Maybe it's Cornish.

Not sure what for, though . . . You understand it, Jack?' She shook her head, so he continued his search and found a Cornish–English dictionary, typed *gweres* into the box provided, and hit ENTER. There was a wait of a few seconds before it provided the answer.

Help.

They all stared at the screen for a few seconds.

Chloe spoke first. 'Call him.'

Itch hit the numbers and listened. 'Straight to voicemail.' He stood up and started walking around the room. '*Help*. In Cornish. Why would he send that? Is he a Cornish speaker?'

'Don't know,' replied Jack. 'Never used any in class. And he's not from Cornwall.'

'So no, then,' said Itch.

'So why send it in Cornish?'

'Because . . .' Chloe spoke slowly. 'Because maybe he's trying to disguise his message. He's with someone who won't understand *gweres* but would understand *help*.'

'That's it!' exclaimed Jack. 'You must be right. He's in trouble. Let's find Danny.'

The three of them ran down to the kitchen, where Danny Stein was running a makeshift control centre. Three laptops open on the table showed real-time images of the town and the academy – now surrounded by flashing lights.

'Danny – Mr Watkins is in trouble! Look!' Itch

held up the phone. 'It's Cornish for *help*. Something must have happened! You have to tell Fairnie!'

Danny kept his eyes on the screens. 'Hang on, Itch.' He spoke into a microphone on one of the computers. 'No, sir! No sign here – just checking reports from the campsites now. Will get back to you.'

Fairnie's disembodied voice squawked through the small speaker, 'Got that, Danny.'

Danny looked up. 'What's up?'

Itch held up his phone again and translated. Even before he'd finished, Danny's gaze had returned to scan an email.

'Middle of a big op here, Itch, as you can see. Can it wait?'

Itch was annoyed. 'I'll just text back then: *Sorry you need help. Hope you can wait a bit as we're busy. Hope it's not serious.*'

Now it was Danny's turn to be cross. 'Which of these guys do I reassign, then? We think a chemical fire might be started in town, possibly at your school. And we've been told that if it's the isotope caesium-137, then it's radioactive. And that's a threat to everyone. Call your teacher and find out what the problem is.'

'I've tried that. No reply. And it's not caesium-137 – I've seen the picture,' said Itch.

'Where did you see it?'

'On her phone.'

Danny sighed. 'I'm not changing our plans because you've seen a picture on a mobile phone. I'll make a note of your teacher's text and tell one of the team to call round when they can. OK?'

'But when will that be?' said Itch, still agitated.

'The clue is in the phrase *when they can*, Itch . . . When they've worked out whether there's a caesium fire about to explode in town. Got it?'

Itch turned and left the kitchen, followed by his cousin and sister. He led them into the lounge, where Jude was watching TV.

'What's up, Itch? You look bothered,' she said, pausing her film.

He told her about the text and Danny's response to it.

'Show me . . .' Jude looked at the screen. 'Shame your father's not here; I'm sure he'd know. But there's not much we can do, Itch. Fairnie's got his hands full and we're all locked up. I'm sure Mr Watkins will be OK – there'll be some innocent explanation.' She smiled. 'Sure you don't want to watch this? You'd like it, I'm—'

''S OK, Mum. We're fine, thanks.' And they trooped back to Jack's room.

'Before you say it, Itch – no, you're not going out there,' said Jack.

Itch flushed at being so easy to read. 'Well, I was thinking . . . what would Cake do? And I think I know what the answer is. He wouldn't just sit here.'

Chloe looked appalled. 'Itch, are you mad? There's a reason we're in lockdown, and that's because it's dangerous out there! Danny was right – they have to find Shivvi and the caesium.'

'So we do nothing? Is that what you think? Watkins is in danger and you think we should just sit here on Facebook?'

Jack sighed. 'You've never understood the meaning of *can't* or *shouldn't*, have you?' she said.

'I just don't think I can sit here, that's all. Danny's not interested, my mother is watching TV. Who's left?'

Jack and Chloe glanced at each other; they'd seen that look before.

'So,' said Shivvi, 'how far will I be travelling? These rocks – where are they hidden?' John Watkins squirmed in his seat and said nothing. 'Come on, you can tell me. I'll find out from your friend as soon as he's here, you know. It'll save so much time.'

Apart from smashing Watkins's phone and switching all the lights off, she had barely moved for half an hour. The only light in the room came from the gas fire, its yellow and blue flames casting flickering shadows across the room. Periods of intense silence were followed by fast talking and taunts.

'All you have to do is sit there and talk to me, *sir*.

And tell me what I want to know.' She half smiled again.

'What do you want with the 126?' asked Watkins weakly.

'Oh, now let me think. I know – I'll put it in my element collection and display it in a case so all the crazy element hunters can come and see it. How about that?' Watkins was silent again. 'I'll think of something,' said Shivvi.

'What's Flowerdew got to do with all this? You working together?'

'He has nothing to do with this any more. But he did tell me about your friend and his rocks, which was nice of him. Itch is a strange boy, don't you think? Really weird. There's loads like him at Greencorps, you know. Smart at one thing, usually oil, and useless at everything else.'

'He's a sweet and very brave boy,' said Watkins gently. 'I admire him very much.' There was a silence.

'Good,' said Shivvi. 'Well, he'll be here soon. And then we'll see how brave he is.'

The sound of approaching footsteps sent her rushing over to the gas tap, extinguishing the flames. She grabbed a napkin and shoved it into Watkins's mouth, then crouched in front of him with the baseball bat pointing at his head, her expression fierce. She didn't need to say anything.

The footsteps paused outside, and there was a

crackle of police radios. The doorbell rang twice, followed by sharp knocking on the door and the lounge window.

'Mr Watkins! It's the police. Are you there, Mr Watkins?'

Shivvi repositioned the baseball bat so that it was against John Watkins's mouth. He sat completely still, his eyes closed.

The police moved away and reappeared at the rear of the house. 'Mr Watkins! Are you there?' They tried the back door, rattling the handle a few times.

'Unlike the dumb security fools you had here, I actually locked the door,' Shivvi whispered in Watkins's ear,

Watkins didn't open his eyes, and although the fire was out and the temperature in the cottage was falling fast, sweat beaded his forehead and he was trembling.

As the police walked away, Shivvi lowered the bat. 'You can light the fire again now,' she said.

Chloe was pleading. 'Itch, you don't have to do this. Please. Just wait for one of the team to call by. I'm sure they'll sort it out.'

Jack was being practical. 'We can't get out anyway, Itch. Lockdown, remember?'

'I know all this,' he said. 'I'm going to talk to Danny again.'

Jack looked at Chloe, and then followed him down the stairs.

They could hear Danny calling and coordinating the other members of the team, and when they reached the kitchen Jude was watching events over his shoulder.

'What's happening?' asked Itch.

'Not much at the moment,' said his mother. 'The academy is surrounded and the town is full of police and fire crews. But no sign so far. Any more word from Mr Watkins?'

'No,' said Itch, 'and Danny doesn't think it's an emergency. So Mr Watkins will have to wait. Even if it looks as though there's plenty of people who could check on him.'

Without looking up, Danny Stein spoke into one of the laptops: 'And Itch is asking again about someone to check on Watkins.'

Moz's voice came back. 'Yes, we've got that. Tell him a patrol car's been round, and it's all quiet. Lights off, no sign of anyone.'

'Got that. Will pass it on.' Danny looked up. 'OK? Happy now?'

'They've done what they can,' said Jude. 'He'll be fine. Maybe he sent you that text by mistake.'

Itch looked unconvinced. 'OK. Whatever. Sounds unlikely, though. Couldn't they break in and check? He could be unconscious or something?'

'Itch, that's it, mate. OK?' said Danny. 'Now let me get on with my job, please.'

'And you should be getting to bed,' Jude told Itch.

'OK,' he said. ''Night.' And he and Jack disappeared up the stairs. They had reached the landing when they heard Danny talking to Fairnie.

'Battery on a laptop failed. Just getting one from next door. I'll be off comms for a minute.' They heard him unlock the back door. Meanwhile Jude had gone back to the film – they heard it start up again.

Itch grabbed Jack's arm. 'Now,' he mouthed. Jack shook her head, and he looked exasperated. 'OK, I'll go on my own,' he whispered, and ran to his room.

Jack followed and saw that he was pulling on a jumper. 'You can't, Itch. The whole thing is stupid.'

'I'm going. I'll check he's OK and come straight back. He wouldn't have asked for help if he didn't need it. It's the right thing to do, Jack; that's all.'

Jack sighed heavily. 'OK. I'll come with you.'

Itch smiled at her. He ran to Jack's room, where Chloe was reading. She looked up and he put his finger to his lips, then left before she could protest. He ran back to his room and grabbed Jack with one hand and his rucksack with the other.

19

They sprinted away from the house. As they crossed the road, they heard the back door bolts lock again; they really were on their own. For the first time since the events of the summer, Jack and Itch had no protection, no security, no guardian angels to watch over them. Terrified and exhilarated in equal measure, they flew down the road towards the golf course. They were aware that the cameras outside the house could pick them up at any time, but Itch's guess was that all Danny's attention was on events at the academy. As far as he was concerned, the cousins were safely in bed.

They kept low across the deserted golf course – two crouched silhouettes. The distant flashing lights of the emergency vehicles reflected off the low cloud, but Itch and Jack were concentrating on their flat-out, heads-down charge for the beach. They caught their breath by the beach huts, then jumped down the steps onto the sand. Keeping as close to the cliffs as possible, and thankful it was low tide, they scrambled over the rocks towards the canal.

They hadn't spoken since leaving the house; they were running too fast to chat. But now, standing at the end of the beach by the huge boulders that marked the start of the path up to the canal, they needed to work out what they were doing. They gasped for breath, thrilled by their freedom, but also petrified.

'What happens now?' asked Jack eventually, once her breathing had slowed.

Itch shook his head – he still couldn't speak. He was weaker than he had been before the radiation sickness, and Jack had always been fitter than him anyway. 'Are there any lights on?' he asked at last.

Jack climbed up on a rock and peered cautiously over the canal. 'Don't think so,' she said. 'The whole row looks dark. Actually, wait . . .' She straightened a little. 'Difficult to see properly, but maybe there's a dim light downstairs. What do you think?' They changed places.

'Could be,' Itch said. 'Let's go closer.'

The path to the canal was a gentle climb to a set of locks. The old waterway carried on inland, with towpaths on either side. A few narrowboats were moored close by, but there were no signs of life; in fact, Itch and Jack hadn't seen a soul since leaving the house. They walked slowly up the path till the cottages were in full view. Jack was right – there was a soft glow from Watkins's living room. They ducked down at the top of the path, their line of sight blocked by a barge.

'Could just be a security light, Itch – doesn't mean there's anyone there.'

He nodded and set off across the lock gates that crossed the canal. The gentle V-shaped beams took them to the towpath on the other side, where he pointed at the sandy path that led into the dunes. It looped around the six cottages, with small offshoots to each back garden. The total darkness of the first five cottages emphasized the indisputable glow that was coming from the sixth.

Jack and Itch opened the small gate that led to the roofless house next to Mr Watkins's. They crouched behind the low fence, close to the wind-eroded brickwork. The big window of their teacher's lounge was a metre away, curtains drawn. They listened.

Silence.

'Call Mr Watkins again. Last time,' said Jack, and Itch dialled the number.

'Voicemail. Same as before,' he told her. 'Let's try the kitchen.'

They stepped over the fence and, ducking below the curtained lounge window and back door, reached the kitchen window. It was dark and curtain-less, and they could see that the kitchen was empty.

'We either go in or go home,' said Jack.

They looked at each other for a moment, each knowing that they weren't about to give up. Itch stood up and tried the back door.

It was open.

They quickly stepped inside and, heart racing, Itch opened the kitchen door.

The light was coming from a small gas fire at the far end of the lounge, its flames just adequate to illuminate the figure of their form teacher sitting in the armchair. He was crying.

'Mr Watkins!' Itch called, but as he ran over, he heard a gasp behind him. Spinning round, he saw Shivvi's arms close round Jack's mouth and chest. She pulled Jack's head back and held it there.

'Hello, Itch. Hello, Jack. Good timing. Thought you'd be a while yet, but you both moved fast,' said Shivvi. 'I'm impressed. We've been waiting, John and me. Haven't we, John?' She reached over and yanked the gag out of Watkins's mouth.

'I'm so sorry,' he murmured. 'So sorry – she broke in and I . . . She took my phone. That's how you got that text.' They saw now that he had been tied to his chair with thick rope around his chest and feet.

Jack coughed and retched, and Shivvi eased her head forward. 'You *are* a pretty thing,' she said. 'Let's hope your cousin's famed stubbornness doesn't cause anything to happen to you.' She held Jack's head back with one hand and lifted the baseball bat with the other.

Itch exclaimed and started towards her. 'No! Leave her alone! Please – she's done nothing, she doesn't know—'

'Yes, but *you* do,' said Shivvi, stepping back and pulling Jack's head back further. She retched again, arms flailing. 'It's very straightforward: you tell me where the rocks are or I'll break the rest of your sweet cousin's fingers. One by one.'

Itch and Watkins both cried, 'No!'

'And then her toes. And then . . . who knows?'

'You wouldn't do that!' said Watkins, shaking again.

'You forget who smashed Lucy Cavendish's face.'

'So that really *was* you.'

'Yes, and you should thank me, Itch. That was punishment for what she did to Jack in the hockey match. Not a nice girl.'

'You're mad,' said Itch quietly, 'and I never knew.'

'Maybe,' said Shivvi, 'but I have Jack and I have a baseball bat. Are you going to tell me where the 126 is? I don't have much time, but I can break bones very quickly. You'd be amazed . . .' She raised the bat.

'Stop! Of course I'll tell you!' shouted Itch. 'Just let her go!'

Shivvi released some of the pressure. 'That didn't take long, did it?' she laughed as Jack gasped for air.

Itch wanted to go and help her but the bat pointed at him. 'No. Stay.' Shivvi let go of Jack, who fell to her knees, her hands clutching her throat. 'Hands on the table, please, Jack, where I can see them.'

'I'm not going to do anything,' she croaked as she gently placed both hands on Watkins's coffee table.

'No, but *I* am.' Shivvi raised the bat above Jack's fingers. 'The address, Itch. Tell me now!'

'OK! All right! The well at the Fitzherbert School! They're down the well! Leave her alone!'

Watkins gasped, and Jack started to cry.

'Where's that?' shouted Shivvi. 'Tell me!'

'Just outside Brighton! Now, let her go.'

Shivvi lowered the baseball bat and Itch went to his stricken cousin.

'You shouldn't have told her,' she sobbed into his ear. 'Oh, Itch, what are we going to do now?'

Shivvi ordered Itch to sit down at Watkins's computer. 'Show me,' she said, and he showed her the location and the history of the Woodingdean Well.

That took two minutes, Itch thought. *All that struggle, pain and vomit, and I just told her where they are after two minutes.* He kept glancing round at Jack, but she seemed OK. *But what else could I do?* he wondered.

'Hands back on the table,' Shivvi ordered, and

Jack wearily complied. 'Any clever moves from you, Itch, and—'

'Yes, I get it,' he snapped. 'I've worked out that you'll do what you say. And that you're mental. I'm doing what you asked, aren't I?'

'Print that off,' ordered Shivvi, and Itch clicked on a map of Brighton, and on the cross-section of the well from a local history page.

She studied the information. 'Where does the water start?' she asked.

'At the horizontal bit, four hundred feet down. Then another eight hundred and eighty-five feet to the bottom. Best of luck with that.'

Shivvi ignored the sarcasm. 'You got them all the way down there?' She whistled and said something in Malay that sounded to Itch like a pretty strong swear word.

She noted something down on a pad and checked her calculations on Watkins's computer. 'I guessed they might be in a mine or underwater somewhere, and I've prepared for most eventualities I could think of, but I never thought you'd have made it so difficult. I'm impressed, schoolboy, I really am.' Itch said nothing. 'Flowerdew said you were an idiot. Like so much he told me, it turned out to be wrong.'

'You're working with Flowerdew?' said Itch, sickened just to hear his name.

'We met. I killed him.' Shivvi smiled. 'Ooh, that

sounded good. I'll say it again. We met, I killed him.'

'You . . . killed Flowerdew?' Itch was stunned.

'Pushed him off his oil rig,' said Shivvi, enjoying the sight of the three shocked faces. 'I know you're all glad really. Did everyone a favour . . . Tell me I'm wrong.' She glared at her prisoners, challenging them.

'Prison would have been fine,' said Jack; 'prison for ever maybe – but no one deserves to die like that.'

Shivvi spat. 'Pathetic, Jack. You're even weaker than you look. My only regret is that he didn't live to see me get hold of his precious 126.'

'Well, you'll have to be quick,' said Jack.

'And why would that be?'

Jack turned and looked directly at Shivvi. 'Because the school has just been sold, that's why. To a Spanish firm. It's in Mr Watkins's newspaper.'

Another string of Malay words, and Shivvi read the article, which was still open on the table.

'OK – we leave now. But first, a few photographs please!'

From a black holdall she produced a long, heavy, carefully wrapped package. She removed the canvas cover slowly, followed by some bubble wrap.

Before half had been peeled away, Itch exclaimed, 'Caesium! You *do* have it!'

'Sure do,' said Shivvi, and she held out the metre-long silver and glass tube. It had a red wax seal over a label written in Russian. CCCP was stamped on both ends, and through the glass they could see a large lump of silvery metal submerged in an oily liquid.

'When I hunted around for some elements to impress the schoolboy here, I found some very dodgy people. They had some boring stuff, but they also had things like this.' She held it up to catch the light from the fire. 'It melts when I hold it – look.' As they watched, the solid silver metal began to change to a liquid gold.

In spite of the danger, Itch found it beautiful. 'Melting point 28.44 degrees,' he said. 'Never seen that before.'

Shivvi lowered the tube. 'Classic, Itch, really classic. You'd better hope that's the only caesium reaction you see. They think I'm about to drop it at the CA, but that would be a waste.'

Watkins cleared his throat. 'What would happen if you dropped it?'

'A big fire, very quickly,' said Itch.

'Correct. And I have a few of them to keep me going.'

He looked into the bag and counted at least five other tubes. 'Where did you get them?' he asked.

'When you mix with criminals and thieves, it's really not difficult, you know. You should try it sometime, schoolboy.' Shivvi walked over to where Jack knelt with her hands on the table, caesium in one hand and the baseball bat in the other.

Jack tensed and cowered a little.

'Sit there and take off your jacket,' Shivvi ordered, pointing to a chair.

Gingerly Jack stood up and went over to the upright wooden chair.

'Jacket off. Quickly.'

Puzzled, but in no position to argue, Jack unzipped her coat and dropped it on the floor.

From the depths of the holdall Shivvi produced a brown waxed waistcoat and threw it over. 'Put that on.'

Jack looked at its many pockets and zips, puzzled. When she had put it on, Itch suddenly realized what they were for. Shivvi stepped in front of her and slotted the caesium tube into one of the deep pockets, and he felt the blood drain from his face.

Mr Watkins had got it too. 'Dear God . . .'

'I know,' said Shivvi. 'It *is* good, isn't it. I got it from one of those clothes shops for old people.' She reached for the thick elastic band on the waistcoat's breast pocket and snapped it over the top of the caesium tube, then grabbed some rope. 'Tie her to the chair.'

'Like hell I will,' said Itch. He used one of his dad's 'oil-rig phrases', and Shivvi laughed.

'Except that when it comes to saving your cousin, you've already shown me you'll do any-thing. So save your big talk for when you need it.

Tie her up.' She brandished the bat and Itch did as he was told.

'Sorry,' he whispered as he passed the rope around the chair, Jack's chest and the caesium. He kept it loose, but Shivvi didn't seem to mind.

'Step away,' she said, and produced a phone. Taking pictures of the terrified Jack, she said, 'These will come in useful. Cornwall's first suicide bomber! Might not make your parents' mantelpiece, but you never know who might need to see them.' Turning to Watkins, she added, 'And if the police turn up, if I even hear a siren, Itch and Jack die. Understand? You tell anyone where we are heading and you'll be saying goodbye to these brave, stupid children. Got that?'

Watkins nodded.

'You're worse than Flowerdew,' said Itch.

'Thank you – I hope so,' Shivvi said. 'Now, schoolboy – untie her.'

Itch did so, and Jack shakily got to her feet.

'Jack, you stay with me. You walk ahead, school-boy. If you do anything stupid—'

'Shut up, Shivvi. I get it, OK? I told you, I get it.'

'And one more thing. Empty your rucksack. Now.'

Itch hesitated briefly, then undid the straps and tipped tubes, packets and tins onto the floor; a small glass phial broke as a piece of iron rolled on it.

'Anything nasty?' asked Shivvi.

'Helium. Just helium,' said Itch.

Shivvi laughed and picked up the baseball bat. 'Time to go.' She turned to Watkins. 'I'm sure you wouldn't want to say anything, *sir*, but I'm afraid I can't take that risk'.

She swung the bat. It hit Watkins just above his left ear.

20

They walked slowly, terrified of the caesium tube and shaken by the attack on their teacher. Itch led the way; behind him came Shivvi, leading Jack with a rope around her neck.

'Faster, children, or I might need to break something else,' Shivvi urged, irritated.

By the lock gates, in the light of a single streetlamp, they saw two parked cars – a small Fiat and a large old Peugeot estate. Shivvi manoeuvred Jack round to the back of the Peugeot. She opened the boot, revealing a space full of boxes and crates, and gestured to Itch.

'Climb in, schoolboy. It's smaller than I wanted but I had to help myself to a new car after your friend Lucy spoiled things. Don't get too comfy – Jack's coming in too.'

Itch clambered in carefully and lay with his head against a metal tank. He had to curl up with his knees on either side of a large box.

Shivvi unzipped Jack's coat and untied the caesium, replacing the tube in her holdall. 'Now you,' she said, and pushed her into the boot. Jack had to lie on her side, her legs on top of her cousin's.

Shivvi produced handcuffs; one set she locked around Itch's ankle and a side handle. Another set fastened their wrists together. 'That should do it. Enjoy!' Throwing a tarpaulin over them, she slammed the boot shut. Next she placed the holdall on the passenger seat, started the car and drove away.

'We've found a way out of bad stuff before, Jack. And we will this time.' Itch sounded more confident than he felt, but he knew his cousin was already traumatized. He felt every shake, every one of her trembles as they bounced along the road out of town. Her face was centimetres from his, and if they failed to brace themselves against the bumps, their heads clashed painfully. Itch managed to put his free arm around her, and eventually she reacted to his reassuring closeness and stopped shaking.

'You can wipe your nose on my jacket if you like,' he whispered.

'You're such a gentleman,' Jack whispered back.

'Thanks. I hope they find Mr Watkins soon. That crack sounded bad. Really bad.

'Do you think he'll be OK?'

Jack could feel Itch's shrug. 'Once those photos get out,' he said, 'no one will be able to do anything, will they? I mean, they wouldn't risk it, would they?'

'Not if they think I'm dressed like a suicide bomber.'

'So Mr Watkins won't say anything, but my dad knows where the rocks are,' said Itch. 'And if they guess that the secret is out, he'll tell Fairnie.'

'Or Chloe will. But if anyone shows up, Shivvi's said she'll kill us! Watkins *has* to pass that on!' Jack was starting to shake again.

'I'm sure he will, Jack. He's *supposed* to pass that on. They'll get the message.'

'If he's conscious,' said Jack.

'If he's conscious,' agreed Itch. 'But I imagine the cow will repeat the warning when she sends the messages.'

The car bumped and swerved, and the equipment in the boot shifted, pulling Itch's ankle. He winced and tried to shift his weight, his leg cramping.

'Sorry about your elements,' said Jack; then, remembering the canister of gas that had got them out of Flowerdew's car, 'You haven't got any more of that xenon, have you?'

Despite the pain, Itch smiled. 'I'd settle for some painkillers right now.'

★   ★   ★

In the cramped and stifling boot and ignoring the fact that they were virtually on top of each other, Itch and Jack both dozed fitfully as the car sped, they both assumed, towards Sussex. Every few minutes a crate or metal canister slid into them and they would both jolt awake.

'Need to pee,' said Jack.

'Me too,' said Itch. In the darkness under the tarpaulin he raised his head slightly. 'Need the toilet!' he shouted above the talk radio station Shivvi had been listening to for hours. She hadn't spoken since the car left Cornwall, but to his surprise pulled over almost straight away. They heard the brake go on and the door open, triggering the in-car light. Then they heard Shivvi walk away from the car.

'Maybe she needed to go too,' said Itch.

'We haven't got a plan, have we?' said Jack.

'No. Not yet,' said Itch as the Peugeot boot opened and Shivvi removed the tarpaulin. She unlocked the handcuff on Itch's ankle and removed some bags which had slid out of place.

'One minute. That's all,' she said. The baseball bat was back in her hand.

It took Jack and Itch a while to ease their way out of the boot, every muscle and joint aching.

'This'd be a lot quicker if you'd help,' said Itch, but Shivvi ignored him. Eventually they clambered out and held their handcuffs up to

Shivvi. She shook her head.

'You go together. Over there.' She indicated some trees by the verge of the lay-by.

They both looked horrified.

'Together? Are you joking?' said Jack, appalled.

'You can't be trusted. Deal with it.'

Itch stepped forward and got the baseball bat in his chest. He pushed against it. 'Fine. We will. We've been through quite a lot together. Using the same bush as a toilet won't bother us. In fact, it's a good idea because we'll take turns, it'll take longer, and we aren't really in a hurry. As long as you can deal with that.' He glared at Shivvi, who smiled.

'Nice speech, schoolboy. And a good point.'

A lorry thundered past but no one looked at it. Shivvi unlocked the cuffs. 'Hands on the car,' she said to Jack. Then, to Itch, 'If you take one second longer than one minute . . .'

'I know. You really do like your threats, don't you,' said Itch. 'I'll be as quick as I can.' He ran towards the trees.

Shivvi stared at Jack, who refused to meet her gaze.

'Quick enough for you?' Itch said, running back.

'Your hands. Now. Spread the fingers,' Shivvi said, holding the bat just above Itch's fingers. 'Go,' she told Jack, who ran off.

They stood in silence, Shivvi on one side of the

bonnet, her back to the road, and Itch on the other side, the bat pressing his knuckles into the bonnet.

'If you'd told me back in school where you'd left the 126, all this unpleasantness would have been unnecessary, you know. It really is all your fault,' Shivvi said.

Itch was silent. *And that's essentially what I think, anyway, it really is all my fault,* he thought.

'Now it's too late. You're my insurance,' said Shivvi. 'They'll leave me alone while I have you two.'

Itch wasn't sure about that. The value of the rocks was so high, the potential for a new energy source was so great, he could imagine that the government, MI5 – whoever was making the decisions – would think they were a price worth paying. *Maybe we are expendable,* he thought. *Now that they know where the rocks are, maybe they'll do anything to get them.* But he said nothing.

'Ten seconds or the schoolboy will need that finger splint of yours,' Shivvi shouted to Jack.

'Coming!' she called, and ran back to the car.

'Open the boot and get in,' ordered Shivvi. 'You first, Jack.' The bat pressed harder against Itch's hand as he watched his cousin lift the tailgate.

'Can't we sit in the back? You can handcuff— *Ow!*'

Shivvi had ground the bat into the back of his

hand; her eyes sparkled. 'Don't give me an excuse to push any harder, schoolboy. The bones in the hand are quite fragile, you know. Ever snapped a chicken wishbone? It's a bit like that.'

'I'll get in the boot,' said Itch.

When Shivvi had repeated the handcuffing, the tarpaulin was thrown over them and the tailgate slammed shut. As the car pulled away and the radio was turned up, Itch twisted slightly so he wasn't breathing straight into Jack's ear.

'Never wanted to be this tall, anyway,' he said, and he felt Jack smile.

'How long till Brighton?' she said.

'No idea. Didn't see a sign. It's five hours to London, but I don't know the route to Brighton.'

'She obviously thinks we have to hurry.'

'Maybe she's right,' said Itch. 'If the school has been sold, it could be closing any day. Maybe it's closed already.'

Jack adjusted her weight and leaned her head on Itch's arm. 'Tell me about the Fitzherbert School,' she said.

Itch had described his break-in and had reached the discovery of the well when he realized that she had fallen asleep . . . Although he knew he was exhausted, Itch felt wide awake. He thought of Chloe and how terrified she must be now; of Mr Watkins lying in his cottage, bleeding; of Colonel Fairnie and the team that had protected him for so long. *And then I had to spoil it by escaping. From my own house.*

It was still dark, but Itch became aware of more regular street lighting flashing past – he had managed to push the tarpaulin away slightly – and he thought Shivvi was driving slower too. He nudged Jack awake.

'I think we might be near,' he whispered. 'We're stopping lots. Traffic lights, I think.'

'What's that funny noise?' asked Jack; a rasping sound was coming from the front of the car.

'Dunno. It's her breathing, I think, but it sounds weird to me.'

Jack winced. 'I have pins and needles everywhere. Don't know what she's got lined up for us, but I can't wait to get out of here.'

'Same,' said Itch as they bounced over a speed bump. 'Ouch. Again.'

'Any idea what this stuff is that's banging into us?' asked Jack.

'Seems to be ropes and equipment of some sort . . . She said she'd realized I must have dumped the rocks underground or underwater, so presumably it's whatever diving and climbing gear she could bring with her.'

'Wasn't she a diver for Greencorps?'

'That's what it said online.'

'How deep is this well?'

'It's 1,285 feet. The Empire—'

'– State Building underground,' finished Jack. 'I remember Mr Watkins telling us the story.' They were both thinking of their form teacher as the car slowed and stopped.

'Here we go,' said Itch.

'I can't wait,' said Jack.

21

It was just after six a.m. when Shivvi Tan Fook drove the Peugeot into the car park of the Fitzherbert School. In spite of the darkness and the early hour, it appeared busy. She had watched from the main road as the school lights were turned on and the large, imposing front doors were opened. A number of builders' trucks and lorries had driven in, followed by a few cars.

'What the hell?' muttered Shivvi. 'Might as well join in.'

She parked next to a pickup marked McAFFREY'S BUILDING SERVICES, reversing up against the school wall. Warning signs and bollards lay piled in the back of the pickup; in the front, the driver was holding a steaming cup of coffee, the flask propped up against the windscreen.

Looking down to hide her words, Shivvi addressed Jack and Itch in the back. 'Any noise or movement from you two and Itch loses a kneecap.'

Itch felt Jack tense.

The driver of the truck, a large man in a tight sweatshirt, nodded in her direction and she wound down her window. A cold blast of sea air blew in, and she called over to him, 'Early start!'

His window opened. 'Eh?'

'An early start!'

'Aye,' he said, surprised to be engaged in conversation. 'Big job, this one.'

She looked around. 'How long do you think it'll take?'

The man shrugged. 'Dunno. They reckon nine months. Two for the destruction, the rest building.'

'When do you start?'

'We won't take the place down till after Christmas, but clearing work has to start now. It's the end of term soon, so we can get on with it. Like I said, a big old job.' He drained his mug. 'What are you doing then?' he asked. 'You a student or a teacher or what?'

'Oh, er, a returning student. An old girl. Wonderful school!' Shivvi beamed.

The driver shrugged again. 'Looks like a dump to me,' he said. He tipped out the coffee dregs then, opening the door, jumped out and walked into the school.

Shivvi shut her window, and Itch and Jack heard the strange breathing noise again. They wondered if there was something wrong with her.

'Listen up, you two,' she said. 'Here's how it's going to be. You're going to help me take some kit into the school. If we are asked, it's for the building work. Then I need you to show me where the rocks are, schoolboy. Once I've got them, I'll let you go. Really.'

She waited until the car park was clear of people, then opened the door and walked round to the boot. She pulled back the tarpaulin, and Itch and Jack shrank away from her.

'Morning. But before I can let you go, and while you're safely tied up, I'll need to attach one of these.' Shivvi produced two of the caesium metal and glass tubes. 'One each, this time!'

They both flinched as she unzipped Itch's jacket and rested the old Soviet metal casing on his chest.

'No!' called Jack, and the baseball bat, from nowhere, crashed into her ribs. Shivvi pushed her hand onto Jack's mouth as blinding pain shot through her body. Wide-eyed with agony, she gave a guttural moan and bent as close to double as the boot would allow.

Shivvi leaned over till she was only centimetres from Jack's ear.

'Stupid girl. It should have been his kneecap, but your ribs were closer. Keep quiet.'

Itch was clasping the caesium to his chest with his free hand, terrified that the tube might roll off

248

and smash against one of the metal cases. The slightest crack in the glass, any seepage of the protective oil, and the reaction would be instantly explosive.

Shivvi produced rope and masking tape. 'I'd lie very still if I were you . . .' She leaned over Itch. 'Undo your shirt,' she said and, holding the caesium in place, strapped the tube to his skin with some masking tape.

The caesium felt heavy and cold. Peering down, Itch could only see the glass and silver end of the tube, but he knew the metal inside would soon be melting from dull silver to oily gold. He did up his shirt as instructed, Shivvi finished attaching a second tube to Jack.

'OK,' she said, 'I'm uncuffing you. Neither of you wants to try anything. Clear?'

They both nodded quickly.

Itch climbed out first; his heart lurched as he felt the caesium drop and settle against the tape, but it held firm, and he helped Jack out. With their coats now on top of the tubes, the cousins looked bulky but, unless you noticed the look of terror in their eyes, not suspicious. Shivvi unloaded four crates and her holdall of caesium tubes. She rested the baseball bat on the bag and, from the back of the McAffrey truck, helped herself to a toolbox and a wheelbarrow, into which she loaded the crates and holdall, with the tarpaulin over the top.

'Bring that rucksack of yours,' she told Itch. 'I might need it.' He hitched it onto his back. 'Now – stay close to me.' She looked at them both. 'It is important that you understand: if either of you speaks or tries to attract attention, I'll smash one of your caesium tubes. Whichever is closer. OK? Let's go.'

With Shivvi pushing the wheelbarrow, the three of them walked up to the dilapidated entrance of the Fitzherbert School.

The lights were on everywhere, and their arrival caused no comment. In the big reception hall, two more builders were examining a chart; behind them, by a large, elaborate staircase, a battered statue of the Virgin Mary gazed forlornly into the distance. Itch shivered. He remembered how he had almost bumped into her on his way to the well to dispose of the 126; how, sick with radiation poisoning, he had asked her for luck.

'Thanks for nothing,' he muttered.

He jumped as Shivvi, loud in his ear, said, 'Where now, schoolboy?'

'This way,' said Itch, turning left past the school office. 'The labs are this way.'

Chloe woke with a jolt. She had slept in her clothes, and it was a few seconds before she remembered why. She had tried to stay awake – listening to every creak and movement of the house, hoping it was the sound of Itch and Jack's return; she recalled seeing 3.30 a.m. on her clock. Now it said 6.05, and she sat bolt upright.

'Please, please let them be back,' she said, and ran towards Itch's room. Finding it empty, her stomach knotting with fear, she sprinted to Jack's. She already knew that her cousin wouldn't be there, but she had to check. Seeing the bed untouched, Chloe stumbled back to her room. She sat on her bed and started to cry. Then, hands shaking, she grabbed her phone and rang Itch.

'Pick up, pick up, pick up,' she said as she listened to it ring. As it went to voicemail, she gave a cry of desperation and sat there, paralysed with fear. When her phone suddenly bleeped and vibrated, her heart leaped, and she stared at the text and photo and was nearly sick. Her hand to her mouth, she read it again:

I have Itch and Jack, who are wired to explode. If I see any police, or anyone tries to stop me, the caesium will detonate. Do not get in my way.

The photo showed Jack sitting on a chair with a large metal and glass tube strapped to her chest. Chloe's eyes filled with tears, and she ran to her parents' room.

Ten minutes later, the security team, realizing they

had been duped both by Shivvi's threat to blow up the school and by Jack and Itch's escape, sat dejectedly around the table in the Coles' kitchen. Danny Stein, having unwittingly let the cousins out, had tendered his resignation and was already on his way home. A white-faced Colonel Fairnie had just been dealing with a furious Jude Lofte.

'Anyone reached Nicholas Lofte yet?' he said, throwing his phone down on the table.

'Just got him now, sir,' called Moz from the front room. 'His mobile was off, but we got the hotel to wake him.'

Fairnie took the phone and related the events of the night, briskly and without apology. He told Nicholas what Mr Watkins had told them – the teacher had come round on his way to hospital; and about the threat made to Itch and Jack. Fairnie was ready for another justified assault on his competence, but not for what Itch's father said next.

'I know where they're going, Colonel.'

'I'm sorry?'

'I can tell you where they are heading.'

'Hold on. I'm putting you on speakerphone.' He pressed a button on the handset and placed it on the table.

'Listen up, everyone. Nicholas, normally we'd wait for a secure line, but there isn't time. Tell me what you know.'

The MI5 team stared at the phone. Nicholas Lofte's voice rang out in the kitchen.

'The rocks are down a well in a school in Brighton. It's the Fitzherbert School.' There was a long pause as the officers took in the information. As if reading their thoughts, Nicholas added wearily, 'It's a long story . . .'

Half a mile away from the Fitzherbert School, the local police commander was informed by the Metropolitan Police chief that there was a major kidnap and robbery in operation at the local school, but that under no circumstances should any patrol cars or officers go near; in fact, all police activity should be diverted away from the Fitzherbert School. There had been no demands made by the kidnapper other than to be left alone. For those reasons, no lines of communication were possible or even desirable. He was told to alert the fire brigade to the possibility of a perilous caesium-based fire. Obviously the school would need to be closed. Despite his questioning, he was told there were no further details available at the moment. This was, he was told, going to be a major operation and all resources at his disposal would be needed. There was to be no media involvement or comment in any way – there must be no leaks to the press. A media blackout had been requested. An MI5 team was on its way from London and would be with him shortly, armed police teams needed to be mobilized immediately. In case he hadn't got it first time, he was reminded that none of this operation was to be visible from the school.

The police commander rang his wife to cancel their lunch.

As Itch led the way along the corridors towards the science labs – through, he noticed, new security doors – his head was spinning. *I can't believe I'm here again*, he thought. *After all I did, after all the secrets I've kept, this headcase is going to try and get the 126 back to the surface. This time I'm not bent double and vomiting blood, but I just* can't *go back down there.*

Every echoing step increased his dread. A man in stained work overalls walked past them with a tool-box in one hand and a drill in the other. Every part of Itch wanted to run up to him and tell him what was happening, but he knew Shivvi would carry out her threat. So he and Jack kept their heads down.

The corridor snaked left; the science department posters appeared on the notice boards. Last time they had been a welcome sign to Itch that he was heading in the right direction; now they indicated that the moment of reckoning was closer. He came to the scrappy piece of carpet spread under one notice board, and stopped. Behind him, Jack and Shivvi stopped too.

'It's down there,' Itch said quietly, pointing at the floor. 'This is the top of the well. The rocks are down there.'

In a second, Shivvi was at his shoulder. 'Under this carpet?'

Itch nodded.

She looked around. 'This the end of the extension?'

He nodded again.

She wheeled the wheelbarrow towards the safety doors, placing some bollards and a DANGER! HIGH EXPLOSIVE! sign in the corridor outside. Shutting and bolting the doors, she hurried back.

Itch and Jack leaned against the wall, supporting the caesium tubes with both hands. They watched as Shivvi threw back the carpet, revealing eighteen planks of wood glued together. Using a chisel to prise them apart, she exposed the steel cap locked into the top of the Woodingdean Well. It was three metres across, with a recessed circle in the middle – the same one Itch had struggled with.

Eighteen screws, he remembered, *and you twist, you don't pull.*

With the drill in her hand, Shivvi walked to its middle and, crouching, started work on the screws. One by one they flew or rolled across the floor, each one seeming to come out faster than its predecessor.

Itch couldn't help thinking of his own long battle and comparing it with the extraordinary speed of

Shivvi Tan Fook. *Not vomiting blood and fainting all the time must be a huge advantage,* he thought.

With all the screws out, Shivvi squatted above the handle, grabbed it with both hands and began to unscrew the well cap. It had taken Itch ages to free the old, rusted thread and move the cap. It took Shivvi less than a minute. The screeching of the metal threads rubbing against each other was followed by a huge clanging noise as the cap came free and Shivvi dropped it on the metal plate. The sulphurous stench from the well made her cough and retch, and she put her hand over her mouth.

'Let's hope she's violently sick and falls down the well,' Itch murmured to Jack.

She thought about that. 'Why don't we push her down?' she whispered. 'Would that be wrong? We probably could . . . Like Hansel and Gretel. And she's the wicked witch,' she said.

'Who got pushed into the oven?'

'Yup.'

'It might be possible,' said Itch, 'but if we messed up . . .'

Jack shivered.

'And it's probably wrong too, I suppose,' he added.

'Come here, you two.' Shivvi was removing boxes from the wheelbarrow and arranging diving equipment around the open well. They shuffled forward.

'I'm going down for the rocks,' she said. 'I don't need you for that, but I can't leave you here either. I need to make sure you don't run off to the nearest teacher like you normally do. You're coming down with me.'

Itch and Jack both gasped as if they'd been punched in the stomach.

'I don't want to go down there again,' said Itch, swallowing hard.

'Not you, schoolboy. I'm taking Cousin Jack.'

Now it was Jack's turn to recoil. 'Me? But what can *I* do . . . ?' She looked at Itch, horrified.

'You're my insurance, Jack. And you won't need to "do" anything. Just hang there looking pretty. You have one good hand, don't you?' Shivvi laughed, and Jack squeezed her eyes shut. 'But first I do need to deal with you, schoolboy. Put your rucksack down and walk!'

Itch let it drop, and Jack grabbed his hand as they were herded towards the labs. They passed the woodwork room, and then the metalwork room. The last room in the extension was the science lab, and Shivvi urged them inside. The glass cabinet containing jars and bottles of chemicals was still there, Itch noticed. This was where he'd found the sodium – the container marked *Na* – that had provided the blast he had needed to send the 126 to the bottom of the well, 1,285 feet down. Alongside the potassium and calcium, a new sample of sodium had been added.

He took all this in as Shivvi herded them both to the far corner of the lab, past the benches with gas taps and bottles of acid in neat, traditional rows. In the corner, a metre from the end of the last workbench, stood a large enamel basin. Two copper pipes ran along the floor joining them.

'Kneel down.'

Slowly, carefully, holding the caesium tubes with both hands, they knelt down on the cold floor. Shivvi produced the two pairs of handcuffs, snapping one on each of Itch's wrists.

'Itch, lock yourself to the pipe.'

He shuffled forward; as soon as one cuff had shut around the pipe, he felt the baseball bat in the back of his neck.

'And the other one! Quickly!'

He hooked the second cuff to the pipe and locked it. Twisting his head round, he found Shivvi's face centimetres away from his.

'You do nothing. You say nothing. If I hear so much as a footstep from up here, you'll never see your sweet cousin again. You'll get out of here, but *she* might not. Am I clear?'

Itch was tempted, and was close enough to head-butt her or spit in her face, but instead he just glared. Then he nodded.

Shivvi peeled off a strip of masking tape and

slapped it across his mouth. Hunched and chained, Itch listened as she and Jack walked off down the corridor.

'I'll be all right,' Jack called.

Itch thought it was the least convincing thing he'd ever heard.

22

In the corner of the Fitzherbert School science lab, chained to the pipes between the sink and the bench and on his knees, Itch was starting to sweat. This was partly due to the overactive heating system, which had taken to blowing hot air into the lab but mainly because he thought the caesium tube was beginning to slip.

He felt the sweat prickle on his back, then trickle down his spine. By the time it was running in rivulets down his sides, he could feel the masking tape losing its adhesiveness; the caesium was definitely shifting.

Itch was getting desperate, the sweat now blurring his vision. He tried to wipe his eyes with his arm, but the movement caused the caesium tube to drop again. Quickly he sank down and felt the glass and metal hit the wooden floor and push against his chest. But the noise it made sounded wrong: the metal clang was accompanied by a brittle crunching sound. If the glass broke, it would be a matter of seconds before the caesium exploded.

He found a position on his side that supported the tube and eased the pressure on the damp tape. But when a fresh trickle of – what? Sweat? Oil? – ran from his stomach and down his leg, he started to panic. He pulled his handcuffed right hand as hard as he could away from the pipe. It made a loud clanging noise, but he didn't have much choice. He had wanted to wait till Shivvi was safely down in the well, but time was running out. The cuff bit into his hand, but nothing else moved. More moisture ran down his leg, and he pulled against the handcuff as hard as he could. The skin of his hand started to sheer off; at the moment he felt no pain, but he knew that would come soon enough.

The silver arm of the handcuff was embedded in the skin above his knuckles; blood oozed from the wound and dripped onto the floor. Itch knew he couldn't stop now: he pulled again. This time the pain shot through his body and he swallowed his cry, screwing his eyes shut. When he could, he opened one eye. The cuff was over the knuckle of his forefinger but had made a deep gouge in the other three. He had made his hand as thin as possible, but it was still too big.

The fear of turning into a fireball gave Itch new strength: squashing his fingers together as tightly as he could, he yanked his hand hard through the steel. With a snap and a stab of pain that shot right through his body, his hand came free. His middle finger hung limp, and a huge flap of skin had sheared off his knuckles – but before he could register the full extent of the damage, he was tearing at his shirt buttons, spraying blood everywhere. When his shirt was open he leaned back to support the tube and pulled at the masking tape that held it in place. He had only removed two strips before it came free. He stopped it from crashing to the floor with his damaged hand, crying out as he was forced to move his broken finger. His eyes wide with fear, he listened for Shivvi, but there was no noise from the well. He eased the caesium to the floor and, slowly but as firmly as he dared, rolled it a little way away from him. He studied the contents through the glass: the oil, moving in the casing, with the molten, liquid-gold caesium.

It looked intact. It looked full. It wasn't leaking.

Itch lay on the floor, his breathing wild, and cradled his bleeding hand on his chest.

At the well head, Jack waited for Shivvi to work out what she was doing. For the first time, she thought, the Malay was unsure how to proceed. The hole in the steel plate did not look big enough for her diving equipment to fit through; Shivvi had been doing her strange breathing routine again – she appeared to have some kind of inhaler in her mouth – and was sorting through ropes and what looked like buoyancy devices. Again, Jack found herself wondering if she could just push her in. Shivvi was standing close to the opening, but it was quite small, and she wouldn't necessarily fall right through. And with Itch chained up, the risk of failure was too high.

Her mind apparently made up, Shivvi gathered all the ropes she could and handed the holdall to Jack.

'OK. Lost some kit in the car swap, but it can still work. Take out the tubes and put them in one of the crates.' She indicated the now empty boxes in the wheelbarrow.

As carefully as possible, Jack eased the caesium tubes out of the bag with her shaking and damaged hands, and placed them in a wooden crate. There were four in total, each one glistening with oil and silver.

'Now take yours off and put it with the others,' ordered Shivvi.

Jack, surprised, didn't need to be told twice. It was a tricky operation with her right fingers still in splints, but she managed to remove the tape and ease the tube out of its pocket. She added it to the others and took off her suicide vest.

She was expecting Shivvi to shout at her, but she didn't seem to notice; she had the baseball bat back in her hand.

'You're going down first,' she told Jack. 'I'm doing the dive, but I need you there too. Let's go.' She pushed the bat into the small of her back. 'There's a metal ladder along one side. I'm going to lower you down and you grab hold when you can.'

Jack felt expert hands passing a rope around her waist and chest.

'It's tight – you're going to have to trust me. Move.'

Jack looked around. On the other side of the security door, life was continuing as normal; on this side, her cousin was chained up, and she was about to be lowered into the deepest hand-built well in the world. On the notice board was a sign saying: TAKE CARE AT ALL TIMES. IF IN DOUBT, DON'T!

Trust me, I wouldn't, thought Jack, and walked to the edge. The truth was that she was scared out of her mind – the well opening loomed dark and terrifying at her feet – but she was determined to show no fear to Shivvi. Itch had gone down here on his own, and got sick with radiation poisoning; if this is what she had to do to help her cousin, then so be it.

And if I could stop my legs shaking, that would help, she thought . . .

'Turn round,' said Shivvi.

Jack turned to see that she was holding the rope in one hand and the bat in the other. 'I hate you,' Jack said quietly, and Shivvi laughed.

264

'Of course you do! But you should be nice to me for a little while longer.' Producing a third set of handcuffs, she closed one end around Jack's un-damaged hand. 'Down you go. Now.'

Jack sat on the steel plate and edged closer to the hole. The strip lights on the ceiling lit up the well for several feet, revealing moss, bricks and the narrow ladder Shivvi had mentioned. She sensed the ropes around her tighten, and Shivvi's boot in her back. Willing herself to stay calm, she eased herself towards the edge, her legs now dangling over the abyss.

'Here we go,' said Shivvi, and gave her a shove.

She shot downwards, her scream echoing around in the darkness. She gasped as the rope jolted, breaking her fall fifteen feet down. The nylon cord cut into her ribs and, instinctively, she grabbed for the rope above her head with her good hand, and spun in space until her eyes adjusted. The narrow metal ladder slowly materialized, and she reached for it. Hooking her right thumb around a rung, she pulled herself closer. Her feet found another rung, and she let go of the rope and grabbed the ladder with her left hand, the handcuffs banging against the metal.

'Now lock yourself to the ladder,' Shivvi called down, 'and quickly. I'm dropping the rope.' Jack barely had time to lock the loose cuff to a rung before she felt the rope go loose and saw its end snake past her into the darkness. She pulled herself close to the wall; it was clammy, some of the bricks slimy with moss. Jack suddenly felt a rising panic. Trapped and handcuffed inside a well, four hundred feet above where Itch had said the water level was, with her cousin locked in the science lab and a sadistic escaped prisoner in charge . . . things were just about as bad as they could get.

She counted fifteen rungs above her and only five below before the light from above was lost in the darkness. She was gauging the strength of the rungs when a bright light appeared above her and another rope spiralled past. Within seconds, Shivvi appeared, now wearing a shiny black diving suit. A hooded jacket and high-waisted trousers were topped by three torches shining powerfully from a headset. On her back was the holdall. She paused only long enough to reach out and check that Jack's handcuffs were secure, then began to abseil down the Woodingdean Well.

As Itch's breathing calmed, the pain from his hand started to kick in. Tearing off some of the masking tape, he tied his forefinger and broken middle finger together; the pain was so intense he nearly passed out. He was sure he'd had some painkillers in his rucksack – as they were in a zipped pocket there was a chance they had survived the shakedown at

Mr Watkins's house. *Just a pity Shivvi has it, then*, he thought.

Gingerly he pushed back the flap of skin that had been gouged out by the handcuff. It was bleeding less now, and he looked at his other hand, still chained to the pipe. Now that the threat of turning into a fireball was past, Itch knew he wouldn't be able to force that one through the cuffs.

But he couldn't just stay here and wait for Shivvi to return. The thought of seeing her with the radiation-proof box containing the rocks of 126 in her hand was making Itch very restless. He pulled at the pipes with his good, but cuffed hand. He swivelled round so that he could kick at the pipes, but from a sitting position his efforts were wasted.

Enraged by his weakness, Itch made himself think again. In the past his rucksack had delivered stench weapons and xenon gas when he needed them; without it, he had no access to any chemicals that might help him. He still had the tellurium packet in his jacket pocket, but that wouldn't be any use now.

Come on, Itch, you're in a science lab! He closed his eyes. *There must be something!* he thought. He looked around. There'd be cutting equipment somewhere, and lubricants too, but all out of reach.

Then he remembered coming into the lab – the rows of jars in the cabinet at the front, *and the bottles of acids on the work benches.*

Itch stopped pulling on the pipes and sat still. *Which acids? And in what order?* He was sure there were three, and that sulphuric acid had been the first in the line. Was the next hydrochloric acid? Or nitric acid? He wasn't sure – he couldn't be sure – but at least he was going to do something.

But even with his height, Itch couldn't quite stretch far enough to see the bottles on the lab bench. He reached out with his damaged hand as far as he could, but the throbbing pain forced him to pull back. He waited a few moments and tried again, but he was millimetres short. *I need longer fingers!* he thought. Would his belt work as a lasso? He didn't fancy throwing a leather strap at bottles of acid, but he was about to have a go when another thought struck him.

Removing one trainer, he slid his hand inside. The pain was excruciating, but the shoe gave him a few precious extra centimetres. At full stretch, he pushed his shoe across the bench until he touched glass – he heard it clink against the bottle next to it. Now he hooked the trainer around the back of the acid – whatever it was – and pulled. Centimetre by centimetre, a glass stoppered bottle came into view. He pushed it to the very edge of the bench. The label said HNO_3.

'Nitric acid,' said Itch. 'Nasty. Very nasty.'

Taking his hand out of the trainer, he found he could pick up the bottle with his thumb and little finger. It was small, but the glass was thick and heavy, and another spasm of pain shot along his arm. He managed to set the nitric acid down on the floor before crying out. He managed to bite most of it back – but it was enough to scare him rigid again.

Keep it shut.

When he thought his hand could bear it, he picked up the bottle and put it next to the pipes. He shifted his weight uneasily, suddenly nervous. He remembered a demonstration where a small copper coin was added to nitric acid. The results were spectacular: the acid had turned green, and clouds of brown nitrogen dioxide fumes appeared. He also recalled that the experiment had been conducted behind a safety screen by someone wearing protective gloves.

He put his trainer back on and tied the laces as best he could: he was going to need to get away from this fast. Without safety gloves, glasses or screen, his plan was unbelievably dangerous. Nitrogen dioxide was toxic, and could kill him if he got it wrong. The lack of ventilation in the lab only added to his worries.

But you know you're going to do it, so just get on with it, he told himself.

He wondered how long he could hold his breath for. Years ago, in the sea, he and Chloe had had a competition; however, buffeted about by the

Atlantic waves, they had both soon given up. When getting rid of the rocks down the well, he had had to hold his breath, but had no recollection of how long that was. His plan now, such as it was, was to hold his breath and use a very few drops of nitric acid – just enough to get the reaction going. With luck, the copper pipes would corrode quickly enough for him to pull the cuffs free.

A formula ran through his head. Out loud, he muttered, '$3Cu$ plus $8HNO_3$ equals . . . I think it's something like $3Cu(NO_3)2$ plus H_2O and with lots of NO_2,' he said to himself, 'and that's the easy part.'

Removing the glass stopper, Itch held the bottle just above the copper pipe that held his handcuff fast. This in itself was painful, but he forced himself to focus as the clear liquid flowed along to the neck of the flask. He righted it too soon, and the acid streamed back. He tried again, and this time a single drop escaped and fell the few millimetres to the pipe.

He took a deep breath and held it. Immediately the liquid bubbled and turned a greeny blue. A few wisps of brown smoke appeared, and Itch instinctively started to pull against the pipe.

Too soon, idiot! Patience! Try again!

Turning his head away, he risked taking a new breath, as the fumes hadn't reached him. With renewed focus, he rested the bottle on the pipe and tipped it up again. This time he allowed more acid to flow, and the reaction started again with new ferocity. The pipe bubbled, and Itch shut his eyes as tightly as he could. And pulled . . .

Outside the Fitzherbert School, everything looked normal. The morning traffic, most with headlights still on, made good progress on its way to Brighton, Woodingdean or beyond. It takes time to set up a police cordon properly, particularly one that has to surround such a large area as the Fitzherbert School and its grounds. But all around Brighton, police officers were racing to take up their positions. Some were heading for the nearby Tesco car park; some joined the dog walkers out on the heathland around the school; others were intercepting parents and pupils on the school run. Slowly, life around the school was coming to a halt.

23

Shivvi Tan Fook was Greencorps' most experienced diver. Recruited from the streets of Kuala Lumpur, she had, in addition to her innate underwater skills, become a hardy survivor and a first-class thief. Rising through the ranks of the multinational operation, she developed a reputation for ruthlessness that brought her to the attention of Nathaniel Flowerdew. Between them they ran the Greencorps operation in the Nigerian delta, siding with the government against the warring ethnic groups, and united in their greed and determination. She ran a team of fearless women divers who became her gang, her protectors. Shivvi and Flowerdew had both been involved in the disastrous drilling operation that had cost many lives; he was the instigator, she its executor. Even in Lagos, the oil-pollution capital of the world, with three hundred spills a year, it had caused outrage.

To no one's great surprise, Greencorps had protected their senior man; Shivvi had gone to prison, and her diving sisterhood was disbanded.

Now, as she lowered herself into the depths of the Woodingdean Well, she was motivated by the desire for revenge. Revenge on the company that had left her to rot; she had already taken her revenge on the man who should have been in that prison – the man who had told her about the 126 and Itchingham Lofte. She'd had the idea of enrolling as a student in order to get the information from the boy, and she might have succeeded if it hadn't been for Lucy Cavendish. Now, with Flowerdew gone, she could help herself to the wealth and power she deserved.

At three hundred feet down, she slowed her descent. The horizontal tunnel that led off the main shaft was close now, and she needed to be ready. According to Itch, the water started at the bottom of this drop, but her torches picked out nothing but bricks, moss and sludge. She angled her head so that the powerful beams shone down: no water. Eighty feet from the bottom her rope ran out, and she had to use the metal ladder. Shivvi could now see that the bottom of the shaft was covered in mud and broken bricks but was dry. She was so absorbed in looking for water that she nearly missed a run of five broken rungs, snapped through the middle like twigs. She stopped just in time and, guessing the drop was no more than three metres, unhooked her holdall and other ropes, letting them fall to the bottom. They landed with a thud, and Shivvi risked a jump. She needed to avoid snagging her delicate neoprene diving suit, but she was in a hurry. Her KEEP OUT notice by the security doors would only work for a while. She needed to be back up before the school day proper started.

She landed cleanly, her heart racing. Where was the water? As she straightened, she found she was staring down a large tunnel that ran off horizontally from the main shaft. Circular and about ten feet in diameter, it was thick with sludge and refuse. Pieces of wood and crumbled bricks were strewn across Shivvi's path as she stepped slowly into the shaft. Her lights picked out green mosses like wallpaper covering the entire tunnel – but it was all dry.

'Itch, you son of a gun. You've actually made this a whole lot easier than you thought . . .' Shivvi had been expecting to swim along this section and then prepare for the toughest dive of her life, down the remaining eight hundred and eighty-five feet. She had never done more than six hundred, and when she'd discarded some of her equipment because of the size of the well opening, she had wondered if the dive was even possible. But with every step the realization took hold that the sodium explosion had cracked the walls somewhere and the water had seeped away.

The horizontal shaft was around thirty feet long, then it dropped out of sight. How much water was left? Might it be dry all the way to the bottom; if so, did she have the equipment for the climb? As she approached the edge, she sensed moisture in the air, and the smell of old, dank vegetation. There was water down there somewhere.

Shivvi had dived in extreme conditions before, but never anything like this. Over four hundred feet below the ground, she stood at the mouth of the circular shaft, looking down into the void. Her lamps were picking up dark reflections far, far below her, and she threw a piece of broken brick over the edge. Several seconds passed before a splash was heard – the water was there all right, but three hundred feet away? Four hundred? The rungs continued down this shaft, but as Itch had never come this far she didn't know how useful they would still be.

She had brought her diving sled with her, which could help get her to a predetermined depth, but she was beginning to think that it would be useless here. This would be a climb *and* a dive; she just wasn't sure how much climbing and how much diving was involved.

A moment's hesitation . . . How much did she really *want* this? Was it worth risking everything for? She thought of the Ikoyi Prison and the daily humiliations she had faced there. She thought of the life Flowerdew had enjoyed while she languished. And then she thought of the unparalleled power and wealth that lay in front of her. She was here first and it was there for the taking.

With the ropes around her and her fins tied around her neck, Shivvi Tan Fook stepped down onto the first rung.

Walking swiftly towards the Fitzherbert School, Flowerdew, Loya and Voss were looking at their messages. They had all received the news from their driver, now parked a few streets away.

Police arriving from everywhere.

'They can't be here for us, but it's not good news.' Flowerdew was frowning.

'Maybe someone has recognized you, Dr Flowerdew?' suggested Voss.

'Maybe. But unlikely,' he said. 'There hasn't been a photo of me on the news or anything. No, it's Shivvi, I'm sure of it. She must have found the location of the rocks after all. And, in her own stupid, bumbling way, has been found out. Damn it to hell.' He kicked the hubcap of a nearby car.

'Let's not get overexcited,' Loya said.

'I thought that's what you Latin types did all the time,' snapped Flowerdew. 'I'll kick what I want.'

The two agents exchanged glances and Loya shook his head, urging silence.

Flowerdew was striding up the school drive.

'Either Shivvi is on her way,' he muttered, 'and they have arranged a welcome party, or . . . she's already here.'

'And diving?' asked Voss, following close behind.

'It's what she does,' replied Flowerdew. 'That and losing.'

'Let's find her,' said Voss as they hurried up the steps. 'And remember — we say we are from the hotel group Mondo if we are challenged. *Assessing development . . .*'

Shivvi wasn't sure how deep she was when she came to the water. She had stepped and sometimes slithered her way down the rungs built into the well wall by its nineteenth-century constructors. She looked up — she was maybe three hundred feet down from the horizontal shaft, and the black, impenetrable water was now at her feet. She adjusted the lights on her helmet with one hand as she fitted her fins with the other. The rubber foot pockets slipped over her feet, the long blades point-ing down towards the water.

She continued the pre-dive breathing routine that she had started in the car. She was in a hurry, but if she got this wrong she could die. She had done this all her life, and it came naturally to her. She took big breaths from deep in her stomach, focusing first on the exhale, then on the inhale. She emptied her lungs completely, then filled them to capacity. After two minutes she put on her black silicon mask and shrugged the empty holdall onto her shoulders.

Calm. Steady. Focus. One enormous breath.

She slipped into the water.

The cold was shocking. Even though she was prepared for it, and her suit was the finest money could buy, it still hit her like a punch to her face. She knew that the cold would channel most of her available oxygen to her heart and brain; also that her clock was ticking. Her record was nine minutes and forty seconds, but that was in warm water, with no baggage. This time the water was freezing and she would have to carry the rocks back to the surface.

She pushed down. Her lights penetrated only a short distance in the total blackness of the well water, but just far enough to see each row of bricks as she descended. Her fins cut huge swathes through the water, giving great thrust with little effort, her legs staying as straight as possible and kicking once per second. She was streamlined, her chin tucked into her chest as she concentrated on the rows of passing bricks. Instinctively, she emptied her mind.

Bricks . . . blackness . . . kick. Bricks . . . blackness . . . kick.

She felt the familiar chest pain that stayed with her for the first couple of hundred feet ease off, only to be replaced by a constant pain between her ears.

As she sped lower, she used air held in her mouth and throat to feed into her cheeks, using them as an air reserve. Moving her tongue, neck and jaw, she moved the air into airspaces in her sinuses and ears; here the pressure wouldn't compress the air as much as in her chest. It was a trick called *mouthfill*, which she had learned as a teenager, diving in the South China Sea. Without it she would have had to return to the surface by now.

Bricks . . . blackness . . . kick.

Shivvi was feeling dizzy now; her eyesight blurred; she had to fight away the stupor. *Bricks . . . blackness . . . kick.*

How deep was she? Surely the bottom was not far away; she noticed that the well walls were crumbling and dissolving.

Bricks . . . blackness . . . kick.

Her lungs were being squeezed down to the size of fists and the pain was overwhelming. She hadn't experienced pressure on her eardrums like this before, but she stuck to her routine. Lights were popping in her eyes, and finally her rhythm faltered.

The first thought of failure entered her mind now: her chest wall was on the point of collapse; her lungs would be filling with fluid, mostly blood. Getting back to the surface – for her, always the start of the dive, where the real work began – was going to be an almighty struggle.

She had given herself just three more kicks when

she hit the bottom. It happened very quickly – she had clearly been falling faster than she realized – and suddenly she was in the mud, surrounded by old rusty winch machinery. Terrified of tearing her suit, she floated back up a few feet and, with all the control she could muster, pushed down again. This time the well bottom emerged slowly, and she saw wooden planks, rusted chains and a large circular cable. And, there, half submerged in mud and slime, amid the tattered remains of an old rucksack, a polythene and lead radiation box.

In the lab and on his knees, Itch pulled desperately at the copper pipe that held him fast. He knew he had only seconds before he would be overcome by the toxic cloud that was billowing around him. At first the copper was unyielding, but as he tugged, he felt it soften. With a new burst of energy, he pulled against the pipe, but he got the angle wrong and the handcuff slipped, shooting away from the corroding reaction. Frantic now, his chest beginning to burn and the heat from the reaction adding to his discomfort, he dragged the cuff back along the pipe till he felt it dip into the reacting metal. If his eyes had been open he would have seen the fumes enveloping his head and circle around the lab. With another almighty heave, he felt the pipe suddenly give way. Water shot everywhere and he fell backwards, gasping.

He opened his eyes. The pipe had ruptured and the handcuff had been pulled through the broken copper, but the fumes were everywhere: as he breathed in, his lungs burned and he choked. Spinning round, then slipping in the water, Itch sprinted away from the lethal haze that had settled above the sink.

He stood in the corridor outside the science lab, wheezing and gasping for air. He was coughing and retching, and his eyes were stinging, but he knew he'd got away with it. A broken finger, a gouged hand and some inhaled NO_2 – but he'd escaped. He wiped his eyes with his sleeve, the handcuffs banging against his chin.

You're fine – now find Jack.

He ran past the metalwork and woodwork rooms, and came to the well opening. Remembering Shivvi's threat to Jack, he tiptoed onto the metal plate and peered down.

Jack was about fifteen rungs down and, seeing the light change above her, she glanced up. She looked exhausted, her face tear-streaked. Itch put his finger to his lips and Jack saw the cuffs dangling from his wrist. She beamed, the relief lighting up her face.

'She's down there,' she said softly. 'Don't know where exactly. But she's been gone a while.'

'Can you get out?' Itch whispered.

Jack showed him the cuffs. 'How did you get free of yours?' she asked.

'Nitric acid. But it's no use down there – the fumes would kill you before you could get out.'

Jack suddenly saw Itch's head whip round.

'Jack, there's someone coming!' he said, and disappeared.

She tensed, and then saw Itch's head above her again. 'We're gonna be fine,' he said quickly, and was gone.

The noise was coming from behind the new security doors that Shivvi had shut: first a rattling of the handle, then pushing, followed by fists banging. Itch could hear voices, indistinct but urgent. He stood there, frozen in indecision: if they were teachers, their ordeal could be over; if they were police they'd be safe, but the rocks would have to be handed over. That, he quickly concluded, would be better than Shivvi escaping with them, and he ran towards the double doors. He was about to call out when he felt the blood drain from his face and his legs go weak.

On the other side of the door he heard a voice shouting, 'Come on – surely you've got something to get these doors open with!' and he knew he and Jack were in even more trouble.

It was Nathaniel Flowerdew.

24

A thousand thoughts and a thousand curses ran through Itch's head.

He's here! Greencorps let him escape!

The last time he and Jack had seen their former science teacher was when they'd anaesthetized him with xenon gas. Soon after that, Flowerdew had been arrested but then freed by Greencorps agents. Itch had hoped never to hear that sneering, arrogant voice again. He remembered how Flowerdew had stolen his first piece of 126; the blinding pain when Flowerdew had banged his head repeatedly against the wall of the Cornwall Academy lab; his casual indifference to the radiation poisoning he and Jack had suffered.

Now he listened in horror to the conversation on the other side of the door, and wondered what he could do.

'Let's find another way in,' said a Spanish voice,

and Itch heard the footsteps retreat. He ran back past the well to the science lab, where the corridor ended and a fire door marked the end of the school extension. That was the only other entrance, and he knew they'd be there in minutes.

What should I tell Jack? Oh help! He sprinted back to the well. He couldn't think of any way to make this easier – she would find out soon enough anyway.

'Jack, it's Flowerdew! He's here and trying to get in the fire exit.' Jack cried out in alarm but Itch said, 'I'm going to hide. I've got a plan. Be brave.' He didn't wait to discuss it with her – he didn't actually have a plan yet, but he knew he had to think of something – and fast.

He grabbed his rucksack and, with greater force than was wise, pushed the crate of caesium tubes into the woodwork room, avoiding a huge tub of sawdust by the door. Next he retrieved the tube that had been strapped to his chest from the science lab, adding it to the others. Running back to the well, he saw the tarpaulin and grabbed it. Underneath were Shivvi's discarded clothes and, in the pocket of her jeans, her mobile. The sound of a door being forced made him jump. He hesitated. *What would Cake do?* Then he thought, *To hell with it*. He dialled 999 and put the phone back under her T-shirt. As the fire door splintered, Itch dived into the wood-work room.

* * *

One thousand two hundred and eighty-five feet below, Shivvi Tan Fook had pulled the radiation-proof box free and managed to push it into her holdall. Even in her oxygen-depleted state, the significance of what she was doing – of what she had just claimed for herself – sent a kick of adrenaline through her body.

They were hers. All of them. The pieces of 126 that would change her life were finally hers.

With her chest bursting and her head feeling as though it would cave in with the pressure, she hooked the bag over her shoulders. The ascent was always more of an effort – fighting gravity with less oxygen in your system – but this would be the worst. She felt anchored to the well bottom and her vision was going again.

Routine. Method. Control.

Calm. Steady. Focus.

With a supreme effort of will, she pushed up. She never looked for the surface anyway, but this time she knew there would be no point: the only thing visible was the murky water right in front of her. Her lights were dimming slightly as she felt for the well wall.

Bricks . . . blackness . . . kick. Bricks . . . blackness . . . kick. There was hardly any air left anywhere in her body; lights were popping in front of her and her legs faltered. She knew she had to reach what divers called 'neutral buoyancy' – the seemingly weightless state between floating and sinking. When you're going down, after neutral buoyancy, you hit freefall; when you're coming up, you can stop kicking. Ordinarily she knew where to expect it – about thirty feet from the surface – but the weight on her back had changed that. She felt she was kicking and clawing her way through treacle. Was she still going up? She checked the wall.

Bricks . . . blackness . . . kick. And now she felt light. Either she had started to hallucinate or she had reached neutral buoyancy. She stopped kicking and reached for the rungs on the well wall. 'Shallow water blackout' often caused fainting as the lungs expanded again and the oxygen pressure dropped. The rungs steadied her as everything else wobbled.

She had seconds left, and she half clawed, half swam her way to the surface. She opened her mouth wide and sucked in the stale well air as though it was the sweetest, purest oxygen. After clinging to the rungs for a minute she felt strong enough to climb the rest of the way up to the horizontal shaft.

And then her torch lights went out.

The commander's officers alerted him to the three figures who had been seen running from the school entrance to the extension. They reported a tall young man in a suit, a larger bearded man in a coat and a third wearing a black cap over his curly white hair. Photos had been taken, checks were underway.

Every hostage situation he had been called on to handle had all involved engaging the hostage-taker as soon as possible. *Negotiate. String it out. Get the hostages safe*; it was the established procedure and it usually worked. But here he had a hostage-taker who didn't want to see anyone, never mind actually talk. And now three unknown men were forcing their way into the school extension where they thought the well was situated.

He took a call from MI5. A man introducing himself as Colonel Jim Fairnie told him that a ferociously radioactive substance had been hidden under the school and was probably in the process of being brought to the surface. He explained that the hostage-taker was an escaped prisoner from a Nigerian jail and that she had two teenagers wired as suicide bombers. Their safety was paramount but he was to make sure his cordon held. He needed to keep the rocks right there.

The commander, stunned at the escalation of the threat facing his officers, volunteered the news of the three men who had run from the school for the extension. He repeated the descriptions he had been given; when he mentioned the man with a cap and white curly hair, the MI5 colonel's sudden intake of breath was unmistakable.

25

Loya forced the emergency exit open, and Flowerdew and Voss charged in. Loya followed, pulling the door shut behind him. The three men looked around, and Flowerdew took charge.

'Science lab. Poky. Useless. And stinks – nitrogen dioxide, I'd say.' They walked slowly along the corridor. 'Metalwork room . . . woodwork room. What a dump. No wonder they're pulling it down.'

Loya and Voss entered each room tentatively, but Flowerdew strode on. He turned the corner past the woodwork room. And stopped in his tracks.

'I think this is what we are looking for, gentlemen,' he said, taking in the discarded wooden planks, the wheelbarrow, the toolbox and the pile of clothes on top of the discarded diving equipment. 'I know who uses this gear . . .' He smiled as he picked up the inhaler-like respiratory sports trainer that Shivvi had used to strengthen her lungs and get her breathing going. He stepped onto the large metal plate and stared at the hole in the middle. Loya and Voss joined him.

'The Woodingdean Well,' said Flowerdew, 'and my guess is that our friend Ms Tan Fook is down there doing our hard work for us.' He leaned over the hole.

'Well, well, well – if you'll excuse the pun – she's even gift-wrapped a present for us! Hello, down there!' The two agents appeared at his shoulder, staring down at the manacled figure of Jack. 'This is, unless I'm very much mistaken, one of the hideous Lofte cousins. Jack, to be precise. And you're right, it *is* a stupid name for a girl. Hello, Jack! Remember me? We have some unfinished business, don't we? And where's that half-witted boy? He down there too?'

Fifteen feet down, Jack had heard the approaching steps and knew what was coming. Her legs and arms were screaming with cramp, but she stood as still as she could, head down. She mouthed every foul word she had ever heard, but Flowerdew could see no reaction to his taunts. It drove him mad, as she knew it would.

'Hey, Lofte, I'm talking to you! You *are* still alive, I suppose?' Finding the plastic respirator in his hand, he let it drop. His aim was straight, and it hit Jack on the head, bouncing off down the well. She flinched but still refused to look up. Flowerdew was about to throw more things at her when Loya pulled him back.

'What do you think you are doing? Are you mad? Not only do you appear childishly cruel, but if you're right and Shivvi is down there, do you want to advertise our presence?' A string of Spanish curses, and Flowerdew had got the message.

'You're right,' he said. 'I'll stop throwing things at her. For now, anyway. Presumably Itch is tied up further down. Having a nasty time of it, I hope. That Tan Fook girl can be quite vile if she's pushed, you know. Better check around though, just to make sure.'

Loya nodded at Voss, who headed back towards the labs. He checked the smelly science lab, looking under the benches, and walking through a huge pool of water in one corner near a basin. Tutting to himself, Voss repeated the cursory examination in the metalwork room and, finding nothing untoward, entered the woodwork lab.

In the seconds that he had available, Itch had thrown the tarpaulin over the caesium, and himself into the wood store. It was a small cupboard behind the teacher's bench at the front of the classroom. The absence of future work meant that supplies were low, and so there was room for Itch to fold himself into the limited space. It meant he was standing on a small pile of timber, while leaning diagonally across a rough plank that poked splinters into his cheek. He reached out to pull the door shut, and the handcuffs banged against the handle; in the confines of the cupboard it sounded like a clanging bell and Itch froze. The men's voices carried on regardless and he exhaled slowly.

The shutting of the door had stirred up a cloud of sawdust, and he had to shut his eyes and mouth quickly. When it had settled, he brushed his hair with his hand, and showers of fine powder fell around his face again . . . As he listened to the voice of the hated Flowerdew, Itch suddenly realized that he *did* have a plan after all. Spitting out sawdust, he allowed himself a little smile.

But now the footsteps were coming closer again, and Itch braced himself for discovery. He found a long piece of wood with some nails in it at one end, and closed his good hand around it. The steps sounded slow and meandering – not the walk of a man who was searching for a dangerous intruder. They continued past the cupboard, then stopped; Itch's hand tightened around his makeshift club.

In the woodwork room, Voss was glancing under the teacher's bench. It gave him a view under most of the other benches and, seeing nothing suspicious, he shrugged and went to rejoin Loya and Flowerdew.

'Nothing?' asked Loya.

'Nothing,' confirmed Voss.

'Good,' said Flowerdew. 'Now the only issue is whether Tan Fook makes it out of the well before we have company. Anyone fancy going to "help" her?'

Loya looked down. 'Our equipment has not arrived yet – we weren't expecting to be going down there so soon. Without light it would be tricky, but without climbing and diving gear it would be stupid.'

'What's wrong with stupid?' asked Flowerdew. 'Stupid gets the prize; stupid might just be the only chance we have.'

'You fancy it?' said the Argentinian.

'If that's what I have to do . . . hell, yes.'

The older man, Voss, snorted. 'Look at you in your Savile Row suit and polished loafers!' He waved dismissively at the Englishman.

'You have a better idea, *Boer seun*?' snapped Flowerdew, and Voss squared up to him.

Loya quickly stepped between them. 'I'm impressed you know how to insult a South African, but calling him a farmer boy is a little lame, don't you think?

'He seemed to understand.' Flowerdew kicked out at the wheelbarrow. 'We didn't know the cops would be so close. We're not dressed for an underground expedition, damn it. We'll have to wait. But if it takes too long, we put the lid on.'

'And trap them all down there?' said Loya. 'Really?'

'Listen, do you want these rocks or not? Is Argentina a proper nuclear power? Your uranium's dull but this is spectacular. You'll be a national hero and no one will worry how we obtained them. And neither should you. If the police get close, we put the lid on and walk away. Then we come back and pick up the goods when we are' – he turned to Voss – 'appropriately dressed.'

A cry from the well sent them all hurrying to the edge.

Exhausted, shivering and weaker than she'd ever felt, Shivvi had climbed the rungs to the horizontal shaft. The total darkness had slowed her considerably, but she could feel her way up, and painstakingly hauled herself clear of the water. When the rungs stopped, she nearly lost her footing and felt the rocks shift in their box, pulling her back down. But she found the top of the shaft and hauled herself up, collapsing on the floor of the tunnel.

'You're not stopping now. Get up,' she said aloud, the words bouncing down the well and along the shaft. She stood up, removed her fins and mask, and felt for the side wall. With one hand running across the mossy bricks, she picked her way along. As she approached the final set of rungs that would take her to her new life, she could see faint light. It was coming from four hundred feet away, but her eyes, now accustomed to complete blackness, detected any change. Shapes and colours only returned slowly, but she quickened her pace. At the foot of the first shaft, she looked up the narrowing tunnel leading to a tiny hole of light.

Almost done. Nearly there.

The only remaining problem was the broken rungs – five of them. She had jumped past them on the way down. Going up would require balance and strength, and Shivvi wondered if she'd used up all her reserves.

The bottom rung was intact. She adjusted the astonishing weight of the bag on her back and stepped onto it. The next five rungs were snapped, but the two metal stumps holding each crosspiece in place remained, like pegs in a counting game. Using them like crampons in the side of a mountain, Shivvi clung to the wall and edged her way up. They all held, but on the last stump her leg slipped, and the metal tore her diving suit, cutting deep into her thigh. Shivvi cried out but held firm, pushing herself up to the next complete rung as she felt the blood start to flow down her leg.

Looking down, alerted by the cry, Jack saw movement and knew that Shivvi was on her way back. The light above her dimmed as Flowerdew, Loya and Voss appeared once more at the well mouth, but she resisted the urge to look up. They swiftly disappeared again, and Jack suddenly thought of Boggis, Bunce and Bean waiting for

Fantastic Mr Fox. She smiled. *I hope your plan's better than theirs was, Itch*, she thought.

Slowly, relentlessly, Shivvi climbed the rungs, and it slowly dawned on Jack that this was her moment. She could push her straight back down. One push, one kick. It would be easy.

Itch too had heard the cry. It sounded like Shivvi, but he couldn't be sure. Either way, Flowerdew and his buddies would be focused on the well now. He was no use in this cupboard, and slowly he edged the door open. The woodwork room was deserted, as he thought it would be, but with just one thin wall between him and Flowerdew, Itch felt extremely vulnerable. Any noise and it would all be over. He straightened up, careful not to shift any of the planks he had been standing on; an avalanche of timber was a distinct possibility.

On trembling tiptoe, Itch crept out of the cupboard. Mindful this time of his dangling hand-cuffs, he carefully pushed the door shut behind him. A thin layer of sawdust had landed on the floor – some from the cupboard, some from Itch – and he crouched down. With his finger he drew a five-sided shape in the dust, touching each corner in turn.

Fuel; heat; oxidizer; dispersion; confinement. He nodded. *I think that's right.*

Itch's mind flew back to the homework he had done for Mr Watkins describing an explosion in a flour mill in Kentucky. A grain elevator had developed a fault, and an electric spark had ignited a cloud of particles, causing an explosion that had blown the roof off the building. Itch had drawn a complicated picture of how the spark had arced into a small cloud of flour. The resulting explosion had shaken loose more dust, causing a secondary, more powerful explosion. Mr Hampton had explained that a mixture containing fine dust is more combustible because there are more exposed surfaces to react with.

Itch had finished the work with a diagram of 'The Dust Fire and Explosion Pentagon'. This represented the five conditions needed for a dust explosion: combustible dust for *fuel*, an ignition source for the *heat*, *oxygen* in the air, *dispersion* of the dust particles in sufficient quantity and concentration, and *confinement* of the dust cloud.

The mill in Kentucky had all five; the Fitzherbert School in Sussex had all five.

Crouching low, Itch looked around for the tubs of sawdust. There were two – the accumulation of many terms of sawing and chopping. One was near him at the front of the room, the other next to the door; each tub was large enough for him to crouch behind. He scuttled to the closer of the two, cradling his damaged hand as he moved. With his back to the plastic tub, feet and good hand planted firmly on the floor, Itch pushed.

To start with, nothing happened. The tub held fast, stubbornly stuck to the wooden floor. Then it shifted, making a scraping sound. Itch checked but, on hearing the uninterrupted conversation from the other side of the wall, continued his gentle pushing. After a few minutes, his tub was next to the other one, a metre from the door. He caught his breath, and was about to head back for the caesium tubes when shouts from the well froze him to the spot.

Manacled to the fifteenth rung, shaking with exhaustion, cold and cramp, Jack was running a calculation through her head. *Would I rather Shivvi had the rocks or Flowerdew? What would Itch want? I could push her straight back down – and she knows it.*

Jack screwed her eyes shut. She knew the answer: she couldn't do it. She couldn't kill someone, even if that someone was Shivvi. Jack stood as far to the left of the rung as she could.

From her body language, she hoped Shivvi would realize she was letting her through. She was allowing her to pass, letting her take her stolen rocks to the surface. She had decided not to be brave or stupid. Let Flowerdew and his cronies deal with her, Jack didn't have the strength to fight. Or to play Hansel and Gretel.

A few rungs from Jack, Shivvi had paused. Step by step she neared the surface, and as Jack had swung out to the left, Shivvi moved right. As her head drew level with Jack's feet, she hesitated again. But Jack wasn't even looking. She was staring rigidly at the wall, waiting for Shivvi to pass.

Just hurry up and get on with it.

The old ladder creaked and shifted. It had been sturdily built for the many miners who dug out the soil for the workhouse well, but that was more than a century ago. As quickly as she could, Shivvi climbed alongside Jack. The holdall with the rocks nudged Jack's shoulder and she clutched the rung even tighter. Shivvi's hips rubbed against Jack's arm as she passed. She said nothing.

Finally clear of Jack, just a few feet from the surface, Shivvi accelerated. The holdall was unlikely to make it through the hole at the top of the well while it was still on her back, she realized, so two rungs from the top, she slipped it off her shoulders. Balancing precariously, she pushed it up towards the opening. It went through vertically, then toppled sideways with a clang as it hit the metal plate.

The clang was followed by a thump and then a scraping noise. Alarmed, Shivvi pulled herself to the surface.

'*Now! Now!*'

As soon as her head and shoulders emerged, she felt strong hands grab her from behind and haul her out.

'Get her down!'

Thrown to the floor, both Loya and Voss held her down. They had been expecting a violent struggle, but Shivvi's strength was gone. As her own ropes were secured around her body, Flowerdew, holdall in hand, stood over her. His face was triumphant; hers was distorted by shock, rage, and the deep lines left by her mask. Her diving suit was torn, and blood poured from the gash in her thigh.

'Hello again' – Flowerdew smiled – 'and thank you so much for doing all the hard work for me.' He rattled the box. 'That must have been some dive down there. I really couldn't have done it without you.'

'But I pushed you off the rig!' gasped Shivvi. '*I saw you fall!*'

Flowerdew leaned closer. 'I have friends, you see . . .' He indicated Loya and Voss. 'Friends with a helicopter.'

A string of curses was cut off when Loya forced thick tape over Shivvi's mouth. Flowerdew reached over and added another strip, covering her nose as well. Shivvi immediately started struggling for breath. She had been breathing hard anyway, and with her mouth and nose enclosed, she couldn't fill her lungs quickly enough.

He ignored her distress. 'You thought you didn't need me. You thought when I told you about the rocks that you could do it on your own. How's that going, by the way? Me and my new friends here worked it all out, you see. I located my old laptop in Brighton, where that idiot Itch threw it. Didn't take long to remember that Watkins taught his nonsense here once upon a time, and when we found out about the well underneath . . . it was all too easy.'

Shivvi was struggling now. Her eyes bulging, her arms straining against the ropes, she was making strangled, gurgling noises. Loya started to take off the tape, but Flowerdew shouted, 'No! Leave her – she had it coming. Let's see if she can still hold her breath for ten minutes or whatever she said it was.' He looked at his watch. 'I'll time it from now.'

Next door, Itch was listening, horrified. He hadn't chanced a look, but it was clear from the shouts and Flowerdew's sickening speech that the 126 was back on the surface. And his old science teacher had it in his hand.

Time for the plan. It was now or never. He had hoped that the 999 call would bring help, but he couldn't wait any longer. Maybe the call hadn't even got through.

And if the police think we're still rigged up with caesium, they might not risk an attack anyway, thought Itch.

He crawled back to the tarpaulin-covered crate of caesium.

'This could go so wrong . . .' he whispered as he

lifted it off the floor. It was extraordinarily heavy, and he felt the tubes shift. Praying that the one that had been strapped to him was indeed undamaged, he staggered, bent double, to the door. As gently as he could, he set the crate down again.

Knife. He ran over to the teacher's desk. Saws and chisels hung from a rack on the wall. Even better. He picked the sharpest-looking blade he could find, as well as a useful-looking axe. Timing was going to be everything. Surprise would be useful too. *And luck*, thought Itch. *As much luck as there is going.*

A memory of some small bags in the science lab was strong enough to tempt Itch to pay one more visit. Next to the door, packed up for disposal, he assumed, were four small packs: two marked *Al*, two marked *Ti*. Aluminium and titanium.

'My firelighters,' he muttered.

Itch picked them up, one after the other, weighing them like bags of sugar. They were in powdered form, but heavy enough to make it a difficult balancing act, especially with his damaged hand.

Unloading them carefully in the woodwork room, he laid the four bags alongside each other. He sliced them open, then transferred one bag of aluminium and one of titanium powder to each tub, sprinkling the grey powders around like icing sugar on a cake. The aluminium was lighter coloured and finer, the titanium darker, with a more granular texture; they covered the sawdust in little swirls and peaks.

'Just to be sure.'

Dusting his hands off on his trousers, Itch pushed the nearest tub of sawdust out of the woodwork room and positioned it just out of view, round the corner from the well, careful all the while not to let his dangling handcuff bang against it. He repeated the operation with the second tub. The shouting at the well had masked the scraping of plastic on wood, and Itch returned one final time to the woodwork room.

Placing the axe on top of the caesium tubes, he used the good fingers of his bad hand to lift the crate under his arm. He carried it through the door and crouched behind the tubs of sawdust. His heart was racing, his mouth dry and the pain from his broken finger was pulsing again, but he barely noticed it. He picked up a caesium tube, the slopping oil and chunk of grey just-solid metal glistening in his hand. *You'll do*. He replaced it on top of the others.

He was ready.

26

In the special ops van, the police commander had listened, horrified, to the conversation in the school. Itch's 999 call had been patched through to his radio, and he and his colleagues strained to follow the conversation. The words were muffled through Shivvi's discarded clothes, but it was clear that there had been a struggle, that Shivvi Tan Fook had succeeded in bringing the radioactive material to the surface, and that they now appeared to be in the hands of Dr Nathaniel Flowerdew.

'We have to move,' he said. 'We can't just sit here,' and he called his chief constable. He was put straight through. 'Sir, the cordon is complete and armed units and bomb squad are ready. Fire and ambulance are here too. We've had a 999 from one of the kids inside – we need to go in.'

The chief constable had one of those voices that everyone around the phone could hear.

'Absolutely not. The orders are from the top, I'm afraid. This is now a national security issue and we are to "contain the situation" until the army units and SAS arrive.'

'And the kids in there? What are we saying to them?' The commander realized he was almost shouting and calmed himself down. 'With respect, sir, we can't just sit here while two children are at the mercy of an escaped prisoner and a psychopath!'

'You can and you will. I'm sorry, but there it is.'

The commander ended the call and threw his phone against the van wall.

Once again, Alejandro Loya made to unstrap some of the tape from Shivvi's mouth, but again, Flowerdew erupted in fury.

'I said to leave her! She cheated on me!' He moved to stop Loya, but Voss stepped in, his hand planted in Flowerdew's chest.

'Back off,' said the South African. 'You are not in charge here.'

Flowerdew, for all his education and fine clothes, had long ago learned to fight dirty. His knee found the agent's groin and Voss dropped to the floor, gasping. 'I'll show you who's in charge,' he seethed. 'We have the rocks, the Loftes are down the well, and Tan Fook here is going straight back to join them. We throw her down and put the lid on. Clean, simple. Clear?' He snatched up some more tape, slapped another strip over Shivvi's mouth and nose, and held it on.

Her eyes widened and she tried to push him away, but her strength was gone. It took only fifteen seconds for Shivvi's eyes to roll back in her head.

Now, thought Itch, horrified. *Absolutely now*. He had just witnessed a murder, and if he didn't move quickly, he'd witness another. The thought of Shivvi being thrown down the well on top of Jack was too terrifying, too appalling – he couldn't let things go any further. It had been difficult even shifting the tubs but now, somehow, he had to tip them over. If Flowerdew, Loya or Voss had been looking, they'd have seen him run out in front of the sawdust, stick his foot at the base of the one-metre tub and, with his good hand, pull hard. It lifted a few degrees, and Itch risked his damaged hand to provide some extra leverage. The pain shot through his arm again, but he ignored it. Slowly the sawdust was falling towards him, and as he felt the weight of the tub shift, he stepped out of the way. With an enormous thud, the tub crashed to the floor. A cloud of fine sawdust mixed with titanium and aluminium powder billowed around Itch as he pushed the crate of caesium along with his foot, guiding it to a point just in front of the spilled sawdust.

He risked a glance up. Flowerdew and Loya had been wrestling on the other side of the well, while

Voss was writhing on the floor; Shivvi's body was still lying on the well plate. It was a few seconds before they realized what was happening. Unable to believe their eyes, they seemed paralysed. Itch had started on the second tub when a bellow of rage from Flowerdew made him look up again. This one wasn't shifting, so, in the few seconds he had left, Itch took the axe to it. With swift blows he hacked into the plastic.

The haze of sawdust, aluminium and titanium swirled around the corridor, the rays of the rising sun hitting the particles as they eddied through the air. Flowerdew, with Loya just behind him, raced past the prone body of Shivvi; he would reach Itch in a matter of seconds.

One final blow to the tub, and Itch dropped the axe. Picking up a long glass and metal tube, he held it at arm's length like the Olympic torch and shouted at the top of his voice, 'Caesium! It's caesium!'

The onrushing Flowerdew skidded to a halt, putting his arm out to stop Loya going any closer. Before they had time to recover, Itch skipped round them to the well plate. They turned just in time to see him take aim and, underarm, in the style of a ten-pin bowler, throw the caesium canister. It flew through the air and spun, end over end, through the clouds of wood and metal dust towards the tubs and the crate. The caesium slithered up and down through the oil as Flowerdew and Loya and Voss watched, transfixed.

'Dust explosion . . .' mouthed Flowerdew as he realized what was happening and dropped to the floor, reaching for the holdall.

The glass and metal tube of caesium hit the ground a few centimetres short of the second tub. It sent a small puff of sawdust up into the air. The glass fractured, then split open, the oil pouring into pools on the floor. As the freshly exposed caesium met air for the first time, it caught fire with a rush of bright blue flame. In a matter of seconds, the powdered titanium and aluminium ignited and the brilliant white flames caught the billowing clouds of sawdust.

Fuel; heat; oxygen; dispersion; confinement.

The windows of the extension blew out, flames roaring through and engulfing the roof in seconds. The walls of the woodwork room collapsed, creating further fuel for the fire, and the secondary explosion tore through the security doors and into the main school. Everywhere the fire found tinder-dry nineteenth-century wood. The classrooms were first to burn: glue, pencils, books, desks, chairs, lost uniforms and pupils' artwork – all dissolved by the raging flames. In the school office, the phones and computers popped and melted; in the lobby, the statue of Mary was felled by collapsing timber. The staffroom and the head's office were the next to go, with generations of school photos hissing and spitting before being engulfed in the inferno.

Within minutes, the whole school was ablaze.

The fire-fighters, already wearing their specialist breathing apparatus, were on the scene in moments. They had had barely an hour to apprise themselves of the dangers of caesium fires; two fire engines, with a rescue unit close behind, had raced up the school drive and pulled up as close as they could to the fire. As the flames spread through the upper floors, the first fire-fighters – the forward rescue unit – entered the Fitzherbert School extension.

When the caesium hit the ground, Itch had been sitting on the edge of the well. As it exploded, he had slipped below the surface. Two rungs above Jack, he held onto the ladder with a fierceness that made his whole arm ache. The skin on his good hand had been scorched in the seconds that it had been above ground as his legs and other hand had found the ladder. He wrapped himself against it.

Above the roar of the blaze he yelled to his cousin, 'They were going to throw Shivvi down on top of you! I had to do something!'

'Caesium?' Jack's voice was weak with exhaustion and pain.

'Yes,' shouted Itch, looking down to see what state his cousin was in. 'And a bit of sawdust and aluminium. And some titanium.'

The heat from the flames was building fast. The raging fire lit up the well, and now Itch could see Jack's sweat-streaked face and trembling body.

'I think we'll be safe down here. They'll come for us soon, Jack! I dialled 999 ages ago. It won't be long now!' In truth he had no idea how long it would be, and guessed that Jack knew that. But he had had no choice but to act: returning to this hideous well was the price of saving Jack – a price he was happy to pay. He looked up at the seething flames and felt a wind pick up; the fire was beginning to draw on the air in the well. It was a thick, acrid wind, and Itch wondered if they might actually suffocate before they burned.

He wasn't sure how long he hung there. He called to Jack and shouted reassurances, but was getting fewer words back. He was just about to try edging closer to her when the well went dark. Itch looked up and saw a masked figure peering down at them.

'Here! Down here!' he shouted up. 'They're here, Jack!'

'You go,' said Jack feebly. 'You can go now.'

'We leave together, Jack – we leave *together*. And I can hardly walk through flames anyway, can I?'

The masked fire-fighter stepped over the edge of the well and appeared to float downwards – he was, Itch realized, being lowered on a line. Two more of the crew peered down at their colleague. Itch started to climb, and a protective blanket was passed to him. He wrapped himself in it as best he could and climbed closer to the raging heat. He could make out the face of the man in the suit now; he looked calm, impassive, as though he had done this a thousand times before. He was talking, but Itch couldn't hear a word. The fire-fighter waved him upwards and he climbed one more rung and felt himself being hoisted out of the well. He heard his hair crackle and squeezed his eyes shut. Suddenly he was enveloped in another blanket; the world went black and he felt himself being carried by many hands. He heard shouting above the roaring and hissing, as strong arms took him away from the school. Itch felt the temperature drop and, assuming they were clear of the fire, started to shout.

'You have to get Jack! She's still in there!'

He felt himself being lowered to the ground and the blanket was removed. The sight of the burning school shocked him; a fierce glow filled most of the windows as the flames ate their way through the building. On the lower floors the windows were starting to break and the fire reached upwards. Six fire engines were now outside, pouring their jets of water into the flames. The extension was fully ablaze and Itch, terrified, tried to explain that Jack was chained to the ladder. One fire-fighter pulled his helmet off.

'We've got her. The line rescue team will sort it, son, we've got her. Don't worry. Leave her to us.' The man's face was covered in sweat, but he managed a reassuring smile.

Itch watched as more fire-fighters entered the collapsing extension.

'I'm not going anywhere till Jack's out, OK?' he shouted above the noise.

The fire-fighter nodded. 'Don't do anything stupid, all right? Stay here.' And putting his helmet back on, he ran back into the flames.

Don't do anything stupid, thought Itch. *Bit late for that now.*

One of the newly arrived ambulances stopped near Itch, and two paramedics jumped out.

'Come on, mate – we need to get you out of here,' shouted the first.

'We'll sort you out in the ambulance,' cried the second, who kept glancing at the inferno.

'I'm not going till I know my cousin is safe!' yelled Itch. 'OK? When she's out, we'll go.' He said it with such ferocity that the ambulance crew didn't question him further; one dressed his burned hand and the other snapped the handcuffs off with wire cutters. Water cascaded down on the extension as clouds of steam and billowing black smoke drifted towards them – but there was still no sign of Jack.

'Come on! Get her out! What's happening in there?' he shouted.

No one was listening. More fire crews were arriving all the time, and the school was encircled with high-rise ladders. But Itch didn't care about the school.

'I started the fire to *save* her, not *kill* her! What's taking so long? Get her out of there!'

A paramedic put her hand on Itch's shoulder as they watched the conflagration.

Then he heard a shout, and four fire-fighters emerged through the billowing flames and smoke, carrying a figure tightly wrapped in smouldering blankets.

'Jack!' shouted Itch, but the paramedic held him back.

'Let them do their work,' she said. 'You'll just get in the way.'

Itch knew she was right, and watched as his cousin was taken into another ambulance. One of the fire-fighters turned to look for him, and gave him a thumbs-up.

Itch turned to his paramedic. 'OK, I'll go now,' he said.

27

Itch and Jack were treated at Crawley hospital in Sussex, then trnsferred to St Thomas's Hospital in London. Jack was treated for exhaustion, minor burns, badly bruised ribs and smoke inhalation; her broken fingers needed re-strapping. Itch too needed treatment for smoke inhalation and minor burns. The doctors who tended to his broken finger listened in horror as he described his escape from the handcuffs using nitric acid.

'You are one lucky kid,' said a nurse as she escorted him back to his room.

'I have to say, it doesn't really feel like it,' said Itch.

He wanted to visit Jack, who was in the next-door room, but was told she was sleeping. Instead, he had a visitor waiting. The familiar figure of Colonel Jim Fairnie stood looking out of the small window.

He turned as Itch entered. His smile was warm,

the relief evident. 'Itch! It's really good to see you.'

The nurse left them, closing the door behind her. Itch stood there awkwardly, not knowing whether to shake the colonel's hand, sit down or get into bed. Then he wasn't sure whether to return the greeting, apologize for running away or ask after the team. So he simply waited and tried a smile.

'I'm sorry you've had to come all the way here,' Fairnie said, 'but they have a great team, and my bosses are just across the road. Quite a few of them want to talk to you.'

'Are these politicians or spies?' asked Itch.

'Both, I'm afraid. This is some security scare, Itch, and there's a lot of interest in the men with Flowerdew.'

'One was Spanish,' said Itch, 'or South American. And a South African. That's what it sounded like.'

'Listen, Itch,' said Fairnie, who was uneasily stroking his moustache with thumb and forefinger. 'I need to say . . . we let you down. We fell for Shivvi's little trick and didn't give you the protection you needed. I'm sorry. The whole team are sorry. We are just so pleased to see you alive.'

Itch shuffled his way over to the chair and sat down, noticing now that his rucksack had been put under his bed. 'Not your fault. We ran away, remember?'

'Yes; that didn't help.'

'I thought Mr Watkins was in danger and I couldn't get anyone to take it seriously.'

'And you were correct,' said Fairnie. 'He was in danger. It would have been better to wait but . . . I understand why you felt you had to take matters into your own hands.'

'Thanks,' said Itch. 'Bet Mum isn't quite so understanding.'

Fairnie smiled. 'I think that's a fair summary of her position,' he said. 'And Mr Watkins will be OK – but only just. He was badly concussed.'

'All my fault,' murmured Itch.

'No,' said Fairnie firmly. 'Shivvi's fault.'

There was a brief silence before Itch said, 'You know Shivvi found the rocks – dived to the bottom of the well and somehow brought them up. You've got them by now, I imagine?' They held each other's gaze, then the colonel looked away.

'When the—' he began.

'*Please* tell me you've got them. They're not still there? And wait, you said *this is some security scare*. It's still going on?' Itch was leaning forward now, his voice suddenly tense.

'When the school building was safe to enter, our teams scoured the extension,' said Fairnie. 'There was no sign of the radiation box. Or Flowerdew. I'm afraid they've gone, Itch.'

Itch was horrified. He sat with his hands over his mouth, speechless.

Fairnie continued, 'The police have played back the footage taken from the supermarket car park. They sent me this – I think you should see it too.'

Handing over his phone, Fairnie watched as Itch pressed PLAY. The screen showed the school extension in the moments after the explosion. The initial blast could be seen burning through the windows of the labs, and then the secondary explosion blew the windows and fire door out. A few seconds passed before a tall figure appeared at the door, his jacket and white hair on fire. He was struggling to carry a holdall, which was also burning. He fell to the ground and rolled around on the grass, eventually putting all the flames out. He then half ran, half hobbled out of shot, swapping the bag from hand to hand.

The film stopped and Itch stared at the final frozen image. He enlarged it with his fingers. Flowerdew, his face blackened and burned, teeth gritted and hair smouldering, was glancing around to see who had noticed his escape. No one had.

And in his hands . . . a charred and smoking bag containing the eight pieces of element 126.

Itch was in despair. 'I might just as well have handed them over back at school! Why bother with the kidnap, the escape and the radiation poisoning? What was the point of it all? The sickness. The bone-marrow transplant! All useless. A maniac in charge of the world's most powerful rocks. A psychopath who has just become a nuclear power. Stop me if anything I've said is wrong, please . . .' He stared at Colonel Fairnie, but the man just shook his head sadly.

'No, all you've said is true. Airports and ports are being watched, and all Flowerdew's known contacts are under twenty-four-hour surveillance; given what happened before, the Nigerian embassy, in particular, is under observation. That's where we expect him to try first. He needs help – probably medical attention too, judging by the burns on his face. All hospitals in London are being monitored and his picture has been sent to every officer in the UK. He's going to find it very hard to move any-where, Itch, but I know that doesn't count for much—'

'No, it counts for absolutely nothing,' said Itch, 'and you know it. You failed, I failed, he won. And that's pretty much it. What happened to the others?

Fairnie shook his head. 'Shivvi is dead; she was suffocated. We found her with tape covering her mouth and nose. The other two men are badly burned. They can't talk yet, and we don't know when they're going to be able to, but they are in custody in a burns unit on the other side of town. Fire teams got to them just in time. They're lucky to be alive.'

'Yeah, well, I can't say I'm that bothered either

way,' said Itch, and he stormed out, determined to see Jack.

A policewoman was sitting outside her door. 'She's still sleeping,' she told him.

'Well, I'll wake her up then,' he said, and he opened the door.

Jack had been washed and her wounds dressed. She lay on her side; like Itch, she had anti-burn ointment smeared over her burned skin. Her face was red and blotchy. Itch went over to the mirror, and saw that he had burns on his forehead and his hair was singed; with a sinking feeling, he noticed that his eyebrows were gone again.

Mum is going to go mental. Really, properly nuts, this time.

He sat down on the chair next to Jack's bed, and she opened her eyes.

She smiled. 'Hi . . .' She started coughing, and Itch put his hand up.

'Don't speak, Jack. It's the smoke . . . Just listen.' He got to his feet and paced around the room. Jack sat up, rearranging the pillows and watching him as he walked.

'Flowerdew got the 126. And disappeared. He's gone – they lost him.' Jack croaked a few words, but Itch put his hand up again. 'Really. Save your voice. After everything . . .' He felt tears well in his eyes, but he wasn't going to let Jack see, and he went over to stare out across a bleak wintry London skyline.

He was about to continue when Jack spoke.

'Itch, you saved my life.' She broke off to clear her throat. 'If you hadn't done that thing with the caesium, Shivvi would have been thrown down the well and we'd both be dead. So let's start there . . .'

She coughed again and Itch passed her some water. 'Shivvi's dead, by the way,' he said. 'Flowerdew killed her.' Jack looked stunned.

'Fairnie just told me,' added Itch, and they sat there in silence, both wondering if it was OK not to feel sad.

'She was a cow,' said Jack, 'a wicked, cruel, evil old cow. But I'd rather be able to visit her in prison to tell her so.'

'But it all seems so *useless*, Jack. Everything we did, and they let Flowerdew go! He's out there. After all we went through, he's out there selling the 126.' A few choice oil-rig words, and Itch slumped back into the seat.

The door opened and Fairnie stepped in. 'Parents are here, if you're up to it,' he said. Jack nodded; Itch sighed. 'Your family seems to have grown somewhat, Itch. You'd better come and see.'

Itch exchanged glances with Jack and, shrugging, left the room.

Jack's parents were waiting outside, and Itch briefly embraced his uncle and aunt. 'Yes, I'm OK!' he said in reply to their expressions of concern.

'Look, sorry . . . Thanks for coming . . . Think Jack's doing well . . . I'll just . . . see my folks . . .' And he went back to his room—

And felt like he had walked into one of those surprise parties that you only see on television. Arranged around the bed was his mum, dad, sister and older brother, Gabriel.

'Gabe! Chloe! Hi! Wow – I didn't know you were all coming . . .' He hugged his sister first and whispered, 'We'll talk soon.'

She nodded and wiped her eyes. 'Brought you some clothes,' she said. 'Hope I chose the right stuff.'

Itch smiled, then hugged the rest of his family. 'I'm OK really, all things considered,' he told them, and sat down on his bed.

'Let's have a look at you,' said Jude, and she sat down next to him.

'I know I've lost my eyebrows, by the way – just to save you pointing it out.'

Gabriel laughed. He was tall, of course, with long brown hair tucked behind his ears. 'I think you should just shave them off and be done with it. It'll be your trademark,' he said.

Chloe and Nicholas laughed, but Jude looked sad. 'When is this going to stop, Itch? You could have died in that well twice now! Why did you run off when you knew how dangerous it was?'

'Look,' said Itch, 'I'm sorry. Mr Watkins was in

trouble and no one would listen, but if I'd known—'

His father stepped in. 'I think everyone realizes they should have listened, Itch.' He waited for Jude to say something else, but nothing came.

'You're not going to spoil Christmas, are you, Itch?' said Gabriel. 'I've only just broken up, and here we are on another Itch emergency.' Everyone laughed.

'I'll do my best not to ruin Christmas,' said Itch. 'I don't try to ruin *anything*, you know. Bad stuff just seems to happen.'

'Yes, but some people invite trouble, Itch.' Jude looked first at her younger son, then at her husband. 'I'll go and get some teas.' And she headed out of the room.

'What was that about?' asked Gabriel.

Itch looked at his dad. 'Have you said anything about . . . ?'

'I've started.' Nicholas sat down where Jude had been. 'It'll take time.'

Gabriel glanced enquiringly at Chloe, who shrugged. 'You've started *what*? *What'll* take time?'

The door opened, and Fairnie put his head in and nodded at Nicholas, before retreating again.

'You've got a visitor,' said Itch's father. 'Next door with Jack. Chloe, you go too – we'll have our tea here. Go.'

Puzzled, Itch and Chloe got up and left. In the

corridor they passed their aunt and uncle again.

'Just off to get some tea,' said their Aunt Zoe, and they disappeared round the corner.

'What is it with tea all of a sudden?' said Itch. Chloe opened the door to Jack's room, and they both walked in. Itch pulled up short. 'Lucy? What are you doing here?'

Lucy Cavendish, sitting beside Jack's bed, smiled awkwardly. 'Hello, Itch,' she said. She wore jeans and a black hoodie, her crazy hair tied back with a black band. Her face was still bruised from Shivvi's attack, but make-up covered some of the damage. She got up when Itch and Chloe came in, and they all stood looking at each other.

'Lucy came up with my parents, Itch,' Jack explained. 'She wants to talk to us.'

Itch and Chloe sat on the end of Jack's bed and Itch turned to Lucy. 'Well, you look a whole lot better than when I saw you at the Oscars. How's the nose?'

Lucy smiled again. 'Yes, it's better than it was. I was a mess, I know, but . . .' She stared down at the floor for a long time before continuing. 'Look, I've come to apologize. To all of you. To Jack especially, but all of you. I—' She fell silent and bowed her head; her shoulders started to shake.

She sat down again, and Jack tried to reach an arm out to her; Itch and Chloe waited for her to look up. She found a tissue in her pocket and wiped her eyes, then cleared her throat.

'I've come to apologize to all of you for everything. For being foul to you, Itch, and for attacking Jack. For all of it. I can't believe quite how vile I was.'

'We couldn't believe it either,' said Itch. 'You were always so nice. There weren't many people at school who smiled at me, so I remember when someone does. And you did. A lot.'

'Yeah, well . . . My dad was still alive then.'

There was silence in the room.

'Your dad?' said Jack. 'I didn't know he was . . . didn't know . . . well . . .'

'It's all right, Jack. You didn't know. No one knew.' Lucy took a deep breath and looked steadily at Itch. 'I'm Cake's daughter. Cake was my dad.' She bit her lip as tears poured down her face.

Jack, Chloe and Itch looked at each other in disbelief. Chloe gasped, but Itch spoke first.

'You're what? You're Cake's daughter! Are you sure?'

'Itch!' said Chloe.

Lucy, through the tears, snorted and laughed. 'Yes, Itch, I'm sure! He was my dad!'

'Sorry,' said Itch. 'It's just that . . .'

'I know, I know. It's true. The hippy dude who spent his time wandering around selling stuff; he was a runaway dad. *My* runaway dad. He wasn't around much when I was growing up. Mum says he scarpered when I was a baby. I saw him

323

occasionally, and we'd go on trips, but then he'd disappear again. But he made contact with me a few years ago and we met up whenever he was in town. He'd show me his collection of elements and the weird stuff he'd been trading. I even went out to that horrid caravan a few times.'

The Loftes looked at each other, all three remembering the horror of finding Cake's body at the St Haven mine.

'He made me promise not to tell anyone, including Mum. Anyway, when I hadn't heard from him for a while, I went back to the mine and found out what had happened. A woman from the shop told me how three children had been asking for directions. She thought it was suspicious so she followed them to the mine.' Lucy reached for her tissue again. 'She saw the three children – a tall boy and girl and a shorter girl – with a body at the foot of one of the heaps, but they ran off, and then the police came.' She blew her nose. 'She said she thought they'd killed him or been responsible for his death in some way. I knew it was you guys. I thought . . . I thought you'd killed my dad.'

She started to cry again, and Jack swung herself out of bed. She put her arm around Lucy, looking at Itch and Chloe. They all had tears rolling down their cheeks.

'It wasn't us, Lucy—' Jack began.

'I know that now, Jack! After our ride in the

ambulance, it seemed unlikely that you'd killed Dad. I went and talked to your dad, Itch, and he told me what had happened. But I was so mad with grief I needed someone to blame. Every time I saw one of you guys, I imagined Dad lying there with you three all around him. I just had to do something to hurt you back. It sounds stupid saying it like that, but it's how I felt.'

'I don't think it sounds stupid,' said Chloe.

Lucy smiled at her. 'It was so great that you were buying stuff from him, Itch. You were his favourite customer. He was always asking after you . . .'

Itch didn't trust himself to speak, and just nodded. Eventually he cleared his throat. 'Shivvi . . . how did you find out her real name? How did you know she was Shivvi, not Mary?'

'I broke into her house. I realized that she was watching the hockey match when I . . . when I trod on Jack's hand. I'm so sorry, Jack!' And the tears started again. Lucy looked stricken.

'Stand up,' said Jack. For a moment Lucy thought Jack was going to hit her, but she slowly got to her feet. Even before she had straightened fully, Jack hugged her. After a moment of surprise, Lucy put her arms around Jack and both girls started crying again.

'You were saying . . . ?' said Itch.

'In a minute . . .' said Chloe in a whisper. 'They won't be long!'

Itch looked puzzled, but waited for the hug to end. 'You realized Shivvi was watching the hockey and saw the stamping,' he said. 'So you thought it must have been her who attacked you as some kind of punishment?'

'Yes,' said Lucy. 'And when I was in the house, I recognized her cycling gear. Then she was talking to someone in Malay on Skype . . . And when she left, I went on her computer . . . I know it was stupid to break in . . . And I found some sandals with her name on. She must have had them in prison or something.' She paused for a moment, then went on, 'You know the rest.' She smiled weakly.

'When you stood on that chair and pointed at Mary, that was pretty demented,' said Jack. 'I thought you'd gone crazy.'

'I *had* gone crazy . . .'

'But then you said "Shivvi Tan Fook", and everything went mad.'

There was a knock, and Fairnie came in. 'People to see Itch, I'm afraid. You too, Jack. And the doctors will be keeping you in overnight certainly – maybe for a few days. Your folks have gone to their hotel, but they said they'd be back. I'll show you where they are, Lucy.' He stood with the door open.

'Can we have one more minute?' asked Jack.

Fairnie nodded and disappeared.

'We have lots to talk about,' she told Lucy.

'We'd love to hear more about your dad,' added Chloe. 'If you want to tell us, of course.'

'I'd like that very much,' said Lucy. She hugged Jack and Chloe and then, more awkwardly, Itch.

'You'll come back, won't you?' he said.

Lucy pulled her hood over her hair. 'Soon as they let me . . .'

Itch watched the sky lighten around London. Up early, as usual, he felt like he was pacing a cage. The knowledge that the 126 was out there had kept him awake for most of the night. The meetings with the MI5 team hadn't taken long: Itch repeated his story many times, telling them everything he'd heard about the men with Flowerdew – which wasn't much. It was clear that they expected him to sell the rocks quickly and then to leave the country. With radioactive material unaccounted for, specialist army teams were on standby, and the Prime Minister had asked to be kept informed of any developments.

While security was tightened elsewhere, it had disappeared from Itch and Jack's life. With his secret out and the 126 gone, there was no need for them to be protected from anybody.

Except my mother, thought Itch. He opened the door and headed down the corridor, stopping to look at a picture of some beach huts and then read the names of all the strangely named wards.

Walking on, he passed a few nurses and porters, who ignored him. Itch smiled. He hadn't been ignored for ages.

'Itch!' called Jack, peering out of her room. 'What are you doing?'

He came back and sat down on her bed. 'I was being normal,' he said.

'I doubt that very much,' she told him. 'What's happening, anyway? How did you sleep? You look rubbish.'

'Thanks. I know. Badly, of course. I kept thinking of Flowerdew and the 126. Eventually I gave up and got out of bed.'

'Why don't we go for breakfast?' said Jack.

'What?'

'Breakfast. The stuff you eat in the morning. There'll be loads of places along the river! We could be tourists!'

The idea of the two of them being tourists was so ludicrous that Itch laughed out loud. 'Sure! Are we allowed?'

'They want to keep an eye on us, but it isn't a prison. Just tell that receptionist.' Jack pointed at the woman sitting at a workstation, working her way through piles of paperwork. 'Might want to get dressed first, though . . .'

'Oh yes,' said Itch. 'See you outside.'

The blast of cold air as they left the hospital took

their breath away. The sun was barely up, and their breath billowed steam out in front of them. They walked, laughing, towards the Thames, enjoying the thrill of knowing that no one was watching them.

'Not sure I'm dressed for this,' said Jack. 'Didn't realize how cold it was.' She'd put all her clothes on, but she still wasn't warm enough.

Itch was shivering too, and rummaged in his pockets. 'I've got five pounds. If we see a coffee shop, fine. Otherwise it's the hospital stuff, OK?'

Jack nodded and they headed along the river bank. A few early dog walkers and joggers passed them. No one paid them any attention. They were chilled but exhilarated. A barge eased its way downstream, passing a police launch heading the other way. Across the river the Houses of Parliament glowed yellow in the weak sun and Itch was astonished; he had expected everything to look grimy and stark, but early-morning London was quite beautiful.

'I'd race you to the bridge,' he said to Jack, 'but everything's starting to hurt. I'll sit here for a sec – you go on.'

'No, I'll join you. I'll start coughing again in a minute and my ribs are hurting.'

They sat down on a bench and felt the cold seep through their clothes. They stared across the river, knowing precisely what the other was thinking.

It was Itch who voiced it first. 'Still can't believe

Lucy is Cake's daughter. I mean, I believe her, but I never . . . all that time . . .'

'Imagine your dad disappearing,' said Jack, 'and then turning up but having to keep it a secret. Did Cake ever talk about family to you?'

'I asked him, but he never said anything. Why didn't he mention Lucy?'

'Dunno,' said Jack, 'but if his reappearance was a secret from Lucy's mum, it had to be a secret from all of us, I suppose.'

'That time he was sick, the last time we saw him before . . . he died . . . he said to you, *You remind me* . . . and then stopped. I didn't really think about it at the time, as he was clearly ill. But he must have meant you reminded him of Lucy.'

'Really?' said Jack. 'Can't see that. We are both girls, I suppose. And the same sort of age.'

'Yeah, maybe that was it,' said Itch, smiling. He watched as a couple of warmly clad walkers strode past. 'They've got hats and scarves on. We should get back before we get flu and have to stay here for Christmas.'

They stood up and started walking back towards the hospital, looking up at the London Eye.

'Reckon we're too early for London coffee sellers,' said Jack. 'Looks like it's hospital tea after all . . . Itch?' She had continued without realizing he was no longer with her. She turned and saw him staring up at the huge white wheel of the London

330

Eye. Jack recognized the look. She was sure he wasn't simply admiring a tourist attraction.

Suddenly apprehensive, she walked back to him. 'What is it, Itch?'

'Remember we had Flowerdew's laptop?' said Itch. 'When I was on the train to Brighton, I went through his files. Documents, videos, photos – the usual stuff. He had hundreds of photos. Some were of Cornwall and his house. Most were of what I guess was Nigeria – oil rigs, apartments, men in suits, that kind of thing. But there were photos of that too.' He pointed at the Eye.

'Is that such a big deal?' said Jack. 'Millions of people take pictures of the Eye.'

Itch shook his head. 'No, these weren't taken from down here on the ground, or up there in the pods. They were taken from inside a building, look-ing out. In those pictures, the Eye was the view from the window.'

They walked on, now staring at the huge grey-brick building adjacent to the Eye.

'They're flats, Itch,' said Jack. 'Can we go back and talk about this? We are both shivering and I'm hungry. Come on.' She tugged his arm.

'Here's the thing, Jack. I recognized the views from his house in Cornwall – we've both been there. The Nigerian photos showed posh rooms and stunning views. And then it was London. Smaller rooms, and then views of the Eye.'

Jack started to steer Itch back to St Thomas's Hospital, suddenly aware of both the cold and how exposed they were out on the wide Thames path.

'So Flowerdew has a flat here. Is that what you're saying?'

They walked on a few more paces before Itch replied, 'I think so, Jack, yes. Cornwall, Lagos, London. And I bet he hasn't run for the ports. If he's kept the apartment a secret and he needs medical help, I reckon Flowerdew is right here. Right now.'

'Great,' said Jack. 'Just great.'

28

Dr Benedict Adebayo had received the call at 3.20 a.m. He wasn't on duty that night, and was both surprised and annoyed to be woken in the early hours of Sunday morning. He was about to switch off his phone when the words CALLER BLOCKED made him reconsider. The only people he knew who blocked their number were his wife and the Nigerian embassy. As his wife was sound asleep next to him, he reckoned he should take the call. He crept out of the bedroom, shielding the glow from the phone. As soon as he was downstairs, he took the call.

'Yes?'

'It's Felix. Can you visit a friend of ours? It's not life-threatening. Burns, smoke inhalation, that kind of thing.'

'Well, they need a hospital, then,' said Adebayo.

'Not possible, I'm afraid. He's at 2223 the

Moorhouse Apartments. Soon as you can. This is from the top, Benedict. Sorry to wake you. Goodnight.'

Dr Adebayo had left a note for his sleeping wife and driven the short distance to the apartments at County Hall. Most of his night calls were to more scary places than this block on the south bank of the Thames, but even here, with late-night stragglers and homeless beggars, he felt vulnerable. Particularly with a case full of medical supplies.

He pressed the buzzer by the entrance, glancing around. London was lit, the Eye was lit, but this doorway was shadowy and smelled of vomit. A rattle from the intercom, then silence.

'Hello? It's Dr Adeb—'

There was a buzz, and the door clicked open. He heard the intercom go dead and stepped inside. He took the lift to the second floor, and followed the signs through a maze of corridors to room 2333. He had no idea who might be behind the door, but if the embassy had requested his help, this patient must be important. He took a deep breath and rang the bell.

Within seconds the door swung open. Adebayo peered into the room; it was well lit, but he couldn't see anyone.

'Well, come in then,' called an impatient voice from behind the door.

Tentatively Dr Adebayo entered the flat. Thick

dark velvet curtains were pulled across two windows; ahead of him was a large brown leather sofa and an ornately carved low table. On the sofa lay a battered and burned holdall. The door shut behind him and, turning, Adebayo gasped.

The man standing behind the door was horribly burned. His face was black and blistered red, the skin on his right side peeling and bubbling. At least a third of his hair had burned away, leaving brown stubble and more blistered, oozing skin. The contrast with his remaining curly white hair was shocking. His burns stretched down both arms, and he had smeared on some cream, clearly with little effect. Both hands were roughly bandaged; one held a tumbler of whisky.

'I need help,' said Flowerdew, and started coughing.

'You do,' said the doctor, 'and next door there is—'

'NO! No hospital! I thought you knew that! You can bring the medics here – that's the way it's going to be.'

'I'm not sure I can—' started Adebayo.

Flowerdew came closer. 'Oh, you can. I know you can – you've done it before. The embassy are very grateful for all the extra services you have performed over the years. And you are grateful for the cash, I'm sure. What do I need?' As he spoke, his lips started to crack and bleed.

Benedict Adebayo approached his new patient slowly. He smelled of smoke, burned hair and whisky, but more than anything else, the doctor sensed danger. 'Have you been in a fire?'

'Oh, brilliant, Sherlock. Yes, well done indeed. They've sent me a bright one here. Listen, chum, I've been in a fire and driven sixty miles to get here. I am in great pain and coughing my lungs up. I know you have the expertise at St Thomas's, and I want some here.'

'What's your name?'

'Dr Nathaniel Flowerdew. Didn't they tell you anything?'

Adebayo sighed. He was wishing he'd paid more attention to burn assessment while he'd had the chance; he felt worryingly out of his depth. He was sure that the thicker the burn, the worse the prognosis, and from what he could see of Flowerdew's right arm, he was in trouble. 'OK, well, if you go to hospital they'll be able to sort out most of these burns. If you stay here you could be permanently disfigured. Stared-at-in-the-street disfigured. It's your choice. I can see who is around to come here, but it won't be as good. Really. Nowhere near as good.'

Flowerdew didn't hesitate. 'I can't go to hospital – I'll never come out and I'll lose my cargo. Get whoever you can. I'll take my chances.'

Adebayo shook his head. 'OK, I'll get who I can. Have you taken any pain relief?'

'Oh yes, lots,' said Flowerdew, pointing at some tablets on the table and coughing again.

'Good. You need to keep warm and wrap some of those burns in cling-film. What's this ointment? It needs to come off fast.'

Flowerdew moved away. 'OK, I'll deal with that. I'd rather you went and got a team together to sort me out. I'll pay ten thousand for everyone you bring, twenty for you. How long will it take?'

The doctor thought for a moment. 'I could assemble a team in a few hours.'

Flowerdew reached out a hand, wincing as he did so. 'For ten k, I expect the best. Not some junior doctor riff-raff. I hope that's clear.'

Adebayo nodded. 'Of course. Do you have cling-film? I could—'

'You could get out and find me a team of medics who'll sort this out.' Flowerdew pointed to his face and arms.

'Of course.'

Dr Adebayo hurried away from room 2223.

After warming up on a hospital breakfast, Itch and Jack were heading back to their rooms when their families – minus Gabriel, who was still asleep – arrived. The adults announced their intention of doing some sightseeing as soon as the doctor had been round, before driving back to Cornwall at lunch time if they got the all clear.

So, when the consultant came to check on Itch and Jack, along with her assistant, she found she had an audience. She was a large middle-aged woman in a tweed jacket and she looked around, smiling curtly.

'You need to stay with us a little while longer,' she told them both. 'I'm sorry if that's inconvenient for your folks, but smoke inhalation and burns need to be carefully supervised. I'm sure all will be OK by tomorrow or Friday at the latest. How's the coughing?'

'Better, thanks,' said Jack.

'And you?' she asked Itch.

'Same.'

The bearded assistant, whose badge said DR C. DREVER, peered at him, eyebrows raised. He was clearly expecting more detail.

'My hand still throbs. And I'm coughing a bit, and I'm weak. But I'll be fine.' Itch was about to raise his own eyebrows in return but then remembered he didn't have any.

'Jolly good. Well done,' said the consultant, and then she was gone, bustling importantly to the next room. Dr Drever followed in her wake, scribbling notes.

Jack's parents announced that they had to return home today, and Jude said she had to prepare an important case for Friday. It was agreed that they would head back to Cornwall with Gabriel, and leave Nicholas, Chloe and Lucy to come home with Itch and Jack. Lucy's mum had already told her daughter to come back 'when you've sorted everything out'.

So with the grown-ups gone, Itch, Jack, Chloe and Lucy sat in the now-open coffee bar in the hospital foyer.

'Go on, Itch – tell us what you're thinking,' said Jack.

Lucy passed round the pastries she'd bought, and Itch told her and Chloe about their walk past the London Eye earlier that morning and the photos he remembered from Flowerdew's laptop.

'Well, I reckon Flowerdew might be in that block next door; that's it, really.'

'What if he *is* there?' asked Chloe.

'Well, maybe he has the rocks. He might have sold them already, of course, but if they are there . . .'

'And if you got them back? Then what? You've already tried getting rid of them,' said Jack. 'The deepest well couldn't keep them hidden for long.'

'I know,' said Itch, 'and I remember Flowerdew talking about the destructive power of the 126 . . . How it could do good things – provide clean energy, et cetera – but that its capacity for destruction would win out eventually.'

'But how can you actually get rid of radioactive rocks,' asked Jack, 'when nuclear waste is buried for hundreds of thousands of years before it becomes safe?'

'Spallation,' said Lucy.

'What?' said Itch.

'Spallation,' she repeated. 'It's the only way to make them safe. You basically bombard them with neutrons and they break apart. Into something safe.'

There was a silence around the table before Chloe laughed. 'You've been out-geeked, Itch! Never thought I'd see it! Go, Lucy!' They all smiled.

'I've never heard of it,' Itch said to Lucy.

'Why would you? I only know because Dad worked at the Rutherford Appleton Laboratory near Oxford for a while. He took me in sometimes. It's quite a place. He was always talking about this kind of stuff.'

'You discussed spallation?' asked Chloe. 'Really?'

'Well, it wasn't much of a discussion really. More of a lecture. But he was a passionate scientist before everything got too much for him.'

'Cake said he studied English,' said Itch.

'His story was that he dropped out of college, but that was only half true. English was his second degree, and he fell out with the tutors and had some kind of breakdown. When I was about ten, he had a job at one of the target stations at ISIS – that's part of the Rutherford Appleton Lab; I loved it there.'

'Why was he called Cake?' asked Chloe.

'It's another science thing, I'm afraid. He was obsessed with nuclear power, and Yellow Cake is a powder made of uranium, I think. He was boring everyone with it so much, they started to call him Cake. And he quite liked it, so it stuck. In time, everyone called him that. Including me.'

'So,' said Itch, 'if you put the 126 into . . . whatever they have at ISIS . . .'

'Big tubes, basically,' said Lucy.

'Big tubes, then . . . and then bombard it with particles, it stops being 126? And stops being dangerous?'

'Think so.'

'Wow,' said Itch.

'I never like it when he says that,' said Chloe.

Outside again, Itch and Jack had led Chloe and Lucy to a vantage point behind a souvenir stall. They stood with their backs to the Thames, looking up at the block of flats. It had previously been an oil company's head office, and still looked like it should have a corporate logo on the front rather than THE MOORHOUSE APARTMENTS. Many of the windows were strung with fairy lights; a few had Christmas trees that were visible from the street; the rest were bleak and empty or had drawn curtains.

'You think he's in there?' said Lucy, stamping her feet to keep the circulation flowing; the day was sunny but still cold.

'The photos on Flowerdew's laptop were taken from one of those windows. I'm sure of it.'

'And if you knew where he was, what then?'

Itch looked at Lucy. 'I'd go and get that box. And then take it to your ISIS lab. Then I'd spallate them or whatever the word is.'

'That's about right,' said Lucy. 'Well, that sounds easy, then.' She laughed.

A few people were coming and going from the apartments, always pressing a buzzer and waiting for the door to be released. Itch put down his ruck-sack and studied them, in between surveying the windows and glancing up and down the paved pathway. Jack and Chloe had lost interest and were browsing at a nearby souvenir stall.

'Jack! Jack! Come here! Look!' Itch was beckon-ing, and they scurried over to join him behind the Union Jack tea towels. 'There . . .' He was pointing at three men approaching the apartments from the direction of the hospital. 'That guy at the front with the beard. He was the doctor who came round with the hospital consultant. I'm sure of it!'

'*Drever*, I think it said on his label. Yes, that's him.' They watched as the men buzzed their way in.

'Stay here!' said Lucy, and she suddenly set off up the path to the entrance. She got there just as the door was closing and shoved a foot in the gap. Pushing it open, she saw Drever and his companions waiting for the lift. When it arrived, she followed them in and waited for Drever to press the *2* before selecting the *3*. They all stared at the teenager who had joined them, but Lucy just smiled and then kept her head down.

The lift stopped at the second floor, and as the door opened, the men's conversation began again. Lucy heard the man called Drever ask, 'So how bad is he?' as they headed down the corridor. She jammed her foot in the lift door as it closed so that she could hear the rest.

'Bad,' said another man. 'Second- and third-degree burns to his face and arms. Hair loss.'

She heard a whistle, and then Drever's voice again: 'Where's 2223?'

Lucy smiled and allowed the lift doors to shut. On arrival at the third floor, she stabbed the 0 button and waited for the lift to return to the ground floor. She flew out of the building and straight towards her relieved friends.

'What was that about?' asked Itch. 'What the hell were you doing? We were just thinking of coming and finding you!'

But Lucy was still smiling. 'Drever would have recognized you or Jack. It just occurred to me that I could find out what was going on. And I did.'

'You *what*?' exclaimed Jack. 'What happened?'

'They all got out on the second floor, looking for room 2223. One of them said the man had second- and third-degree burns.' Lucy looked at her new friends.

'Wow. You're fast!' Itch was impressed.

'So what now?' she asked.

'Call the police?' suggested Chloe. 'Wouldn't that be good?'

'I could have done that last time,' said Itch. 'The whole point was to get rid of the rocks. I thought I'd done that, but here we are again.'

'Lucy, you know your dad left a note for Itch . . .' said Jack.

Lucy's mouth dropped open. 'You're kidding. What did it say?'

'I've got it at home,' said Itch. 'He told us to get rid of the rocks and trust no one.'

'Sounds like him,' said Lucy.

'That's why I threw them down the Woodingdean Well. What would he do now?' Itch wondered.

'I think he would try to get them to his old colleagues at the labs. And blast them to bits.'

Itch nodded. 'Then that's what we should do.' He looked at Jack, who was staring at the river. He knew what she was thinking; he was thinking it too: *This is unbelievably dangerous and stupid. They are ruthless criminals, we are schoolchildren.* But who else would do what had to be done? If he could put the rocks out of harm's way, for good this time, he knew he had to take the chance. But he wanted Jack to agree.

She looked pale and nervous, but she nodded. 'OK. I was too ill to help much last time, so I'm in. Let's try, anyway.'

Itch turned to Chloe, but she put her hand over his mouth. 'Don't even say it, Itch. You're not leaving me behind again. You did that last time and I hated it. I'm in too.'

Itch was trying to say *Mum and Dad will go mad*, but it came out as 'Mmmngndmdg'. He pulled his head away.

'I'm coming. And I'll be useful.'

Jack touched Itch's shoulder and he turned. 'Itch. We are doing this. The four of us. Deal with it.'

He half smiled. 'Right. OK, let's see if we can find that 126 again.'

Dr Benedict Adebayo had two very nervous colleagues with him. It had taken him some time to find medics good enough to help fix his difficult patient. Eventually the promise of easy money worked its magic. He had found an ex-colleague, Drever, who worked at St Thomas's – who had, in turn, recommended a burns unit specialist from Mount Vernon hospital called Reith.

Both doctors were now wondering if they'd made the right call. Flowerdew was on his bed, in pain and shouting. He also looked a lot worse than he had at four a.m. that morning, Dr Adebayo thought. The skin on his arms and face was turning black. They had rigged a bag of saline drip on a stand, the tube disappearing into the patient's left arm.

'Of course I can't lie still, you idiot. Give me a sedative or something!' The whisky had made him aggressive and Adebayo realized that he needed to act fast.

'Pass me some diamorphine, Charles – quick.'

Drever passed the loaded syringe to his colleague, who was swabbing a small area of Flowerdew's upper arm.

'This should take the edge off things,' Adebayo said, pushing the needle in and watching the painkiller disappear into his patient's veins. 'We can dress your wounds, but really you'll need skin grafts, I'm afraid. I can arrange that, but I can't do it in your flat. There is a discreet hospital I know—'

'OK, book me in. How long would I have to wait?' Flowerdew was already sounding calmer.

'I will need to check. Not long, I'm sure, but a few days maybe.'

Flowerdew had just closed his eyes when there was a knock on the door and everyone jumped. Adebayo's colleagues cried out in alarm, and Flowerdew tried to sit up.

'Who . . . ? No one . . .' He lay back again, the effort too much.

Adebayo went to the door and peered through the security fish-eye lens.

'Who is it?' called Reith, a small bony man with slicked-back greasy, lank hair. He had been sweating already and the knock at the door had started a virtual river down his face.

'It's that girl from the lift. And she's carrying someone.' Adebayo opened the door slightly. 'Yes?'

Lucy Cavendish was standing there, with Chloe in her arms. 'Hi. Please can you help me! My sister just started groaning and saying her head hurt. Mum's out and I can't find any painkillers. I heard you talking in the lift and realized you were doctors.' Chloe started groaning.

'There's a hospital next door – take her there.'

'Oh please, sir! Just a paracetamol or something. Do you have kids? Calpol would be great. We only need tablets and water and we'll go. Sorry if it's not convenient.'

Adebayo hesitated. 'Oh, well, quickly then. Sit there – I'll get you something.' He indicated the sofa, and Lucy laid Chloe down.

A slurred voice from the bedroom called out, 'Who was it?'

If Adebayo had been watching his new arrivals, he'd have seen them tense.

'Just some kids from upstairs. I'm getting them some painkillers.'

'Didn't know we had kids upstairs. Come in here!'

Adebayo handed over some tablets and a glass of water, then hurried back to the bedroom. Flowerdew, his eyes still shut and fighting the sedative now, said, 'Describe them. I've got a small security team on the way – they can keep unwanted visitors away.'

'Two girls, sisters. Sixteen and thirteen maybe. Ignore them – you need to rest . . .'

'Where are the rocks?' whispered Chloe. Lucy shrugged. She looked around the room and then, taking the glass of water with her, went into the kitchen. There was a whisky bottle and an open packet of biscuits on the counter, but apart from that it appeared empty. Lucy reached inside her jacket and pulled out a small plastic pot with a screw lid. Checking the door, she opened the whisky and sprinkled some white powder inside. She replaced the top and shook the bottle.

'Lucy?' Chloe was watching her. 'What's that?'

'Something your brother gave me. He said to drop it into Flowerdew's food if I got the chance. But he hasn't got any food so the whisky will have to do!'

'What is it?'

'*Tellurium*, apparently.'

'What does it do?' asked Chloe.

'No idea – but maybe we'll find out.'

An open door led into a guest bedroom and Lucy, her heart racing, peered inside. The single bed was made up but untouched, the room barely furnished. She slid open a wardrobe door: some old coats and a pair of boots, but no holdall. She had just returned to the kitchen when one of the doctors appeared.

'What are you doing?' Reith's voice was whiny and thin. 'Thought you just wanted water.'

'I just topped up,' said Lucy, smiling. 'Look.' She held up the tumbler, but the man wasn't interested in the water.

'We'll be going then,' said Lucy, and she walked at speed back to Chloe. 'Come on – drink this and then we're off,' she said, unnecessarily loudly.

'Charles, come in here,' called Adebayo, and, still staring at the girls, the thin man went back into Flowerdew's bedroom, staring at the girls as he went.

As soon as he had disappeared into the room, Lucy whispered, 'If the holdall is here, it must be in there! With him!' She pointed at Flowerdew's bedroom and Chloe raised her eyebrows, staring at Lucy.

'But we need to get out. Now. That man gave me the creeps,' she said.

'But we need the rocks!' whispered Lucy.

A cry of pain came from the bedroom, followed by raised voices. Both girls got up and made for the front door; they paused for a moment outside Flowerdew's bedroom.

There was a string of abuse from Flowerdew, and Chloe peered in. It was dark, with the curtains shut and a bedside light illuminating Flowerdew's burns. Two doctors were holding his hands and feet while a third tried to clean the wounds, looking up as the door opened. Chloe gave him a thumbs-up, and he waved her away irritably.

As she turned, there on the floor, right against the wall, she saw a holdall. A grubby, blackened holdall! She froze, rooted to the spot, her heart hammering in her chest. She knew she had to be quick, but she could barely move.

'Well, get out! Out!' shouted the doctor.

As though released from a spell, Chloe ran from the room and grabbed Lucy by the hand. 'It's there!' she whispered, her eyes wide, her breathing short. 'But we have to go! What do we do?'

The sound of movement from the bedroom sent them both scurrying for the door. Lucy pulled it open, and they ran out into the corridor, nearly crashing into Itch and Jack.

'Chloe!' cried Itch, but her hand was over her brother's mouth again.

'You were right!' She was speaking in an urgent whisper, glancing from her brother to her cousin. 'The rocks are in there, just inside the bedroom door. But so is Flowerdew and the doctors. They're trying to treat him – he's got a drip in him or something – but he's shouting and yelling so much . . .' The sound of breaking glass and more bellowing from inside the flat drew them all to the door again.

'I put the latch on,' said Lucy. 'It's not shut, look . . .' and she pushed gently. The door edged open. They listened nervously: the flat was silent.

'Itch?' Jack was watching her cousin. 'What do we do?'

'We walk in. That's what we do.' He handed his rucksack to Jack.

'No, Itch . . .' She tried to pull him back, but he was already inside.

The door to Flowerdew's bedroom was open, and Itch paused briefly to listen again. He could hear Flowerdew's breathing – loud but regular – and the doctors whispering.

'When can we leave?' asked one. 'We've done all we can. Now, while he's asleep?'

'We stay until our job is done,' insisted another. 'He's paying us well. We owe him.'

'And he owes *me*,' said Itch quietly, and walked into the bedroom. In one quick glance he took in the prostrate figure of his former teacher, the attentive medics and the blackened holdall.

'Hey – who are you?' called Adebayo.

Like a porter collecting the luggage, Itch bent

down, slid his hand through the straps, lifted and left. It took three seconds.

'Hey – come back!'

Itch flew from the apartment as fast as his terrifyingly familiar load would allow him. Chloe, Jack and Lucy didn't need telling: they were already sprinting for the lift.

29

The stairwell and the lift shaft were next to each other. As they ran down the corridor, they could hear the lift moving, climbing.

'Stairs! Take the *stairs*!' called Jack. They flew past the ornate brass doors, where the floor indicator sign was already showing 2. They pushed open the fire doors and took the stairs two, three at a time.

Itch hoisted the holdall onto his shoulders and followed. He was already one flight down when, above him, he heard the lift door open and voices talking. He hurried on down the stairs, aware of the radiation box banging against his spine. Ahead of him, Jack, Chloe and Lucy were pushing open the entrance doors.

'Where now?' asked Lucy.

'There!' said Jack, pointing at a sign that said WATERLOO STATION.

They set off along the river walkway. Itch

glanced back at the apartment block, but could see no signs of pursuit. He headed under an arch and along a covered passage past some stalls. Behind him, he heard the rocks rattling as they were jolted around in their container.

'Where are we going?' asked Lucy, glancing at Itch as they ran.

'Underground,' he said.

'Then where?'

'Not sure. But west. Let's get out of here first.'

They pushed their way through slow-walking sightseers who seemed to be conspiring to get in their way. The queues for the Eye and the street performers were all seemingly intent on slowing them down too. Itch turned to look behind again, and saw three men – two with buzz cuts and one with a ponytail – pushing their way through the crowd. They shuffled, ran and dodged their way along the path, veering right under a bridge when they saw the Underground sign. Running across a roundabout and avoiding the taxis, they leaped up the steps up to the station, running along the concourse looking for the tube entrance.

'Who's got money?' Jack called over her shoulder.

'I have!' said Lucy, and handed her purse to Itch.

They'd reached the top of the steps leading to the Underground when they heard a shout. Spinning round, Itch saw the three men close behind them now.

'Go!' he shouted, but even as they started down the stairs, he knew they wouldn't have time to buy tickets and escape. Their best bet was to leap over the barriers and hope they could lose their pursuers in the tube system.

The lobby was busy, the electric barriers opening and closing as passengers swiped cards or inserted tickets. The ticket office was closed, and long queues had formed by the ticket machines. Underground staff stood at the barriers. They were trapped.

'Itch, *do* something!' cried Chloe.

He glanced round at their pursuers. They were pushing people out of their way, provoking angry cries.

Itch knew they would be caught in seconds . . . 'Jack!' he said suddenly, an idea forming in his head. 'Do that thing you did at Marylebone Station. With burned-hair guy!'

Jack got it immediately, remembering how she had escaped from a Greencorps agent by telling a stranger she was being followed. She took Chloe's hand and grabbed a man with LONDON TRANS-PORT and RAYMOND written on his badge.

'Please help me!' she cried. 'Those men are following us! I'm scared!' She pointed at the rapidly closing men and she stood behind Raymond, holding onto his shoulder.

'What?' spluttered Raymond, a stout man in his fifties who had dealt with fare-dodgers and security scares before, but had never been asked for protection. Jack was actually taller than him, but she and Chloe took cover behind him.

The first man – who had a ponytail – approached and made a grab for Jack.

'Hey! No – what do you think—?' Raymond pushed his attacker away, but now the man's two companions had appeared; one shoved Raymond against the ticket barrier. Instantly three more London Underground staff arrived, shouting and reaching for their radios. One pushed Raymond's assailant and got a fist in the stomach; wheezing and gasping for breath, he dropped to the floor. A crowd of passengers gathered around, watching, or filming the action with their phones; others were running for the exits. More London Transport staff appeared on the other side of the barrier.

One of the newly arrived attackers, a short-haired blond man turned away from Raymond and caught sight of Itch and Lucy standing just away from the mêlée and peeled away from the fracas. Itch stood in front of Lucy and looked around him for help, but the staff were concentrating on the fight around Jack and Chloe. The man grinned as he approached, a silver tongue stud glinting in his mouth.

'Itch, he's got a knife!' shrieked Lucy, and Itch caught sight of the blade in his hand.

Passengers scattered as he approached, making a throat-slitting gesture with his knife.

Walking backwards, Itch and Lucy quickly hit the wall, Lucy and the holdall first, then Itch pressed up against her. The man lunged at Itch, who got a kick in before he was grabbed and spun round. Itch felt the serrated knife at his throat cut him, and Lucy screamed, 'OK! OK! Here!' She was taking the holdall from her shoulders when suddenly there was a roar of rage from behind them. A voice he recognized. Itch, his attacker and the knife all went flying, felled by a rampaging Nicholas Lofte.

'Dad!' As Itch picked himself up, he felt his throat and looked at the blood on his fingers. He guessed it wasn't a deep cut, but when he saw the knife on the ground, he grabbed it. His father had the knife-man with the tongue stud pinned down on the floor, but was taking blows to the stomach and face. The dark-haired third assailant abandoned the struggle by the barriers and flew at Lucy and Itch, but he pulled up short when he saw the bloody knife in Itch's hand. Instead he went to help his colleague, who was losing the fight with Nicholas. Itch looked around frantically for Chloe and Jack, who were now protected by Raymond and a circle of London Transport staff, all shouting and swearing at their ponytailed attacker. Realizing that he wasn't going to win this battle, the thug ran to join the fight with Nicholas.

Itch, Jack, Chloe and Lucy were finally in a position to escape, but were reluctant while Nicholas was fighting three thugs on his own.

Itch had never seen his father fight before; he was amazed by his skill and strength. He had seen them applied to sport, to housework and to play-fighting his children, but nothing like this. His punches were powerful and accurate, most hitting his attackers in the stomach or neck. But there were three of them and just one of him.

'I can't just watch,' said Itch and ran over. 'Come on, everyone! Help him! He's my dad!' He looked at the crowd of passengers and Underground staff. 'Well, what are you waiting for!' He heard his father yell with pain and launched a kick at the nearest thug. It connected with ribs and the man howled.

'Just run, Itch!' shouted his dad.

'No way!'

'Itch, look!' called Chloe. A group of Underground staff were advancing on the men. Nicholas had his arms around Tongue Stud's neck and was kicking out at the others, but they swept his legs out from under him. He crashed to the ground, taking Tongue Stud with him.

'Leave them alone!'

'We're calling the police!'

'Stop! Stop! Stop!' Two passengers started shouting at the attackers and then began throwing their shopping at them. Others joined in, and within seconds the men were being pelted with books, perfume, jeans, newspapers, chips – anything that came to hand.

'Go now!' Nicholas shouted, before disappearing under a barrage of fists and feet.

'Whatever you're running from,' shouted Raymond at Jack, 'I'd just go now. We'll try to sort this!'

Itch glanced at Chloe, who looked stricken at watching their dad fight. She watched the small gang of staff and passengers close in around the struggle, but when one of the attackers lashed out at the shoppers, she nodded at Itch.

'OK,' she said, and followed Jack, Lucy and Itch in vaulting the barrier. The crowd at the top of the escalators parted, and the four ran for the moving staircase taking them deep under the London streets.

'Bakerloo, Jubilee or Northern?' called Itch.

'Just get on the first one,' suggested Jack.

'Bakerloo is good if we can,' said Lucy. The sounds of trains thundering and clattering filled the air, but they couldn't see a sign. 'Here!' she called, and they ran down some steps and onto a platform. There was a scattering of waiting passengers, and the electronic sign said: NEXT TRAIN TWO MINUTES. They huddled together at one end of the platform, breathing heavily. They all looked terrified. Itch slipped the holdall from his shoulders and they all stood around it in a protective circle.

'Is it safe, Itch?' asked Lucy. 'The radiation box. Does it leak?'

'I think we're fine. It's been underwater, but I don't see how that would affect it. When we were at the mining school, Dr Alexander chose that box to house the 126 when we brought it in; my guess is it's still secure.' Jack and Itch exchanged glances. 'But if anyone feels sick, tell us straight away, OK?'

Everyone nodded.

'Itch,' said Jack, 'the knife . . .'

He had forgotten he still had the knife in his hand, and hastily tucked it away in his jacket. He wondered if anyone had noticed a teenager running through the station with a bloody knife.

'What if we're still being followed?' asked Jack.

'Let's hope we're not,' said Itch.

'Hope your dad's OK,' Lucy murmured. 'He must have been coming back to the hospital and seen what was happening.'

'Whatever,' said Jack. 'He saved us.'

'Again,' added Itch.

More passengers arrived: backpackers, shoppers, families.

NEXT TRAIN ONE MINUTE.

'Who were they?' asked Chloe, still breathless.

'Flowerdew's little army of helpers,' said Itch, aware of his throbbing hand now.

360

'Wasn't expecting you to just grab the rocks like that,' said Jack.

'I wasn't either,' he admitted. 'But I reckoned Flowerdew was tied up to his drip – and asleep, as it turned out – and the doctors wouldn't care about the 126.'

'Still pretty stupid.'

'Still pretty stupid,' agreed Itch.

They were all studying the faces of the people on the platform while willing the train to appear. Chloe peered along the platform. She nudged Itch, and he followed her gaze. At the far end, a tall black man in a long coat was reading a paper. 'He was looking at us,' she whispered.

They all tensed and studied the man she was talking about.

'He's looking the other way now,' she told them.

'On purpose maybe,' said Lucy.

Lights in the tunnel behind them and the sound of a train approaching made them look away. Lucy went to hoist the holdall back onto her shoulders, but Itch stopped her.

'My turn. Seriously,' he said.

'But your fingers—'

'Are OK, thanks. And so are my shoulders.'

The train had stopped and the doors opened. They were relieved to step onto it – it felt as if they were stepping away from Flowerdew, away from danger.

At the other end of the train, the tall man, still reading his paper, stepped onto the Bakerloo Line train to Kilburn Park. Via Paddington.

'Eight stops,' said Chloe, 'then Paddington. What happens then?'

'Train to Didcot,' said Lucy.

They were sitting in the last carriage, Itch and Chloe on one side, Jack and Lucy on the other.

'They're pretty regular. Used to catch them with my dad – then you take a cab to the Rutherford Lab.'

'What was that powder you gave Lucy?' Chloe asked Itch.

His eyes lit up. 'I forgot! Yes, the tellurium. Did you use it?'

Lucy smiled. 'Yes – put it in his whisky. There was no food to sprinkle it on. I think he's drinking quite a lot of it. Is that OK?'

Itch laughed. 'Who knows? It could be fun!'

'Have you poisoned him?' said Chloe.

'No, that's going a bit far. And illegal. This is more . . . interesting. Tellurium, element fifty-two. Atomic weight 127.6. Melting point 449 degrees. Boiling point 988 degrees.'

Jack mimed a yawn. 'And the interesting bit?'

'It makes you stink of garlic for a week,' said Itch, and everyone laughed. 'And not just ordinary garlic either. Really smelly, rotten garlic. It seeps through every pore and there is nothing you can do about it. Wherever he goes, he'll stand out. He can't hide.'

'Sweet,' said Jack.

As they stopped at Charing Cross, Piccadilly Circus, and Oxford Circus, the train filled and emptied again.

At Regent's Park, policemen showed up on the platform, scanning the carriages. They were concentrating on the more crowded centre carriages, and missed the Loftes and Lucy, who had slid down in their seats as low as they could.

'What if the police get on at the next station?' asked Jack.

'Bet it'll be like that everywhere,' said Jack, 'but we get off soon.'

'Four more stops,' said Lucy. 'Baker Street, Marylebone, Edgware Road, then Paddington.'

'So let's split up,' suggested Itch. 'They're looking for the four of us together, so at the next stop, Chloe and I will get off and get into the next carriage.'

'Good idea,' said Jack.

'*The next station is Baker Street.*'

When the door opened, Itch and Chloe let a few passengers out first, then Chloe stepped off. She took a few steps along the platform to the next carriage, ducked round a policeman, then got straight back on again. Itch hurried after her with the holdall, hiding behind a vast American before getting in at the far end. He caught his sister's eye through the crowd and she gave him a thumbs-up. She peered through the door between the carriages at Lucy and Jack.

'*Stand clear of the closing doors.*'

Two more stops, and then Paddington. Lost in the middle of the crowd of strap-hanging passengers, Itch peered into the next carriage along.

And stared right into the eyes of a tall Nigerian. Who smiled.

30

'Keep walking. Fast!' Itch led the way, marching along the platform at Paddington. 'I think we're being followed! Might be one of Flowerdew's old Nigerian mates,' he called to Jack.

Instinctively she turned and scanned the crowd heading for the mainline station. Chloe and Lucy followed her gaze, not knowing what they were looking for.

They assembled at the ticket machine and Itch told them what he had seen. They all glanced around but saw nothing suspicious.

'How much money do we need to get to . . .' Itch tailed off.

'Didcot,' said Lucy, choosing tickets on the machine. 'It's OK – I came prepared.' She fed it with notes and coins, then gathered up the pile of tickets. 'Train in six minutes. Looks like a slow one, but at least we'll be out of here.'

'I can't see the guy from the tube,' said Itch, still looking around. 'Maybe I imagined him. Let's just go.'

'Platform Eight,' said Lucy.

On the train they sat facing each other in the first group of seats they came to; Itch squeezed the holdall under his seat and Jack put his rucksack beside her. The carriage was empty apart from a family at the other end, arguing furiously over who should sit next to the window. Itch, Jack, Chloe and Lucy waited anxiously for the train to pull out of the station; they were expecting their pursuer to board any minute. But no one came.

'Bet I know what you're thinking,' said Jack.

'I bet you do too,' said Itch, and he described his train journey to Brighton for Lucy's benefit. By the time he got to the part where he had been vomiting blood at the Fitzherbert School, Lucy's eyes were wide and she had a hand over her mouth.

'I understand what you did with the sodium and the rocks back at the well,' said Jack. 'Blasting them to the bottom was a neat trick. But explain what we are doing at this laboratory again? Does it blow them up?'

'Not exactly,' said Lucy, 'and I'm hardly an expert. It's just stuff I heard from Dad and his friends – they talked about this kind of thing all the time.' She stopped and looked out of the window for a few moments. The train had stopped again. 'At this lab they have a vast number of huge tubes and magnets arranged in what they always used to call "target stations". Probably still do. They have a thing called a synchrotron and it shoves beams of protons down the tubes and they look at what stuff is made of. At their atoms, I think.'

Itch interrupted. 'So this is Cake – your dad – and the guys at ISIS. What were *you* doing there?'

'Just tagging along,' Lucy told him. 'Some dads take their kids to football matches – mine took me to a particle accelerator.'

Jack was going to make a sarcastic comment but thought better of it, especially when she saw Itch's look of rapt attention.

'They'd all sit around the control room telling rude jokes about hot cells and interlocking tubes, and I got a bit bored. Then, one day, they were talking about a dangerous type of plutonium they'd found and how they were going to deal with it. My dad used the word *spallation*. I only remember because I asked him what it meant and he said it was like firing a marble into a bag of other marbles. The plutonium was the bag of marbles, and the neutron beam was the single marble. It blows them apart into smaller pieces. And those small pieces are then safe.'

'And that's what we can do to the 126!' said Itch, excited. 'We'll blast it with neutrons.'

'If they let us in.' Jack wasn't convinced.

'If the old team are there, they'll remember me,' Lucy said. 'I used to be quite the golden girl there. But if it's all new guys now, we've got a problem.'

'And how easy is it to get something into this target station and zap it with your death ray?' asked Jack.

'Jack, that's hardly—' began Itch.

'No idea,' said Lucy, 'but impossible sounds about right.'

The train pulled into Didcot, and they were the last to alight. They watched as the passengers headed through the station to the car park. Some were met by friends and family, a few got in taxis; there was no sign of the man from the tube.

'OK, let's go,' said Itch, and they set off along the platform.

They went into the station building, past a deserted coffee stall and a closed newsagent's. They were level with the ticket office when Itch pulled up sharply. Jack and Lucy almost walked into him.

'What is it?' asked Jack. 'Oh . . .' They all smelled it now as they stood at the platform gate to the station, inhaling what felt like lungfuls of rotten garlic.

'What's that stuff I put in Flowerdew's whisky?' said Lucy.

'Tellurium,' said Itch.

'And what's it make you smell of?'

'Garlic. Very bad garlic.'

'Then he's here. Flowerdew must be here!' cried Jack, horrified. 'But how did he find us?'

'I guess that guy did follow us to the mainline station after all . . .' Itch guessed. 'And if he knows we're at Didcot, he's probably worked out where we're heading.'

They all glanced around, looking into every corner of the station concourse, but they couldn't see anyone.

'There are toilets there,' said Chloe, pointing to a door beside the ticket office. Jack started to walk slowly towards it, sniffing.

'Wouldn't go in there, son,' said a man behind the counter, speaking through the glass. 'Gentleman been taken proper sick. Looks in a bad way.'

Jack let the 'son' go. 'Was he on his own?' she asked.

The ticket man shuffled some timetables and rearranged some hairs over his balding head. 'No, there's someone with him – a doctor, he said he was. Just as well really. And there's a car too, I think; Land Rover Sport – big grey thing over there.' He pointed to the car park: peering round, they saw it idling in the taxi rank, the red-haired driver studying his phone. They hurried back onto the platform and tucked themselves in behind a large timetable board. Through the white-slatted fence they could see the Range Rover and hear its engine ticking over.

'Flowerdew must have been waiting for us,' said Itch.

'Then he was taken ill. What a shame,' said Jack.

'But we're stuck,' said Lucy. 'We can't get out without the driver seeing, and any time now that monster will be coming out of those toilets.'

'Got any fireworks left in your rucksack?' asked Jack.

'Shivvi made me tip a lot of my stuff out, but some survived – chuck it over.'

Jack threw the rucksack and Itch caught it.

'Still got the bismuth that Shivvi had . . .' He held up the sparkling stone.

'Great,' muttered Chloe. 'You could throw it at someone. Anything else?'

Itch produced packets and pots with labels on, while the others glanced nervously in the direction of the toilets. 'This would help, definitely,' he said, glancing at the *B 5* pocket and feeling inside. He drew out a small bag of powder and looked intently at it. 'But this might be better!'

'Plan?' said Jack.

'Possibly . . .'

'What is it?' asked Lucy.

'Boron. Or, to be specific, boron carbide powder.'

'And?' said Jack. 'Forgive our ignorance . . .'

'It messes up engines,' said Itch. 'But we need to get the driver out of the car first. Who's the fastest runner?'

'Probably me,' said Jack, looking at Lucy, who nodded.

'Your cough OK?'

'Getting better.'

'Ribs?'

'Painful, but OK.'

'Could you kick his car or something and not get caught?' asked Itch.

There was a slight pause before she replied, 'Maybe. Yes, I suppose.'

'Right. Lucy and Chloe, stay here with the rocks and the rucksack. Be ready to run for it. Come on, Jack.'

The two cousins went into the station entrance again, where the smell of rotten garlic was as strong as ever.

'We might not have long before they come out of the toilets,' said Itch. 'Whatever you're going to do, do it now!'

Jack took a deep breath and walked towards the Range Rover, where the driver was still looking at his mobile phone. She found a ten-pence piece in her pocket and, as she drew level with the Range Rover, dug it into the paintwork. She scraped it along the side, the sound of metal on metal surprisingly loud, the silver-grey paint flaking off in small twists and curls.

Perfect, thought Itch. *Now run for it.*

As Jack took off, Itch saw the red-haired driver start. He leaned over to the passenger window but couldn't see anything. He jumped out of the car, looked at the damage and, seeing Jack heading out of the car park, set off in pursuit. He was short but powerfully built, and showed enough speed to worry Itch – but Itch had a job to do. He ran towards the unlocked Range Rover, opened the front door, and was assaulted by the smell of garlic here too.

Flowerdew had been here all right.

He located the bonnet release and popped it. Running round the outside of the car, he lifted the lid and looked for the oil tank. He remembered that you weren't supposed to take the lid off while the engine was still warm, but thought he didn't have much choice.

Slowly, the black plastic warm to the touch, he twisted and released the oil cap; there was a little hiss as it came away. From his jeans pocket he produced the bag of boron carbide and tipped it slowly into the opening. He knew it would destroy the engine – the granules scoring the cylinder walls – but he didn't know if there would be a bang or smoke. He assumed not, but put the lid back on quickly anyway.

A taxi had pulled up behind the Range Rover;

the driver looked crossly at the big car blocking his space.

'Not mine,' Itch mouthed to him, and closed the bonnet just as a cry from Lucy made him look up.

Jack was running back through the car park, the Range Rover driver barely two metres behind. She looked scared, hot, and was clutching her ribs. The red-haired man, his face a picture of crimson fury, was gaining on her all the time. Itch looked around desperately for inspiration.

'Itch!' shouted Jack as the driver reached for her. His fingers touched her jacket collar but she dodged out of the way.

They were just metres away now, and Itch, pointing at the red-haired man, shouted at the taxi driver, 'It's his! The Range Rover is his!'

The cabbie studied the chase in the mirror. As Jack flashed past him, he opened his door. His timing was perfect. There was a crunch of bone and flesh on metal and glass, and the man collapsed on the ground, blood pouring from a head wound.

'Yes!' said Itch, punching the air.

'Shouldn't park in our space,' said the taxi driver, climbing out and checking his door for damage. 'We keep telling them, but they don't listen.'

Jack was standing bent double and holding her ribs. She was fighting for breath, but smiled at the sight of her pursuer knocked out cold. Lucy and

Chloe came running, carrying the rucksack and the holdall.

'Can you take us to the ISIS labs!' called Lucy. 'I've got twenty pounds. Please, it's urgent!'

The taxi driver, a young man with a stubbly beard and cropped hair, looked at her. 'You in trouble?'

'Not really,' said Itch, 'but we are in a hurry.'

The cabbie looked at them all and then at the twenty-pound note in Lucy's hand. 'OK, get in,' he said. 'Bags in the boot.'

'If it's OK with you, we'd like to keep them with us,' said Itch.

The man shrugged. 'Suit yourselves . . .'

They were dropped outside the ISIS reception. Inside, the small Christmas tree shone brightly; a woman behind the desk was on the phone. They looked around the vast complex of buildings, which stretched, like a small town in every direction.

'Looks like a university campus,' said Itch. 'I went to see Gabriel's once – it was just like this. But with supermarket trolleys everywhere.'

'It used to be an airfield, I think,' said Lucy. 'The D-Day gliders left from here. There are still old tunnels around somewhere.'

'Guys,' interrupted Jack, 'can we get on with this? If he's guessed where we're headed, Flowerdew will make his way here somehow. Let's find your death ray and blast these rocks to . . . whatever it is we are blasting them to.'

'I think you need to stop calling it a death ray,' said Itch.

She shrugged. 'Well, whatever it is, let's find it. Who are you asking for, Lucy?'

'The main guy was John Kett. I'll see if he's here.' Lucy went up to the desk and smiled broadly at the woman, whose badge said ANITA. 'Hello!' she said.

'How can I help you?' said the woman.

'I'm looking for John Kett, please,' said Lucy. 'He works in one of the target stations. Well, he used to, anyway.'

'One minute,' said Anita as she scrolled through a list of names on her computer. 'Sorry – no one by that name here. What was the nature of your visit?' Her eyes moved from Lucy to Itch, Jack and Chloe. Both Itch and Jack were suddenly conscious of their burns, finger splints and bandages.

We must look a really bad group of people to let into a place like this, thought Itch. *She might just call security and throw us out.*

'My dad worked here a few years ago and his friends always said to drop by. So . . . I have.' Lucy smiled weakly, and they all noted a softening in Anita's body language.

'I see. Is there someone else I can try?' she asked.

Lucy thought for a minute. 'Well, there was a crowd of them. Bill Kent was one; Tom . . . er, Tom

Oakes was another, I think. Could you try them?' Lucy turned to the others; they were all silent and tense. If they couldn't get past this point, their plan was lost.

'Bill Kent is here,' said Anita. 'I'll try him. Who should I say is here?'

'Lucy Cavendish. Tell him I'm Cake's daughter.'

'I'm sorry?'

'Cake's daughter,' Lucy repeated. 'He'll remember.'

And remember he did. Within five minutes, an electric buggy was pulling up outside the reception and a young woman in a thick coat was beckoning. They trooped outside.

'Hi. I'm Tilly,' she said. 'I work with Bill and Tom. Jump in – I'll take you to them.'

Itch punched Lucy gently on the shoulder and she smiled. They climbed aboard; Itch and Chloe sat behind Tilly, the holdall at their feet, with Jack carrying the rucksack, and Lucy at the rear, facing backwards.

Itch twisted round to speak to Lucy. 'Now, remember what we agreed – no mention of the rocks!' he whispered.

'But there's a chance they might help us,' she pointed out.

Itch shook his head. 'Are you mad? *Trust no one* – that's what your dad said. They might simply turn us in.'

'Dad would have trusted Bill and Tom. He *did* trust Bill and Tom.'

'But how long ago was that, Lucy? Seven years? Eight? They're not going to blast our rocks just because we ask them to.'

'And we don't have time to argue with them,' added Jack.

Lucy was silent as they rolled silently along, following signs for TARGET STATION FOUR. 'OK,' she said eventually, 'but if we're stuck, we ask for help.'

'Maybe . . .' said Itch.

'Here we are!' said Tilly. 'Target Station Four! It's pretty much brand new.'

In the large open doorway stood two men. The buggy stopped in front of them, and the older of the two, grey and slightly stooped, waved.

'Hello,' he called. 'I'd recognize that hair anywhere! Lucy Cavendish! It's great to see you.'

They climbed off the buggy and Lucy shook hands with him awkwardly.

Itch read the swinging ID card around his neck, which identified him as BILL KENT, with a photo taken before his hair had turned grey.

'Bill Kent,' he said, acknowledging their glances. 'How do you do . . . You like you've been in the wars . . .' He was staring at Itch and Jack.

'These are my friends, Itch, Jack and Chloe,' said Lucy. 'They . . . had an accident.' She didn't elaborate, and simply made the introductions.

Kent beckoned his colleague over. 'And this is Tom Oakes – remember him, Lucy? He had slightly more hair when you saw him last, I'd wager.' He was younger, thinner, and blushed at the reference to his baldness.

'Lucy, hi.' The accent was American. 'Last time you were here you sat on my glasses. Good to see you again.'

'What's in the bag?' asked Bill Kent. 'Looks heavy.'

Itch was staring at Lucy; both scientists studied the holdall.

'Oh, just some Christmas shopping,' she said, and changed the subject. 'I was telling them about my dad's work here and wanted to show them round. Would that be possible?'

'Well, normally it would need to be approved,' said Bill Kent, 'but under the circumstances . . . I'm sure no one would object. Seeing as it's you!'

Tom Oakes agreed. 'Sure. It's not as if letting kids in will get us into any trouble! Itch, it's good to meet you.' He was staring at Itch with interest, and just nodded at Jack and Chloe.

'How is your father these days, Lucy?' asked Kent, ushering them inside. 'We still talk about him, you know.'

Lucy hesitated, but before she could answer, she was distracted by a loud 'Wow!' from Itch.

Tom Oakes had led the way into a vast,

cavernous, fiercely lit building. Itch's jaw dropped. High metal walkways crisscrossed above their heads, with bright red steel girders lining the ceiling. On the ground, a baffling maze of huts, cabins and steel cupboards were interspersed with pink, orange and yellow blocks. And running straight through the middle of the building was a steel tube like a huge air-conditioning duct, with a diameter Itch put at a little over 1.5 metres. It came into the target station two hundred metres away, and then twisted round and ended at a huge pod just in front of them. At the far end of the building, a low arch bore the words, painted in enormous red letters: SITE INCIDENT. FIRE. EVACUATE HALL. DIAL 2222.

Itch's eyes darted around, not knowing where to look first. 'It's like a cathedral . . .' he whispered.

Bill Kent appeared at his side. 'Impressive, isn't it?'

Itch nodded.

Without waiting to be asked, the ISIS man pointed at the steel tube, tracing its route through the target station. 'So the beam enters the building at the far end there – an offshoot from the other target stations. As you might know, it starts in the particle accelerator, and the proton beam is travelling at eighty-four per cent of the speed of light. It is focused by those huge magnetic coils you see stuck around the pipe.' He pointed to large gold-coloured loops of wire that surrounded the tube at regular intervals. 'And this pod is where it hits whatever we have for testing and examination.'

They stood in front of a large egg-shaped hull, all polished steel and glass, with shower-hose style cabling running between brass bolts and hoops.

Itch, with the rocks at his feet, thought he might as well just ask directly. 'Does it do spallation?' he said.

Kent looked at him in surprise. 'Spallation? Sure. We've done that in the past. Tom! He's asking about spallation.' He beckoned the American over. 'Why do you ask? That's pretty advanced stuff.'

'Oh, just curious,' replied Itch.

'Well, what we do is, we load the product into the pod and fire the beam—'

Itch interrupted. 'If you had a dangerous radioactive material that you needed to destroy, would it do that? Could it do that?' His voice was a little more high-pitched than he intended, and he tried a smile to offset it.

Again Bill Kent was taken aback by the question, but it was Tom Oakes who answered: 'Why, yes, certainly. It would cause an inter-nuclear cascade, and the radioactive material would disintegrate into fission products.'

'And does that mean the dangerous stuff would be made safe?'

'Well, yes, I suppose so. You would have to do tests, of course, but—'

'And how do you load the pod?' Itch realized he

was pushing it, but the thought of Flowerdew arriving with his goons gave him an overpowering sense of urgency.

As it turned out, Tom Oakes was only too keen to show off their toy. 'It's quite fun, this, actually,' he said, demonstrating. 'The material goes in the guide tube here . . .' He pulled a thick, grooved steel tube out from the pod door; it was about twenty centimetres wide, with thick insulation. He pushed his arm into the hole, like a conjurer showing that a box is empty. 'When you push the tube through the target door, your material appears inside. You can see it through the glass here.'

He showed them a head-height window in the pod. The steel guide tube had opened alongside a small crane, similar to some Itch had built from his dad's childhood Meccano set.

Oakes rubbed his hands together with excitement. 'This is the best bit!' He put his hands into two lined holes in the pod's control system. 'In here are the manipulators – handles that you can spin and twist to operate the crane. Watch.' As they peered through the glass, the metal crane inside the pod swung over to the empty guide tube and its pincers opened, looking for something to pick up. 'My right hand is controlling the pickup and my left the swing of the crane. I'd now place whatever the material is on this base' – he indicated a small, bolted metal plate – 'and then lock it all in place.' Pulling his arms out of the pod, he swung a lever. 'It's a Castell interlocking system. Once it's in, it's in. That's it and you can't touch it. And then' – he smiled at his audience – 'I'd retire to the control room.'

'Which is where we should go now, Lucy,' said Bill Kent. 'There are a few other people here who remember you from all those years ago.'

'Is that where they fire the beam from?' asked Lucy as they headed up one of the metal staircases.

'Yes – we have four crews who work twenty-four hours a day,' said Kent as they followed a set of six narrow pipes that ran round the wall.

Their footsteps echoed and clanged as they made their way towards a control room high up in the corner of the building. Lucy went ahead with Kent and Oakes; Itch, Jack and Chloe hung back. Itch was carrying the holdall, and as he swapped hands, the rocks rattled again. It was an ominous sound – a deep rumble that made him feel sick. It was the sound of violence and death. He couldn't wait to destroy them.

'That was almost a lesson in how to use his kit,' said Chloe, interrupting his thoughts.

'It was, wasn't it,' said Itch.

'Is this do-able?' asked Jack. 'Can you get the 126 into that pod, and then fire the beam? How does that work?'

'Well, let's hope we can find out,' said Itch, 'because if we can, it'll happen here.'

They were approaching a door marked NO ENTRY and RADIATION HAZARD. Kent had one hand on the handle.

'So how is your father, Lucy? I don't think you said . . .'

31

Lucy looked down at the metal floor and stuffed her hands in her pockets.

'I'm afraid he died.'

Chloe touched her arm.

'My God,' said Kent. 'When? What happened?'

Both scientists looked stunned. Kent recovered first. 'I'm sorry, Lucy – you don't have to tell me, of course . . . I'm just so . . . We are just so shocked . . .'

She looked up again. 'That's OK. It was a few months ago. Radiation poisoning.' Itch could tell that she was doing her best to sound matter-of-fact.

'Radiation?' said Kent, flabbergasted. The ensuing silence suggested the scientists expected more detail, but none was forthcoming. Lucy was just staring into the distance and biting her lip.

'I am so sorry,' said Oakes. 'Please accept our condolences.'

Lucy nodded, and there was silence for a few

moments before Kent spoke again, smiling kindly.

'Let's see if we can rustle up some tea,' he said, and opened the door.

In the windowless control room, Lucy was introduced to the technicians and scientists; it seemed that many of them remembered her father. Itch looked around at the array of monitors that formed the control room. Three men and a woman were glued to computer screens; the rest were listening to Lucy.

Tom Oakes peeled away from the reminiscing and stood at Itch's shoulder.

'Basically we control everything from here,' he said. 'We fire the beam, we shut it down. We open the building, we shut it down. We monitor all the experiments in all the other target stations; we are number four – of four. We hire out the equipment to whoever wants it, as long as they fulfil our strict research conditions and make their results public. Targets one and two are running at the moment, three and four are waiting for new projects to arrive.'

'So there's nothing you're working on at the moment?' asked Itch.

'No, just maintenance today – some of the tube's panels are being inspected tomorrow – so we have a reduced staff. We expect new work next week.' The American walked past another operator. 'Jenny, this is Itch. He's with Lucy. Just showing him around.'

The woman called Jenny barely looked up from her screen but nodded in Itch's direction.

'Where is the beam controlled from?' asked Itch. 'Is there a beam controller?'

'Yes, that's Jenny.' Oakes pointed to the BEAM ON/BEAM OFF light above her panel and the key by her left hand. 'She turns the key, the beam is on. There's a built-in pause of up of two minutes before the beam hits, then we are up and running.' He smiled. 'OK?' He turned back to join his colleagues, who were listening to Lucy.

'And he always used to say, *Remember the golden rule of chemistry, Lucy,*' a slight, greying woman with glasses on a chain round her neck was saying: '*Don't lick the spoon!*'

Everyone laughed – though no doubt they'd heard the story countless times before.

Lucy looked around the control room. 'This has changed so much. I really used to love coming here . . .'

Itch stood next to the beam controller woman and wondered if he could make it work. He glanced at Chloe and Jack; they looked pale and exhausted. The technicians were still chatting to Lucy:

'So when do we get to see your dad, Lucy? How is he anyway?'

Itch saw her swallow and look down. Gasps and shocked expressions greeted the news of Cake's death.

Jack, turning round to look for Itch, mouthed, 'Go now.'

As the control room listened to Lucy's account of her father's death, Itch realized that she was telling – and considerably elaborating – the story for a reason. All the staff were distracted. Jack was right: now was the time.

He took his rucksack from Jack, and picked up the holdall. The handles strained with the weight, but Itch was careful not to let the rocks rattle around. Dr Alexander had shut them in their lead-lined box of high-density polythene. They had been submerged underwater, blasted by fire; now they had one last journey to make.

Every one of his footsteps along the high metal walkway sounded to Itch like the banging of a gong. He was going as fast and as quietly as he could, but was sure he was making too much noise. He looked down at the shiny beam tunnel. Signs of the maintenance crew were everywhere: replacement panels and pipes lay on the floor, ready to be fitted. Where the walkway turned left, Itch went down the steps to the pod.

As he stood in front of it, peering through the thick glass at the empty plate where the 126 needed to go, he realized his mistake. He banged his head against the pod in frustration. *OK, clever guy with a new bone marrow – how are you going to get the rocks out of the box and into the pod? Smart move.* He looked around but saw nothing that he could use to mask the radiation. He needed gloves, tongs and a radiation suit. He had nothing.

He checked his rucksack: there were a few cloths he had used to wrap things in, but that was it. There was no more time to spend being careful. Flowerdew was surely on his way – and who knew how long Lucy's distraction would last? He pulled open the guide tube and knelt down in front of the holdall. He wrenched it open and lifted out the large radiation box. When Dr Alexander had first shown it to him, it had been white and pristine; now it was dirty grey, and covered in dents.

It had four clasps, all rusted solid. Itch stood up and kicked at the fastenings; they came loose immediately, and popped up when he flicked the clasps with his thumb and forefinger. His hands started to shake as he mimed the procedure of lifting the rocks out of the box and dropping them into the pod's guide tube. Like a rugby player picturing the route his conversion kick will have to take, Itch imagined lifting and letting go.

How long do I have? Twenty seconds? Thirty? How much radiation can I cope with? In his weakened condition, presumably the answer was: none at all.

But it was too late to change the plan; it was now or never. It was him or no one.

He lifted the lid.

For a moment – one heart-stopping moment –

Itch could see only seven rocks. The thought that they might not all be there should have occurred to him; Flowerdew had had the rocks long enough to swap or change them if he had wanted to. But as he shook the box, all eight rearranged themselves. Charcoal-black, different sized, jagged-edged.

One, two, three, four, five, six, seven, eight.

Itch breathed in again, and a stewed, steamy smell came from the box. As he moved his hand closer, he sensed the heat generated by these un-remarkable-looking rocks. A moment's hesitation and he had the largest one in his good hand. Its weight didn't surprise him – he had been lugging the box around long enough; but it seemed extra-ordinary that one individual rock the size of a potato could be so heavy. Itch stood and dropped it into the waiting tube. As it rattled against the steel, he swung round to get another. The next one was egg-sized and smoother than the first, silver flecks in the 126 catching the fierce neon lighting as he dropped it in again.

Must be quicker. This is your body you're messing up.

He stooped, picked up and dropped, picked up and dropped, picked up and dropped. Each rock was in his hand for no more than two or three seconds. Three left, and the guide tube was filling up. With each passing second Itch imagined the radiation cutting through him, seeking out his new bone marrow and taking it down. He picked up the last three rocks together and dropped them into the tube; he had to rearrange them with his hand to make them all fit. With all eight secured, he rammed the tube shut.

Allowing himself one deep breath, Itch stared through the glass at the front of the pod. The tube had emerged alongside the small crane, and Itch shoved his hands into the manipulator sockets, as Tom Oakes had shown him. They found the control handles, but his damaged right hand throbbed, and he wondered if he would be able to flex his taped fingers well enough.

Spin and twist. That's what Oakes had said. Itch jabbed with his left hand and the crane swung wildly. Pulling with the right made the crane dive, the claws opening automatically. He felt a trigger on both handles; pulling them made the claws close, pulling again made them open. After a couple of trial runs, Itch thought he had enough control to start the transfer.

He swung the crane over the drawer and swooped. After one aborted attempt, he successfully picked up the first rock, swung it over to the metal plate and set it down in the middle. His hands were clammy, his face dripping with sweat, but he needed these rocks in position *now*. He had to speed up. He swung the crane again and again, each time finding a rock and swinging it into position. He was building a small, if uneven, pyramid, just as his father did with barbecue charcoal. He had four at the base, two on top, and was twisting his right hand, picking up the seventh, when his broken finger caught on the control handle. As he flinched, the crane dipped down and hit the pile. The 126 in its claws slipped and fell. Horrified, Itch watched as the small mound collapsed, the more spherical rocks rolling off the plate and down the beam tunnel, out of sight.

Itch stood and stared through the glass. Four rocks were visible, three had disappeared, and one was still in the tube. If the beam was fired now, would he destroy the 126 with only half of it on the target plate? He had no way of knowing for certain, but he suspected that the answer was no.

He leaned his head against the glass. *This feels like failure. I could try to fire the beam, but if it misses the rocks, is it worth the risk?* Itch tried using the manipulator again, but the crane couldn't access the rocks that had rolled away. There *must* be a way of reaching them.

He ducked slightly and peered into the tunnel. He thought there was slightly more light there than before, so he walked round the pod and followed the tunnel that carried the proton beam for twenty metres. He ran his fingers along the steel as he walked; it felt cool. He came to some gleaming pipes arranged on the ground – ready, he assumed, for inserting into the tube. He had seen these from the walkway but hadn't worked out what they were.

Of course, there's another way in! That's what the maintenance teams use!

He stared up at the tunnel. There was a panel in front of him that was due to receive the new piping; now that he was up close, he saw that it was stencilled with BEAM THRESHOLD ADJUSTMENT. He pushed against it and it swung in on four hinges.

I'm in.

Itch had dropped the rucksack, and had got one knee and two hands into the opening when he smelled the garlic. Putrid, rotting garlic – and it was coming from inside the tunnel. Scarcely able to believe his senses, he hauled himself up and peered inside. Looking right, the tunnel darkened and snaked away to the left. Looking along it, Itch saw nothing at all. Blackness.

But he heard plenty.

He heard the sound of a man forcing himself through a steel tube.

The beam tunnel may have been a metre or so in diameter, but its walls were thick and there wasn't much room inside. As his eyes grew accustomed to the gloom, Itch could make out the slowly disappearing feet of Dr Nathaniel Flowerdew. Propelling himself with elbows and knees, he had pushed himself along the tunnel and was now only a few metres from the pod. Itch could hear his laboured breaths and the occasional yelp of pain as he slithered towards the 126. Itch was scared, nauseated and furious all at the same time. And now he couldn't help himself.

'You're like a slug leaving a trail of slime,' Itch blurted out, his voice deadened by the closeness of the tunnel walls, 'but *you* leave a trail of stench. Everywhere you go.'

Flowerdew jumped, banging his head on the roof of the tunnel. Now in the slightly expanded space of the pod, he roared with anger and twisted his head round to try to see Itch, but the tunnel seemed empty.

Itch had dropped back out and run back to the pod. Looking through its glass screen, he stared in astonishment and revulsion at what he saw. Flowerdew's face was lit by the ferocious neon of the lab, and the true extent of his injuries was apparent.

His face was blistered, some of it black, some lobster-red, oozing with fluid that ran down his face like sweat. The skin over his right cheek had started to fold and peel away, leaving a loose flap of pink skin. Flowerdew moved around, picking up the rocks with his bandaged hands and scooping them, one at a time, into a long black flask. He didn't seem concerned by the radiation hit he must be taking. Catching sight of Itch, he yelled again, but no sound penetrated the thick steel and glass that surrounded him.

What if I could turn the beam on now? What does it do to people? Itch had no idea, and as he had no access to the beam, it wasn't a choice he had to make. But Flowerdew had sought the rocks of 126 for the third time and now he had them in his flask. If Itch didn't do something immediately, they would be gone again, possibly for the last time.

Running back to the opened hatch, he found a short length of metal piping and rammed it into a pocket, then climbed back into the tunnel. Flat on his stomach, he pulled and pushed his way along the tube. It wasn't easy: as soon as he tried to get a purchase on the walls, his spine cracked against the roof. Metre by metre, pushing his rucksack along in front of him, he closed in on Flowerdew. He had no idea what he was going to do when he got there, but he had to stop him.

Twenty metres away, Flowerdew was prising the last rock out of the guide tube.

'Time to give up, Flowerdew!' shouted Itch. 'The rocks aren't yours. Put them back. Go and get some medical help; your face is a mess. And did anyone tell you that you stink?'

The last rock rolled into Flowerdew's flask and he turned slowly, filling the tunnel. What light there had been from the pod disappeared. Now the only illumination came from the hatch door behind Itch, and he was blocking most of that.

'That's *Dr* Flowerdew! *Dr* Flowerdew! You never

got that, Lofte, did you? Always the cocky know-all with the idiot sister and cousin.'

Itch heard the clang of metal on metal as Flowerdew felt his way along the tunnel with, he assumed, the flask in one hand. The smell of garlic was getting stronger.

'You're a criminal, Lofte. A thief, a poisoner, an arsonist – you tried to kill me back at the well. You deserve a long stretch in prison.'

'You killed Shivvi and were going to throw her down the well!' shouted Itch. 'On top of Jack! You're a monster, Flowerdew . . . I know what you did in Nigeria. All those people died because of you; *you* should be the one in jail!'

'Losing your cousin down the well would have been the best thing for her, Lofte. That's how we got rid of our rubbish in Lagos, you know.' Flowerdew was breathing heavily, and Itch knew he couldn't be far away; the clanking and the garlic stench were both getting stronger. 'You find something useless, you get rid of it.'

Itch was shaking with anger. The pain and anguish of the last six months were boiling up inside him. The kidnapping, the radiation, the bone-marrow transplant, the Russian attack, the caesium – all of it was Flowerdew's fault. He crawled along faster, grazing his elbows and knees. He was about to launch himself at Flowerdew when he was struck, hard. A flash of metal – the flask, he realized

– and he was hit again – heavy blows to his forehead. He tried to back away, but a third blow hit him above his right eye, followed by a fourth. He felt blood start to run down his face, and lights started to pop in front of him.

'Not so pretty now, Lofte,' cried Flowerdew, breathing heavily, 'and I haven't even started yet. When I find your cousin—'

Itch's vision cleared and, leaving the rucksack, he launched himself at the shape in front of him. He pushed with his feet, bounced off the tunnel roof, and his head cracked against Flowerdew's. The sound of skull on skull was shockingly loud, and they both fell back, stunned.

Itch was still trying to clear his vision when a bright light shone in his eyes. Flowerdew had a small torch between his teeth, and before Itch could react, he reached out with a bandaged hand and grabbed him by the hair.

'This is what I have been dreaming of doing,' he said through gritted teeth; 'what I should have done a long time ago. I had a go back at the academy, but this time it's for real.' With his fingers tightly wound in Itch's hair, he slammed Itch's face into the tunnel wall. Itch heard the crack of his nose and the clang of steel as pain flooded his head. Flowerdew flung him left, then right, each time smashing his head against the walls.

Itch blacked out before Flowerdew's fingers had let go of his hair.

When he came to, he heard Flowerdew say, 'That was fun,' and felt himself being hauled, centimetre by centimetre, back towards the pod.

As the light grew stronger, Flowerdew dropped the torch. 'You're in a bad way, Lofte. Such a shame.'

As he was pulled and jolted down the tunnel, Itch opened his eyes. He gasped in pain as his split ear rubbed along the side of the tunnel. He could tell his face was a mass of blood, and when he tasted it flowing into his mouth, he coughed and spat it out.

'Welcome back, Lofte,' said Flowerdew. 'This will be so much more fun if you're awake.' He carried on crawling backwards and dragging Itch with him. 'The proton beam, as you appear to know, will break things down. If it's a metal like tungsten, it'll work on that. If it's a person like – oh, I don't know . . . you, maybe – it'll work on that too. When the particles hit, they'll cause a complete breakdown of your central nervous system. Instantly. I don't know if it's painful, as no one has survived to tell the tale. Probably not, unfortunately.'

'You'll never get the beam to work.' Itch was coughing and spitting again.

'Oh, I think I will. Don't you worry about that,' said Flowerdew.

They had reached the pod. At least, Itch thought, the pain was waking him up. He realized that Flowerdew was planning to leave him here, then turn on the beam. He had at last learned something from his old science teacher – the neutron beam in this tunnel would kill you if you were in the way. He had to get out.

Flowerdew was still holding Itch by his collar. Itch was face down, his right hand resting on his back, his left hand trying to ease his passage towards the pod. His arm rubbed against his jacket pocket, and he felt the hard steel of the pipe he had picked up; the fingers of his left hand closed around it.

'You're going to have to stay here, Lofte.' Flowerdew was breathing, and now speaking, through gritted teeth. The stink of the tellurium garlic was stronger than ever. 'I'm glad you woke up so I could tell you what I was doing. I'm going to destroy your central nervous system, and then, when you're dead, I'm going to sell the rocks. I've tried to sort this out before but you got in the way. That won't happen again.'

To his surprise, Itch started to laugh. 'But I *have* got in the way. I *am* in the way. You can't get past me. This tunnel is too small. You're trapped.'

'But that, dear Itchingham, depends on whether you're conscious or not, doesn't it? I'm sure you'll flatten out if I hit you hard enough.'

Itch felt Flowerdew move and heard the rocks rattle around in the flask. His 'club' was ready again. Itch realized he was going to have to do something now – before Flowerdew did. Pulling the steel tube out of his pocket, he rammed it into the first part of Flowerdew he could find. He heard the soft squelch as the tube skewered Flowerdew's inflamed ear – and then a howl of pain.

Flowerdew swung wildly with the flask, missing Itch's head by millimetres and hitting the steel wall. A sound like a vibrating gong filled the tunnel, and somewhere Itch registered that it was odd no one had come to check what was going on. Flowerdew missed again. He was flailing blindly now, and Itch smashed the pipe down onto one of his damaged hands. Flowerdew dropped the flask and, in one movement, Itch caught it and rammed it into Flowerdew's forehead. His head bounced against the wall and he lay still, out cold.

His pulse racing and his whole body trembling, Itch grabbed the flask and put Flowerdew's torch in his mouth, nearly gagging on the saliva that was still on the ribbed handle. He could see his old teacher's slumped form against the pod glass, blood and body fluids smeared in an arc where he had collapsed. But he was still breathing, and Itch knew the man might not be out for long. Itch had the rocks, but Flowerdew had fallen precisely where the

126 needed to be placed. He couldn't destroy them without destroying the man too.

'I want you in prison, not dead,' he murmured.

Itch banged the wall of the tunnel in frustration, then tried to move Flowerdew. He tugged at his jacket, then pulled at his arm, but soon realized that he couldn't shift him. He was wedged there, and Itch's strength was spent. He paused to get his breath back, and heard the *drip drip* of his blood hitting the steel floor.

'I need help.'

Retreating back along the tunnel, Itch put the flask in his rucksack and opened the hatch. The light outside was blinding, and he waited a few seconds before jumping to the ground. As he landed, the jolt reverberated through his smashed nose, broken finger and every cut and bruise he had just received from Flowerdew. He gently dabbed his face with his sleeve; the fabric came away soaked in blood. Itch took a deep breath and hobbled away towards the control room.

32

By the time Itch had made his way up the stairs with his rucksack, he could barely limp along the high walkway. Each step seemed to echo and crash through a deserted building.

Where is everybody? he wondered. Surely the others would be wondering where he was. He looked down at the beam tunnel, half expecting to see Flowerdew stagger out of the hatch, but nothing was moving. He reached the control-room door.

NO ENTRY. RADIATION HAZARD.

'You don't say,' said Itch and, pressing gently on the handle, opened the door a few centimetres. Silence. Nobody. As he eased it further he saw only empty chairs and unmanned consoles. Itch knew something was wrong. Hesitating, unsure, he listened. There was a swallowed, gulping cry, and he swung the door open. Itch gasped.

Jack, Chloe and Lucy, together with all the

terrified scientists and technicians, were on their knees, hands behind their heads. Five men with guns stood over them – men he recognized. There was the short red-haired man who had chased Jack at Didcot station and got a door in his face – the bruise on Jack's forehead indicated that he had already exacted revenge for that humiliation. There were the three men who had attacked them at Waterloo, and the one Itch had thought was Nigerian, who had followed them on the tube. They all stared at Itch, but it was the Nigerian who spoke.

'Where's Dr Flowerdew?'

Itch looked at Jack, Chloe and Lucy. They were smiling now, but their eyes were red-rimmed and they were clearly terrified.

'So pleased to see you,' said Jack quietly.

'You look terrible,' cried Chloe.

'Shut it!' ordered the Nigerian. 'Where's Dr Flowerdew?'

'Who are you?' asked Itch.

The man grabbed a gun from one of his associates and flicked off the safety catch. 'You don't seem to realize who is in charge here,' he said, then walked down the line of kneeling hostages and pointed the barrel at Lucy's head. The technicians tensed, and Lucy bit back a scream, her eyes wide, her whole body shaking. 'Last time. Where's Dr Flowerdew?'

'OK! OK! I get it!' said Itch. 'He's in the tunnel. Down there. He's . . . not very well.'

The gun lowered slightly. 'Does he have the rocks?'

Itch swallowed. 'Yes. He has them. He took them from me. We fought but I managed to escape.' He didn't look at Jack, Chloe and Lucy in case they realized he was lying. He just stared at the Nigerian and hoped he believed him.

'Show me.' The man waved his gun towards the door. 'Show me where the rocks are. Girls come too.'

Itch watched as his sister and cousin helped each other up, then Chloe helped a still-trembling Lucy to her feet.

'Go!' shouted the Nigerian, and Itch led the way out, glancing briefly at the haggard faces of Bill Kent and Tom Oakes.

The American nodded slightly as Itch headed back out onto the walkway.

They walked along in single file. The Nigerian had left only the ginger driver in the control room; all the other men were following behind, their heavy footsteps echoing around the building.

Itch slowed so that Jack was within earshot. 'They're in my rucksack. In a flask,' he whispered. He had no idea if she'd heard him.

Now they were on the steps leading down to the pod and the tunnel, and the empty radiation box was being inspected by the Nigerian.

'So where are they then?' he snapped. 'Where's Flowerdew, and where are the rocks?'

Itch knew he was running out of time and had run out of choices. He pointed at the beam tunnel.

'Get in there!' came the shouted command. The Nigerian waved his men towards the open hatch. 'I want the rocks and Dr Flowerdew.'

As the men clambered in, Itch stepped back and reached for Chloe's hand. Startled, she soon realized what it meant: they were in serious trouble. She in turn found Jack's hand, and Jack held Lucy's. The four of them stood there together, not moving.

When they find Flowerdew hasn't got the 126, thought Itch, *that might be that. They won't need us and they won't want witnesses*. He squeezed his sister's hand and closed his eyes. *Failed. Failed. Failed.*

There was a shout as one of the gunmen emerged from the tunnel again. 'He's here! We've got Dr Flowerdew but he's in a bad way! Out cold.'

Flowerdew's feet appeared, and he was pulled out of the tunnel.

'What about the rocks?' snapped the Nigerian. 'I need the rocks!'

Flowerdew, bleeding from his ear and his hand, was laid down on the floor and his pockets checked. 'Nothing. And nothing in the tunnel.'

Flowerdew coughed, then spat blood. He tried to sit up but fell back, cursing viciously. 'Where are you, Bello?'

The Nigerian crouched down beside him, trying unsuccessfully to hide his revulsion at the sight and smell. 'We were just looking for the rocks, Dr Flowerdew.'

'Do you have the children, Bello? Do you have the children?' Flowerdew croaked.

'Yes, all four. They're here – my men have guns on them.'

'Then you have the rocks. The boy has them. Search him!'

Bello turned to face them. He noticed for the first time that all four were holding hands. A flicker of a smile crossed his face.

'Of course.' He walked up to Itch. 'You have them. Do you give them to me or do I have to put a bullet in your sister's head?'

Itch sensed defiance flowing from the others, but he knew it was time to stop. He glanced at them: Lucy, her hair as wild as ever, was staring ahead, not trusting herself to look at anyone. Jack caught his eye, scared but angry too – her face flushed. She mouthed something, but he couldn't make it out. Chloe, he could feel, was shaking but trying hard not to show her terror. He tried a smile, but he knew it was unconvincing. She smiled back anyway.

Itch slowly took off the rucksack, the guns following his every move. He placed it on the ground in front of him.

'Open it,' ordered Bello.

'You open it,' said Itch, and a pistol grip hit him on the back of the head. It was Tongue Stud from the tube; he was grinning wildly.

'Next time it's your sister,' said Bello. 'Open it.'

Itch bent down and opened the rucksack. Even now he wondered if the bismuth might help; whether he could use his sample of tin, or his iron filings . . . But looking at guns pointed at him, even Itch had to concede defeat. He pulled out Flowerdew's large flask, set it down on the ground in front of him, then retreated.

There was a pause before Flowerdew spoke. 'Count the rocks, Lofte. I need to know they're all there.'

'But you *know* they're all there,' said Itch. 'You put them in the flask in the first place.'

'But then you took them, you see.' Flowerdew had clambered to his feet. 'And who knows what you did with them!' Even though it made his face bleed, he was smiling. 'Let's see them! I want to see all eight!'

Everyone knew what Flowerdew was asking. The boy with the bone-marrow transplant, who couldn't afford any more exposure to radiation, was being asked to handle eight pieces of 126.

'Come, come – why so slow?' Flowerdew stepped forward as his mouth started twitching. 'They may be the most radioactive rocks ever seen, and you may think you've pushed your luck already' – his voice was quieter, more menacing now – 'but I think you can cope with just a teensy bit more.' Another leer; more blood seeped from his cracked lips. 'Let's give that new bone marrow of yours something to work on, shall we?'

No one moved.

'Now, Lofte!' Flowerdew was shouting. 'On the floor. Count them!'

Itch looked at the gunmen. 'It'll expose everyone here to dangerous levels of radioactivity. Everyone. You want me to take the top off?' He stepped over to the flask, putting his hand on the cap. 'Really, you want this?'

Bello and the others stepped back, unsure.

'It's not their call, Lofte, It's mine. Remove the lid and count the rocks,' Flowerdew repeated.

Itch picked up the flask again. He held it out in front of him, its astonishing weight straining his tired arms. *If I open this, it will probably kill me – and maybe make everyone else very sick. Not good.* 'No thanks,' he said, putting it on the floor again.

Everyone tensed. Flowerdew stepped closer, his eyes narrow slits. 'You'll do as I say, Lofte.'

'*I'll* count them.' Jack had stepped forward.

'Excuse me?' said Flowerdew.

'If you need them counted – which you don't – I'll do it. Give me the flask, Itch.'

Then Chloe and Lucy stepped forward too. 'We'll count them too.'

Itch was dumbstruck.

Flowerdew walked along them as if inspecting a military parade. 'Very touching, but you all miss the point. This has all been about Itch. *His* rocks, aren't they? You're in trouble because of him. I could let you three go – that wouldn't matter because it's all about *him*.' He spat the last word as he picked up the flask and slammed it down on the floor in front of Itch. '*You* open the flask – *you* count the rocks.'

'It'll kill him!' cried Chloe.

'You're a monster,' shouted Lucy.

'You've got five seconds,' said Flowerdew.

Itch stepped towards the flask and crouched down.

'Five.'

He picked it up again.

'Four.'

Bello stood behind Chloe, the muzzle of his gun against her head.

'OK, I get it!' shouted Itch.

'Three.'

It was as if he could feel the heat through the flask. His head was spinning. How long would it take for the radiation to affect him this time? Well, he was about to find out . . .

'Two!'

'I'm doing it! I'm doing it!' Itch was frantic. 'Put the gun down! I'm doing it. Look!' He gripped the flask between his legs and tried to turn the lid, but his hands were too weak.

'ONE!' yelled Flowerdew.

'IT'S STUCK! IT'S STUCK! JUST WAIT!'

And a gunshot rang out in Target Station Four.

Jack and Lucy screamed; Itch yelled, 'No!' and spun round in time to see Chloe fall to the floor, blood spraying in an arc.

'Chloe!' cried Jack, and she and Lucy ran over to her cousin. Chloe had fallen with Bello on top of her; all Jack could see was one leg and the top of her head.

'Oh God, Chloe!' shouted Itch as he tried to take in what had happened. 'Get him off her! Where's the blood coming from?' A steady stream of dark red blood was pooling just centimetres from Chloe's head; her hair was thick with it. 'Grab his arm! Pull together!' he told Jack and Lucy, and they hauled Bello off her. As he flipped over, they saw a huge hole in his skull, above his forehead.

And Chloe opened her eyes.

With a cry of relief, Itch spun to see where the shot had come from; the other gunmen had hit the floor, doing the same.

A noise like thunder from above – the sound of footsteps pounding along the metal walkway. Putting the flask in his rucksack, Itch threw himself down, then crawled over to his sister. She flung her arms around him; she couldn't speak, she could barely breathe. He glanced up at the walkway and his heart leaped.

'It's Fairnie! And' – his voice caught – 'and Sam, Moz and Kirsten, I think!'

Itch and Chloe watched the MI5 team, wearing helmets, protective goggles and bulletproof vests, thunder across the walkway from the control room. As fire was returned, they all hit the floor, but their weapons reappeared above the handrail.

'Itch! Over here!' called Jack. She and Lucy were crouching behind a large metal portable office.

Itch took Chloe's hand and they ran to join them, collapsing on top of each other.

Jack was smiling. 'Never seen anything sweeter,' she said, hugging Chloe, Bello's blood smearing both of them.

The firing was intense now, bullets ricocheting dangerously around the building. Bello's men were retreating along the tunnel, using it for cover. They were looking for an exit, but were pinned down by steady raking fire. Moz emerged above the rail, and as he fired, the others continued along the walkway, jumping down the steps. Their combat boots squeaked on the floor as they ran straight past Itch, Jack, Chloe and Lucy.

'Stay low!' shouted Fairnie as he ran past.

'Stay out of it!' added Kirsten, and gave them a thumbs-up.

'I think we will,' said Itch, and Chloe managed a smile.

The firing continued for many more minutes but, like a passing thunderstorm, seemed to be moving away. The four of them stayed huddled together, not daring to move. It had been quiet for a few seconds when they heard pounding feet and saw legs running on the far side of the tunnel.

Sam Singh ducked underneath and emerged, grinning. 'Nice to see you guys again. We've accounted for all of them apart from Flowerdew.' He pointed at Bello's splayed body. 'His mates gave up once they'd taken bullets in the legs and buttocks. But no Flowerdew. Seen him?'

'Not since you started firing,' said Lucy, sounding scared again.

'Itch,' said Sam, 'where's the 126?'

'Of course, you're rescuing the rocks too,' said Itch. 'I thought it might be just us you wanted.'

'Unfair,' said Chloe.

Itch paused. 'Fair point. Sorry.'

'No worries,' said Sam.

'In my rucksack. Need to see them?' Itch showed him the flask.

Sam spoke into his mic. 'Rocks are here. Kids safe.' He listened briefly to the reply. 'Right, keep low. Let's assume he's still out there. Let's meet in the control room.'

He led the way back to the steps and they ran at

full tilt along the walkway, no one looking anywhere other than immediately in front of them. Chloe followed Sam, Lucy tucked in behind Jack and Itch, exhausted, lagged behind. They all crashed into the control room, where Tina Greaves was tending to the released scientists. They all cheered as Sam led the party inside. The body of the red-haired gunman lay against a computer terminal, his head covered by a white coat; blood leaking through in three places.

Despite the weapon hanging from her neck, Tina embraced Chloe, Jack and Lucy.

'Are we safe?' Itch asked her.

She pointed at the monitors: they showed Fairnie, Moz and Kirsten on their way back, without Flowerdew. 'No,' she replied, 'but you're OK.'

'What's the difference?'

She held up her machine gun.

'Fair enough.'

Itch turned and went to look more closely at the monitors.

Lucy came over to join him. 'What happens to the rocks?' she asked.

'What do you suggest?'

She shrugged. 'Not much we can do. Hand them over, I suppose.'

Itch was silent. Lucy was right. He was relieved to be alive – relieved all of them were alive – but he hadn't achieved what he'd come here for.

'What would your father have done?' he said.

'If Cake was here, what would he do now?'

Lucy thought about it. 'I don't know. I honestly don't know. And you know what? I'm not sure I care.' Itch looked shocked, but she continued, 'Itch, this is about *us* and *our* decisions, not my dad. I loved him very much, but he was always running away. And making the wrong decisions. *He* couldn't have done any of this. You're far braver than he ever was. He would be very proud of you.'

Itch was staring at the floor when Chloe and Jack joined them.

'You all right, Itch?' asked Jack.

'Yeah, fine. Never been better. Now, group decision needed. Colonel Fairnie will be here any second. He'll want the rocks – it doesn't seem we have much choice.'

'You're going to hand them over?'

'Does anyone feel like running?' Itch looked at them all in turn: they were exhausted. No one said anything. 'I will if you will – I just don't know where we'd go any more. And hiding them doesn't seem to work . . .'

They looked up as Fairnie, Moz and Kirsten came into the control room. The colonel headed straight for Itch and smiled. 'Good to see you all again. We'll need to get some medics in to check you over, but Flowerdew is still missing—'

'We put tellurium in his whisky. He'll stink of garlic for a while. That might help.'

413

Fairnie laughed. 'Did you indeed! Nice work! We think he's in one of the tunnels under the labs, but there are quite a few to cover. Maybe we'll sniff him out.' He made to leave, then turned back. 'Oh, just one thing . . . The 126. Where did you say you'd put it?'

Itch smiled. 'Well . . .' he said, reaching for his rucksack – but Fairnie put out his hand to stop him.

'You do whatever you have to do,' he said quietly. He looked Itch straight in the eye. 'My team are going to hunt for Flowerdew. We'll be gone for a while. *Do what you have to do.* Do you understand?'

Itch looked stunned. 'Do you mean . . . ?'

'I don't mean anything. I need to go and find Flowerdew. Be careful.' The colonel nodded at them, and stroked his moustache as if about to say something else; instead, he went back to his colleagues.

Jack spoke first. 'Was he telling you to go ahead and kill the rocks?'

'Sounded like it,' said Itch. 'What else could he have meant?'

They watched the MI5 team head out along the walkway. Sam had stayed behind and was keen to get the scientists away as soon as possible.

'There's a police coach outside, everybody,' he announced. 'Let's go!' And he herded them out – a few supporting each other – through the rear door.

One by one they left the room, some waving at Lucy as they did so.

'What do we now?' asked Chloe.

They all jumped as the door opened again and Tom Oakes came back in. 'Apparently I can help . . . in your, er, undertaking.' He went over to the beam controller's console. 'Jenny has had to leave with the rest of them, so there's just us now.'

Itch, Jack and Chloe were all too stunned to move, so Oakes walked over. 'You all look as though you've seen a ghost. I once worked with your science teacher at the Mountain Pass mine in California many years back. Henry Hampton and I go back quite a long way – he told me about you, Itch. I know it's all supposed to be top secret, but you'd be surprised how many scientists know all about Itchingham Lofte.'

Itch didn't know what to say.

Oakes smiled. 'Come on, we need to whomp this sucker.' He led them over to the console. 'You can see the whole tunnel from here. Unless you object, I'll put the rocks in the pod and you fire the beam. It's the quickest way, and we don't have a lot of time. Also, we don't know quite how your 126 will react.'

'You know about—?' began Itch, but Oakes shook his head.

'Later. When all the rocks are in, you'll see it on the screen. I just need to get the beam intensity right . . .' He keyed in some figures, his hands moving deliberately. 'That should do it. When I give the signal, turn this key and leave. Now the rocks, please. I have to catch that bus.'

Still in a daze, Itch gave Oakes the flask, and he ran out of the control room; when he reappeared on the monitors in front of Itch, he had donned a protective helmet and gloves. The four of them watched as, expertly, he used the crane to load the 126 onto the target plate.

'Wow, he makes it look easy,' said Itch. 'I think he's done it.'

They saw Oakes giving the thumbs-up before he ran out of view. The middle monitor showed a close-up of the eight rocks. Jack, Chloe and Lucy looked at Itch, whose hand hovered over the key.

Staring at the rocks, he said, 'This is for all the misery and pain you've caused. We're better off without you.' Then he added, 'And this is for you too, Cake. I got rid of them in the end . . .'

He put his hand on the key. Jack rested her hand on his, and Chloe and Lucy placed theirs on top. Itch, the bow of the key in his fingers, turned the key through ninety degrees. Lights started to flash everywhere, but the BEAM OFF light was still illuminated; another twist of the key, and BEAM ON flashed at them. Everything seemed to start humming.

The rocks now disappeared from view as thick steel barriers came down within the tunnel, leaving

Itch staring at screens that showed lots of flashing lights but not much else.

'Death ray on,' said Jack.

'Didn't he say *turn the key and leave*?' said Chloe.

'He did,' said Itch.

'Shall we go, then?'

Itch nodded. 'I suppose so.'

Two minutes after they had turned the beam on, the protons hit the pieces of 126. The reactions released pulses of neutrons, and the temperature climbed quickly. The smallest rock started to glow red immediately, swiftly followed by the other seven. As their atomic weight tumbled, they rapidly turned blue-white before seeming to melt into each other, folding into a molten lava-like puddle. The temperature continued to climb, and some of the 126 began to vaporize; it snapped and sparked as the extraordinary amount of energy released made all the instruments in the target station light up.

A convulsion in the pod sent a shock wave through the tunnel, and the whole building shuddered. With nowhere to flow, the molten rock heaved and pulsed with released energy; tremor after tremor hit the deserted target station.

The 126 was splitting.

Under the neutron bombardment, it was being torn apart.

33

Itch clicked his front door shut and walked down the hill towards the beach. A fierce wind and steady rain were blowing in off the Atlantic, and he kept his head down, hands shoved deep into his pockets. He walked quickly, inhaling the salty air deep into his lungs. By the time he'd reached the golf course his hair was plastered to his face; by the time he got to the beach huts he was soaked through. He stood watching the mountainous surf; slate-grey water and pale foam smashing into the sand and rocks. He had always loved high tide on wild days, partly for the show but also because there weren't any surfers around to make him feel useless.

The roar of the surf was so loud, he only heard the footsteps at the last minute. He turned to see his father jogging towards him, waving cheerily. Nicholas was, unlike his son, appropriately dressed, with a cap pulled low and a thick jacket that

Itch was sure had seen duty on many an oil rig.

'Hey, Itch. Where you heading?'

'Don't know really – just somewhere.'

'Getting out of the house?'

'Something like that.'

They stood watching the surf in silence for a moment, before Nicholas touched Itch on the elbow. 'Come on, let's walk. Can't hang around in this weather, and you're barely wearing anything. Your mother would have a fit.'

'If she was here, she would,' said Itch. 'But she's not, is she?' He hadn't meant it to sound so angry – though he saw no reason to apologize.

'I know it's been bad, Itch, and that's my fault. Most of it, anyway. I'm hoping she'll be back soon. I'm sure she wouldn't miss Christmas with you guys.'

They continued along the high path, walking close to the cliff edge and looking down onto both the town's beaches. Row after row of Atlantic rollers were piling in; low cloud obscured the horizon.

'Where's she gone?' asked Itch.

'A friend's,' said his father. 'Not far.' The path dipped towards the beach. 'I should have told her about leaving the rigs sooner, but it seemed . . . too risky. I never thought she'd like me working with Jacob Alexander. And as it turned out, I was right.'

'Does Dr Alexander know—?' began Itch.

'He knows everything. And that you spallated the 126.'

'And?'

'Well, first up he can't believe you got to use the ISIS particle accelerator. He's rather jealous, I think. And impressed. But of course, he'd love to have had the 126 to work on himself. He keeps telling me how he analysed it on the X-ray spectrometer; he's shown me the printout of the readings. It took a while for him to accept that I knew where the rocks were, but he's a family man. He said he understood and would probably have done the same.'

'Wow . . .' Itch's phone bleeped, and he took it out. 'It's Chloe. Wants to know what I want for Christmas. She's in town.'

'I know,' said Nicholas. 'I told her I was coming after you. Listen, Itch, I just want you to know that our little group of scientists are doing some great work. There are some South African mines we've found that you would *love*. Our team have discovered some new thorium deposits to look at. We were thinking of getting an expedition together, and wondered if you might like to come. To, you know, help out.'

'OK, nice idea,' said Itch. 'But that's *radioactive* thorium you're talking about, Dad, and I reckon I might have had a lifetime's radiation in the space of a few months.'

Nicholas laughed. 'Fair point! And what will your mum say?'

'If she comes back, she might not like it.'

'She *will* come back, Itch. Trust me.'

'Did she leave because of what I did? Did she go because we disappeared to the ISIS lab? She must have gone mental.'

'No, absolutely not. She was cross about that – so was I – but she left because of me. Because of . . . us. She says she can't trust me, and I understand that, but we're working on it, Itch.' Nicholas looked at his son, resting his arm around his shoulder. 'She didn't leave because of you. OK?'

Itch nodded. 'All right. You might want to tell Chloe that too.'

'I'll do that.'

As they neared the beach, they were hailed by a familiar figure. Wrapped in a vast yellow waterproof, John Watkins was waving a walking stick in their direction, and Itch took off as soon as he recognized him. Watkins stood smiling, his face mottled with bruising and a thick bandage showing under his cap.

'Itch, my good man! How terrific to see you!' Watkins called out as he approached. He had to shout over the noise of the crashing waves.

There was a brief awkwardness, covered by a handshake. 'You got away! My God, I was so scared for you all, and so cross with myself for not helping you.' Watkins was still holding onto Itch's hand, and tears filled his eyes. 'I've been trying to think what else I could have said—'

'Sir!' interrupted Itch. 'We're sorry we got you involved. Who was to know Shivvi was so loopy, so dangerous?'

'Well, we found out soon enough,' said Watkins, touching his bandage gingerly.

'How bad . . . ?' began Itch.

'Bad enough. I was kept in for tests – X-rays and the like – and I need to go back for more. But I'm sure I'll be fine. Ah, your father's caught up! Hello, Mr Lofte! Terrible day!'

Nicholas shook him warmly by the hand. 'May we walk with you? We seem to have the beach to ourselves, after all?'

'Delighted!' said Watkins. 'Though I won't stay out much longer. There's only so much soaking I can take at my age. I feel the cold nowadays.' He paused to look out to sea. 'The academy, as I'm sure you'll know, has been in uproar. What with Lucy's exposure of Mary as a fraud, Shivvi's escape, your kidnapping and the fire in Brighton, I don't suppose anything has been taught at all. And there are mocks on the horizon too!'

'You know Shivvi died?' said Itch.

'Yes, I heard.'

'Flowerdew killed her.'

'Yes, I heard that too.'

There seemed nothing else to say.

'Does everyone know it was me? The fire, I mean?' asked Itch.

'Not really. Well, officially the fire was blamed on Flowerdew and the men he was working with – the papers were quick to blame the Argentinians – but everyone here guessed you were mixed up in it somehow. But you and Jack have been kept out of the story. Once I heard you were both OK, I must say I mourned for the Fitzherbert School. To see my old school in flames . . . Oh my.' John Watkins looked quite overcome for a few moments as he rested on his walking stick.

You look old, thought Itch. He had been about to say he got the idea for the sawdust fire from one of his lessons, but thought maybe that could wait.

The three of them turned back in the direction of the canal. If anything, the rain was settling in and the clouds darkening.

'I can offer tea and biscuits,' said Watkins, the rain dripping off his nose. 'Why don't we all dry off at the cottage – we're nearly there anyway.'

'That sounds great – thanks,' said Nicholas. 'If you're sure it's no trouble.'

'Not at all – it'll be nice to entertain Itch without him getting kidnapped.' Mr Watkins smiled at Itch, but the memory of what Shivvi had put them through was still painful, and Itch's smile was forced.

'I hope you've got plenty of biscuits,' said Nicholas, pointing to two figures running towards them along the canal path. Chloe and Jack, struggling with shopping bags and umbrellas, were waving from the lock.

'The more the merrier!' said Watkins, clapping his hands together.

'Hi, Itch! Hi, Uncle Nicholas!' called Jack when they reached the canal. 'We guessed you'd be heading this way. Hi, sir! How's the head? It looks painful . . .'

Mr Watkins beamed at Jack. 'I'll be fine. I'm tougher than you'd think, Jack. Follow me: we're all having tea.' He bustled into his cottage, where he produced towels for everyone. Jack, Itch and Chloe got the fire going while he and Nicholas talked in the kitchen. A small Christmas tree stood in the corner, lit by a string of flashing reindeer. Every time one of the cousins looked at them, they burst out laughing.

'They have to be the worst lights ever,' said Chloe quietly – though as it turned out, not quietly enough.

'I can hear rude comments about my lights from a thousand metres, young lady!' called Watkins's voice from the kitchen. They all laughed again, and Chloe flushed.

Itch looked around the room. Get Well cards mixed with Christmas greetings along the bookshelves, and a few festive angels hung from lampshades.

'Hasn't been very Christmassy at home yet, has it?' he said. 'What with Mum leaving, tests at the hospital, police visits and everything.'

Chloe nodded. 'I've just bought you a present, though. Which you'd better like, as I've hardly got enough money left for Gabriel's now.'

'And it is really smart,' said Jack. 'If you don't want it, I'll have it!'

Itch was pulling a face at her when his phone buzzed. He was reading a text from Lucy when his dad came back in.

'Just had Colonel Fairnie on the phone,' said Nicholas. 'He's been at Lucy's and wants to come over. Say goodbye, I guess. Mr Watkins says that's fine. They'll be here shortly.'

'Lucy just texted me,' said Itch. He noticed Jack and Chloe grinning but ignored them. He turned to his dad. 'Has everything gone from next door then? Can the Cole family move back?'

'I think the Coles are happy where they are by the golf course,' said Nicholas.

'Even after Chloe and I got it blown up?'

'Yes, even after that!'

Mr Watkins came into the lounge carrying the tea tray. 'Coming back to school on Monday, Itch? There's only a few days till the end of term . . .'

'S'pose I should. It'll be strange to just walk in

and then walk home again, with no protection. To be honest, I'm dreading it. People like Bruno and Darcy have been waiting to have a go for months; well, now's their chance.' He looked glum.

'We'll watch out for that, Itch. I'll tell the staff and talk to the usual suspects. It'll be fine. We'll sort it.' Watkins sat down heavily in an armchair and cleared his throat. 'I should let you know . . . I've decided to take early retirement. I'll be leaving the CA at Christmas.'

'But sir . . . !' said Itch and Jack together, but he raised a hand.

'I told Dr Dart yesterday. I realized in hospital that I wasn't sure I wanted to go back. The whole Mary business has shaken me. And the doctors say I need to rest up. I need these tests in the new year, apparently. And it's all a bit much really—' He broke off, eyes filling with tears.

The doorbell rang and he got to his feet, happy for the distraction; Itch and Jack exchanged bleak looks.

The wind and rain followed Colonel Jim Fairnie and Lucy Cavendish into the cottage before Watkins hurriedly shut the door. They stood dripping on the mat and smiled at the assembled company.

'We only walked from my car,' said Fairnie, 'but look at us!' He wiped his face with his sleeve.

'Hi, Itch! Jack! Chloe!' Lucy grinned broadly as

she peeled off her jacket. She embraced Jack and Chloe while Itch put another log on the fire.

'Itch, can I have a word?' asked Fairnie. 'And before I take my coat off . . . outside, maybe? We can sit in the car.'

'Oh, OK. Sure,' said Itch, glancing at the others. He shrugged and grabbed his jacket, which was still soaking wet. 'Can I wear yours?' he called to his father.

'Of course,' said Nicholas, coming in and acknowledging Lucy and the colonel. 'It'll be more use than your flimsy one.'

Itch pulled on his father's black, waxed, three-quarter-length coat; it seemed to swallow him up.

'See? A perfect fit.' Nicholas grinned.

Fairnie opened the door and followed Itch out-side. The rain was easing, and they stood looking across the canal to the beach and sea beyond. 'I'm going to miss this,' said the colonel. 'I love this beach.'

'A beach and a battleground,' said Itch. 'That was quite a shootout on the rocks.'

'Ah, the Russians, yes. That caused quite a stir. A Mafia gang, essentially, as it turned out. They were going to drug you and smuggle you out of the country. Great embarrassment that they got so close. MI5 had no idea they were here.'

The rain started up again, and they walked briskly over to Fairnie's car – parked where Shivvi had left hers just a few days earlier. Itch could still feel the weight of the caesium strapped to his chest, and shivered. Fairnie's car bleeped and the doors unlocked. Itch slid into the passenger seat.

'I came to say goodbye.' Fairnie shut his door and turned to face Itch, his damp clothes squeaking on the leather seat. 'It's been . . . quite an adventure.' His face creased into a broad smile, and he wiped the rain from his moustache. The car windows were steaming up, and he started the engine to activate the climate control. 'When I was put in charge of your security, I knew it would be risky because what you had found was so extraordinary. And that looking after a schoolboy who lived at home and went to the local academy would be . . . sensitive.'

Itch watched the windscreen de-mist slowly as the warm air blew against the glass.

'And I know we made things difficult for your mum and dad. I'm sorry about that.'

Itch shifted in his seat. 'Yeah, well. You know she's left, don't you?'

'Yes,' said Fairnie quietly. 'Yes, I heard that. I'm sorry about that too, Itch.'

'Not your fault – and not mine either, apparently.'

They sat watching the rain thunder down onto the windscreen for a moment. Then Fairnie spoke again: 'I've just come from Lucy's house, as you know. I've been talking to her mum. They have quite a story, I can tell you. What did you think when you found out that Lucy was Cake's daughter?'

Itch laughed. 'Amazed. Stunned. Still can't quite believe it. But it was Lucy who knew about spallation and ISIS. They all knew Cake there. It's funny, but—' He broke off to clear his tightening throat. 'The 126 killed him. He didn't realize what he had until it was too late, and it killed him. I did my best to dispose of the rocks, but it turned out I hadn't dealt with them either. Then . . . then . . . Cake's daughter shows up, and because of her and what they did together, we knew what to do.'

'I was relieved to see the results of those tests you all had done,' said Fairnie. 'No radiation damage this time.'

'No. Just broken bones, burns, cuts. That kind of thing.'

Fairnie nodded. 'Lucy's mum is quite upset that Lucy didn't tell her about her father's death,' he said. 'Understandably, I think.' He paused. 'Families are complicated sometimes.'

Itch sighed.

'By the way,' said Fairnie. 'Lucy's room is full of chemicals and powders, you know; drives her mother mad.' He smiled. 'Reminds me of someone.'

Itch nodded and looked slightly awkward. He changed the subject. 'It was pretty cool when you showed up at ISIS, by the way. I thought we'd had it. How did you find us?'

'CCTV at Paddington showed us which train you got. MI5 and ISIS have worked together in the past – it wasn't difficult to sort that bit out. It was Sam Singh who briefed us on spallation, but he doubted you could do it.'

'Well, I wouldn't have been able to if you hadn't let me. I thought your job was to get the rocks for the government . . .? I was sure you were going to take the rucksack . . .'

'That was the plan – those were my instructions. But when the team were tooling up for the ISIS rescue, Kirsten said she had never seen anyone with such determination and courage as you, Itch. Then – and I remember her words exactly – she said, "I'm glad the kid is on our side." Moz then added that he thought you were right and that maybe no one could be trusted with the 126. So we took a vote.'

'You did *what*?'

'I know – most irregular. But then everything about this operation has been irregular. We took a vote. And it was unanimous: we would help you if we could. Officially, you'd started the beam before we got there, and it was too late to stop the reaction. That's what we've written in our report, and that's the way it is . . .'

A long silence was eventually broken by Itch. 'Wow. Thanks, Colonel Fairnie.'

'No worries. ISIS are less happy. They've essentially lost a target station; the whole area around the pod is being filled with concrete. There's so much energy coming off the disintegrating 126 that it was considered the safest option.'

'Oops,' said Itch. 'Is it safe?'

'It is now.'

'I've done some work,' said Itch, 'and I think the 126 breaks up into element sixty-three, which is europium, with assorted bits of promethium and terbium.'

'Can't say I've heard of them, Itch.'

'Well, europium is cool. I'd quite like some of that. It's next on my list.'

'I'd leave that batch of it alone, if I were you,' said Colonel Fairnie with a smile.

Itch nodded. 'And that scientist Tom Oakes was helpful. Basically showed us how to destroy the 126. Will he be OK?'

Fairnie smiled again. 'Think so. As you know, he was an old friend of your science teacher, Mr Hampton. He seemed to know all about you. Given that it's an official secret, there's a lot of gossip about you and your discovery.'

'Which doesn't exist any more.'

'Precisely.'

'Would you thank the team for me?' said Itch. 'I'll miss them. Particularly at school. We're going back

431

on Monday and, whatever Mr Watkins says, I know who'll take advantage of you guys not being there . . .'

'I think you'll be fine,' Fairnie reassured him.

'Trust me,' said Itch. 'The second Darcy and co. realize you're gone . . .'

'I think you'll be fine,' the colonel repeated.

Itch looked at him, puzzled. 'OK . . . And Flowerdew? What do you know about him?'

Fairnie winced. 'Used the tunnels to get away, I'm afraid. Our biggest failure, and one reason why I'm not completely stepping down from this assignment. When he resurfaces again, he'll find life very difficult; he's an internationally wanted man.' He handed Itch a card. 'Call me anytime you think you might need me.'

Itch gazed at the number.

'And now I need to go,' said Fairnie.

'You're not coming in again?'

'No. Would you say goodbye for me? You're the one we came to protect, and I can honestly say it's been a privilege, Itch. You're a remarkable boy. Like Kirsten said, I'm glad we're on the same side.' He held out his hand and Itch shook it.

'Thanks for everything, Colonel Fairnie.'

'I'm sure we'll meet again.' The colonel smiled.

Itch nodded and got out of the car. He stood and watched as Fairnie drove out of the car park, the tail lights bright through the swirling rain. He ran back through the puddles, relieved that no one would query the moistness in his eyes. They all looked up as he ran in and took off Nicholas's oil-rig coat.

'Where's Fairnie?' asked Jack.

'He said he had to go. And he says goodbye.'

Jack looked surprised, but Mr Watkins chose that moment to produce a tray of home-baked cookies.

'A festive favourite,' he said. 'I need your reviews, please.'

The smell of cinnamon and chocolate filled the room, and everyone suddenly felt hungry. Watkins passed them round, and it was clear that they were a hit. While the others were discussing the recipe, Lucy came over and sat on the arm of Itch's chair.

'You OK?' she asked.

'Sure . . .'

'I've got you something. I hope you like it.'

Itch flushed. 'Oh. Er. I'm sure—'

Before he knew what was happening, Lucy had put a small, heavy package in his lap. Then she kissed him on the cheek. 'Happy Christmas, Itch,' she said.

He froze. Somewhere he registered that Jack and Chloe were grinning and giggling, and that his father and teacher had stopped their conversation. But mainly he was aware that he had gone bright red. He busied himself with unwrapping the present.

Inside was a shiny button of a silvery-grey metal-like material. On one side it was almost flat but on the other it tapered to a point.

'It's silicon,' said Lucy.

Itch heard Chloe whisper, 'How romantic!'

He held the silicon up to catch the light from Mr Watkins's Christmas tree. It sparkled and gleamed.

'Your mouth's open, Itch,' Chloe told him.

'It's beautiful . . .' he said. 'Like a Christmas tree decoration. Where did you get it?'

'It was my dad's. I found it with his stuff and I thought you should have it.'

The silence in the room was eventually broken by Mr Watkins.

'More biscuits, anyone?'

The rain eased as they all headed back along the cliff path. Nicholas asked to see the silicon. He weighed it in his hand and rubbed its smooth surface.

'A nice gift,' he said. 'That must mean a lot to you. Do you have silicon?'

'Yes, but not like this,' said Itch. 'And it was Cake's.'

His father nodded.

'And it was delivered with a kiss,' giggled Chloe.

Itch punched her on the shoulder.

'Still the element collector then?' said his father.

'Of course,' he replied. 'What else is there to be?'

Acknowledgements

Many people made this Itch adventure the wild journey it turned out to be. My high-class, top-of-the-range scientific advisers were once again Paddy Regan, Professor of Nuclear Physics at Surrey University, and Andrea Sella, Professor of Chemistry at UCL. Their advice was, as ever, indispensable. Every school should have a Paddy and an Andrea on call, and then all would be well. It is fair to say that the spallation process (making its debut in fiction, I think) is pretty advanced stuff, and it, along with the numerous bangs and flashes, would not be here without them. Research scientist Dr Jonathan Speed has joined the ranks too, with comment and the rare ability to make a jelly baby scream.

The STFC Rutherford Appleton Laboratory at Harwell provides the backdrop to the conclusion of the story, and for the purposes of this book I have built them a new (simpler, less secure) facility at no cost to the taxpayer. Lucy Stone, Dr Martyn Bull, Dr Chris Frost and Dr Andrew Taylor, thanks for your time, tour and the glimpse of a world where the UK is a world leader.

Gary Gates at the London Fire Brigade made sure my fire-fighting procedures were up to date, and Laura Storm, Master Scuba Diver, generously gave me insight into her extraordinary work. Having access to Gordon Carrera, the BBC's security correspondent, and Danny Shaw, the BBC's crime correspondent, was invaluable, and both answered my enquiries when they had far more pressing concerns to attend to. Thanks, guys. Drs Mary Davies and David Davies honed a few passages of medical ghastliness with wit and, as I recall, Chablis. Bob Digby, Senior Vice President of the Geographical Association, is still the full-time adviser on all things Cornish. Any mistakes are, of course, all my own. I should have paid more attention.

Thanks to Sam Copeland at RCW for wisdom and perspective. To the team at Random House, especially editor and master craftsman Ben Horslen, and Clare Hall-Craggs with Stephanie-Elise Melrose at Publicity for all our wonderful school visits. To Chiggy and Emily Rees Jones at PBJ Management for still being cheerleaders.

And, of course, to my wonderful family. Hilary, Ben, Natasha and Joe have been my biggest supporters and have cheered for Itch, Jack and Chloe from the start. Love always.

Coming in 2014:

The story continues in a brand new adventure starring ITCH.

Turn over for a taster . . .

The armour-plated Mercedes swerved to avoid a pothole the size of a snooker table. The expensive suspension could smooth out the roughness of most roads, but the A1 from the Murtala Muhammed International Airport into Lagos was beyond repair. One wheel clipped the edge of the ruptured tarmac and the jolt shook its passengers. They grabbed the leather arms of the car's upholstery and the loud cursing came in French and Dutch. Christophe Revere and Jan Van Den Hauwe, the co-chairs of oil multinational Greencorps, were not happy.

'Dammit – don't they know how to build roads here?'

'The answer to that, Christophe, is clearly no. The only way things get done here is through bribery and corruption. We know that much, surely?'

The Frenchman smiled and chanced another sip of his expensive brandy. 'We do, Jan – of course we do. We caused most of it, I believe.' He dabbed his lips with a handkerchief and checked his seat belt. The onboard satellite TV was tuned to a finance channel; both men watched the continuous scroll of information across the screen.

'More European madness, Christophe! Those Greeks . . .'

Another big swerve, and some of the spirit splashed onto the carpet. Revere closed his eyes as if in prayer. 'Give me strength . . .' he muttered.

Both men peered through their own tinted windows at the road outside, but the streetlights and neon advertising weren't bright enough to pierce the darkened glass. Ahead, the view through the windscreen was clearer, the powerful headlights illuminating a nightmarish, crazy night-time rush hour.

'It's gone midnight, for God's sake! Why so busy?' Van

Den Hauwe aimed his question at the chauffeur, who spoke into his intercom, though his eyes never left the road.

'It is always like this, sir.' The driver glanced in his wing mirror as he pulled first into the outside lane, and then – to gasps from his passengers – into the other carriageway.

'What the . . . !' The oncoming traffic, now heading straight for them, swerved out of the way with barely a blast on the horn or flash of headlights. As though it was normal.

'Big hole in the road, sir,' said the driver. 'We call it "Mama's Dig". Everyone knows about it.'

The Dutchman shook his head. 'You actually have names for the potholes? This is one crazy country.'

The driver smiled. 'Yes, sir. You got that right!'

In front, their security team – in a polished four-by-four – seemed to be having an easier time, easily weaving between the holes in the tarmac, the dawdling, ancient saloons and the racing sports cars. It sounded as though the driver's hand must be glued to the horn, with yells and gestures aimed at any motorist who really annoyed him. On one occasion the barrel of a gun appeared from a passenger window, aimed at the driver of a soft-top BMW trying to overtake – who quickly dropped back behind the four-by-four and the Mercedes, leaving the Lagos road at the next exit.

The traffic thinned as most cars took the filter for downtown Lagos; the small Greencorps convoy continued south, following signs for Tin Can Island.

'I'm nervous about this meeting, Jan,' Revere said to his colleague. 'Who says this new Head of Police is trustworthy? And why do we have to meet so far out of town? I don't like it.'

Van Den Hauwe swivelled slightly to face him. 'I don't like it either, but after the spill, and Flowerdew's' – he searched for the right word – 'insanity, we have to get control of this town again, Christophe. It used to be ours, but not any more.

If we can buy ourselves the Head of Police – well, it's a start. He sounded willing. Which is why we're both here.'

The car swung left, following a sign for the Apapa Oworonshoki Expressway, and a dark expanse of lagoon was briefly visible through the Mercedes' windscreen. It was the driver's sharp intake of breath that let his passengers know that all was not well. They looked up from their glowing phone screens.

'What? What's up?' asked Van Den Hauwe, but the empty road ahead gave him his answer.

'We've lost our security,' said Revere calmly.

They leaned forward to peer through the windscreen, but the twin headlights just picked out the dirt-covered tarmac, a few telegraph poles and an empty road.

'Where did they go?' shouted Van Den Hauwe. He pressed a button on his door; the window slid down and he put his head out into the sweltering night. The smell of the sea, along with oil and burning rubber, filled the car, and Revere pulled him back inside.

'Someone's paid them to disappear. I think we should go back,' he said. 'Back to the airport.'

The driver was looking worried now. The Mercedes might have all the safety features that money could buy, but he knew that Lagos was a lawless town, and if there was a price on your head . . . He swung the car round.

'Not much traffic for an "expressway",' said Van Den Hauwe quietly.

Revere nodded. 'None at all. I imagine we'll have company shortly.'

They were accelerating into a corner when the first of the pick-ups shot out in front of them. Three silver and grey Isuzu Rodeos spun on smoking tyres till they were facing the oncoming Mercedes. The Greencorps men were already braced and holding the leather straps that hung from the ceiling, but their seat belts snapped tightly around them as their driver stood on the brake. The car had an impressive stopping distance, but the pick-ups were too close, and there was a sickening metal-on-metal thud of a collision. While the air was still filled with sand and smoke, black-clad figures jumped out of the trucks.

'Back! Back! Back!' yelled Revere, and the driver threw the car into reverse. It pulled away from the tangle of bumpers and backed up to the edge of the road. As they spun away from the pick-ups, new headlights cut though the dark. Three more trucks hurtled round the corner and screeched to a halt, cutting off the Mercedes' escape.

'Looks like someone wants to talk,' said Van Den Hauwe.

'Let's hope that's all they want,' said Revere, and the Greencorps men sat and waited.

Palmeitkraal, Western Cape, South Africa

'Catch!' shouted Chloe.

'Why?' said Itch as the ball went sailing past his head, bouncing into the dusty scrubland.

'You could at least have tried,' said his sister.

'I could have, yes,' said Itch. He was on his hands and knees, scraping earth and stones towards him with both hands. Great clouds of dark sand and dust swirled around him, much of it settling in his wavy blond hair and sticking to his sweat-soaked T-shirt.

'Does Dad know what you're doing? I'm sure he said you're not allowed to do illegal experiments.' Chloe walked over to her brother, looking over his shoulder.

'No, you said that,' said Itch, packing soil around a glass jar.

'It is illegal, though, isn't it?' persisted Chloe.

'In England it is. But we aren't in England, are we?' He looked up and smiled at her. 'Come on, Chloe. I've always wanted to try this – give us a break.'

'If it's illegal at home, it's probably illegal in South Africa – have you checked?'

'OK, let me ask . . .' Itch looked theatrically around the hilly terrain: the low evergreen vegetation, the patches of bare sandstone and deserted old mine dwellings. 'No, no one around.' He smiled again. 'I'll just have to get on with it.'

Chloe sighed. 'Yeah, 'cos "just getting on with it" has been so great for you in the past. What did you say you were doing?'

'Stump removal,' said Itch.

'But I don't see any tree stumps.'

'Well, the key word is removal. It'll remove anything, I think.' He measured out some white powder into the jar.

'Looks scary,' said Chloe.

'Really?' said Itch. 'It's only KNO_3.'

'Itch, I don't play your stupid games. In English please. I know K is potassium . . .'

'Potassium nitrate. Or saltpetre.'

'And the other powder?'

'Secret.'

'Let me guess. It goes bang?'

'Can do,' said Itch. 'If you mix them together and set fire to it.'

'That's what I was afraid of,' said Chloe, walking away to retrieve the ball. 'Sure you wouldn't prefer to play "catch"?'